Learn
your
Lesson

Learn
your
Lesson

kandi steiner

Published by Kandi Steiner, LLC
Edited by Elaine York/Allusion Publishing, www.allusionpublishing.com
Discreet Cover Design by Staci Brillhart
Formatting by Elaine York/Allusion Publishing, www.allusionpublishing.com

To the caretakers,

 the givers,

 the ones who so selflessly protect and cherish,

 who love with their whole heart,

 who are generous with their attentiveness

 in ways that impact others more than they could ever

 know...

  This one's for you.

Chapter 1

Yes, Sir

Will

"You've got to be fucking kidding me."

I growled the words, ripping my mask off as I skated past our wide-eyed assistant athletic trainer. She was new to the team, joining us for her first season, and I didn't mean to make her pale as a ghost with my reaction to the message she'd delivered — but I couldn't help it.

Grumpy was my natural state of being lately.

And I was *extra* grumpy at the moment from being interrupted in the middle of our practice by a trainer telling me my daughter was here.

Ava was my fucking world. Other than hockey, she was all that mattered to me. I looked forward to every minute I got to spend with her.

The issue was that she should have been at home right now with the newest nanny I'd hired — not standing in the penalty box.

I tried and failed to school my breathing the closer I got, both frustrated by a clear sign my latest nanny had bit the dust, and worried something might have happened to Ava. But she looked content as could be, perched on the seat inside the box, pressing up onto her toes to get a better look at the rink through the glass. She was watching the rest of the team as they ran drills, her mop of dark brown curls falling out of the ponytail I'd tried to wrangle them into earlier that morning.

Like me, my daughter didn't smile much. It was an unfortunate side-effect to having me as a father and the only steady parental figure in her life.

But right now, her eyes were big and filled with excitement — well, as much excitement as she was capable of showing, anyway. The kid loved hockey just as much as I did, and any time I let her come to the arena, she lit up like I'd taken her to Disney World.

Except this time, I hadn't let her come. This wasn't an approved visit.

She was supposed to be at home — playing house or running in the yard or swimming in our pool.

Instead, she was watching pucks fly.

And it wasn't her nanny standing beside her and making sure she didn't fall.

It was Chloe Knott — her kindergarten teacher.

She stood out like a sore thumb, not just because the stands were empty, but because that woman wouldn't be able to blend in *anywhere* no matter how hard she tried.

Her bright copper wave of hair was lobbed just above her shoulders and parted down the middle, her brown eyes framed with thick, dark lashes that dusted her rosy cheeks every time she blinked. Other than that blush, her skin was like porcelain, pale and smooth like she bathed in sunscreen every morning before leaving the house.

She wore a long black skirt with white polka dots and a white t-shirt with a rainbow on it. Under the rainbow, it said *no rain, no rainbow.* Jade green arches dangled from her ears to complete the look, and they shimmered in the stadium lighting the closer I got.

I remembered the relief I'd felt in my chest the first time I'd met her, how she'd warmed at the sight of Ava as if she were her only student. Chloe had bent down to her level, looking her right in the eye and talking to her like an adult. She'd managed to get my daughter to smirk, and I'd felt the weight on my chest dissipate.

It was one thing to have Ava in a half-day of early learning last year, but to have her officially in school had put my emotions through the wringer. I didn't want her to grow up. I didn't want to have to face everything that came with school — bullies, friendships breaking down, the struggle of learning.

I wanted her to hold onto her innocence forever, to always stay this young.

"I'm so sorry, Mr. Perry," Chloe said when I was close enough to hear her. She smiled apologetically, her coral-painted lips curving up just a fraction as she looked at Ava and then at me. "I didn't know what else to do."

I could put the pieces together before I even got an explanation.

After the run of bad luck I'd had with nannies over the summer, I'd made sure to let Miss Knott know when I hired a new one. I'd also written consent for Miss Knott to be able to drive Ava to me should anything happen.

She had already been added to my approved list from when she'd tutored Ava in the first semester of the year, as my daughter had struggled with speaking in front of a class of twenty kids. When Ava finally started

3

feeling comfortable, she excelled — but I didn't revoke Miss Knott's access even now that we were in the second semester, because I had a feeling I'd need her.

The fact that I couldn't depend on anyone I'd hired to care for Ava thus far made me grind my fucking teeth.

To me, it was simple — if you had a job, you did that job. Properly. End of story.

Apparently, that was asking too much.

When I joined Miss Knot and Ava in the box, I immediately shut the door behind me just in case a puck came flying our way. And even though it didn't do much to block out the noise of practice, I was instantly aware of how the three of us fit in the tight space.

I was particularly aware of how close I stood to Chloe.

The modest skirt and t-shirt she wore did absolutely nothing to hide her curves, and I was as irritated as I was surprised by the fact that I noticed those curves at all. I cataloged the way her ample breasts stretched that damn rainbow on her chest, how her hips made that polka dot skirt flare, how soft her arms and legs were...

I thought that side of me was dead. I hadn't so much as cast a woman a second look since my wife passed, other than to take care of my needs when I had to.

But the awareness buzzing beneath my skin proved my theory wrong.

Because I was *very* attuned to my daughter's teacher at the moment.

"What happened?" I grumbled more forcefully than I meant to.

"Hi, Daddy," Ava said, not bothering to take her eyes off the rink.

I softened, just a bit, leaning in to sweep her hair off her face and kiss her cheek. "Hey, Pumpkin."

Chloe lowered her voice a little, all while keeping a close eye on Ava to make sure she didn't fall off the bench she was standing on.

"I tried calling," she explained, her eyes sympathetic. "No one came to pick Ava up. We tried the number you left us for Ava's new nanny, and when that failed, we tried your cell, and then the emergency contact you have on file. When we didn't get an answer, I took it upon myself since I had your permission on file. I tried your home address first, but no one was there. So..."

"You came here," I finished, pinching the bridge of my nose on a sigh. The emergency contact I'd put down was my uncle — the closest thing I'd ever had to a father, since mine had been a shell of himself after my mother passed. But my uncle was a lineman, a dangerous electrician job that fulfilled his thrill-seeking nature, and he was on the road more than he was home anymore.

"I'm sorry," she said again, and when I looked at her, she was biting her lower lip as if *she'd* done something wrong. She was also wringing her hands together, nervously tucking her hair behind her ear only to untuck it again, and shifting side to side.

I'd never seen someone wear their anxiety like that — especially when they were doing someone a favor, not being a burden in any way.

I blew out a breath. "Not your fault I seem to have a knack for finding the worst nannies in the world."

"It's okay, Daddy. We are doing our best."

Again, Ava didn't take her eyes off the rink when she said those words. When I messed up, which was often, those were the exact words I used. Now, she was echoing them back to me, and Chloe smiled, glancing at my daughter before her eyes found me again.

5

I couldn't even find it in me to be pissed off — mostly because, at this point, I was just *tired*. I'd tried everything, from personal recommendations from my teammates' wives to working with a recruiter.

So far, every nanny I'd hired had either been unprofessional, under qualified, or unavailable for the hours I needed them.

I'd dealt with everything from older women who couldn't keep up with Ava's energy to younger women who pretended to be a nanny only to attempt to shoot their shot with me when Ava was asleep.

Why was this so goddamn difficult?

If Jenny were here, she'd know what to do.

Then again, if Jenny were alive, we wouldn't need a nanny in the first place.

My chest tightened the way it always did when I thought about my late wife, the mixture of complicated emotions all too familiar.

"It's *me* who should be sorry, and I am," I finally said to Chloe, ruffling my kid's hair before I looked at her teacher again. "Thank you for bringing her here."

"Of course."

Chloe's eyes flicked between mine, those impossibly wide brown irises watching me with uncertainty.

"I can watch her," she offered suddenly, her voice louder than it had been. The offer seemed to surprise her as much as it did me, because she nervously grabbed her elbow with the opposite hand. "I mean, it seems like you're a little tied up. Unless you want to call her nanny?"

"Oh, I want to call her *ex* nanny many things," I grumbled.

Chloe smiled. "I'm happy to take her to my place, or to yours — whichever you'd prefer."

I tilted my head to the side. "Really? I'm sure you have plans."

She snorted at that — like actually *snorted*. "Trust me — I have nothing better to do."

I grabbed the back of my neck, looking at the time on my watch before I glanced behind us at where practice was in full swing. I knew if I needed to leave, Coach McCabe would understand. It was rare for me to ask for *anything*, and I was a leader on the team.

But I didn't *want* to leave. We had a big home game tomorrow night against a team fighting us for a spot in the playoffs, and I needed the ice time.

"If you're sure you don't mind… just this one time," I clarified quickly. "And I'll pay you."

"That won't be necessary."

"I'll pay you," I reiterated.

Chloe offered a soft smile, her fingers twiddling with her skirt. "Yes, sir."

My nostrils flared at that, for a reason that was entirely inappropriate, and I mentally slapped myself before turning my attention toward Ava.

"You're going to go spend the afternoon with Miss Knott, okay?" I said, lifting her into my arms so I could look her in the eye. "And I'll pick you up after work."

"Can't I stay here?"

She didn't whine those words. In fact, she said them as if she didn't actually care what I responded with. Her lips were turned down, her eyes seemingly bored.

She had my feigned indifference down pat.

I hated that I'd rubbed off on her.

"Not today, Pumpkin," I said, kissing her temple. I sat her down then, squeezing her hand. "But if you behave, we can talk about you coming to the game tomorrow."

She considered that, and then nodded, but still didn't show any emotion when she said, "Okay."

Chloe arched a brow at Ava, then at me, and shook her head on a soft smile. "Don't worry about picking her up," she said. "I'll bring her home around six?"

"That would be perfect."

I wondered if she heard the relieved exhale leaving my chest. I'd seen her in action at the school, knew about her outstanding reputation as a teacher and a babysitter, and remembered all too well how she'd helped my daughter find confidence to speak in the first semester of tutoring. The way Ava was too shy and uncomfortable to speak those first few weeks of kindergarten was something I hadn't been equipped to deal with, but Chloe had found the solution easily.

Knowing Ava was with her meant I could focus on practice.

Of course, I still had rage for my former employee simmering under my skin — but I'd deal with that later.

"Maybe you could have dinner with us," Ava said, and she did so on a shrug that indicated she didn't care either way. "Chef Patel always makes too much food for just me and Daddy."

I tried to give my daughter a warning glare that would tell her not to put me on the fucking spot like that, because as much as I was thankful for her teacher stepping in to help, I wasn't eager to have *anyone* joining us for dinner.

Chloe peeked up at me, and for a moment, I thought she looked pleased by that idea. But the second she saw my face, her smile dropped.

She cleared her throat. "Oh, that's okay, sweetie. You and—"

"You're more than welcome," I cut in. I hoped the words didn't sound as forced as they felt, that she didn't notice how much my teeth gritted together when I said them.

At that, Chloe tilted her head a bit, as if she could read right through the lie.

Then, she smiled. "Okay, then. Dinner it is."

I blinked.

I hadn't expected her to take that offer seriously.

I certainly hadn't expected her to accept it.

And something about her satisfied smile as she took Ava's hand and led her through the tunnel told me she knew it, too.

Chapter 2

The Furthest Thing from Cool

Chloe

"Your house is like the circus Daddy took me to," Ava said, standing just inside the front door of my small home with her Tampa Bay Ospreys backpack still strapped to her shoulders.

She didn't seem particularly excited about the observation.

Then again, this kid was rarely excited about *anything*.

Her curly hair — which was almost as long as her father's — had completely fallen out of her hair tie at this point, and she swept it out of her eyes as she looked around at the organized clutter.

I couldn't fault her for her assessment. Between my current knitting project, my half-sewn skirt I was working on, the paint-by-numbers craft I'd started and then abandoned after three glasses of wine, and the array of colorful cat toys strewn throughout the house — it kind of *did* look like a circus.

"A circus, huh?" I asked, taking her backpack and hanging it by my door. "Well, we better be on the lookout for acrobats and tigers."

"There's one!"

Ava pointed at Nacho just as he came scampering over from somewhere in the back hallway, his fluffy orange tail flicking back and forth. The cat wasn't scared of anything, not even a kindergartner, and he trotted right up to Ava and arched against her leg.

"This is Nacho," I told her as she bent to pet him. She didn't smile like most kids would when having their fingers running through silky fur. She didn't say *awww* or giggle, either. No, she wore the same look of indifference I was used to her showing in class.

Now that I'd been around her father a few times, it was easy to see the apple didn't fall far from the tall, thick, muscular tree.

Still, even this was an improvement over where she'd been at the beginning of the school year. Will had hired me to work with her after school in the first semester, as she had lost her confidence to speak once she was in a class with twenty other students.

I learned quickly that Ava just needed a little patience, and, honestly? Indifference. She didn't want the baby talk and the nonstop attention. She didn't need cookies for a job well done or an over-the-top celebration.

"He's soft, isn't he?" I asked.

Ava nodded, and it wasn't long before my other two fur children joined us.

"This one is Pepper, and that one is Coconut," I told her, signaling to each of them.

Pepper was a gray striped tabby and the skinniest

of the three, no doubt the runt of his litter. He had more energy than any five-year-old I'd ever taught.

Coconut, on the other hand, was standoffish and untrusting of everyone — even me. She curled her tail underneath her as she sat beneath my sewing table, a full ten feet away from us, her bright blue eyes narrowed and assessed Ava.

I didn't mean to become the stray cat mom. It just sort of... *happened*.

Pepper was the first. I saw him on the side of the road on my way home from work one day, and when I'd taken him to the local animal shelter, they'd told me that if I left him, he'd be put down.

The memory of that still made me angry and upset today, but then again, I understood. They were overrun. They didn't have space.

And so, he became my first baby.

Nacho showed up at my back porch a few months later, meowing for food with his fur matted and gunk in his eyes.

I'd no sooner taken him in before Coconut appeared in my backyard, although she'd stayed distant for weeks before she'd graced us with her presence inside. I'd left food for her on the porch and made sure she had water, too.

It took two weeks for her to let me close enough to pet her.

Then, when the temperature dipped below sixty one night — a rarity in Tampa — she'd croaked a meow at me when I opened the door and sauntered inside like she already owned the place.

Now, I was a certified cat lady at the ripe old age of twenty-six.

"Do you have any pets?" I asked Ava.

"No. Daddy says cats are assholes and dogs are too much work."

I slapped a hand over my mouth to stifle my laugh. I was fairly certain her *daddy* wouldn't approve of that language, but I was also pretty sure he didn't know how to filter himself around her. She probably didn't even know asshole was a "bad word."

"He's not wrong," I told her. "You hungry?"

Ava nodded, standing from where she'd been scratching Nacho behind one ear. The fact that she wasn't trying to pick him up by the neck told me she had more restraint than most of the children I taught.

"I'll make us a snack," I said, nodding toward my abandoned artwork on the coffee table. "Any chance you can help me with that? I started it the other night, but I'm not very good at painting."

Just as she didn't like baby talk, I learned early on with Ava that she also didn't respond to what I referred to as my "teacher voice." Where I was usually sing-song sweet and peppy with my kids, Ava responded better when I spoke to her like an adult. She liked an even, emotionless tone.

I couldn't imagine why.

An image of her father crossed my mind as Ava sat on her knees, picking up the paintbrush and wetting it in the cloudy glass of water before she wiped it over one of the dry paints. We'd experimented with watercolor last semester, and I was impressed she remembered just what to do.

She then promptly started painting all over the place, no care for the numbers or lines on the butterfly image.

I just chuckled.

Better for her to make a mess of it than for it to sit unfinished on my table for months.

I turned on my Bluetooth speaker as I rounded into my kitchen, putting on a kid-friendly, but not annoying, playlist. That was literally the name of the playlist on Spotify — Kid Friendly, Not Annoying.

That last part was essential, since I spent most of my day listening to either kids or cartoons singing.

I could keep an eye on Ava through the window cut out in my kitchen, only a bar and a couple of stools between us. Not that I really felt like I needed to. Out of all my students, Ava was the easiest to handle.

So, with her occupied and my hands mindlessly working to make us a snack tray, I let my thoughts drift to Will Perry.

The man was a magnetic force.

Tall as a tree, muscles like a bull, and the saddest golden-brown eyes I'd ever seen.

The first time I'd met him, I'd had to actively work to keep myself from drooling. He was an exact replica of the cover model for one of the Harlequin romances I'd snuck into our house when I was fourteen — one I'd kept hidden from my mother and grandmother and re-read more times than I could count.

His chestnut hair was long and unruly, flowing to his shoulders and highlighted by the sun with strands of gold like he was Hercules. He had the kind of jaw that could cut glass, it was so sharp, and though his pouty lips never did curve into a smile, that didn't make it any less difficult to not stare at his mouth.

He was just... beautiful. Achingly so. The way the last sunset on a beach vacation is.

I didn't have to hear his life story to see that he'd been through pain. He wore it like armor, his lips in a thin line, brows furrowed, hand tight around his daughter's like he didn't trust anyone to properly care for her.

Judging by how fast he'd gone through a half-dozen nannies since Ava started school, he had reason to feel that way.

Today, that severe gaze of his had been tinted with anxiety.

And so, without even thinking twice, I'd offered to help.

Not that I *wouldn't* have helped even if I *did* stop to think before opening my mouth. I was so desperate for something to do with my spare time that I'd jump at practically any opportunity. There were only so many nights I could spend sewing a new outfit, knitting a scarf that I'd never wear because it's too damn hot in Florida anyway, or bingeing the latest true crime podcast.

You could go on a date, a voice whispered in my brain, but it was snuffed out by the louder voice that reminded me all the reasons that wasn't a good idea.

The most prevalent being that my matriarchy would likely disown me.

I grew up in a house ruled by scorned women. My mother was a single mom, raising me to be independent from the time I could walk in some sort of effort to spite my father and every other man on Earth. *She* was brought up by a single mom, too — my grandmother, who was not too shy to remind her daughter what a constant disappointment she was for following in her footsteps despite my grandmother's warnings.

After my father left, Grandma moved in with us. And between the two of them, I was surrounded by an ever-present reminder that all men were trash.

And after the one experience of my own with the opposite sex in college? I had to agree.

I didn't think of boys much when I was younger, but when I turned thirteen, something inside me just... *clicked*. I was instantly boy crazy, hyperaware of every time a boy so much as looked at me, let alone brushed past.

By the time I was in high school, I was sneakily watching romance movies on my laptop and hiding books in my room like they were paraphernalia. I spent multiple nights a week under my comforter with my eyes wide as I read Wattpad stories. I listened to the few friends I had tell me stories of dating and going to first, second, or third base with my phone in hand, feverishly taking notes.

But I knew better than to even *try* to date in my household.

It wasn't until I left for college that I had enough guts to kiss a boy. It was slimy and gross and didn't do much for me, but I didn't want to be a virgin my entire life, so I let the guy have his way with me in the back bedroom of a house party.

My head hung off the bed the whole time, and he had an old Chingy song playing on his speaker.

It hurt at first. Then it was just uncomfortable.

It lasted approximately forty-eight seconds, and to this day, I still counted them as the worst of my life.

Add in the fact that the jerk bragged to his friends the next day before promptly making me out to be some kind of *Stage 5 Clinger*, as he'd put it, and it was then that you could say my appetite for romance was snuffed out like a match flame.

It had devastated me that my mom and grandma were right.

I'd wanted so desperately to have the kind of love I'd seen in *The Notebook*. I'd even dreamed about something as hilariously inevitable as the stubborn, helplessly love-sick situations in *No Strings Attached* or *Friends with Benefits*.

I wanted to be the average girl who turned the head of the billionaire, or the shy bookworm who got the quarterback, or the cool advertising account manager who fell for her childhood best friend.

But I didn't have a childhood best friend.

I was the furthest thing from cool.

And my only experience with a boy had left a taste in my mouth so sour, I still wasn't rid of it even seven years later.

So, here I was, twenty-six and devoted to my life as a teacher. I didn't watch romance movies anymore, but instead indulged in crime documentaries. I didn't listen to love songs, but to podcasts about how cool ants are. I didn't go on dates, but instead spent my evenings with my three cats and my current project — be it sewing, knitting, painting, or some other craft I saw on social media.

To some, I knew it seemed an unfathomable existence. It sounded lonely and pathetic.

But I *liked* being alone. I liked throwing my all into my classroom, into the students whom I had the chance to plant seeds with at the perfect age for them to sprout. I never felt lonely, not with my cats, my mom, and my grandma.

I did, however, feel stuck sometimes — like I wasn't living life, but rather that life was living me.

"Oops!"

I blinked out of my thoughts as Ava sent the glass of murky water toppling, and instead of moving to clean it, she just looked over her shoulder at me.

I smirked, grabbing the tray of fruits, veggies, and crackers I'd put together and bringing it with me into the living room — along with a towel.

"Don't worry, my little angel bug," I said, pressing the towel into the wet carpet. "Life's no fun without making a mess once in a while."

Chapter 3

Mr. Turkey

Will

Chef Arushi Patel was proof that angels were real.

It had been Uncle Mitch who'd first found her. Shortly after Jenny died, when I could barely keep my kid alive and drag my ass to work, I came home one day to find her in my kitchen. My uncle knew I needed help, but he also knew I wasn't capable of seeking it out myself.

A normal, well-functioning person would have been shocked by a stranger in their home.

But I was numb to everything at the time.

I hadn't so much as questioned her presence, tending to Ava as Chef Patel cooked me my first hot meal not from a drive-thru in weeks. When I finished eating, she cleaned up the kitchen, crossed her arms, arched a brow at me, and said, "We doing this?"

I'd had her on a weekly payroll ever since.

Tonight, she was whipping up an elevated version of chicken nuggets and macaroni and cheese — something Ava loved, but I could also tolerate, with Chef putting her spin on it. The chicken was always well-cooked and juicy, seasoned to perfection without too much breading, and the pasta was so good I'd licked my plate clean the first time she made it. Add in that she always somehow found a way to sneak in vegetables and get Ava excited about them, and you could say Chef was first on my short list of things in life I was grateful for.

"Thank you for accommodating an extra guest," I said to her as I sat at the kitchen island, wincing a bit as I did. Practice had been brutal, and so had the last few games. January was when every team in the league started getting a clearer picture of whether they had a shot at the playoffs or not, and we were hungry for the Cup this year.

"Are you kidding? I'm just happy you *have* a guest." She shook her head as she stirred the pasta. Her black hair was pulled into a tight ponytail that swung a bit as she did. "I was beginning to worry you didn't have any friends."

"I have plenty of friends," I grumbled.

"Uncle Mitch doesn't count."

"I have my team."

"Oh, that's right," she said, leaning a hip against the edge of the stove and tapping the wooden spoon against her chin. "I think I met a few of your teammates. One time. In the five years I've known you." She pointed the spoon at me. "You must be so *close*."

I leveled her with an unamused look as she shot me a wry grin. Chef Patel loved to give me shit.

I'd never tell her that I secretly liked it, too.

At the rink, I was all business. I always had a team to wrangle and a game to win. Somehow, in the last nine years, I'd gone from a decent rookie, to a promising rising star, to a fucking train wreck, and then to the best goalie in the league.

I was now a veteran player for the Tampa Bay Ospreys, and for the first time since I'd been a part of the franchise, we had a real shot at the Cup.

My sole focus rested in getting us there.

Which didn't leave much time for *friends*.

My teammates were like family, though. I may not have shown it as much as I should have, or in the ways most people were used to — but they knew I loved them. They knew I was there for them. Hell, if it wasn't for me slapping them upside the head sometimes and making them think straight, half of them would probably be sent down to the AHL, or completely wiped from *any* league.

I would push them. I would remind them of their priorities. I would show them how to play better, faster, stronger.

But no, I wasn't going to party at the local puck bunny spots after a win, nor was I going to crack open a beer and shoot the shit at a barbecue in the off-season.

I didn't *want* friends.

I wanted a team.

I wanted the Stanley Cup.

And I wanted my daughter to be okay.

That last part was always the most difficult of the equation. Not only was I struggling more often than not to be a good, present father with a career that demanded so much of my time and attention, but I also apparently had a massive ineptitude when it came to finding a nanny to help me balance it all.

A heavy sigh left me at the thought of Ava standing in the car line waiting for the *last* sorry excuse for a nanny I'd hired — the one I'd promptly *fired* just thirty minutes ago. Actually, I'd let Chef Patel do the honors. She was all too eager after I'd told her what happened. Chef thought of

Ava like her own daughter at this point, and she never did like that nanny.

I wasn't too proud to admit that I wasn't exactly the easiest guy to work for, but I also wasn't going to apologize for laying out the expectations I had for my daughter's caretaker.

It shouldn't have been so fucking hard to find a competent female figure for Ava to connect with and look up to, to learn from and feel safe with.

But fuck if it wasn't the most difficult game I'd ever played.

The security system announcing that someone was at the front gate shook me from the thought. I tried not to groan out loud as I pushed the button on my phone app that granted access, but Chef Patel chuckled — which told me I didn't succeed.

"It's just dinner," she said in a way a mother might scold a child for throwing a tantrum over cleaning their room. "Besides, I looked up your *friend*," she added, waggling her brows. "She's quite pretty. Don't think you'll have to suffer too much."

I ignored that comment and made my way to the driveway just in time to see Miss Knott opening the back door of an old Honda Accord.

Chef was wrong.

Miss Knott wasn't *quite pretty* — she was fucking gorgeous.

Even after what I could assume was a long day of herding little brats at the private school she taught at, she still had a glow about her. I'd been annoyed that I'd even noticed her shapely body when she'd come to the rink earlier. Now, with practice over and nothing else calling my attention, it was all I could do not to stare too hard at those curves as she bent down to help Ava out of her booster seat, the swell of her ass framed perfectly by that damned polka dot skirt.

Fucking Christ.

She handed Ava her backpack as I straightened my shoulders and brought my eyes *away* from her backside. My daughter slipped the straps over her shoulders with a blank stare, dragging her feet a little on her way over to me.

"Hey, Pumpkin," I said in greeting, ruffling her hair when she made it to me. "Have fun?"

"Yeah," she said — in the way someone might sound if they were telling you about a root canal. "I painted a butterfly."

"A butterfly? That sounds pretty. Can I see it?"

"Nacho threw up on it," she said, and then she was heading inside without further explanation or waiting for me to follow. "Guess you were right. Cats are assholes."

She disappeared inside the house with me internally cursing myself for how blatantly unaware I was of my mouth around my kid. I heard Chef Patel greeting Ava inside at the same time I heard a soft giggle behind me.

I turned slowly, cocking a brow when I found Chloe with one arm crossed over her abdomen and the other covering her mouth as she fought back another laugh.

"Find that amusing, do you?" I asked.

"Oh, immensely so."

I shook my head, nodding toward the front door. "Please, come in."

I really did try not to grit the words, but I was fairly certain I failed in that attempt as Chloe smirked to herself and led the way inside. She paused once she was in the foyer, and I shut the door behind us.

"I didn't even think to ask if you had a booster seat," I said.

"Always have one in the car."

"You have kids?"

Her cheeks flushed red enough you'd have thought I asked her if she was wearing panties.

"No. Just like to be prepared as a teacher, and a babysitter. I take care of my neighbor's kids sometimes."

I nodded. "Well, thank you. For bringing her to me, and even more so for taking her to your house while I finished up at the rink."

I pulled my wallet from my back pocket, thumbing out a few hundred-dollar bills and handing them to her.

Chloe blanched, blinking before her wide eyes slid to mine. "That's entirely unnecessary."

I blinked back at her, but didn't smile or drop my hand.

With an exasperated sigh, she took the money, slipping it inside the purse she had on that looked like a gold coin. She snapped it shut again before folding her hands together.

"Um, would you like something to drink?" I asked, so out of practice having a guest in my house I was practically breaking out in hives.

"Wine would be great."

Shit.

Chloe smirked at my expression. "You don't have wine, do you?"

"He doesn't drink," Chef Patel said, rounding out of the kitchen and wiping her wet hands on a dish towel. She threw it over her shoulder before stepping down to greet Chloe with an outstretched hand and her million-dollar smile. "Fortunately for you, I do — and I have a stash in the kitchen."

"You do?" I asked.

Chef rolled her eyes at me, then looked at Chloe and pointed her thumb my way. "No one better on the ice. But at home? This one's about as observant as a turkey."

I narrowed my eyes. "A turkey?"

"Gobble, gobble," she said with a saccharine smile, and then she hooked her arm through Chloe's and led her toward the kitchen. "I'm Arushi Patel, but you can call me Chef."

• • •

Dinner was served a short ten minutes later, Chef Patel making sure we were all settled and taken care of before she kept herself busy cleaning up the kitchen. I was thankful she was still close enough to where we were in the informal dining area that she could help me carry the conversation with Chloe because I was as good at small talk as I was at braiding my daughter's hair.

I must have worn my discomfort on my sleeve, too, because as soon as dessert was cleared away, Chloe smiled into her napkin, blotting at her lips before folding it on the table. "Well, I'm sure you're ready to relax. I'll get out of your hair and be on my way."

Before she could stand, Ava said, "But I wanna show you my room."

Chloe's eyes shot to mine before she smiled at my daughter. "Maybe we could save that for another time."

She was doing that thing again where she shoved her hair behind her ears only to immediately fix it the other way, her lips pinned between her teeth, weight shifting from one hip to the other.

"You're more than welcome to stay," I said, clearing my throat.

"Oh yeah?" She smiled like I'd told a joke. "Pretty sure you just checked the time on your watch for the tenth time since I got here."

Chef Patel sucked her teeth at me as she cleared our dessert plates. "Manners of a goat."

"First I'm a turkey, now I'm a goat?"

That almost got a smile out of my daughter, and then my phone was ringing. I frowned down at Carter's name on the screen before standing and excusing myself out the back sliding glass door that led to our pool.

"Okay. You win. Why don't you take Miss Knott up to show her your room?" I said to Ava. "I'll be right back."

I thought I heard another joke at my expense from my darling chef before I shut the door behind me and accepted the call.

"What?"

Carter barked out a laugh. "Well, hello to your grumpy ass, too."

I rolled my eyes. "What do you want? It's a school night."

"How's my favorite girl?"

"Currently as close to happy as she gets because she's showing her kindergarten teacher around our home."

There was a brief silence before he said, "Um... care to elaborate on why her teacher is there this late?"

"Not even a little bit. What do you want, Fabio?"

Carter Fabri was the closest thing I had to an annoying little brother. The kid had rolled up as a rookie last season with a feather in his hat and a grin the size of his home province. As much as he gave me gray hairs, I liked his attitude. I liked that when he was here, he was dedicated — no matter how much he partied in his off time.

The problem was that he wasn't here long.

He rode the bench for a lot of his first season, coming in for sporadic line changes every now and then before he was sent down to the AHL to help them with playoffs. He came back to training camp for this season and stuck around for a few months, but he just wasn't quite where he needed to be to stay put.

And so, he was back with our AHL affiliate once again.

I knew he had it in him to secure a permanent spot here in Tampa, he just needed to grow up a little bit. He also needed to get laid more or find some kind of way to beef up his confidence. As a center, he needed to be a leader. He needed to call the shots and communicate with his linemates without any hesitation.

As it was currently, he had the backbone of a grasshopper.

"I sent you a film clip," he said, and my phone buzzed in my ear with the text arrival. "I need some Daddy P tough love because I'm about to lose my mind if I can't figure out why this shit keeps happening to me."

Daddy P was the nickname bestowed on me by my team. Daddy for obvious reasons, and P for Perry — or Pickles, depending on who you asked, because I was "cool as a cucumber."

The Pickles side of that argument clearly hadn't seen me at my lowest.

I watched the clip, seeing the error immediately. He'd cleared the puck up the middle only to lose control and have the opponent take it the other way and score.

In other words — a turnover.

He wasn't back checking hard enough, and I told him as much, coaching him through the scenario and giving him some drill homework.

It took nearly thirty minutes to get him off the line, and as soon as I did, my phone rang again.

This time, it was Maven — fiancée to Vince Tanev, one of our right wingers and, in an interesting twist of events, a good friend of mine.

Well, as good of a friend as I let into my life, anyway.

"What?" I answered.

"Don't *what* me, you prick."

The difference in how she responded to my greeting compared to Carter wasn't lost on me. Maven King was feisty. I liked that about her.

"I heard another nanny bit the dust today," she said. "Was just calling to see if you needed me. I have a lot going on with the foundation right now, but I should be able to move things around to help."

I pinched the bridge of my nose on a long sigh, feeling like an asshole — which was nothing new.

"Thank you," I said. "I might take you up on that. Let me try to figure something out, but if I can't..."

"I've got you," she said. "You can take her to school in the morning before pre-game skate?"

"Yeah."

"Give me a call after and let me know if you need me to pick her up. I could bring her to the game with me, too."

I nodded. "Thanks, Mave."

My head was pounding by the time I ended the call, and I made my way back inside to find the kitchen spotless and a note from Chef on the counter.

Pre-game pasta is in the fridge.
See you in a couple days, turkey.

I dragged my sore ass upstairs, nearly forgetting Miss Knott was still here until I heard her voice coming from Ava's room.

I frowned, the words familiar as I crept closer, and when I made it to the door, I paused at the sight of her sitting against Ava's headboard reading one of her favorite bedtime books.

My daughter was already sound asleep, one arm around her Ospreys stuffed animal fish, her mouth half-open and a little drool coming out.

Chloe startled when she saw me, glancing down at Ava with a soft smile before she carefully slid off the bed, replaced the book on Ava's shelf, and tiptoed toward me. I waited until she was out of the room before I took her place, bending to kiss Ava's forehead and turn on her night light.

I met Chloe in the hallway, and she waited until we were away from Ava's room before speaking in a whisper.

"I hope you don't mind, but after she showed me her room, she was already yawning. I ran a bath for her, checked on her a couple times, and laid out some pajamas for when she was finished. She brushed her teeth without me asking, and then asked if I'd read to her."

I couldn't articulate why, but there was a thick knot in my throat.

This.

This was what I had been looking for, what I needed. Someone who had common fucking sense. Someone who knew how to handle kids — no, not just any kid. *My* kid.

Someone who could figure out what needed to be done without asking me for a fucking play by play.

"How attached are you to your job?"

Chloe blinked at my question, and then chuckled. "Very much so. Why? Are you going to try to get me fired?"

"No, I want to hire you."

She blinked again. "Oh."

Her fingers wound together at her waistline, and I let out a long sigh. Not only had I burdened this woman, but now I'd made her uncomfortable.

Fan-fucking-tastic.

"I'm sorry," I said. "It's a stupid idea. Of course, you wouldn't want to leave your position."

"No," she agreed.

I nodded, leading her down the stairs, and she followed on my heels for a moment before jogging to walk by my side. She tripped a little over her feet in the process.

"But that doesn't mean I can't work for you, too."

I paused when we hit the bottom stair, arching a brow. "Are you saying you'd be interested?"

"What are you looking for, exactly?"

I blew out a breath. "A nanny," I said honestly. "I need someone to get her up on the mornings I can't be here, the ones when I'm traveling with the team. She needs after-school care, sometimes weekends, sometimes weeknights."

She chuckled. "So... like all the time?"

I grimaced, shaking my head and walking toward the front door. "It's not possible, I know. It's just... you'd be surprised how what you did just today and tonight has far surpassed any other nanny I've had."

"You're really bad at letting people speak for themselves."

I turned, nearly knocking her over when I did because I didn't realize she was following so closely. My chest knocked against hers, and she let out a surprised laugh as I steadied her with my hands on her arms. She peeked up at me through her lashes with her cheeks burning pink.

From this angle, those curves that were already haunting me were on prominent display — especially that heavy bust of hers. She was soft in a way nothing else in my life was, and without meaning to, I stroked her arm with my thumb.

Then, I promptly cleared my throat and stepped back, scowling.

"I doubt you'd have time for everything I just listed."

"You'd be surprised to know just how much time I have," she said on a chuckle, tucking her copper hair behind one ear. She folded her arms across her chest then. "Let's give it a try. One week — starting tomorrow. Whatever you usually ask of your other nannies, I'll do. As long as you're okay with her coming to my house?" She smirked. "I *do* have three asshole cats."

"Three? Good God." I shook my head, but then studied her, looking for red flags or warning signs. I already knew she was competent and good with kids. She did still look a bit flushed from me touching her, but she wasn't trying to seduce me — which was a pleasant change.

And at this point, what other choice did I have?

"Are you allowed to do this? With her being your student."

"Absolutely. I've nannied for many of my students."

"Really?" That honestly surprised me.

"It's a private school," she reminded me. "The parents can be quite..."

She didn't have to finish that sentence for me to understand. Just in the times I'd dropped Ava off, I'd witnessed the overbearing mothers who wanted to have a whole parent-teacher conference there in the car line. I'd also witnessed the fathers dropping their kids with barely a glance as they yacked away to someone on their cell phones, already doing business before eight AM.

"Let's just say it's not a problem," she assured me. "I'll let the principal know, of course, just so all the information is on the table. She'll want to be aware. Other than that, Ava might have to hang around with me a little bit after school sometimes, or go in early with me, but she's easy to handle. I'll give her a job to do and she'll be happy."

There was that damned knot in my throat again because she already knew more about my daughter than any other nanny I'd had.

Ava didn't want attention. She didn't want you to watch her play or entertain her. She wanted something to do with her hands and to be left the hell alone.

No idea where she got that from.

"One week," I agreed. "But you have to be honest and tell me if it doesn't work out. I don't want to take you from your boyfriend or anything."

At that, her lips curled, eyes searching mine. "No boyfriend, Mr. Perry."

The words were soft and timid.

And for some reason, they sent a jolt straight to my cock, just like hearing her say *yes, sir* had earlier.

I ignored the sensation, nodding as I opened the door for her while surmising that I needed to get laid soon so I didn't keep having fantasies about my kid's teacher and now, possible nanny. It wasn't hard to find a woman to warm my bed, but I didn't do it often — not until my agitation got to a point where I had no choice but to find a release that wasn't my fucking hand.

Apparently, that time had come.

We walked to Chloe's car, and once we reached it, I asked, "How much?"

"To nanny the easiest child in the world?" She tapped her chin. "Oh, I don't know. Five grand a week."

I considered the price for only a split second before I held out my hand. "Fair."

Chloe gaped at me, laughing at my hand before she swatted it away. "I was *joking*."

"I'm not."

"That's... *ridiculous*. That's far too much."

"To know my daughter is safe and cared for, I'd pay four times that price."

She softened, her brows sliding together, and I hated the way she looked at me in that moment so much that I opened her car door and ushered her inside.

"I can take her to school in the morning, but I'll need you to care for her after. I'll send you an email with the gate and house codes, but I have to get everything changed since I fired my previous nanny today. It might take a couple days, so if you don't mind taking her to your place until then?"

"Not a problem at all," she assured me.

"I'll make sure she has extra clothes. I have a friend who can come get her and bring her to the game."

"I could take her," she offered. "I mean, if you want. We need to test out every scenario, right?"

I nodded. "Fair point. I'll have a ticket for both of you at the box office."

She rolled down her window when I shut her door, the old car firing to life.

"See you tomorrow, Mr. Turkey," Chloe said with a wink.

And then she reversed out of the driveway, giving me a headache while simultaneously saving my ass.

Chapter 4

Dead Inside

Chloe

The next evening, I sat next to Ava in club level seats at the Tampa Bay Ospreys arena downtown, wide-eyed and taking in the scenery of my first hockey game.

The energy was palpable.

Fans streamed in from every direction, filling the seats and adding to the noise level with every passing minute. The jumbotron shot off announcement after announcement while the DJ played loud, upbeat music for the teams to warm up to.

I looked around in awe, taking in the various groups of fans. I saw everything from couples and families with young kids to groups of rowdy men sloshing beer and screaming women with hand-painted signs for their favorite players.

The game hadn't even started yet, and the crowd was loud as hell.

Ava stood next to where I sat, pressing up on her tiptoes to get a better look at all the action. As usual, she didn't wear a smile, but just like she had when I brought her to practice, she lit up like I'd never seen her before.

"You really like hockey, don't you?" I asked her.

"Mm-hmm," she said, barely acknowledging me as she watched the players warm up. It was almost seven-thirty, and from what her father had told me, she usually went to bed around eight or eight-thirty. But tonight was a special occasion, and she didn't look the slightest bit sleepy.

I turned my attention back to the ice to where the players were, and I didn't realize I was chewing at the skin on my lip until Ava said something about it.

"How come you move so much when you're sitting still?"

I blinked, then chuckled, blushing a little as I realized she'd picked up on my nervous tics. I had a habit of wringing my hands together or fussing with my hair when I was uncomfortable — had ever since I was a kid. It drove my mom and grandmother absolutely batshit, but I had yet to find a way to control it.

To be honest, I rarely realized I was doing it at all.

"Just like to fidget, I guess," I said. "You know, kind of like the fidget slinkies we have in class?"

"Those are kinda fun." She looked at me then. "Maybe you should carry one in your purse."

I rolled my lips together against a laugh. "Yeah, I probably should, huh?"

"Chloe?"

I turned toward the voice coming from above and behind me, finding a stunning woman smiling at me from the next row up. She had jet black hair styled in tight curls, her honey-colored eyes glowing against her warm brown skin.

"I'm Maven," she said, extending her hand for mine.

"Oh! Hi," I said, standing so I could turn to face her and take her hand. Will had told me about Maven. She was one of his teammates' fiancée and helped out with Ava from time to time.

"Glad to see you made it in okay," she said, and then she leaned over the seats to give Ava a hug from behind and a kiss on the cheek. "Hey, you."

"Hi," Ava said, but she kept her eyes on the ice, as if Maven was bugging her as much as I had been with my question.

"I'm surprised you're not down there on the ice," she said to Ava. Then, to me, she added, "Warmups are about the only time the kids can get their dad's attention before the game."

She nodded toward where a player was making faces at a little boy who couldn't have been more than three years old to illustrate her point, and I smiled.

But Ava just shrugged. "Daddy needs to focus. I'll see him after."

Maven shot me an amused smile, her perfectly shaped eyebrow arching a bit. "Okay, as her teacher... is she always this serious?"

"Afraid so," I mused with a grin of my own at the little angel. "I'm working on her, though."

"Tough to soften up someone raised by Will Perry, I suppose." Maven assessed me for a moment. "Well, I'm just a few rows up, if you need anything," she said, pointing to her seat. When she did, a woman with rich brown skin and straight black hair cut in a sharp bob waved at us. "That's Livia. She's my best friend and also the team's dentist."

I waved back at her, my head spinning a bit.

The team had its own *dentist*?

"After the game, I can walk you to the friends and family lounge. That's where we meet up with the players," Maven explained.

"That would be lovely. Thank you."

"Sure thing," she said with that dazzling smile. "Oh, and... don't be a stranger, okay? Just the way those guys down there are a family, we're a team, too," she said, as if I were a wife or partner to one of the players.

I hoped my skin wasn't as red as it felt.

One last look at Ava had her chuckling to herself, and then she retreated to her seats. I watched her for a split second with her best friend, the way they so comfortably laughed and clutched each other's arms like they had a million inside jokes.

It made my stomach ache.

I longed for a friendship like that.

It wasn't that I hadn't had the opportunity to make friends. I had a few in college. I had some at the school where I worked now. But for whatever reason, I just never... fit in, I supposed. They were nice to me when I was around. If there was a work event, we could all laugh and chat. But it was surface level. It never went deep.

The closest things I had to best friends were my mom and my grandma. We talked all the time, shared inside jokes, and leaned on each other through the good and the bad. Those women had sacrificed so much for me, from their bodies, energy, and time to what little money they had. They'd even gone into debt to put me through college.

I loved them. And I loved spending time with them.

But I could never talk to them about my deepest thoughts and desires, could never be one-hundred percent honest with them. Because so many of the things I thought about, so many of the things I wanted... well, they would never understand.

When I took my seat again, I let myself get lost in the daze of watching players dash this way and that on the ice. There were dozens of pucks on both sides of the rink, and the teams were skating around in a dizzying pattern taking shots on the open net.

My eyes lost focus, the fatigue from the day and the week catching up to me. Starting up the second semester of the school year always felt harder than the first. After the holidays, kids were restless — and so was the staff. We still had months to go, but it seemed everyone was counting down to summer break.

Add in the fact that I unexpectedly took on a second job, and I felt all kinds of off-kilter.

It wasn't a job I didn't feel prepared to take, otherwise I would have said no. I'd nannied for plenty of my parents before and always enjoyed getting to know my students better. I also enjoyed having something to do with my time other than be alone. I liked being at home, liked my crafts and my cats and my peaceful quiet. But in the same breath, I always felt like I was itching for a change in routine.

And this was certainly a change in routine.

It was also my first time nannying for someone as high-profile as Will Perry.

I shook my head at the memory of him dropping off Ava at school this morning. He'd slid a check for five-thousand dollars into my hand when he'd walked Ava to class, and although I'd tried with all my energy not to accept it, he'd insisted.

Five grand.

That was more than I made in a month.

There was absolutely zero chance that I'd continue to let him pay me such an astronomical amount, but arguing with a six-foot-four, two-hundred-twenty-pound goalie on the day he had a game didn't seem like a smart idea.

Besides, that money could help me pay off the student loans my matriarchy was currently buried under. It could help me pay my *own* bills without stress.

That was the life of a teacher that so many left out. You had to love what you did because you certainly weren't going into this career for the money.

I blinked, my vision coming back into focus, and found myself scanning the ice for that beast of a man I was now temporarily working for. I knew from the tiny blue and white jersey Ava was wearing that he was number twenty-eight. It was also fairly easy to spot the goalies, as they stood out among the other players.

When I found him, he was standing off to the side of where all the rest of the team was shooting pucks. He hovered close to the glass, facing the rink, and he skated in place, side to side, with his gaze locked somewhere on the ice ahead of him. Then, he crouched low, dodging this way and that with lightning-quick movements and fast-snaps of his limbs in various directions like he was blocking pucks.

The back of my neck tingled with awareness as I watched him, knowing that under that cage of a mask was the scowl that he wore so easily. He was menacing, on or off the ice — and yet, after dinner last night, I couldn't help but wonder if there was a softness under that hard shell exterior.

The way he cared for his daughter, the way his chef seemed to care for *him* — it just seemed like there was more to him than met the eye.

And the poor man needed help.

That was more evident than anything else. He'd acted like I hung the moon rather than just helped his daughter get ready for bed. I knew he'd had a string of bad luck with finding a nanny, but had it really been *that* atrocious?

I marveled at his poise as he went through his warmup drills, the crowd getting louder and louder. I took my eyes off him long enough to pay attention to one of the announcements on the jumbotron, and when I looked at him again, my eyes shot wide.

He'd moved down to the ice now, onto his hands and knees, and he was stretching like he belonged on an Olympic gymnast team rather than a hockey team.

His hands were braced in front of him, holding his weight steady as he stretched his hips wide against the ice. One leg was bent, the other extended to the side, and he crouched low to the ice before rolling his hips forward and backward in a rhythm that made heat rush to my cheeks.

It should have been illegal for any man to have an ass like that.

And it should have been a felony for him to move his hips in that way, the way that made it impossible not to imagine what it would be like to be beneath him while he did it.

I tried not to stare. Really, I did. I attempted to focus on the other players, on the fans, on the bright orange fish mascot that was now making its way around the arena.

But my eyes kept snapping back to Will Perry.

He had both legs bent now, and he'd roll forward before extending his legs as straight as he could and then bending them again. After a while, he laid in a pancake stretch, his stomach and chest on the ice and his legs spread. But it wasn't a passive stretch, it was *active* — his quads and hamstrings lifting him off the ice a few inches before he'd lower deeper into the stretch.

When he bent his legs and started rolling his hips again, I forced myself to look away.

Now was not the time to fantasize about my new boss — not when I was responsible for his daughter in the seat right next to mine.

Okay, in reality, I probably should *never* fantasize about him.

But he was a hot, professional athlete with a daughter he'd move mountains for.

I might have been celibate, but I wasn't dead inside.

I managed to keep it in my pants through the rest of the warmup, and when the game actually started, Ava took her seat with something that almost resembled a smile.

"Let's go, Daddy!" she screamed, and damn it if my heart didn't melt into a puddle. This kid was so cute it hurt, and the way she loved her father... I knew he was the end all, be all in her eyes.

I was quiet most of the first period, mostly taking in the experience and trying to follow as best I could. I'd never watched a game of hockey in my life, never really watched *any* sport, to be honest, and I found myself taking my cues from Ava.

If she cheered, I did, too.

If she groaned and booed, so did I.

And if she growled in frustration, shaking the stuffed fish in her hands like she wanted to strangle it, I tried not to laugh and failed every time.

We got up long enough for both of us to use the restroom and get some popcorn during the first intermission. No one had scored yet. When we sat back down, I finally asked her, "So, what's with the fish?"

I tapped the ugly thing on the tail, and Ava shoved a handful of popcorn in her mouth before shrugging.

"It's for when we win."

"When we win, huh? What happens then?"

"We throw the fish on the ice."

I blinked, sure I'd misheard her, but she didn't so much as glance my way with the statement. She was watching where they were doing some sort of game with a fan in the stands as the Zambonis smoothed the ice.

"Why?"

Ava frowned a little then. "I dunno. Daddy said it used to be real fish, but that got stinky. So now we throw fluffy fish."

I was even more confused. Fortunately, a fan just above me leaned down and explained, "It's an offering to the Osprey. She's right — it did used to be real fish in the beginning. But several years ago, it shifted to toys. The team donates the stuffed animals to local shelters and kids in need."

I offered the man a thank you before turning back to Ava with a light bulb going off.

She loved hockey, loved this team.

Maybe *this* was a way to get her talking more, to get her to open up a bit.

The game started up again, and I waited until a whistle blew before I leaned over to Ava. "So, what's going on? Why did the guy in the stripes blow the whistle?"

"He's the *referee*," she said, singing the words in an almost exhausted tone. "They were offside."

"What does that mean?"

She looked up at me then, blinking. "You don't know what offside means?"

"I'm afraid I don't know what any of this means," I said, leaning in and whispering like it was a secret confession just for her. "Think you could help me understand? I don't want to look silly."

At that, Ava's eyes widened even more, and she nodded emphatically. "Don't worry. Daddy had to teach me, too."

"So now you can teach me?"

"It's like we're switching places!"

"It is," I agreed with a grin, tapping her nose. "It's a good thing we have each other, huh?"

At that, her little brows tugged inward, and she grew quiet, nodding.

But then a fight broke out on the ice, and she grabbed me by the sleeve and tugged me down to her level to explain why.

Chapter 5

If You Want

Chloe

After the game, Maven and Livia led the way to the area where friends and family waited for the players — and it was absolute chaos.

Wives and partners of the players were everywhere, along with various family members and a bunch of kids running around. It felt like my classroom on Halloween.

The Ospreys had pulled out a win, scoring two goals to our opponents' one, and Ava had heaved her fish with all her might... only to have it land in the section below us.

Fortunately, it seemed all the fans were used to this. Fish went flying the way hats would during a hat trick — a fact Ava taught me halfway through the third period — and if one landed by you, you picked it up and threw it yourself until it made it to its intended destination.

I had to admit, it was quite a spectacle.

Although nothing was as fun to watch tonight as Will having more than two-dozen saves — another term I'd learned from his daughter.

It had been addicting, seeing how determined and focused he was on the ice. I watched him block shot after shot, most of which I felt were impossible to fend off, but he made it look effortless. Whether he had to block the puck with his torso, an extended leg, or his gloved hand — he found a way.

He only let one shot get past him, and I could tell by the way he shrugged off his teammates' assurance that it was fine that it completely pissed him off.

That man. He demanded perfection of himself.

I couldn't imagine how exhausting that must have been.

It had also been the most heartwarming moment of the game, because as he attempted to shake off the goal, Ava had sighed, whispering under her breath, "It's okay, Daddy. We are doing our best."

It was the same thing she'd said yesterday when I'd brought her to his practice, and I wondered if it was a sort of mantra for them.

I loved it.

Even if it made my eyes water every time she said it.

Ava was just finishing up a chicken nugget from the snacks provided in the family lounge — and ignoring every kid who tried to play with her — when Will spilled in from the hallway.

And I promptly stopped breathing.

He was freshly showered, his long, damp, chestnut hair pulled into a low bun at the nape of his neck. That delicious stubble peppered his jaw, his signature scowl firmly in place, his eyes as deep and haunted as ever. He was no longer in his gear, but in a charcoal suit, instead. It was custom fitted and hugged every lean angle of his body, a black tie fastened at his neck, and he didn't have to turn around for me to know those slacks would show off that perfect ass of his, too.

And as if all *that* didn't make it hard enough not to drool, he searched the room with a menacing scowl before softening as soon as he found his daughter.

She ran to him, her arms open wide, and he dropped the bag off his shoulder and slung her up the second she made it to him. It didn't matter that she was five. It was like she weighed nothing in his arms, and he pressed a kiss to her nose before listening patiently as she talked about the game.

He watched her like she was his entire world.

My guess was that she likely was.

I knew from my first meeting with Will before the school year that his wife had passed away in the first year of Ava's life. Every time I thought too hard about it, my eyes would prick with emotion that I'd have to sniff away.

I couldn't imagine losing my husband, especially after having a child.

Then again, I couldn't imagine *having* a husband, either.

My hormones were being pesky little buggers as I watched Ava nearly smile in her father's arms. He had said something to her to make that almost-grin appear, and then she started rambling on with her own stories. It was the most I'd heard her talk.

And I stood there on the other side of the room with a half-eaten cookie in my hand and my stomach flip-flopping.

I'd always wanted a family. When I was younger, I'd imagined having the opposite of what my mom and grandmother had. I pictured a little house with a little yard, a husband who adored me and worked with me as an equal partner, and maybe two or three little ones running around.

Of course, after my one and only experience with a member of the opposite sex, I realized how delusional that dream was.

But just because a dream is nonsense doesn't stop it from existing.

Ava said something that made Will frown a bit, and his gaze scanned the room until he found me.

Those deep brown eyes locked on mine, and I thought I saw his furrowed brows bend even more before the corner of his mouth twitched into the best sort of smile he could manage. He said hello to a few people in the room as he passed, and when he made it to me, he dipped his chin.

"Well, how was your first hockey game?"

"Entertaining and informative," I answered. Then, I narrowed my eyes. "Wait, how did you know it was my first?"

"I told him," Ava volunteered.

"Ah, I see. Ratting me out already, huh?" I reached forward to tickle her side, and she squirmed away with a playfulness in her eyes that was new to me — though she still didn't smile.

"I'm glad you could come," Will said, and when I brought my gaze back to him, I saw the sincerity behind that statement.

"It was nothing. Honestly. I had a great time."

He nodded, his lips pressed together as he checked the time on his watch. "Do you have a moment to talk about the week ahead?"

"You can have me all night, if you want."

I said it as a joke. At least, I *attempted* to say it as a joke. I meant it in the self-deprecating *I'm a loser with no social life, so yeah, I have time* way. Instead, it came out like a poor excuse for a flirt, which promptly made my eyes widen in horror and my cheeks burn so fiercely I felt like I had a sunburn.

Thankfully, Will just arched a brow with an amused quirk of his lips. Then, he set Ava down and told her to go talk to Maven for a moment before launching into what to expect over the next several days.

They were in the middle of a home game stretch, he explained, but since the next games would be on Sunday and Tuesday, Ava wouldn't be allowed to come. He'd need me to be home with her and getting her to bed at the usual time.

I pulled out my phone, taking notes on the times he had practice, the times when he could pick her up or drop her off versus when he needed me to, and when to expect him home to relieve me each evening. He informed me that the gate and house codes would be emailed to me first thing in the morning, and that he'd have a binder on the ins and outs of the house ready for me when I arrived to watch Ava.

By the time he finished speaking, he looked more worried than he had when I'd showed up with Ava at his practice yesterday. He let out a long sigh, his eyes searching mine.

"Are you sure you're okay with this?"

"Mostly."

"Mostly?"

I dug into my purse and fished out the folded check from that morning. "This is too much."

Will glared at the paper in my hand, then slid that glare to me. "Hardly. You deserve every penny for how you're helping me out."

48

"This is almost twice what I make in a month."

That made his jaw clench. "Well, now I'm even more adamant that you take it. You should be paid three times that amount for what you do."

My neck flushed, and I shook my head, looking down at my shoes as I tucked the check away.

"We fly to Boston on Wednesday," he explained. "But my uncle should be able to care for Ava in my absence. I get back late Thursday night, and I have the day off on Friday. Would you have time to discuss next steps then?"

"Of course. I can bring Ava home after school if that works?"

He nodded, and once again, I watched him release a long, relieved sigh. "Thank you, Chloe. I can't... I can't tell you how much this eases my mind, to know Ava will have you while I figure out what's next."

"It's nothing," I promised again.

I folded my hands in front of my waist, and Will slid his into the pockets of his slacks. His eyes searched mine for a moment, long enough that I had to tear my gaze away and look at the floor.

"I find it hard to believe," he said. "That you have the time for this, that I'm not taking you from your friends or..."

He didn't say *boyfriend* this time, and I smiled when I caught the way his Adam's apple bobbed in his throat.

"I lead the life of an eighty-year-old cat lady, Mr. Perry," I said, trying to laugh with the joke at my own expense. "Trust me — you're doing me a favor giving me something to do other than start and quit a new hobby this week."

He almost chuckled, though it was more of a chuff of a breath that left his chest. Then, we were both silent again, his eyes on mine.

At least, until they slid over the length of me, taking in the outfit I'd carefully planned for this occasion.

I didn't have a hockey jersey, but I *did* have a sewing machine and a recurring existential crisis around midnight every night. Thus why I was currently wearing a cobalt blue velvet skirt with a white blouse tucked into it, along with an ocean blue scarf, nude tights, and my favorite Sofft Shauna heels.

My skin burned in every place his gaze touched, and when he dragged it back up to my eyes, I nearly combusted at the cocky arch of his brow.

"Nice skirt."

I was pretty sure my voice was locked in my throat, caged in by sandpaper and a wine cork. Thankfully, I didn't have time to speak before Ava was running toward us, and she ran right past her father until she was standing in front of me with her hands clasped behind her.

"Thank you for tonight, Miss Knott," she said, peeking up at me. "I really liked watching the game with you."

I bent until I was at her level, smiling and tucking her wild curls behind one ear. "Thank *you*, my little angel bug. I'll see you tomorrow while your dad is at practice, and you can explain more of the rules to me. Sound good?"

Again, I could see how she wanted to grin, but instead, she just nodded once and looked proudly up at her father. "See? Told you I taught her everything."

Will reached down for her hand, and I willed my ovaries to not combust at the sight.

"I had no doubts, Pumpkin," he said. His eyes found me, and he tilted his head toward the parking lot. "I'll walk you to your car."

I waved him off as I stood upright again. "That won't be necessary."

"I apologize if that came out like a question," he said, and the way he was looking at me, I knew better than to argue.

I bit my lip against a smile, letting him lead the way, and even though he and Ava were parked in the players' lot, he walked me all the way to the lot at Sparkman Wharf, making sure I was inside with the engine started before he and Ava waved goodbye.

And I sat there with my hands on the wheel and my heart racing, even long after he'd gone.

Chapter 6

Tough Guy

Will

"For fuck's sake."

I gritted my teeth, skating hard and fast across the ice to where Aleks Suter had one of our rookies pinned up against the glass, his forearm pressing hard into the kid's neck. He was spitting something at him in German, and I didn't have to speak the language to know he wasn't complimenting the pigeon on a nice shot.

It had been a hell of a week. With a string of home games and an away game in Boston tomorrow, the whole team was tired. We needed a day off — whether to rest or blow off steam — but we weren't going to get it until Friday.

Which meant until then, I had to deal with this jerkoff and the rest of my exhausted team.

I slid to a stop when I made it to them, grabbing the back of Suter's practice jersey and yanking him backward. I had to immediately step between him and our teammate to stop him from advancing again.

"You fuck up my shot again, and I'll wring your fucking neck," Aleks threatened.

"Bro, relax. It's practice."

"Yeah, well, I don't fuck around in practice like you dumbasses."

"I was giving you the assist!"

"You were wasting oxygen and skating like a goddamn baby giraffe."

I slammed my hand hard into Suter's chest, skating him backward and away from our teammate. He pointed a thick finger over my shoulder at the rookie before shaking me off and skating away like he was just going to get right back to practice.

But I snatched him by his jersey again, dragging him with me to the bench.

Aleks Suter was a big sonofabitch. He was just as tall as I was and built like an MMA fighter, every muscle in his body sculpted by rigorous workouts and skating. Still, I slung him onto our bench like he was a teenager who weighed nothing, narrowing my gaze as he ripped off his helmet and glared at me.

"Cool off," I ordered.

Before I could skate away, he spat near his feet, offering me something between a glare and a cocky grin. The motherfucker was intimidating. He had his last team wrapped around his finger until the moment his general manager booted him, and the only reason he was here was because *our* general manager loved anything that served as a spectacle and got asses in our seats.

But *I* wasn't intimidated by Aleks — not even a little bit.

And I was hell bent on whipping him into an actual teammate who could be useful.

"You're not my daddy," he said, standing, but I shoved him back down onto the bench.

"You're already on two strikes," I reminded him. "One more, and you're off this team and likely out of the league completely. Is that what you want, tough guy?"

His jaw ticced, nostrils flaring as he returned my hard stare. He was like a mustang that refused to break, but I knew that he didn't want to lose hockey.

If I had to guess, I'd say it was the only thing that actually mattered to him.

He didn't realize it, but I saw right through his act. I knew that behind all that anger and aggression, he was dealing with something none of us understood.

I knew because I'd been there myself.

I didn't know *what* he was running from, exactly, and to be frank — I didn't give a fuck. All I needed was for him to rein it in enough to be a good fucking teammate and help us get the Cup. I wanted to help him, the way my mentor helped me when I was in a similar spot.

But unlike my mentor, I didn't have the patience to hold this prick's hand.

I didn't give two fucks if he ended up out of the league — not if that was what was best for this team. But as it stood, Coach McCabe had put his faith in me to give this clown a little guidance, to help him reach his potential.

I'd do anything for Coach because he'd been one of the men to save my ass.

After I lost Jenny, I was drowning. I could barely get myself up in the morning to care for Ava. When I *did* make it to the arena, which wasn't much, I was like a ghost — a really pissed-off, irritable ghost.

Because losing Jenny was more complicated than anyone realized.

Jenny and I weren't ever lovers — not in the traditional sense. She was my best friend, someone I laughed with and trusted. When we felt like it, we fooled around, but that was where we drew the line.

Until things got serious.

She got pregnant.

Marrying her was the easiest thing in the world. Nothing was complicated with us. We had an agreement, an understanding to raise our kid together and still live our lives the way we had been.

But somewhere along the way, I realized I loved her. Not in the passionate way love is portrayed in the movies, but in the comfortable, warm and reliable way. I came to care for her more than anyone else in the world.

And I never got the chance to tell her before she died.

Our goalie at that time was a senior veteran, a beast of a man who had a great career but was on his way out. His name was Sven, and he was trying to prepare *me* to fill his role.

I didn't know how he did it.

I didn't know how he found the patience for me, how he saw past the asshole exterior I knew I wore like a badge of honor.

But he did, and I would never be able to thank him and Coach enough for that.

I supposed getting Aleks in line was one way I could try.

"Listen, I know it can be frustrating when you feel like you're outperforming your teammates. But instead of fighting them, work with them," I chastised. "Teach them. Show them how to be better."

"No, thanks. I'm not a fucking babysitter."

"No, you're clearly the child who needs babysitting," I shot back. "Cool. Off," I repeated, jabbing my finger into his chest. "When you're ready to get serious about this practice and this team, you can come back on the ice."

"Fuck you," he said, standing. "I don't need this shit."

He stormed off toward the locker room, and I let out a heavy sigh before Coach walked over to join me. We watched Aleks disappear down the tunnel, and when I moved to go after him, Coach put a hand on my shoulder to stop me.

"Let him go," he said. "Practice is almost over anyway. Let him get centered for tomorrow's game."

"He's a cancer," I said, turning to face McCabe. "And he's bleeding into every inch of this team."

"He's our teammate," Coach argued, leveling me with just one look. "I know he's not the kind of teammate you prefer, but he's still in Osprey blue. He's still one of us. And you know damn well we wouldn't have the record we do without him."

That made me grind my teeth.

I hated that he was right.

Aleks had a bad rep around the National Hockey League and had since he joined as a rookie four years ago. When rumors surfaced over the summer that he might be traded to Tampa, I'd thought there was no way Coach would allow it. He ran a tight ship around here, and I was certain he wouldn't let some bruiser mess that up.

But as much as he loved to find trouble on and off the ice, Suter was one of the best wingers I'd ever seen. He even had more goals and assists this season than even our star forward, Vince Tanev, which was almost impossible to believe.

The issue was his attitude.

He thought he was better than everyone else, that we were all a waste of space on the ice. He also had a fuse the size of a fucking ant, and any time he blew, we paid for it — like in last night's game, when he ended up in the penalty box and Atlanta scored on us on a power play, leading to a loss.

"Be patient," Coach said, releasing my shoulder.

"I have been," I growled.

"Be *more* patient," he said with a grin, and then he blew the whistle and called practice.

Chapter 7

George of the Jungle

Chloe

Chef Patel and I had become fast friends in the five days I'd taken over as Ava's nanny.

She was the kind of sassy I wished I could be, with a smart mouth and a quick reflex to put anyone who crossed her in their place. She pushed my flavor palette to new heights by introducing me to spices I'd never tasted in my life. And perhaps what I loved most was that I had a woman to talk to who wasn't related to me.

Although, Chef Patel seemed to have the same disposition about men that my mom and grandmother did. When I asked her if she was married, she scoffed and waved her towel at me with a look that answered the question without words.

She'd helped me get acquainted with Will Perry's mansion over the weekend, showing me around the property and making sure I had all the necessary codes. When Ava was with us, Chef Patel would talk to her like an adult — which I appreciated, because that was the same approach I liked to take with her. And when Ava was asleep or otherwise occupied, Chef Patel would whip up a new dish for me to try, all while telling me her fascinating stories about traveling to places like France, Spain, India, and Poland in all her culinary studies.

Currently, she was making what she referred to as a pre-flight meal for Will — who was on his way home.

He had an away game in Boston tomorrow, and the entire team was flying out tonight. His uncle would be watching Ava in his absence, and then he'd asked if we could talk more about the next steps when he got back.

I had no idea what those *next steps* would be.

Will and I had barely had time to talk about whether this position was permanent or not. Between the string of back-to-back home games he'd had and practice in-between, the only energy he had left at the end of each day was reserved for spending time with Ava.

I respected that, and I'd left him alone, doing my best to just take care of his daughter so he had one less thing to worry about.

Now, I found that my stomach was in knots waiting for him to arrive, wondering if my services would no longer be needed. I had no idea if he had been searching for a replacement, for a more permanent option who had better availability than I did. I couldn't imagine *when* he would have found the time to do so, but I still worried, nonetheless.

Because the truth was that I adored his daughter already, and I was going to miss spending this one-on-one time with her.

I was going to miss trying to make her smile. I'd miss listening to her talk me through the beginning of each hockey game before trying her best to get me to let her stay up well past her bedtime — just like she had all week. I'd miss styling her hair — which, God help him, Will tried to do but just didn't have a clue as to how. I'd miss her quiet contemplation when we did crafts, and how she gave me a hug every day when it was time for me to leave, or every night when I put her to bed, depending on the schedule.

I'd just *miss her*.

I knew I'd have her in class still, at least until the summer, but it wouldn't be the same.

I'd also miss Chef, miss her food and her jokes and the way she made me feel right at home from the moment I showed up for dinner after watching Ava that first day last week.

And though I'd never admit it out loud, I'd miss Will, too.

I swallowed, only half-listening to Chef talk me through how she was preparing one of Will's favorite Mediterranean dishes while my heart raced thinking about her boss.

Our boss.

Something about that man called to me, even though the scowl he wore should have made me want to run and hide. Every time he walked through the door, my stomach would flip, heart pumping blood a little faster when his ginormous frame swept into the room.

I told myself it was because he looked like Brendan Fraser circa his *George of the Jungle* days — which may or may not have been my sexual awakening.

I was lost in that particularly naughty thought when the security system announced that the front gate of his property was opening, and I blinked, coming back to the present.

Chef widened her eyes at Ava. "I wonder who that could be."

"Daddy!" she said, and then she slid off where she'd been seated next to me at the kitchen island, abandoning her half-colored image of a unicorn in a field of daisies.

I laughed when I looked at it.

She'd colored the unicorn black.

Will had no sooner stepped through the front door with his giant duffle bag on his shoulder before Ava was running full speed at him. Just like always, he slung her up into his arms like she weighed nothing, kissing her hair and offering her the slightest tilt of his lips.

It was as close to a smile as I ever saw on that rugged face of his.

"There's my girl," he said. "How was your day?"

"Okay. I colored a unicorn."

"You did?"

She nodded. "And at school, we learned about words that whine. Like sink and think."

I covered my laugh with a hand as Will arched a brow at me.

"Words that *rhyme*," I corrected softly, crossing my arms where I stood by the spiral staircase. That made me feel weird, so I uncrossed them and pinned my hands between my back and the wall, instead.

She scrunched her nose. "Oh, yeah. Rhyme," she said. And then she lifted her chin. "Give me a word, Daddy."

"Duck."

Will's eyes sparkled when he glanced at me, and I shook my head.

He was asking for it.

"Tuck," Ava said, and her shoulders squared, showing how proud she was of herself. "Oh, and Daddy's favorite word — fuck!"

Chef Patel said something in Hindi that sounded disapproving, and I just tongued my cheek and cocked a brow at Will.

"You are far too smart and observant for your own good," he said, nuzzling her neck while Ava fought off a grin. It was the closest I'd seen her to losing that fight. "Which means you also know better than to say that word, don't you?"

Ava flushed and nodded.

"You know what to do."

Will sat his daughter down, and as if it was the most natural punishment in the world, she dropped down to the floor and did five pushups — with rather impressive form.

He gave her a high five when she was standing again, and after warning her not to use grown up language until she was older, he ruffled her hair.

"Alright, Pumpkin. Why don't you go wash your hands and we'll have some of that shrimp I can smell that Chef Patel is making for us."

"Harissa shrimp," Chef called from the kitchen. "With butter couscous and quinoa salad."

"You're too good to me," Will called back.

"Oh, trust me, I know. You go wash *your* hands, too," she added, sliding out of the kitchen long enough to point her wooden spoon at him. "I know how smelly that locker room is, and I don't trust any kind of showers taken in there."

He chuffed something close to a laugh, and then when Ava had run off, he let out a long, heavy sigh, his large hand running back through his damp hair.

That movement was tied to something low and electric in my belly. Every time he did it, I had to squeeze my thighs together against whatever kind of magic he cast.

It was then that I noticed the tight lines of his face, the worry etched between his brows. This wasn't his usual scowl.

Something was weighing on his shoulders.

"Long day?" I asked.

He shook his head. "I think I deal with more children than you do, the way my team has been acting lately."

I smirked, but then Will's phone was buzzing, and he frowned at the screen before excusing himself.

Five minutes later, Ava was washed up and was putting her crayons and coloring book away like I'd asked her to when Will rounded into the kitchen on a curse.

"Change of plans," he said, looking at his watch. "Uncle Mitch got called out of town and can't stay with Ava. I need to get her ready and see if Maven or someone can step in."

Chef didn't miss a beat, nor did she ask any questions or check to see if Will was okay. She just said, "I'll box this up so you can eat it on the plane," and then immediately got to that while I was still trying to process.

"Called out of town?"

"He's a lineman," Will explained. "Apparently there was a pretty bad storm in north Alabama last night, and they're calling for help to get power back up and running." He was already pulling up Maven's contact on his phone. "Excuse me, need to make this call."

"I can stay with her."

Chef paused where she was boxing Will's meal into a glass container, something in her face telling me she hoped Will would accept this proposal so he could eat her food fresh. It had to kill her, to go through all that work only to know her dish would be eaten cold on a plane.

"I won't be back until late tomorrow night after the game," he said. "Maybe even Friday morning, depending on what Coach decides."

I shrugged. "I don't mind. My mom should be able to check in on the cats until I get home, and Ava and I *do* go to the same place in the morning," I reminded him.

"I don't want to be a hassle. I'm sure you'd like to be home in your own bed."

"It's really not a hassle at all," I assured him. "It's one night, maybe two. And something tells me your guest bed is probably a decade newer than the mattress I currently sleep on."

I said it with a smile, all light with the joke, but I didn't miss how Will frowned even deeper at the comment like it was something he needed to fix.

"It would be my pleasure," I said when he didn't respond. "Truly. You should sit down and eat, get packed or whatever you need to do before the flight, and leave the rest to me and Chef."

"She's right," Chef Patel said, and she was already scooping the garlic spicy shrimp out of the glass container and onto a plate. "There's nothing we can't handle, and you need to eat and get to the airport. Besides, Maven is in the throes of wedding planning right now. I'm sure any time she gets Vince out of the house for an away game is time she needs to get things done."

The way Chef winked at me told me that Maven likely wouldn't have minded taking Ava at all, but Chef knew exactly the buttons to push on Will to make him do what she wanted.

I chuckled.

"You're sure?" Will asked, his eyes searching mine. "I'll pay you, of course."

"You already paid me," I reminded him. "Yes, I'm sure. I want to. I love spending time with that grumpy kid of yours," I said with a grin. "And it's really not a problem, I promise."

Will let out a long sigh, nodding in surrender, and then Chef was ushering him to the table just as Ava dragged herself back into the kitchen like Eeyore. The two grumps sat side by side at the smaller of the two dining tables, and I shared a look with Chef before grabbing my purse off the bar.

"I'm going to run home and pack a bag real quick," I told them. "And call my mom about watching the cats."

"Three cats," Will grumbled, shaking his head as he forked his first shrimp.

I smirked, stopping by the table long enough to tuck Ava's hair behind one ear. "I'll be back in an hour. What do you say we read the rest of *Where the Wild Things Are* tonight?"

"Okay," Ava said, not even looking up at me. She just scooped up her first bite of couscous, kicking her legs under her seat.

"Okay," I repeated, and then I looked at Will, who was watching me with his brows bent together, his fork hovering over his plate, something I couldn't quite read in those haunted brown eyes of his.

Thank you, he mouthed.

I nodded like it was no big deal, and then turned, scurrying out the door to my car before the unavoidable smile spread on my lips.

Chapter 8

In the Habit of Lying

Will

"**D**on't make any plans for June twenty-ninth."

I blinked at my teammate, Vince Tanev, as he shot those words my way. We were filing off the plane late Thursday night after managing to squeak out a win against Boston. Despite the win, the plane was eerily quiet — which told me the rest of the guys were just as beat as I was.

"When do I make plans, ever?" I replied.

"Aw, shit," Jaxson Brittain said, clapping Vince on his shoulders from behind. We filed off the plane and onto the tarmac, a cool rain greeting us — which was a rarity in Florida. Most of our rain came in the summertime in the form of hot, heavy storms. "Did you and Mave finally set a date?"

"Don't act like my sister didn't already tell you," Vince said, shrugging him off.

"You ever going to stop hating me for loving her?"

"Depends. You ever going to stop making out with her in front of me?"

"Probably not."

I flattened my lips as Jaxson tried to use me as a shield, Vince doing his best to get around me and slug his best friend in the arm. I loved them both like brothers, but like the younger, annoying kind — just like Carter.

"Enough," I told them, glaring at Jaxson when he got in one last flick to Vince's ear. "June twenty-ninth. Got it. Where?"

"Michigan, of course," Jaxson answered for Vince.

"Hey, can you let me have my moment here?" Vince threw up his hands. "Next you're going to tell me you've already filled Carter in on the news."

Jaxson's gaze slid to mine, eyes wide, and Vince let out a long sigh at the answer that silence gave him.

"I'm happy for you, man," I said to Vince, clapping his shoulder and squeezing hard. "Maven is entirely out of your league, but thank God you managed to make her fall in love with you. She's the best."

"Hey, she's pretty lucky she got me, too," he said with a tug on the lapels of his suit.

"Yeah. Lucky she got you to stop kissing your reflection long enough to notice her."

Jaxson barely got the words out before Vince had him in a headlock, and then Jaxson was complaining about Vince fucking up his "flow" as I shook my head on a grin. At least the two of them weren't trying to kill each other on the ice like they were earlier this season. Jaxson had been seeing Vince's younger sister in secret, and when the truth came out, the whole team paid for it.

Just like I'd warned Jax we would, but that fucker couldn't think straight at the time.

"Alright, I'm out," I said, peering up at the drizzly sky. "I'm ready to see my girl."

"Give her a kiss from us," Jaxson said.

"I absolutely will not."

They chuckled as I waved goodbye, stopping where Coach was long enough to confirm when we needed to report for practice on Saturday before I was heading for my car.

I couldn't drive fast enough across town, the fifteen-minute ride to Davis Island feeling like a lifetime. It had only been one night, but I missed Ava any time I wasn't with her.

The usual anxiety I felt over what I would walk into at home was present, too. In the rotation of over a dozen nannies I'd had in the last few years, I'd never known what to expect.

Although even before I pulled into the drive, I somehow already knew this time would be better.

Chloe had kept in constant contact with me, texting me updates from the moment I left the house for my flight to Boston. She informed me by the hour what Ava was doing, sent photos of them working on crafts, and even called me so I could talk to Ava before the game.

She was a fucking godsend.

The fact that she was so quick to step in and help me when Uncle Mitch had to bail told me how much she already cared about Ava. And I didn't have to watch my daughter long to see that she felt comfortable with Chloe, too.

That made my chest pinch, because I had no idea if this was going to continue working, or if I'd have to start all over in nanny-search hell.

Chloe had been sweet to step in this week, but she had a full-time job already. And as much as she insisted it was fine, I couldn't expect her to teach all day *and* take care of

Ava in-between. Sometimes I needed her in the mornings, sometimes in the afternoons, sometimes at night, and many times — all three.

The girl was in her mid-twenties, if I had to guess, and was fine as hell.

There was no way she didn't have something better to do with her time.

There was no way she didn't want to go out with her friends, or be taken out on dates.

I couldn't explain why that last thought made me grip the steering wheel a little tighter, my jaw tight as I turned onto our street. The rain was still coming down steadily, the streetlights blurred above.

And through that rainy haze, I could see Chloe all too clearly.

I could see the home-sewn outfits she wore, the way they always seemed custom fitted to highlight every soft, round part of her. I could see her warm brown eyes, her smile that was bright enough to knock the breath out of me every time she shot it my way. I could see the way her cheeks flushed the prettiest pink when she didn't think I noticed, the way she'd pin her juicy bottom lip between her teeth out of nervous habit, how her hands would play with that silky red hair of hers.

Every time I watched her fidget, I wanted to give her something better to do with her hands.

And the way she looked at me, I could tell she had a crush, too.

Both of which were a big fucking problem.

Still, she had been nothing but professional. I knew *I* could contain my urges. If it meant having her taking care of Ava, I'd happily fuck my hand every night to get out the tension coiled in my muscles. Hell, I'd even suffer through a night at Boomer's, the local club where the puck bunnies hung out, if it meant I managed to control my desire for Chloe.

I didn't know if she could do the same.

But she hadn't given me reason not to trust her — not yet. She hadn't made any inappropriate comments or advances. She'd kept her hands to herself. She didn't seem like she had any ulterior motive.

I wondered if there would always be this part of me that would be suspicious of every woman I came into contact with, if the parade of puck-chasing nannies I'd dealt with had fucked me up permanently.

It was nearly two in the morning when I finally pulled into my driveway, and the fatigue I'd been fighting felt like a hundred-pound weight on my shoulders as I climbed out of my Bentley. I entered the door code and tiptoed inside, doing my best not to wake anyone.

The first thing I noticed was that the house was spotless.

Ava's toys weren't strung from one end to the other, the way they had been more times than I could count. And, judging by the silence that met my ears, she was asleep — unlike the times when various nannies had thought they'd win my heart over by greeting me after an away game with Ava in their arms when I walked through the door.

I left my bag by the door, content to deal with it in the morning, and almost smiled when I took a few steps inside the foyer and saw the banner hanging across the staircase railing. It was bright yellow with blue and green paint that spelled out *Welcome home, Daddy!* There were handprints of different sizes all over it — enough variation that I knew Chef Patel had likely been dragged into this craft against her will — and little stick drawings of a goalie and an Osprey.

I sighed, but not because I was annoyed.

Because I was *relieved.*

Making my way to the kitchen, I poured myself a tall glass of cold milk, chugging half of it before I stood there in a daze. The full weight of exhaustion from the week was settling over me, and I couldn't wait to get a good night's rest and have a day off. I wished it was a day off for Ava, too, but I'd make the most of the time I had with her before and after school.

My eyes caught on a framed picture in the downstairs hallway, just barely visible from where I stood in the kitchen. It was black and white, and I didn't need to be closer to see it perfectly in my mind. I'd stared at it long enough that the image was burned into my memory.

It was of Jenny holding Ava when she was just three months old.

Jenny had bags under her eyes and curlers in her hair, and she was still as beautiful as ever. Ava was sleeping, her little hand wrapped around Jenny's finger.

I'd snapped the photo on my phone — one of the only ones I'd been smart enough to take.

And I'd printed and framed the grainy image about a year after she died, when I finally started pulling my head out of my ass. I filled other parts of the house with photos of Jenny and me when we were younger, too — when we were just friends who occasionally liked to hook up.

I wanted to make sure she was all around as Ava grew up, as if our daughter could somehow get to know her through the three-by-fives and eight-by-tens.

A dark shadow of movement coming down the stairs drew my attention from the wall, my heart lurching into my throat. But before I could so much as tense or grab a weapon, Chloe stepped into the soft light coming from the kitchen, a sleepy smile on her face.

"Congrats on the win," she said, a yawn stretching her mouth as she wrapped her fluffy robe around her tighter. She had on the most bizarre pajama pants I'd ever seen in my life — bright pink with cats and books all over the fabric in a repeating pattern — and her robe was Barney purple, which matched the furry headband holding her hair off her face.

And even looking like a Crayola box had thrown up on her, she still somehow looked enticing.

I couldn't take my eyes off the way that robe revealed she wasn't wearing a bra, or how her thick thighs made those stupid pajama pants swish a little bit as she walked toward me. And without a stitch of makeup on, I could see the flush of her cheeks so easily, could note how her lips were still a soft pink even without lipstick.

"I'm sorry I woke you," I croaked, clearing my throat as she made her way into the kitchen.

She waved me off. "Don't be. I have a recurring existential crisis around this time every night like clockwork."

She slid into a barstool while I blinked at her, waiting for more of an explanation that never came.

"Ava was very proud of you tonight," she said, reaching up to tuck her hair behind her ear. When she remembered she had the headband in place, she crossed her arms tightly over her chest again with a nervous smile. "I hope you don't mind. I let her stay up tonight since we have a pretty easy day tomorrow. But I got her ready for bed in-between periods, and she knocked out as soon as the final buzzer blew."

"It's fine," I assured her.

"She was so excited, even though she was clearly tired," Chloe continued, her eyes crinkling at the edges as she recalled it. "She kept saying, *Daddy scored a goal! Daddy scored a goal!* I think I even saw her smile."

"Bullshit."

"Okay, so not *smile*," she amended. "But less of a scowl, anyway."

I chuffed a little laugh out of my nose at that, tilting my glass of milk one way and then the other before taking a big swig. "Yeah, well — not often that a goalie scores a goal. But with them leaving the net open in the final minutes." I shrugged.

"Yes. Ava had to explain that to me, by the way," she said. "Still not sure I completely understand it. Hockey makes no sense."

"Hey now, no blasphemy in my house."

She chuckled, folding her hands together on the island as her gaze slid to watch them. She cracked her knuckles and began wringing her fingers as silence washed over us.

"Thank you," I said. "For everything. The house looks amazing, and the text updates were very appreciated."

"You act like those things aren't, like, the bare minimum of being a babysitter," she said on a grin.

"The bar is very low, Miss Knott."

I didn't miss the way her skin turned that lovely shade of pink when I said her name like that.

Tonguing my cheek and doing my best *not* to let my mind lead me down the road it so desperately wanted to drive, I drained the rest of my milk, planting my hands on the cold granite countertop and thinking.

"I'm not very good at beating around the bush," I said after a moment. "So... I'm just going to come out with it."

I lifted my eyes to hers. "I want to hire you. Permanently. And I want you to move in."

Her eyebrows shot up so high it moved the fuzzy purple headband.

"I know I pitched this as a temporary thing," I said, holding up a hand before she could speak. "But... I can't explain how much pressure you've taken off me just in this last week. I'll be honest, I haven't even begun looking for a replacement. And to be frank, I don't want one. I want you."

She swallowed at those words, and I cleared my throat, standing and scratching an imaginary itch on my neck.

"Now, I realize this would be quite a change for you. I don't expect you to quit your job or anything — I know you love it. But, living here is the one part that's non-negotiable. With my schedule, I need you here all the time. I'm happy to pay rent at your current residence in addition to your paycheck. You won't be responsible for cleaning, although I appreciate that you took that on yourself this time around. We have a housekeeper who comes once a week. And you'd have your own space," I added quickly. "The pool house has an en-suite bathroom, complete with a soaking tub, as well as a kitchenette."

I stopped talking, then opened my mouth to add something else, but snapped it shut again. I needed to give her time to answer for herself — even if I was tempted to keep listing every perk I could think of to get her to say yes.

The pool house has a huge closet.

You can use any part of the house you want to for your bizarre crafts.

Want a new car? I'll buy it.

It killed me to stay silent, especially the longer Chloe went without answering. Her nervous tics were all I could focus on in that moment — the cracking of her knuckles, the playing with her hair, the back-and-forth criss-crossing of her legs.

They were *so* distracting, in fact, that I couldn't help what happened next.

I didn't realize I'd been moving toward her, not until my hand shot forward and covered hers.

The moment our skin touched, heat rippled through me — sharp and electric. It was like sliding into a hot spring, every cell in my body singing at the sweeping sensation.

I knew right then and there that she was the kind of girl you could get easily lost in.

Chloe stilled, her eyes on where I touched her before she slowly trailed that gaze up to mine.

"You good?" I asked.

The words felt dry and suffocated coming from my throat, but my hand was calm and sure, thumb smoothing over her wrist bone.

She swallowed, her cheeks tomato red now. "Sorry—"

"Don't apologize," I ordered. "Just... tell me it isn't me that makes you this nervous."

"I'm not in the habit of lying, Mr. Perry."

That heat surged to an all-encompassing level, but I didn't remove my hold on her.

"But," she added with a coy smile and a shrug. "To be fair — almost everything makes me nervous. Or at least, makes me do things like this." She tore her hand from mine and illustrated, cracking her wrists and wiggling a few fingers before she tucked her hands firmly between her crossed legs and kept them there.

"You don't have to say—"

"I accept," she butted in.

When I frowned, she dipped her head to catch my gaze, holding it as she straightened her spine.

"I want to be here. I want this opportunity," she said confidently. "If I'm being transparent, I was worried sick the whole time you were gone, thinking you'd come home and tell me you found someone else."

I almost laughed at that, but for me, that manifested in the way of a puff of air from my nose and the slight relaxation of my tight shoulders.

"It won't interfere with work," she assured me. "But... I would feel terrible for you paying my rent."

"Don't," I said immediately. "I want you to keep your space."

"Just in case you fire me?" she teased.

I didn't answer — but honestly.... *yeah*, that was exactly what I was thinking. Right now, Chloe was great. But I'd thought other nannies were great, too.

My trust meter was permanently stuck at negative one at this point.

When I didn't answer, Chloe chuckled, sliding off her barstool and folding her arms over her chest. She tucked her hands tightly in the crevices like she was afraid of what they'd do unchecked.

"When do you want me to move in?"

"This weekend would be ideal."

Her eyebrows shot up in surprise, but then she nodded. "I think we can make that happen. Oh, but I do have *one* condition that's absolutely non-negotiable."

"Name it."

She grinned, stepping a little closer to me — enough that my nostrils flared, hands flexing with the want to reach out and touch her again.

"I won't be the only resident in that pool house."

I arched a brow, trying not to show any emotion, but the moment realization dawned on me, it became nearly impossible.

So she *did* have a boyfriend.

Maybe it was so new she didn't want to tell me before, or maybe she didn't feel like she needed to, but now that she knew she'd be staying here, she had no choice.

It made absolutely zero fucking sense that jealousy licked at my spine. I didn't *want* her — not like that. I wanted a reliable, uninterested nanny who would take care of Ava and leave me the hell alone.

And yet...

I cleared my throat. "That won't be a problem."

"Oh, are you sure?" Chloe asked, smirking.

She reached for her phone in the pocket of her robe, holding the screen toward me.

And where she laughed, I groaned — not sure if this was better or worse than what I'd been assuming.

Staring back at me from that mirror-like screen in her hand were three asshole cats.

Chapter 9

Exactly Zero Interest

Chloe

The weekend flew by in a tornado of boxes and helping hands, both Friday and Sunday filled with Will and his teammates moving boxes for me whenever they didn't have practice or a game.

Their schedule was insane. Friday was a day off after the Boston game, and then they flew out for their away game on Saturday. They returned Sunday morning and still had practice even after the game and travel.

It made sense why he wanted me to move in. How the hell could he take care of himself with a schedule like this, let alone a five-year-old?

I'd tried to help with the unloading, but no sooner would I grab a box than a big, burly hockey player would quickly take it from me — usually with a wink, a smirk, and a reassurance that I should just relax.

Vince Tanev was there, whom I remembered was engaged to Maven. Jaxson Brittain was also helping, and I learned that he was dating Grace — Vince's sister. But apparently Grace loved to travel, and so when Maven and Livia came over on Sunday afternoon with a large basket of wine, cheese, and fruit, Grace didn't accompany them.

"Okay, when Will said he was moving you into the pool house, I was worried," Maven said when she set the basket on the kitchenette counter. She looked around appreciatively. "But this is more like a penthouse."

"It's too much," I agreed, tucking my arms so tight around me they felt like a straitjacket as I watched Vince dump another box in the bedroom after asking me where it went. He swung by where we stood long enough to sneak a kiss on Maven's cheek, who batted him away.

"Like hell it is," Livia argued, propping her ass up onto the granite. "You're saving his ass. If I were you, I'd be asking for a gold card, too. And maybe a G-Wagon."

Maven laughed, and I cracked my neck before blushing when they both swiveled their heads toward me at the loud sound.

God, I was so awkward.

"Listen, if there's one thing I know, it's that you can easily lose yourself when you start getting involved with this team," Maven said, her eyes soft as she approached me. One hand reached out to squeeze my arm. "So, Livia and I are always here to rescue you."

"Starting with a girls' night next week," Livia added, hopping off the counter. "This bitch has wrangled me into DIY wedding crafts, which is utter bullshit considering how much money her soon-to-be husband makes."

"It'll be fun and you know it," Maven teased her.

Livia scoffed. "You can't call anything that doesn't include a peg and a bottle of lube *fun*, bestie."

"Liv!"

Maven tried to scold her, but was bent over in a laugh now as Livia winked at me. I couldn't help it — I cracked a smile.

Who the hell *were* these girls?

I loved them already.

"Anyway, I'm not going through that torture alone. Grace is supposed to be in town, too, so I'm wrangling both of you into it with me," Livia said, pointing at me as she floated past. "We'll text you the details."

She swung out the door, teasing one of the hockey players carrying in my cat tree on the way.

Maven smiled at me when she was gone. "I got your number from Will. I'll add you to our group text. Okay?"

I nodded. "Okay."

"I gotta run. Make sure these boys clean up after themselves," she said. "And hey, Chloe?"

"Yeah?"

"Welcome to the family. We're a bit crazy, but I promise we're fun."

I couldn't explain the way my heart expanded at that comment, at the word *family*. I thanked her, and then she was out the door with a princess wave, walking in stilettos in a graceful manner that would have been impossible for me to achieve.

The rest of Sunday was a blur.

I hadn't packed that much over — at least, I didn't think so. Still, with three cats to get settled and limited time to move things from my house to Will's in-between practices and games, it felt like I had blinked and the weekend was over.

That evening, once Ava was in bed, I put on an episode of the *Stuff You Should Know* podcast — this one about sloths — and got to work unpacking and organizing.

Maven was right. The pool house was more like a *house* house, and it was at least twice the size of the one I was currently renting. The main living area was expansive, with a stained alder ceiling and polished concrete floor. Plush rugs kept the space warm, along with the massive cream couch piled high with pillows I was certain Will didn't pick out, a cozy electric fireplace, and two oversized leather chairs fit for hockey players the size of my new boss.

The living area bled into the dining area and kitchen, which looked fresh out of a magazine with the navy cabinets, gold hardware, and white marble kitchen island. Nacho had already made himself at home on that island, sprawled out and flicking his tail as he watched me unpack a few of my favorite tea mugs.

Pepper was too busy exploring to sit still. I had to be careful with the gigantic glass doors that opened to the pool. As beautiful as they were, they only begged my mischievous cats to test their luck — to see if they could slip through my legs and out that door before I had the chance to close it.

Pepper would be the first to try, no doubt. He had already figured out how to climb up onto the mantel over the fireplace, as well as scale the empty floating shelves Will had told me I could outfit with whatever I wanted to. I was already plotting out which books and art supplies would go where.

Coconut, on the other hand, was still hiding somewhere — likely under the gorgeous king-size bed. Every time I walked through my new bedroom, I stopped and let out a dreamy sigh at the sight of it. It was memory foam and flush with expensive bedding that made it feel like I was sleeping on a cloud.

It felt as strange as it did comforting, unpacking my belongings as the evening slipped by. Something about the pool house, about Will and Ava in *general* felt... natural, like they were family already and I'd visited a hundred times.

Then again, everything about it also felt incredibly disconcerting.

I was trying to discern my confusing emotions when my phone rang, a FaceTime request coming through with my mother's picture on the screen.

With a sigh and a silent prayer to whatever God there was, I propped my phone against one of the giant candles at the kitchen island and took a seat at the bar, tapping the green button to answer the call. Just like always, I'd been texting my mom and grandmother every day — which meant they were fully updated on my situation.

Updated... but not entirely happy.

"You look tired."

I flattened my lips but managed a smile. "Hello, Mom. Nice to see you, too."

"You *do* look tired. Is that man not helping you at all?" Grandma chimed in, poking her head up behind Mom. "Typical."

"I bet he's inside his big fancy mansion stuffing his face and watching sportsball," Mom added with a shake of her head.

"Mr. Perry is probably sleeping," I chastised them both. "He has practice in the morning and usually gets up early to spend time with Ava before school. And I'll have you know that he had half his team helping me move, and I didn't lift a single box."

My mom and grandma gave each other a look, their lips flat and a little hum of disapproval leaving their chests at the same time. They had it down now so they were in sync, like a symphony of suspicion.

It wouldn't matter if a man paved a street of gold for me. In their eyes, he'd still be a man — and therefore, a pest.

It was too easy to see our similarities reflected on my phone screen, from our pale, moonlight skin to the soft, coral pink color of our lips. Where Mom got her father's rich brown hair, I had the same copper tone as my grandma — though hers would go white if she didn't dye it now. All three of us had the same thick, dark lashes and wide brown eyes. Grandma's eyebrows had thinned to be almost non-existent except when she drew them on with liner, but Mom's were still as thick and bushy as mine. Grandma was petite and thin, but Mom was curvy just like I was, her face round and soft where Grandma's was hard and angular.

"How was Rummy tonight?" I asked.

"You would know if you wouldn't have canceled on us," Grandma said, arching a brow. "We had to ask Genevieve to play."

Mom shuddered. "You *know* how I feel about that woman."

Yes. Yes, I did. In fact, I was pretty sure everyone in their little senior community knew how Mom felt about Genevieve. Something my mother excelled at was wearing her mood on her face like a flashing neon sign. It wasn't that she or my grandmother never smiled, just that those smiles weren't always friendly — and if they didn't care for you, you'd know it.

"Thank you for understanding that I had to unpack tonight," I said. I stood a bit taller as the words came out, proud of myself for not apologizing. That was usually my go-to.

Grandma hmphed, waving her hand and walking out of the frame as Mom studied my background.

"Looks nice," she commented. "Have you checked the locks to make sure that man can't get in when you don't want him to?"

"Mom," I groaned, pinching the bridge of my nose. "For the fifteenth time, Mr. Perry is a gentleman and a father. He has been nothing but respectful to me."

"Mm-hmm, and I'm sure that's not part of his master plan to get you in his bed."

My cheeks flamed, and I covered my face with my hands, shaking my head.

"We know better," Grandma called from somewhere in the small home they shared. "You be careful, Chloe May. The last thing you want is to end up pregnant. You still have that pepper spray Grandma got you, right? And you remember the moves from class?"

"Always go for the groin," Mom chimed in. "Or if he comes at you from behind, smash his foot with all your might. It only takes—"

"Twenty pounds of pressure to break a bone," I finished for her on a sigh. "Yes, I know. And yes, I have the pepper spray, Gran, but I'm not going to need to use either. Because Will Perry is a *nice man*, giving me a great job with great pay and a lovely place to live."

They still didn't seem sold on the idea, and their glances at each other told me as much. But what *they* didn't know was that accepting this job meant that I'd be able to do something I'd always wanted to do for them.

Pay off their debt.

It was enough pressure weighing on me as the first woman in our family to go to college. Add in the fact that Mom and Grandma had taken out a heap of loans to ensure

I could do so, and there was a layer of guilt on top of that pressure.

It wasn't from them. They always insisted they were *glad* to help. What did they need money for, anyway, Grandma would titter. But I saw the stress they tried to hide. I overheard the many conversations in their kitchen when they thought I was asleep, when they were struggling to pay their bills or asking for deferments of the loan payments that kept rolling in.

They had sacrificed so much for me over the years, pulling together to raise me as parents when both their partners had deserted them.

We were a trio. I loved them so fiercely it made my eyes sting when I thought too much about it.

Blessedly, the conversation turned from their man-hating comments to them asking how school was, and filling me in on the latest gossip from the Bingo hall. After about a half hour, I started wrapping up the call with the excuse that I wanted to finish getting unpacked and get some sleep for school the next day.

I knew they were worried about me. I knew, even if they didn't say it outright, that there was a part of them worried I was going to get myself into trouble.

But I'd show them. I'd make them proud.

I would save money. I would pay off my own student loans. And I'd save to provide for myself even long after this job came to an end, if that was what happened.

I didn't know why their approval meant so much to me, and tried not to dwell on it as we ended the call. I was exhausted by the time we finally did, and once I was as unpacked as I needed to be, I climbed into my new cloud-like bed with a sigh...

And proceeded to sleep only a couple hours before I was wide awake again.

This was normal for me. It didn't matter how comfortable the bed was. As soon as I woke up to use the bathroom, my brain would start racing.

I knew the key to getting myself back to sleep. I needed to go for a little walk around the house and eat a snack. Unfortunately, I hadn't brought any groceries with me, and hadn't shopped for myself yet. Chef Patel was already spoiling me, making it so I didn't *have* to worry about meals.

The bottle of wine Maven had brought over was tempting, but the last thing I needed was a hangover or to still be drunk on my first morning officially working for Will. And sadly, cheese wasn't going to cure my sweet tooth right now, either.

Throwing my robe over my pajamas, I quietly tiptoed out of the pool house and walked around the pool a few times, the January air cool against my hot cheeks. I smiled at the safety gate surrounding the gorgeous pool. Of course, Will had thought of that, of protecting Ava even if it meant disrupting what most interior designers would claim as the "aesthetic." He was a father first, above everything.

It was quite unfair how hot that was.

My stomach kept growling as I paced, appetite insistent on me finding some sugar. I was debating digging through my purse to see if I had peanut butter crackers stashed in there when the light to the kitchen in the main house flicked on, casting a warm glow over the pool.

I saw Will's shadow next, and I smiled, making my way to the sliding glass door. He'd left it unlocked in case I needed to get inside for anything, but he still jumped a little when I slid it open, his hand gripping the fridge handle tight as he whipped around.

He relaxed a bit when he realized it was me, though the way his scowl deepened didn't do anything to ease my late-night anxiety. The sigh he let out next as he pulled a gallon of milk from the fridge didn't exactly make me feel welcome, either.

The man was harder to figure out than the sewing method for a Victorian bustle dress.

He was the one who asked me to move in. *He* was the one who said he wanted this. And yet, all weekend, he'd grumped about like I was the biggest inconvenience.

"Ah, we meet again," I teased as I slid inside the kitchen, taking my familiar spot at the island. "Only this time, you're not coming home from an away game. Don't tell me you have midnight existential crises, too?"

Will harrumphed, giving me a look before he grabbed a glass from the cabinet. He held one toward me in a silent question, his eyebrow raised, but I shook my head.

"I'm more of a snack girl at this time of night," I said. "Got any cookies?"

Will stared at me for a long moment before plucking a pack of Oreos from the pantry. He slid it in front of me, and I let out a very unladylike groan of approval before ripping the packaging open and popping one into my mouth.

"So," I said when Will just shook his head at me. "Are you changing your mind now that I'm here?"

He frowned. "Of course not. Why would you ask that?"

"Oh, only because you've been alternating between giving me death glares and stomping around here like a grumpy bear the last two days," I said with a shrug, plucking another cookie from the package. I debated dunking it in his milk, but thought it would be better to keep my hand in tact since I had to teach in the morning.

Will let out a sigh, staring at the glass in his hands before taking a small sip. "I'm sorry," he said. "It's not you, it's just..."

He fell silent, his jaw working like he was chewing on the words he wasn't sure how to say.

When his eyes slid back up to meet mine, they were laced with sorrow, with a vulnerability that nearly made me choke on the cookie I'd half-swallowed.

"You have no idea how hard this has all been for me."

He didn't have to elaborate on what *this* meant. It was written in every line of his face.

This poor guy had been battling being a single father, on top of a high-performance athlete, all while flipping through a catalogue of sorry excuses for nannies who only added to his stress.

My bet was he was wondering how long I'd last, wondering how long he could count on me before he'd be back to square one.

I stopped chewing, holding his gaze a moment before I swallowed and nodded. "I think I'll take that milk now."

He poured me a glass, and I washed down the dry cookie in my throat before finding his gaze again. How he could look tired and yet devastatingly handsome at the same time was a very unfair magic trick. Somehow, the bags under his eyes only made him more enticing. Paired with the way his long hair was half-contained by a hair band at the nape of his neck, and half-mussed by what I assumed was him running his hand through it, he looked like a paid model for an underwear ad.

At least he was wearing pajama pants and a white t-shirt.

I probably would have fainted if he was shirtless.

"I'm sorry it's been hard," I finally said when I could speak again. "But... hopefully this is the start of it being easier. Hopefully I can help take some of the pressure off."

He nodded, his eyes finding his hands again. "So... midnight existential crisis, huh?" He cocked an eyebrow when he looked at me again. "This a nightly occurrence?"

"Close to it. Sometimes I go a few days without one, but that's rare."

"And what is it that keeps you awake?"

"Oh, you know, thoughts of how we're a tiny marble of life floating in space, in a universe where there are more stars than grains of sand on Earth."

"Is that all?"

"And how I'm twenty-six and single, with three cats and no real friends, and no real chance of meeting anyone since I'm devoted to my job and have exactly zero interest in going out or talking to men."

He nearly spit out his milk at that last confession, and then blinked several times, wiping his mouth with the back of his wrist before opening his mouth and shutting it again.

"You asked," I said with a smile, and then I dunked another cookie in my milk and popped the whole thing in my mouth on a shrug.

"You act like twenty-six is old."

"I'm not saying it's old," I argued. "I'm just saying that I could have a serious boyfriend if not a husband at this age, but instead I have three cats."

He wrinkled his nose at that, which made me chuckle.

"Why don't you go out?"

"Because it sucks," I said on a laugh, arching a brow at him. "Come on. You of all people strike me as someone who knows that fact, too. When your teammates go out after a game, do you join them?"

"Absofuckinglutely not."

"See?"

"But I'm a dad," he pointed out.

"Well, I'm a homebody," I said, shrugging. "I don't know. I just... I don't like it. I don't like the big crowds of people, or strangers pushing all up on me, sweaty and drunk. I don't find it fun to stand in the middle of a bar or club with lights flashing and music pounding. Trying to scream over the noise to have a conversation?" I cringed. "No, thanks."

"You make some good points there," Will conceded.

"I like being home. Home is... nice," I said with a smile. "It's cozy. I like to sew, or do a puzzle, or hang out with my cats while I read a great book."

"Maybe you should just have friends over for a night in, then."

"Sure. Doesn't help with the dating situation, though, does it? Can't exactly ask a guy from Hinge to come to my place for our first meeting. Not without risking death or abduction, anyway."

That made his face harden into stone, like he was something between a jealous boyfriend and an overprotective father. Not that I'd know what either of those actually looked like — but I could imagine.

"Anyway, it's fine," I said, waving him off. "Anxiety manifests in strange ways. I'm actually okay with this. In about an hour, I'll be soothed and have a belly full of sugar and will go right to sleep."

Will smirked at me — yes, *smirked* — and the sight of that slight curl of his lips made my thighs clench together.

When his eyes slowly raked over me, I nearly combusted.

He never rushed his observation, never seemed ashamed of it. He took his time, his gaze lingering on every spot where a sliver of my bare skin showed, like he had all night to look at me and intended to spend it doing just that.

"I'm sorry about your wife."

That snapped his gaze to mine, and my eyes shot wide.

Did I just fucking say that?!

Sometimes, my mouth moved before my brain did, and now, I was nervously fidgeting and trying to think of something to add to that sentence that would make it less awkward and rude.

I came up empty.

"I just mean, I know you said things have been hard," I finally stammered, my neck hot enough to melt gold. I played with my necklace, plucking it from my skin and running the charm along the chain as if I was scared it actually *would* melt against my skin. "With the nannies. And I can't imagine what you've been through, and I..." I cringed. "I'm sorry."

I closed my eyes shut tight, peeking one open and then the next.

Will just held my stare, his face void of emotion. "Thank you," he finally said.

"What was she like?"

Oh, my God, Chloe.

Stop. Talking.

Will rubbed the scruff on his jaw, cracking his neck one way and then the other. His gaze was focused on the kitchen island now, like his thoughts were far away.

"Wild," he finally answered, and a ghost of a smile touched his lips. "Jenny was absolutely wild. She was a free spirit, never gave two shits about what anyone thought of her. She liked what she liked and hated what she hated. She was the first to dance on the bar or jump into the ocean naked after midnight."

I didn't know why, but my chest tightened, a pinch of jealousy surprising me. The way he looked when he talked about her was the way any woman would dream of being spoken about, like she'd been his entire world.

She also sounded cool — and I was anything but.

The comparison monster only hung around for a moment before I mentally slapped it away, and genuine sorrow slipped in to take its place.

This man lost his wife, the mother of his child.

"How did you meet?"

Will's eyebrows lifted and lowered, like he was laughing to himself at the memory. "At some sorority party in college. You would have hated it," he added with a glance from beneath his brows. "Sweaty, drunk people everywhere."

I smiled.

"I went with some of my teammates, and as soon as we walked in, she hooked me by the arm and dragged me to do shots."

That surprised me, since he didn't drink now. At least, I hadn't seen him drink, and I learned that first evening at dinner that he didn't have wine in the house.

I guessed he'd been different back then.

"Love at first sight?" I guessed.

"Not at all, actually. We were just friends. Best friends," he clarified. "We hooked up a time or two in college, but nothing serious. We'd always laugh it off the next day. When I left college to start my NHL career with the Tampa organization, we didn't think we'd see each other again. But about a year later, she got a job offer in St. Pete. She moved here, we started hanging out, one thing led to another, and we found ourselves in bed together... and then she got pregnant."

My eyes shot wide.

I did not expect *that*.

"I couldn't believe it when she told me, but strangely, neither of us was upset. We were just kind of like... okay, I guess we're doing this. We got married a couple weeks later, just a small ceremony on the beach."

He cleared his throat, standing up straighter and looking at the now-empty glass in his hands.

"I don't know why I'm telling you all this."

"Because I asked."

He lifted his brows, but then fell quiet for a long time. I realized what he meant by that statement was that he wasn't used to talking so much. Maybe not at all.

It made me giddier than it should have to know he felt like talking to me.

But the longer silence fell between us, the more I wondered if the conversation was over. I was just about to drink the last of my milk when he started talking again.

"We loved each other, but not in the traditional way. We had fun together. We had respect for one another. And we knew we'd make good parents." He shrugged. "I was too busy with hockey to care about trying to find a partner, and she seemed content with me — at least for the moment. It didn't make sense to anyone else but us," he admitted. "But that was all that mattered."

"What happened to her?"

Again, the words shot out of me, and I curled in on myself when Will's gaze hardened and landed on me.

"She got on birth control about a month after having Ava. The doctor said she was fine." He swallowed. "But she wasn't. She experienced a blood clot, but the symptoms were so mild... we didn't really know anything was going on. Not until she got really dizzy one day, and felt like she couldn't breathe."

I covered my lips with my trembling hand, eyes watering, heart racing.

He was saying it so matter-of-factly, but I felt the weight in every word. I felt the pain he was barely holding at bay.

"It happened so fast," he croaked. "One moment, she was lying down because she didn't feel well. The next... she had a pulmonary embolism." Will swallowed. "I called 9-1-1, but it was too late."

I closed my eyes at his words, holding back tears I felt like I didn't have a right to shed.

"Thank you for sharing that with me," I finally whispered, forcing my eyes open to look at him. "You didn't have to, but I... I really appreciate that you did."

He swallowed, nodding. "I don't talk about it much to anyone. But... I guess you're a good listener." He paused. "Or I'm just exhausted enough to not fight against telling you the truth."

My heart felt like it was being squeezed in an iron fist.

Two months.

She'd lived for less than two months with her daughter.

It was so impossible to imagine.

"What did you do?" I asked, locking my gaze on his. "After..."

Will cleared his throat and took his glass to the sink, rinsing it and tucking it in the dishwasher. "I think I've talked enough tonight."

I jumped off my barstool. "Yes, of course. I'm sorry."

"Stop apologizing."

"Sorry."

He pointed a glare at me, cocking a brow, though the corner of his lips tilted just a quarter inch.

I shrugged.

It was habit.

"You're welcome to sleep in one of the guest beds, if you can't fall asleep out there," he said, nodding toward the pool house. But I was already stifling a yawn, and I mirrored him, taking my glass to the sink.

"I'll be fine. See you in the morning?"

We were standing so close now, less than a foot between us, and I found my feet rooted in place as I stared up at him.

"In the morning," he agreed.

His nostrils flared a bit when his eyes traveled down, and I knew without looking that my robe was gaping, that the slim spaghetti strap top I wore beneath it did nothing to hide my large breasts.

But I didn't cover myself, didn't back away.

I swallowed, staying perfectly still.

And when Will finally inhaled a stiff breath and tore himself away, I swore I heard him mutter a curse under his breath on his way down the hall.

Chapter 10

Morning Routine

Chloe

In the first full week of living with Will and Ava, I learned three things.

One — my mission to make the two of them smile or, God forbid, *laugh* would prove more difficult than I thought.

It was like living with Sadness from *Inside Out,* except neither of them was capable of showing even *that* kind of emotion. They just sort of floated about with scowls on their faces, even when they declared they were "happy" and "having a good day."

When Will was home for dinner, I'd crack jokes, make them both play silly games with me, and use my napkin to fashion the most ridiculous hats on my head.

The only reaction I got was the two of them sharing a look like I was crazy.

When it was just me and Ava, whether we were on our way to or from school or hanging around the house or watching a hockey game, I was just as unsuccessful. It didn't matter if we were playing or painting or swimming in the heated pool — getting Ava to do anything more than smirk was impossible.

Not even dipping my head underwater and brushing my hair forward, only to emerge and flip it over so I looked like George Washington, did the trick. She'd simply blinked at me, and then floated on her back like the sky was much more interesting.

Still, I wasn't giving up — not on either of them.

One day, I would make them laugh.

The second thing I learned was that my morning routine was much, *much* different from Will's.

My mornings were slow, lazy, and then absolutely chaotic and rushed in the last ten minutes before I had to go out the door.

I usually laid in bed reading for a half hour before I'd drag myself to the bathroom, brushing my teeth and, on the good days, washing my face. If it was a morning Will wasn't around, I'd go in to help Ava get ready for school, and Arushi — er, *Chef Patel* — was usually yelling at us for taking too long to get ready when we were eating our breakfast on the way out the door instead of at the table like she wanted.

When I *didn't* have to help Ava, I'd listen to a podcast and drink tea until Chef was knocking on my sliding glass door with the butt of her spatula, a warning glare on her beautiful face.

Either way, I was usually rushing out the door with Ava in tow.

Will, on the other hand, woke up three hours before he had to be anywhere — and he had a strict routine that he followed.

Because the time he woke up depended largely on how late he got to bed the night before, I'd witnessed all the various stages of his routine. After a week, I could easily surmise the order.

First, he'd drink a full glass of water. Sometimes I watched this from the safety of the pool house, and other times, I'd have a front row show at the kitchen island. I'd have to pretend I was helping Ava pack up her backpack and *not* watching the way his throat constricted, or how his pajama pants hung from his hips in a way that made me feel like I needed to do a set of Hail Marys.

Next, he'd change into athletic shorts and usually nothing else, moving out onto the turf that lined the far edge of the pool. He'd sit and meditate for twenty minutes or so, and then transition into a yoga flow — one I found incredibly distracting when I was getting my supplies ready for the day in the pool house.

For a few days, I didn't know where he went after that portion of his routine. It wasn't until halfway through the week when I needed him to sign a permission slip for Ava to go on a field trip that I found him in the gym connected to the garage...

Jump roping.

It was a sight I would be hard pressed to ever forget. 2000s hip-hop music blasted through the space filled with weightlifting equipment, and when I walked in, I found him in the middle of the room, shirtless, his tan body glistening with sweat, his gaze hard and focused as he jumped rope faster than I'd ever seen anyone do before.

But he wasn't just jumping rope like a warm up.

It was an entire cardio workout.

He'd jump regularly, then one foot at a time, then

both, then whip the rope back and forth before jumping in a circle to the beat of the music.

My perverted brain couldn't help but warp time from my vantage point at the gym entrance. I saw it all in slow motion — the way the taut, thick muscles of his abdomen and chest rippled each time he landed on the concrete floor, how his hair was dampened at the edges, the way the muscles of his forearms and shoulders ebbed and flowed with each swipe of that rope.

It was pornographic.

And when he realized I was there, when he noticed I was watching, he didn't stop.

In fact, I swore I saw a smirk on those plump lips of his before he turned away from me, finishing his reps like he didn't mind the audience.

After his workout, he'd meet us in the kitchen. And where Ava and I typically had the same breakfast, Chef Patel always had a special one for him — one loaded with lean protein, whole grains, and a pile of fruits or vegetables.

I also had a sneaky suspicion that he had a skin and hair routine somewhere in there, because by the time he showed at the breakfast table, his face was glowing, his hair so shiny it looked like it was out of a Pantene commercial.

Needless to say, I did not mind bearing witness to any portion of Will's routine — not in the slightest.

And that was the third thing I learned that week.

I liked watching Will Perry.

And I was fairly certain he liked watching me, too.

• • •

"Livia, you could at least *pretend* to help," Maven said, a smile on her lips even as she rolled her eyes at her best friend — who was currently lying on the floor beside me, swiping through her phone, feet kicked up on the couch.

"And *you* could stop pretending you can't afford to pay an event planner to do this shit for you," she shot back.

Grace laughed, picking up a dried rose and tossing it at Livia. It landed on her forehead, making her flinch, but she just daintily swiped it away before smiling and getting back to whatever she was doing on her phone.

We were currently a half-hour into carefully packing the most gorgeous and elaborate wedding invitations I'd ever seen. They weren't just a slip of paper tucked inside an envelope. Instead, Vince had made hundreds of beautifully unique clay pots, and we were filling them with seeds so guests could turn their invite into a house plant. We also threw in dried flowers and crystals, and of course, the invitation. Even that piece alone was stunning, an opaque, gold-foiled vellum with gorgeous script overlaying luxurious lavender card stock.

The four of us were sitting around a beautiful coffee table in the middle of Maven and Vince's beach house. The evening had been sprung on me in the form of Vince and Jaxson showing up at the house and forcing Will to go with them to a pizza arcade — one they'd rented out for the evening — and of course, bringing Ava along.

Maven and Livia had then introduced me to Grace before promptly piling into Maven's car and dragging me with them.

It had been impossible not to fidget the entire car ride, even despite the way every single one of them went out of their way to make me feel welcome into their group. Still, as nervous as I was, I also couldn't contain my excitement.

They weren't dragging me out to a bar, but to Maven's home.

We weren't going out to dance, but rather were staying in to craft.

I mean... this was right up my alley.

"She does make a fair point," Grace said, assessing the box she'd packed with an unsure wrinkle of her nose. She tilted her head to the side. "I'm not exactly killing it over here."

Maven peeked at the atrocity before glancing at her own, and she let out a puff of a laugh, abandoning the ribbon she'd been tying around her invitation and sitting back on her hands. "Oh, who am I kidding? I hate crafts."

"Says the woman who will spend hours in the garden," Livia shot.

"That's different! My plants are my babies. This..." she said, lifting up the last invitation she'd done with the ribbon looking like one of my students tied it. "Is anything but."

"Can we please abandon ship, then, and go drink a bottle of wine on the beach?" Livia sat up, tossing her phone on the couch. "It's supposed to get cold tomorrow."

"Sixty-five degrees is not cold," Grace said. "Come to Michigan this time of year and you can tell me about *cold*."

"No, thank you," Livia said.

Maven tossed in the towel. "Alright. I'll grab the wine. And tomorrow, I'm hiring an event planner."

"Praise the Lord," Livia said.

But then, her eyes bulged out of her head, and she smacked me across the arm so hard I yelped.

"Look at this bitch!" she said, and then she smoothed my arm. "Sorry, didn't mean to hit you so hard, but damn, girl! What are you, a craft wizard?!"

The other girls gathered around to see where I'd perfectly packed four boxes. Each invitation was assembled with precision, the ribbons tied elegantly, the dried flowers arranged just so. I'd carefully surrounded the clay pots Vince had made with the crinkled packing paper Maven had, and made it so when the guest opened the box, it was like unwrapping a beautiful gift.

"A kindergarten teacher," I answered, clearing my throat when my voice came out so soft I sounded like a mouse.

Talking to kids? Easy. Teasing Will? Fine. But apparently, I was awestruck by these gorgeous women and the confidence they wore as easily as the stiletto heels on their feet.

"And also, a homebody who happens to love picking up a new project every week."

Grace smiled. "I love that. As someone always on the go, I really appreciate the chance to sit still and be at home in my own space."

"You wouldn't know how to *sit still* if Jaxson tied you to a chair," Maven said.

Grace shimmied her shoulders. "That happens to be my favorite way to sit still, actually."

"*Now* we're speaking my language," Livia chimed in, hopping up and wiggling her hips. "Ropes and chains, whips and clamps. Let's go, baby! Get that wine, Mave."

Livia tugged me up off the floor before looping an arm through mine, and the next thing I knew, we were watching the last bit of the sunset over the beach, our toes dug deep into the cool sand, a bottle of red wine split between us.

Grace made a toast to Maven and Vince, we clinked glasses, and then as soon as the first sip was done, Maven turned the attention to me.

"So, how has the first week been at the house?"

"Great," I said. "I mean, Ava is the easiest kid in the world, and Will has been very accommodating."

"Oh yeah?" Livia waggled her brows. "*How* accommodating?"

Grace swatted her arm. "You are too horny for your own good."

But even as the girls laughed her off, their eyes all swung to me, waiting.

My skin felt hot enough to turn water into steam as I traced the rim of my glass with a fingertip. "I assure you, nothing like that. I'm trying *not* to be like the other nannies he's had to go through."

"I already know you're different," Maven said. "And I'm glad he's found you. Poor Will... he's been through hell and back."

The girls fell quiet, nodding.

"I can't imagine," Grace said softly. "Jaxson always pokes fun at him, but deep down, he just wishes Will would open up and talk about it all. It has to be so hard, carrying the burden alone."

"He talked to me a little," I said without thinking.

Again, all eyes shot to me, brows lifting. "He did?" Maven asked, genuinely shocked.

"Not a lot," I said hurriedly, tucking my hair behind one ear. The wind blew it back in front of my face in the next second, and I slid my hand under my thigh to keep from fidgeting more. "But... yeah."

"That's huge, girl," Livia said. "Even when I had him high on anesthesia before pulling a tooth, he didn't say shit to me."

"He already trusts you," Grace assessed. "Probably because of how well you take care of Ava. I mean, Jaxson said you're a natural with her."

"Well, thank you. My mission now is to make her laugh. Her dad, too."

"Okay, well, you might succeed with Ava," Maven said. "But don't hold your breath for Will, alright? That man is stone."

"Mm-hmm, I'll bet he is. In all the right places."

Livia did a little dance in her chair with that comment, her tongue out and hips thrusting as Maven and Grace laughed and chastised her.

I couldn't help the little twinge of possessiveness that came over me when I watched her do it, but thankfully, it receded as quickly as it had come, and then the conversation moved to Grace — to where she was off to next, which happened to be Spain.

It was a magical evening, one filled with bottle after bottle of wine, conversation rich and deep and easy, and laughter that made my stomach hurt. I was perfectly content to sit on the sideline and just listen to them talk, but they always made sure I was *involved*, asking me questions about school, about my mother and grandmother, about how the hell I put up with a classroom full of kids every day.

By the time the boys showed up and Jaxson offered to drive me back to Will's, I was buzzed and smiling ear to ear.

Because for the first time in my life, I felt like I'd found a group of girls I could be friends with.

Will and Ava were both already asleep when I got home, and I no sooner made it back to the pool house and greeted my cats before my phone pinged.

Maven: Welcome to the group text, Chloe!

Livia: Beware of NSFW images at random.

Grace: No, seriously, beware of that. I was with my mom the last time Livia sent a picture of her latest toy. My poor mother is still scarred.

Livia: Or is she curious...

Grace: EW.

Maven: Love you all so much. Thank you for your help tonight. And by help, I'm talking to Chloe only. The rest of you were useless.

Livia: And you love us still. HIRE AN EVENT PLANNER. Goodnight, bitches.

Me: Thank you for inviting me. I had a lot of fun.

Grace: Good, because you're stuck with us now.

Maven: *kiss emoji*

Livia: Feel free to send us photos of that fine ass daddy, too.

Maven: LIV

I laughed, plugging my phone in to charge and dragging my smiley, tipsy ass into the shower.

Chapter 11

You Don't Count

Will

It smelled like a goddamn lemon orchard in my house.

The sweet, tangy scent invaded my senses as soon as I walked in, a candle burning in the entryway and soft voices streaming in from somewhere in the house. I shrugged off my coat, hanging it by the front door before investigating the sound further. When I rounded into the kitchen, I found it spotless — dishwasher running and pans drying on the mat while a podcast of some sort played on a speaker.

I frowned.

Arushi had asked for the weekend off. She had family in town. I'd let Chloe know as much and left money for pizza. But the evidence pointed to her cooking, instead.

"Daddy, look!"

I whipped around to find Ava waddling toward me — and yes, she was waddling, because she was dressed head to toe in full hockey gear.

106

Her curly hair was hidden under a mini helmet, her legs shielded by thick pads, a jersey just a tad bit too big for her swallowing her slight frame.

My eyes shot wide, and then slid to where Chloe was standing at the bottom of the staircase. She covered her smile with one hand, but I swore her eyes were a bit glossy as she watched my daughter teeter over to me.

"Whoa!" I said when she dropped into a low stance in front of me. She had one of my old hockey sticks in her hands, one I'd given to her after a winning game last season, and she stuck her tongue out as she pretended to skate toward me, tapping the stick side to side.

"It's a lightning-fast release from number ten, Ava Perry," she said, sticking her little tongue out. "And the puck goes up and over the glove of Will 'Pickles' Perry! Goal!"

Ava threw her hands up in victory, pretending to skate around me by sliding on her socks across the tile floor. That earned her a hearty chuckle from Chloe, and I tongued my cheek before swooping my daughter into my arms on her second lap around me.

I knew she picked number ten because it was well known that it was her favorite pop star's favorite number. Mia Love was impossible to avoid regardless of who you were or what your musical preference — but especially as the father of a five-year-old girl.

Ava giggled as I swung her high, spinning her around once before plopping her back down. I patted her helmet with the corner of my mouth turning up.

"Nice shot, Pumpkin. I didn't realize I was raising the next Wayne Gretzky."

"I think I'm more like Gordie Howe," she argued, shimmying her shoulders in the way she usually did when she was telling me off. "Look what Chloe made me!"

She did a little spin, holding her arms out to make sure I could see the intricate stitching on the jersey. And when she stopped, she beamed up at me, a wide smile spanning her adorable face.

A smile.

Fuck.

My chest tightened at the sight of it, at how it took up her whole face and shone like spotlight onto me. When I glanced at Chloe again, I knew I wasn't wrong. Her eyes were *definitely* watering.

Honestly, mine would have been, too, if I wasn't emotionally stunted.

I dropped to my daughter's level, bracing my hands on her shoulders as I took in every inch of the mini-sized gear she wore.

"This is, by far, the coolest thing I have ever seen."

"I look like a real hockey player!"

"You sure do," I agreed, tapping the mask of her helmet. "A forward, no doubt."

"Right winger." She dropped into her stance again, tongue sticking out as she pretended like she was gliding down the ice.

I looked around until I found something suitable for a makeshift puck, and when my eyes landed on our paper towel holder, I quickly tore one off and bunched it up, dropping it to the floor.

"Okay, Pigeon. Let's see your moves."

My daughter lit up like I'd never seen in my life for the next twenty minutes or so, batting that rumpled-up paper towel across our kitchen and dining area and scoring on me every time.

Not that I was trying very hard to block her.

Mostly, I was trying to breathe past the knot in my chest at the sight of her having fun, of the way her face looked entirely different when she sported a toothy grin.

After her fifth celly dance — which consisted of her holding the stick above her head and doing some weird wiggle maneuver with her legs — I slung her up over my shoulder and pretended like I was going to toss her into the pool.

"No, Daddy! You'll ruin my outfit!"

All the playfulness left her at the thought of that atrocity, and I slung her back over my shoulder and carried her inside, setting her down just a few feet in front of Chloe.

"Did you tell Miss Knott thank you?"

"A bajillion times," Ava assured me. But then, she turned and wrapped her arms around Chloe's legs, squeezing as tight as she could with all the padding. "Thank you, thank you, thank you!"

"You're so welcome, my little angel bug," Chloe said, hugging her in return. Then, she bent down and looked Ava in the eyes. "How about we go hang this up so it doesn't get wrinkly, and get you in the tub."

"Can I play with my toys?"

"Well, I don't see how we can leave the story of Princess Unicorn and Prince Duck untold after that major cliffhanger last night."

Ava scrunched her nose. "What's a cliffhanger?"

"I'll explain upstairs. Go ahead. Leave this all on your bed and I'll take care of it before I come in."

"Okay!"

Ava ran up the stairs as best she could in her padding, and Chloe stood, smiling at her the entire way before she slowly turned to face me.

"You made that?" I asked, and damn if that knot

wasn't still tight in my throat.

Chloe shrugged, folding her arms over her middle. She was dressed in an oversized knit sweater that hung off one shoulder, her leggings covered in cat hair.

And yet, I'd never wanted to strip a woman bare so badly in my *life*.

"I needed a project," she said, as if it wasn't a big deal, as if she hadn't just made my daughter's entire life with that fucking outfit.

"She was smiling."

That made a grin bloom on Chloe's lips, her cheeks turning a delicate shade of pink. "She *was*, wasn't she?" Then, she threw her fist into the air and jerked it back down by her side, shimmying her hips in her own little celly dance. "Mission one accomplished."

"Mission one?"

"Well, mission two is to make *you* smile," she said, poking her finger into my chest.

I had to fight against the urge to capture her hand in mine and pull her into me, to feel that soft body of hers pressed against me, to slide my hands into her hair and show her how much what she'd done meant to me.

"And then mission three is to make both of you laugh."

"I smile," I said defensively.

Chloe flattened her lips, crossing her arms again. "That little centimeter curve of the right side of your mouth doesn't count."

I scowled. "Who made you the smile police?"

Before she could answer, Ava was calling for her from upstairs, and I could hear the bathwater running.

Chloe shook her head at me on a grin, pointing at the kitchen. "Not sure if you already ate, but there's leftover chicken zoodle stir fry in the fridge."

"Zoodle?"

"You know, like noodles but made with zucchini."

My eyebrows inched into my hairline. "You got my daughter to eat *zucchini?*"

Chloe grinned, satisfied with herself as she shimmied up to me. "Every bite."

It was a miracle, and I knew my face said as much.

"You didn't need to cook," I said. "When Chef Patel takes off, we usually just order in."

"I'm perfectly capable of making a well-balanced meal, Mr. Perry."

"I wasn't doubting you."

"Mm-hmm."

She gave me a sassy look over her shoulder before walking up the stairs. She was halfway up when I called out, "Thank you."

"Ah, so he *does* still have manners."

She winked at me, and then disappeared up the banister.

And I stood there in my kitchen with one hand scrubbing over my jaw, wondering how the hell I was supposed to resist that woman when she did shit like *this*.

• • •

After bath time, I relieved Chloe of her duty, taking over and reading Ava a book.

Of course, I didn't get far into it before she was begging me to join a hockey team, saying she was ready and that Axel Swann in her class was on a hockey team and why couldn't she be, too?

I promised her I'd look into it with my heart squeezing painfully in my chest. One, because I had no idea if I could find a league of girls, or one that would allow a co-ed situation. And two, because the thought of her getting hurt was enough to make me want to lock her in this bedroom of safety until she was twenty.

Still, I would have had to have been blind not to see how much joy just *pretending* to play had brought her tonight. I vowed to actually follow through on this promise and see if I could get her somewhere to play. At the very least, I could hire a coach for her. Maybe I could even fund a small league of girls if we had enough interest.

My mind was still spinning with those thoughts as I read to my daughter. She passed out just a few pages in, clutching her new jersey tight to her chest after begging me to let her sleep with it.

As if I could say no to the first thing to make her smile in I couldn't remember how long.

I kissed her forehead once she was asleep, slipping out of her room and down the stairs with a long sigh leaving my chest. I was sore as hell from practice and the string of games we had, and we had another home game tomorrow night.

We were just a few games away from our bye week — and as much as I hated to rest too long during the season, I was looking forward to the break.

When I made it downstairs, I re-heated the leftovers Chloe had mentioned before sitting down on the couch. I had two *Jeopardy* recordings to catch up on, and I played the first one before taking a bite.

Damn.

How the hell did she make noodles made out of a fucking vegetable taste so good?

I shook the thought from my head, doing my damndest not to think too hard about the woman in my pool house as I settled in for the episode. Being upstairs with Ava had helped me clear my mind a bit, and I remembered staunchly why I needed to stop having fantasies about my kid's nanny.

She was the first *good* one I'd ever had, and I'd be damned if I messed it up because my cock seemed to react every time she did something nice for me or Ava.

Okay, so maybe I was kidding myself with that. It wasn't just when she treated Ava like her own, or when she did something around the house that she really didn't have to, or when she made my life easier by doing what — in her words — was the *bare minimum* of a babysitter.

It was that she was fucking gorgeous.

It was that she walked around here every morning in that stupid robe with no bra on, and that she was sexy as hell even when she wore the most colorful, outrageous outfits. It was that she was witty and quick to call me on my shit. It was that she cared for three asshole cats like they were her kids and listened to more true crime podcasts than anyone I knew. It was that she spent an entire evening with my teammates' partners, even though I knew it was out of her comfort zone.

Every small, ridiculous thing about her turned me on.

Which was a real fucking problem.

"What is *Back to the Future*?"

I blinked out of my haze, finding Chloe sauntering into the living room with a full glass of white wine in one hand, and a half-stitched project in the other. She was freshly showered, her hair damp and held back with a fuzzy headband — which was good, considering she had some sort of goopy green shit slathered on her face.

The giant t-shirt she had on was thin and stretched out like it'd been worn for years. It was navy blue and said

Manifest the Matriarchy. It was so oversized that it made it look like she didn't have pants on, but I caught a sliver of the small sweat shorts she had on underneath it as she walked across the living room.

It was the first time I'd seen her thighs, and from the way my heart stopped beating and my cock jolted to life, you would have thought I was a twelve-year-old boy sneaking my first look at a picture of boobs.

"Do you mind if I join you?" she asked, hesitation making her pause at my lack of reaction to her entering. "I know this is your space, but it gets kind of... quiet out there in the pool house by myself."

I was still gaping at her, because apparently her body broke every fucking cog and wheel in my stupid brain.

"I can go," she said, already turning when I finally found my voice.

"Please, sit," I managed, clearing my throat. "Sorry, long day. My brain isn't firing."

Chloe offered a shy smile before she sat down at the opposite end of the couch from me with her eyes on the screen, completely oblivious to how she'd rendered me stupid. She took a sip of her wine before setting it on the side table.

"What is *Pulp Fiction*," she said. The contestant on my TV mirrored her question, and Ken Jennings confirmed it was correct.

Chloe wiggled her shoulders at me, and I blinked, hoping my neck wasn't as red as it felt.

"That was an easy one," I managed to grind out.

"The easy ones still rack up the cash," she combatted. "Besides, I haven't heard you answer any."

"I'm not in the habit of talking out loud when I'm

alone."

"That's a shame," she said. "I get some of my best ideas that way."

She pulled her cross-stitch into her lap then, picking up where she'd left off on what appeared to be a mushroom design.

I tried to focus on the TV and not on where her bare legs were just a few feet away from me, or how it was perfectly obvious that she didn't have a bra on under that thin t-shirt, but very much failed.

My eyes kept sliding to her where her legs were crossed, to the delicate ankle that bounced a bit as she stitched, to where her thighs hugged each other in a tight seam that I wanted desperately to slide my hand between just to see how warm that nook was.

And if I let my gaze travel up enough, I'd have to fight back a groan at the sight of her nipples through her shirt, at the plump swells of her breasts.

Fuck, I wanted to touch her, to feel the weight of her in my hands, to hear her moan when I bent and took one of those pebbled buds into my mouth.

"I would not have taken you for a game show man," Chloe said when a commercial came on.

I internally cursed and ripped my gaze to the screen, willing myself to calm down before my hard-on became too much to hide.

When I started fast-forwarding through the commercials, Chloe laughed. "Wow. A very *dedicated* game show man. You recorded this?"

I was thankful for the conversation. It helped me release my focus on her goddamn hypnotizing body — even if only marginally.

"I used to watch *Jeopardy* with my dad every night,"

I explained. "Mom was more of a *Wheel of Fortune* fan. But Dad, he loved *Jeopardy*. He was smart enough to be a contestant, too. There was hardly ever a category that he didn't know most of the answers to."

Chloe smiled, laying her cross-stitch in her lap for a moment. "I love that. I bet it was fun for you, to have that time with your dad."

"It was," I agreed, frowning a bit because I hadn't realized how much that small bit of time really had meant to me when I was younger. "I think it became even bigger after Mom passed. Dad was..." I swallowed. "Well, it was hard for him. Understandably. And I think sometimes he just didn't know what to do with me."

She nodded, her eyes on her lap before they flitted back to the screen. We watched the next round play out before I was fast-forwarding through another commercial break.

"I grew up with my mom and grandma," she confessed, something of a smile on her goopy face. "I don't think they knew what to do with me much, either. Other than warn me that men were an evil species, and I should stay far, far away from them."

I arched a brow. "A bit harsh."

"After their experiences, it was an absolute, irrefutable truth to them."

"And you?"

She laughed, picking up her cross-stitch again. "Let's just say I have had little evidence to prove otherwise, at least thus far."

"Ouch," I said, covering my chest like I was wounded by the words. Truth be told, I was a bit. "Am I so bad?"

"You don't count," she said, waving me off.

"And why's that?"

"Because you're clearly a rarity. One of the nice ones."

"I don't think anyone has ever called me *nice*."

"Just because you're grumpy doesn't mean you're an asshole," she said, giving me a look like she saw right through me. "But you also don't count because you're not in the dateable sphere."

Now I really *was* offended — for reasons unbeknownst to me because dating was the furthest thing from my mind. I didn't want a girlfriend. I didn't even want a *friend*. I knew the danger that came with both of those territories. I liked to be firmly in the *fuck and flee* category — and even that was rare.

But all those truths didn't stop my prideful ass from asking, "And why is that?"

"You're unattainable," she said, matter-of-factly. "Your focus is your daughter and your career. Which is admirable," she added quickly, as if she saw the hurt I was masking with a scowl. "But... if you're not on the market, then you don't count. And trust me when I say that most of the men who *are* on the market are... well..."

She didn't finish the sentence, and she didn't need to. I had enough rowdy teammates and memories from college to put the pieces together.

"I take it you haven't had anyone sweep you off your feet, then?" I surmised.

She snorted. "One night with my head hanging off the bed and a Chingy song blasting in my ear was enough for me to realize the only sweeping that would be happening in my life would be me dusting away all my romantic fantasies."

I was as confused as I was intrigued by her comment, but a timer went off on her phone, and she hopped up from her spot on the couch.

"Gotta wash this off," she explained, motioning to the avocado-colored shit on her face. "Enjoy your show. See you in the morning."

"Goodnight," I managed, though my mind was racing now, and I wanted to follow her out to the pool house and question her about everything she'd just said.

Head hanging off the bed... was she referring to her first time having sex?

What the fuck was a Chingy?

And what romantic fantasies did she have... because there was a very animalistic part of me that very much wanted to fulfill them.

But the moment she disappeared out of the sliding glass door, the spell was broken, and it felt like a thousand hands were smacking me upside the head.

Get your shit together, Perry.

Chloe was the first nanny I'd had who checked every fucking box. She was fantastic with Ava, and Ava clearly adored her. Hell, my kid had *smiled* all night tonight.

Wasn't it usually *me* bitching if the nanny came onto me? That was almost always my cue to kick them to the curb.

Now, here Chloe was, completely dedicated to the job and so at home already that she sat next to me in a face mask and the most god-awful pajamas I'd ever seen in my life, and yet somehow, she had me wanting to break my own rules.

It was dangerous, not just because it would put a good thing with Ava at risk, but because I was in no position to be anything *near* what Chloe deserved. That part of me that could be a good man to her, or anyone, had been broken a long time ago.

It died along with my wife, with the woman who had been my best friend.

And that was what messed me up most. I couldn't remember the last time I'd felt like this, that I'd been so overcome with the desire to touch a woman, to hold her, to...

Fuck.

I growled in frustration, flipping the TV off and storming back to my room.

Clearly, I needed to release some tension.

And I one-hundred percent would not do so while thinking about Chloe Knott.

Or so I told myself.

But the moment I was alone, my pants around my ankles and my throbbing cock in my fist, I pumped myself long and slow until the tension coiled inside me ripped through like an electric current.

And I pictured a copper-haired beauty with the curves of Aphrodite on her knees for me, those warm brown eyes watching as I pumped out every last drop on her chest.

Chapter 12

Positive Reinforcement

Will

Somewhat successfully, I managed to snuff out my improper thoughts of Chloe over the next few days.

After I fucked my hand to the thought of her, I'd slept — and woken up absolutely pissed at myself. I felt a whole lot more shame in the bright light of day, and other than having breakfast with her and Ava before the morning skate, I steered clear of my nanny.

The Tampa Bay Ospreys were cruising toward bye week, which meant between games and practice, I barely had time to sleep, let alone anything else. I spent what little time I did manage to have with Ava, including finding a local girls hockey league that she could join once she turned six.

Ava's birthday was July twentieth, and for the first time in her life, she was counting down the days.

As a team, we were finding our rhythm, a playoff run well within reach as we clenched another win at home.

Tonight, we would play our last game before the bye week — and we'd play it in New York.

This was a big one.

New York was on a hot streak, having won their last fourteen games in a row. Their goalie's stats rivaled mine, their defensemen like a brick wall you had to get through just to *make* it to the goal, and they made scoring look easy.

We hoped to end their streak tonight — but it was going to take focus. And a near perfect fucking game.

"Suter," I called at the end of our morning skate, nodding toward the bench. Sweat dripped off my hair and down my neck, my body sore from days of practice and games. I never felt this sore in my twenties — but then again, I never felt as *strong*, either.

Aleks flattened his lips with an eye roll before following me over, spitting on the ice like whatever I had to say wasn't worth his time.

But the truth was he'd been decent over the last week — as decent as he could be, anyway. And after reading an autobiography by one of my favorite coaches over the weekend, I was curious to see if a different approach would strike with our hellcat of a winger.

"What?" Aleks asked, plopping down on the bench and sitting spread eagle with his murderous glare on me.

"Look, even thinking about the words I'm about to say makes me want to kick myself in the balls. I don't do compliments, or *atta boys*, so don't get used to it."

I paused to assess his reaction, and when I noticed his eyebrow ticing up a bit, when he cracked his neck and lifted his chin, I internally smiled.

I had his attention.

"You've always been great on the ice. I don't have to tell you that, nor do I fucking want to, to be honest.

But," I added, sucking in a breath like it pained me to say the words. "Your wrist shots lately have been fucking immaculate. You haven't been afraid to get dirty for us this season, and while sometimes those penalties cost us," I said with a glare. "More times than not, they swing the momentum in our favor."

Suter's brows were furrowed, his jaw tight — and I wasn't sure if he was pissed or absolutely fucking floored that I was saying something nice.

"The truth of the matter is that you've been instrumental in our winning season, and if you keep playing your best, you're going to take us to the playoffs. Maybe even to the Cup. So, keep it up."

Aleks blinked a few times, and then opened his mouth, shut it again, and stood. He pulled his glove off and reached his hand out for mine.

"Appreciate that, man."

Hope flickered in my chest as I shook his hand hard. Maybe this was what he responded to. Maybe having everyone raining down on his ass all the time made him not give a fuck, but a little positive reinforcement got through.

"Don't expect this shit ever again," I said. "And also, just know I think you can do better. I think you can *be* better. I know you have a reputation. I know you probably like it. But you can be rough around the edges and a scary motherfucker while also being a good teammate."

I gave him a pointed look, fully expecting him to suck his teeth and skate off pissed like usual.

But for the first time, he nodded, sniffing and looking away from me like he was indifferent to what I'd said.

But I knew I'd gotten through. He'd heard me.

Halle-fucking-lujah.

"Holy shit! Look what the cat dragged in!"

Aleks and I turned toward the commotion, and I almost cracked a smile when I saw Carter Fabri walking through the tunnel. He traipsed in with all the swagger of a fourteen-year-old, practically bouncing on his heels.

Suter was unimpressed by the arrival, and he made his way back on the ice as I wobbled on my skates toward Fabio. A half-dozen of my teammates shoved past me in an effort to get to our teammate first. They tackled him in hugs and ruffled his dark hair, hitting him with joke after joke as he smiled and hugged every one of them.

This was what made me feel like he could be a leader — a captain, even.

Everyone loved him. Everyone was fired up by his presence. He made his teammates feel good. He made them feel confident.

If only he could match this energy with talent on the ice.

"Cute pubes, Fabio," I teased when I made it to him, rubbing the scruff on his chin before he batted my hand away. He grinned, though, and clapped me hard on the back. "Nice to see you."

"Couldn't let my team play in my city without showing up to support."

Our AHL affiliate was based in New York. My guess was they had a day off, and so here he was, ready to cheer on the team he should have been playing for.

He was less prideful than I was. I was fairly certain I couldn't do the same without throwing myself a fucking pity party.

"So... any of the girls come with you this time?" Carter asked, stuffing his hands into the pockets of his jeans like he didn't care all that much.

"Grace is backpacking in Spain," Jaxson said.

"And Maven makes the most of any away game by forcing Livia to help her get caught up on wedding shit," Vince chimed in. He shook his head. "That woman and her planning. I feel bad for the event coordinator she hired. Poor woman is going to have the shakes when she sees the list my future wife has put together for her."

We all chuckled a bit at that, but I didn't miss how Carter deflated a little when Vince mentioned Livia wasn't here. She was our team dentist, and it didn't take a fucking rocket scientist to see Carter had a crush on her.

Poor guy. He didn't stand a fucking chance with that one. Livia was the kind of woman who would chew him up and spit him out just for fun.

Then again, maybe that's all he wanted.

"Ah, too bad," Carter said. "I'm sure they miss me."

Vince rolled his eyes. "Oh, yes. You're all my fiancée talks about."

"Obviously," Carter said. "You know who *will* be here tonight, though?" He paused for dramatic emphasis, waggling his brows. "Mia Fucking *Love*."

"What?!"

"No fucking way."

"Mia bloody *Love*?"

"As in *the* Mia Love?"

"Bullshit."

"Siiiick!"

All these responses came at once from various teammates, and I had to fight back a snort at the guys who were high-fiving each other as if they had a chance in hell of the biggest pop star on the planet so much as looking their way.

"Ah, she's alright," Jaxson said when some of the team quieted. "But she doesn't have shit on my girl."

Vince gagged. "Bro."

"What are you girls screaming about over here?" Aleks grumbled, finally joining us. He'd skated off to take a few more lazy laps around the ice when Carter showed up — probably because he and Carter didn't particularly get along. Aleks was quick to rag on Carter in the short time they played together earlier in the season before Carter got sent down to the AHL.

My bet was Carter wouldn't soon forget his comments.

"Mia Love is coming to the game tonight," Coach McCabe answered, and I think we *all* shit ourselves a bit because we hadn't realized he'd come out from where he was back in the locker room with the training staff and one of our injured defensemen.

There were some muttered *oh shit's* before most everyone got back on the ice, pretending like they hadn't been fucking around.

"Which doesn't matter to us, because our focus is on winning, right?" Coach added, pointedly — mostly at our younger players who looked quite sheepish.

"What did you say?"

Coach turned to Aleks, who asked that question not in a prickish way like usual, but in an almost out of breath manner.

"Mia Love. Pop star," Coach added, as if that woman needed any introduction. She was the most well-known human on the planet. Her tour last year had grossed more than Elton John's farewell tour.

I watched as Suter's brows slid together, his Adam's apple bobbing hard in his throat.

And then, I swore against all fucking logic that the corner of his mouth curled into something very much resembling a smile.

Not a cocky grin, not a sneer — a genuine *smile*.

It shocked me almost as much as when my daughter did the same the other night, and Aleks wobbled past us and toward the locker room, mumbling something about taking a quick break.

Coach and I watched him go, blinking at his back and then at each other.

"That was interesting," Coach surmised, a thumb pointed over his shoulder to where Aleks had disappeared.

"Or creepy," I volleyed. "I think his smile scares me more than his scowl. What the fuck was that about?"

"I heard they grew up together."

Coach and I whipped our heads toward Carter, and it was like Coach just realized he was there. He grinned and pulled him in for a hug, squeezing his shoulder when they broke apart.

"Who?" I asked.

"Him and Mia."

"No fucking *way*," Vince said, crossing his arms and leaning against the boards. "How does that make sense? He grew up in Germany, no?"

"Her parents were his billet family," Jaxson said, chugging from his water bottle. "Pretty sure he lived with them through high school — at least during the hockey seasons."

Coach's lips turned down in a *huh* gesture, like this was news to him, but nothing too wild to believe. Carter grinned wryly like he knew something the rest of us didn't. And I just blinked.

Because I'd *never* seen that asshole show any kind of emotion that came close to what flashed across his face at the mention of her.

My wheels were spinning the rest of the day, and when we crushed New York four to one that night, we had Aleks Suter to thank.

He scored three times — a hat trick.

He didn't get even *one* penalty.

And at the end of every period, I swore I saw his gaze sweeping the suites like he was looking for someone.

Chapter 13

Apologize One More Time...

Chloe

It was a quiet Wednesday evening in the pool house when Ava came sprinting into my bedroom in a full-blown panic.

Well, as much of a panic as she could show, anyway.

I was kicked back on the bed finishing up my mushroom cross-stitch that I planned to turn into a pillow, periodically texting in the group chat with my mom and grandma. They'd been asking for constant updates since I moved in — and also begging me to come visit. I'd been so busy between school and Ava, though, that I hadn't had the time yet. So, for now, group texts and phone calls would have to do.

I also had a group text with the girls, photos of Grace in Spain the current topic of conversation. Well, that and the photo Livia had sent, which was of a cylinder-shaped object that looked like tall cup covered by a fake vagina.

I wasn't sure I wanted to know what it was for.

The fireplace was setting the mood, and I was feeling Zen in my coziest pajamas — the only set of thick ones I owned, since living in Florida meant I was usually sweating, not shivering. But we'd had a cold front blow in, and it was just shy of fifty degrees as the sun cast its final rays of gold along the pool.

I had the evening off — by strict orders from Mr. Perry, who had all but threatened me to stay gone until Chef Patel called us for dinner. Between school and his rigorous schedule lately, he hadn't had much time with Ava, so he was taking over for the night and wanted me to do whatever it was I would usually do before I became his nanny.

I hadn't fought him. I absolutely adored Ava, but I truly *was* exhausted, and a night to myself sounded like heaven.

I was also maybe still cringing from my last conversation with Will, where'd I'd admitted in an unfortunate case of word vomit that I'd lost my virginity to an old rap song with my head hanging off the bed.

He'd all but avoided me since then, which told me it had been a drastic overshare instead of the silly little self-deprecating joke I'd meant for it to be. The girls had found it hilarious when I provided the play by play in the group chat. Of course, Livia had then demanded a voice note explaining *everything*.

I divulged the details, but left out the part of that being not just my first time having sex, but my *only* time.

So, yes — I'd gladly taken a night off from the awkward tiptoeing around my disturbed boss. Evidence pointed to the fact that I *needed* the night, too, because my midnight existential crises had turned into midnight fantasies about a certain long-haired, muscle-covered man whom I could not stop thinking about.

Trouble. With a capital T.

I needed to rein it in.

Still, it had felt quiet all night. *Too* quiet. And I couldn't help the smile that split my face when Ava slid into my room on her fuzzy, sock-covered feet.

I laid my cross-stitch in my lap. "Hello, angel bug."

Ava had arrived with all the grace of an elephant on roller blades, her eyes wide, breath shallow, hair a mess like she'd run through a dark magical forest to safety. I half-expected her to tell me we had a dragon to fight outside, but instead, she took a moment to compose herself, sweeping her hair out of her face and folding her little hands in front of her lap.

"I need your help," she informed me, her chin tilting up, face completely neutral.

"I'm at your service."

I set the cross-stitch aside and made sure my phone was face down on the bed — just in case Livia sent any other photos. Then, I swung my feet over the edge of the bed, patting the spot next to me.

Ava eyed the bed like she was regretting her choice of coming to ask me for help, but then she ambled over, and I helped her climb up next to me. For a while, she stared at where her legs hung off the mattress, her little toes curling in her socks. She, too, was bundled up — and there was something so adorable about seeing her in tiny gray sweatpants and a Tampa Bay Ospreys blue hoodie that swallowed her slight frame.

"I wanna ask Daddy to come to the thing," she finally said, tucking her hands under her thighs.

I didn't have to ask for clarification to know what *the thing* was.

In class today, I'd reminded my rowdy little munchkins that we'd be having *Donuts with Daddy* on Friday.

I both loved and hated these types of events. On the one hand, it made the kids happy as clams to have their parents, siblings, or grandparents come into the classroom — attendees dependent on what the theme of the event was.

On the other hand, it was hard to avoid very complex emotions when you had children who perhaps didn't have both parental figures in their lives, or who knew their parents were too busy to join for days like this.

Of course, we always made sure to show those children extra love, to not give them time to be too sad when the day came. We'd give them extra treats. We'd give them special tasks. And usually, they brought someone to fill the gap — maybe it wasn't Dad, but it was an uncle, or a family friend.

Still, I could sense Ava's hesitation and anxiety over even bringing this up to her father. I decided to tread carefully.

"Alright," I said. "I think that's a wonderful idea. Your daddy loves donuts, doesn't he?"

She nodded, but her eyes were still on her little feet.

"How can I help?"

Ava shrugged.

"Do you need me to help you figure out what to say?"

"No," she said after a moment.

"Okay. Do you need help remembering what day it is, and what time?"

She shook her head.

For a moment, I waited to see if she'd fill in the gaps. When she didn't, I asked her if I could hold her hand, and when she said yes, I pulled that little hand into mine and squeezed it, waiting for her to look up at me.

"You seem a little nervous about asking," I said. "Is that fair to say?"

We'd talked a lot about what the feeling *nervous* was in the first semester of school — mostly because that was a big emotion for half the class.

Ava nodded.

"That's okay," I assured her. "Feeling nervous is totally normal. Do you know why you feel that way about asking your dad to come to school?"

Ava kicked her feet. "I'm afraid he'll think it's stupid."

My heart swelled in my chest. As much as I hated to hear she felt that way, I was so proud of her for being able to articulate it. It made me feel like I'd done something good because she was learning how to communicate.

"Well, that's a perfectly natural thought, isn't it? Your dad thinks a lot of things are stupid, huh?"

Ava almost smiled at that. I saw how her cheeks pinched as she fought it back. She nodded.

"I bet he'd say my pajamas are stupid," I said, gesturing to the light blue fleece covering me from head to toe. It was a whale and penguin print. "And we *know* he thinks the referees at every hockey game are stupid."

Ava didn't fight her smile that time, and a sort of giggle gurgled out of her.

"But you know what?" I said, nudging her with my shoulder. "I don't think he'll think this is stupid at all. Wanna know why?"

"Why?"

"Because out of all the things in this world that he loves — hockey, food, quiet time — he loves *you* the most."

I tapped her nose with the *you*, and her little cheeks turned pink.

"I think," I continued. "He will be over the moon when you ask him. And guess what?"

"What?"

"I happen to know that your dad is off work that day."

"Because of the bye week," Ava finished for me.

"Exactly. And just think of how lost your dad is without hockey! I bet it'll make his day to get invited to spend a morning with you — his favorite girl. He might even smile."

Ava gave me a look. "Daddy doesn't smile."

"Well, maybe you can change that," I said, patting her leg. "Now, I'll ask again. How can I help?"

"I think I just don't want to do it alone."

"Doing stuff alone can be kind of scary, huh?" I asked. And then I slid off the bed and helped her down, too. "I would be happy to go with you. We're in this together. And if you need me to talk, you just give me the look, okay?"

"Okay," she said, and I could see her shoulders relax, could see how relieved she felt already. "Now?"

"If you want," I said. "It's completely up to you."

Determination slid over her face, and she nodded. "Let's do it."

And this time, it was she who grabbed *my* hand.

I tried not to melt at the gesture, but failed miserably, and decided it was fine to let myself be giddy at that little breakthrough as Ava tugged me though the pool house.

But when we made our way toward the large sliding glass door, I stopped dead in my tracks, panic slicing through my chest.

"Ava," I said, careful to choose my words. "It looks like the door wasn't shut behind you."

"Oops," she said. "I forgot."

Then, she looked up at me with eyes wide as sand dollars.

Realization hit us hard.

"The cats!"

And we both took off in a sprint.

· · ·

Will

"Go ahead. Keep laughing," I said to Chef Patel. "Remember who signs your paycheck."

That made her snort before another fit of laughter, and she hung one hand on her hip, snapping a pair of tongs at me. "Your accountant signs my check, and I bet you wouldn't even know how to fire me if you wanted to. I'd probably get checks in perpetuity."

I grumbled in lieu of answering, not wanting to confirm that she was right.

"Besides, this is the best thing I've seen since you refused to shave your mustache during the playoffs four years ago." She shivered with a bit of a grimace, like the memory brought her both amusement and disgust. "And this sight is far more cute."

"I'm going to have hair on me for days."

"Just don't cough any of it up near my food, and I'm fine with it."

Arushi turned back to what she was doing in the kitchen as I let out a heavy sigh. Apparently, that sigh disturbed one of the *three* cats currently using me as a bed, because the white one meowed and glared at me.

"Don't *meow* me," I warned.

The orange one had been the first to invade my space. Here I was, minding my own business and watching *Jeopardy,* when suddenly I had a furry asshole in my face.

And I do mean a furry *asshole.*

The cat I was pretty sure was named Nacho had jumped right into my lap, twirling until its tail flicked under my nose. It promptly took a seat, and when I immediately tried to remove it, I was met with a hiss that told me I'd better think twice.

I was ready to bark at the damn thing when its companion decided it was best to team up on me. Black and gray striped and far skinnier than the orange fluff in my lap, that one climbed up onto the back of the couch and walked to where I was sitting before curling up on my shoulder like a scarf.

Every time it flicked its tail, I got a mouth full of hair.

And just when I thought I couldn't be in a more nightmarish situation, a third, white cat sauntered into the living room. At first, it slow blinked at me and watched from a distance, but as if it sensed when I was about to stand and shove the other two off me, it bounded over and made biscuits on my house slippers before settling in as if it were a nest.

So here I was, held hostage by three cats that scared me more than any winger ever had.

The one on my shoulders jumped a little when my daughter and Chloe slid into the living room, both of them looking like cartoons as their arms windmilled to keep them from falling once they stumbled upon the sight of me.

The other two cats didn't so much as blink.

Chloe covered her mouth with her hands, eyes flicking from my shoulder, to my lap, to my feet, and then back to my flat gaze.

And Ava was silent for one long pause before she burst into laughter.

It fizzled out of her at first, like she was trying with all her might to fight it. But when it came, it was as if it was a laugh that had been held captive for years, like it was breaking free.

My daughter's face turned beet red as she gave into it, her eyes watering, and she pointed at the cats on me before dramatically flopping onto the other end of the sectional and down to the floor.

Chef Patel ran in like the living room was on fire, and when she realized it was Ava laughing, her eyes softened, hands covering her heart like she'd just seen a barrel of puppies. She looked from Chloe to Ava to me, and though she didn't say a word, I could hear her loud and clear.

At least, until my daughter managed to speak through her fit of giggles.

"Daddy's covered in assholes!"

"Language," I warned, but my attempt at sounding serious was thwarted by the upturn of my lips.

Because my daughter, the one who was unfortunate enough to have a grumpy brute for a dad, was *laughing*.

"I'm so sorry," Chloe finally said, and I realized then that she was wiping tears from her eyes. "They shouldn't be in here. I promised I'd keep them under control and I... I'm sorry."

She made her way over to me, bending to grab the white one first, who let her scoop the thing into her arms.

Its blue eyes sparkled at me, and I swore it smiled in victory.

"It's my fault," Ava finally said once she was able to control herself. "I left the door open."

I let out a heavy sigh, but forced as much of a smile as I could. "It's fine, Pumpkin."

"I think they like you."

I arched a brow. "Mm, lucky me."

Another fizzle of laughter seeped out of her, and when I slid my gaze to Chloe, I saw her eyes well again. She glanced at me, her cheeks turning pink when our gaze met, and just like Arushi, she didn't have to say a word for me to understand those tears weren't from laughing too hard.

It was another part of her mission.

She'd made Ava smile, and now, her stupid cats had made Ava laugh.

The corner of my lips tilted up.

I couldn't even pretend to be mad now.

"Why don't you help Miss Chloe get them back home," Chef suggested to Ava. "Dinner's almost ready." She disappeared into the kitchen then, but not without watching me a little too closely, a smirk on her lips like she was hiding a secret.

"I can take Coconut," Ava offered, reaching up her hands for the white cat.

Chloe blinked out of her daze and smiled, handing off the fluff ball. "Make sure you shut the door behind you, okay?"

Ava nodded and walked carefully toward the back door.

When she was gone, Chloe turned her wide, glossy gaze back to me. "Did you hear that?"

"I did."

"She *laughed.*"

"She did."

"It was so sweet," she whispered. "It was..."

I couldn't respond, but I nodded, my throat tight with emotion.

Chloe covered her mouth, shaking her head for a moment before sucking in a long, deep breath. Then, she turned to assess my situation.

"I really am sorry," she said. "I will make sure this never happens again."

She reached for the cat in my lap.

Which should have been fine, *would* have been fine — if in the process of scooping the orange terrorist up, her hands didn't slide right over my fucking cock.

But they did.

I sucked in a breath I couldn't let go of at the first graze of her warm hand, the thin pajama bottoms I wore doing absolutely nothing to shield me from the touch.

Then, the cat wriggled out of her grasp, doubling down on the fact that it was *not* ready to leave my lap.

"Nacho," Chloe scolded, and she attempted the scoop again.

This time, when she rubbed her hand along my crotch, my cock started to wake.

Fuck.

I ground my teeth together, closing my eyes and thinking about anything that might quell that natural reaction — insects, freezing cold ice, roadkill.

But the cat slipped out of her grasp once more, and Chloe toppled in her attempt to wrangle the thing before it could dig its claws into my couch.

Which left her half-straddling my lap, one knee on the couch cushion next to my thigh, and one hand propped behind my head, those perfect, round, full breasts squarely in my face.

Fucking hell.

"Oh, God, sorry!" She squeaked the words, scrambling off me and leaving her sweet scent behind. She smelled of crayons and chai and sugar.

Once she was standing again, her hands dove for the cat with new determination.

But the cat scampered off before she could grab it.

Which left her grabbing *me*.

"Oh!" she exclaimed, and I clamped my hands around her wrists to stop her from trying to do anything else.

If this woman so much as grazed my cock again, I was going to have a hard time not throwing her over my shoulder and having my way with her.

The cat on my shoulder flicked its tail, as if it were deeply entertained by the whole show. Chloe's face was redder than I'd ever seen it, and she had her eyes squeezed tight, her face pinched up in embarrassment.

I held onto her wrists for longer than necessary, probably just to have *some* sort of control in that moment.

She peeked one eye open and then the next. "I'm so sorr—"

"If you apologize one more time," I threatened, but the warning died on my lips, because suddenly, I was very aware of *everything*.

How the room suddenly felt smaller.

How I could hear her breathing through the silence.

The way my words had softened her.

The way she melted into me.

The way her nipples grew hard beneath the stupid fucking fleece pajamas she wore.

She was still close enough to smell, and I still had my hands clamped around her wrists, and she still had her wide eyes on me, her lips peeling apart slowly as her mouth fell into a soft *o*.

Every breath she took was shallower than the last.

My nostrils flared.

She swallowed.

"What?" she asked, and *fuck*, I'd never heard a one-word question sound so goddamn sexy in my life. It was just a breath, warm and dizzying when it met my mouth. "If I apologize one more time, *what*?"

It felt like a dare.

An invitation.

It felt like she wanted me to follow through on that threat.

Like it turned her all the way on.

And *fuck* if my cock didn't jump with the desire to grant her wish.

But what was left of my common sense forced me to close my eyes, and I let out a hot breath through my nose before releasing her hands.

I didn't dare look at her again. Maybe because I didn't want to see disappointment.

Maybe because if I *did*, I'd cave.

"I've got Nacho!"

Ava's voice made both of us jump, and Chloe snagged the tabby cat from the back of the couch before all but running away from me toward her pool house. She didn't chance a glance over her shoulder.

When she was gone, I cursed, and Chef Patel peeked around the corner with a smirk.

"Don't," I clipped, standing and angrily flicking cat hair off my clothes.

Arushi raised her brows and sucked her cheeks in like she didn't know what I was talking about, dipping back into the kitchen without a word.

Once the cats were wrangled and hands were washed, we all sat down for what I was sure would be the most awkward dinner of my life. Fortunately, Chef Patel agreed to join us at my request, and she carried the conversation with Chloe, allowing me to brood and eat my vegetables in silence.

Just before dessert, I noticed Ava and Chloe sharing some sort of look, and Chloe winked at her, encouraging her with a quiet, *"go on"* that I was fairly certain I wasn't supposed to hear.

My daughter took a deep breath, and then she stood, the legs of her chair scraping against the floor when she did. She held her chin high, looking directly at me in a way that made me feel like I was about to get a lecture.

"Daddy, there's a school thing on Friday. It's called Donuts with Dad. And I…"

She looked nervously from me to Chloe, who just smiled and nodded.

"I was wondering if maybe you'd come," Ava continued. "To my school. To the thing." I opened my mouth to answer, but before I could, my daughter hastily added, "You don't have to. If you don't want to, it's okay. It's probably dumb, anyway."

When she looked to Chloe, her teacher gave her a look that warned she should be honest.

"But I want you to come," Ava added sheepishly, and she sat back down, forking her first bite of the little tart Chef Patel had just sat in front of her. "If you want."

I smirked at her, and then there was a clearing of throats.

Chef stood behind Chloe's chair, and both of them had a whole conversation with me without opening their mouths.

Arushi's eyes were wide and threatening, and she held my dessert in her hand like the way I responded would determine if I got it or not.

Chloe, on the other hand, was nodding and smiling and holding up two thumbs, as if she needed my reaction to not just be a simple yes, but a *resounding* yes, like I'd never been invited to anything so great in my life.

They clearly didn't know me if they thought I'd say no.

But I guess they *did* know me well enough to know I hadn't planned to make any fanfare about it.

I rolled my eyes, dabbing my mouth with my linen napkin before I set it aside and reached for my daughter's hand over the table. I waited for her to look at me, and then I forced a smile that felt so awkward I didn't know if I looked happy or scary.

"I would be absolutely *honored* to attend," I said, squeezing her hand. "Maybe you could wear your hockey gear that Chloe made you, and I'll wear mine to match. And I'll bring the best donuts. We'll make everyone jealous."

"You'll really come?" Ava asked, her eyes lighting up.

"I wouldn't miss it."

My daughter bit her lip on a smile that was coming more easily nowadays, and then she looked across the table at Chloe, who gave her those two big thumbs up that had been directed at me.

Ava shoved her chair back again, and I prepared myself for a tackle hug.

But she sprinted around the table and threw herself into Chloe's arms, instead.

"Great job," Chloe whispered, and she hugged my daughter tight, her eyes shut, the widest smile on her face.

My chest nearly caved in on itself at the sight.

I couldn't place the feeling — how I couldn't quite breathe right, how my pulse was unsteady, my mouth dry and a strange sensation pricking my eyes.

I blinked it away when Chef delivered my dessert, muttering a thank you toward her.

But I felt a monumental shift in that seemingly tiny moment.

Something in this house had changed.

Something in *Ava* had changed.

And it was all because of a certain some*one*.

Chapter 14

Warm-up Humps

Chloe

My classroom was absolute chaos.

Between the little voices, the adult ones, and my *kid-friendly, not annoying* playlist — the noise level was roughly around the decibel level of the Tampa Bay arena during a hockey game or a Mia Love concert.

Desks and tables were pushed together with the tablecloths I'd purchased failing miserably at keeping sugar and sticky goo off the wood. We'd had three milk spills already and one box of a dozen donuts dropped on the carpet — which was the kind that held stains like my mother held grudges.

But it was the most *magical* sort of chaos.

I felt like sunbeams were about to burst out of me as I looked around at it all, taking in the various groups of parents and children. It would be hell to wrangle these little humans once their fathers left, but right now, they were smiling brightly and chattering on and on about what they'd been learning in class.

Their tiny fingers pointed to various areas in the room — our counting posters that lined the top of the white board, the world map and globe that we'd been exploring, the cork board where I proudly displayed their best artwork.

They were so happy, so carefree, so *thrilled* just to share this little bit of their world with their dads.

It was hard *not* to feel your ovaries swelling when you saw something like that.

The dads wore various expressions. Though most of them smiled and asked questions and laughed when they had to clean their kids mouth after a powdered donut incident, some of them sighed and watched the clock and wrinkled their noses at the mess.

This was par for the course.

It was easy to see who'd been forced into coming, whether by their wives or someone else, and who actually wanted to be here.

I made my rounds, making sure I stopped to speak with every parent and paid special attention to the kids whom I could tell were a bit uncomfortable. They may have been five-year-olds, but they weren't stupid. They could tell if their father wanted to be there or not.

One moment, my heart would be full, watching a dad hold his kid in his lap and snap a picture on his phone, or grab two donuts and hold them up to his eyes like glasses to make his child laugh, or reach for his little one's hand and ask them for a tour of the classroom.

The next moment, my heart would be breaking, watching a dad and his son sit in complete silence, or a grandfather try to cheer up his granddaughter who was no doubt wondering why her father couldn't make the time to come, or two kids sitting alone together, eating their donuts and pretending it didn't bother them that no one had come to join them.

I flitted around the room with a smile I hoped could lift any spirit, refilling milk, juice, and water cups, and stopping long enough to chat with each parent and child individually. I made sure to spend extra time with the kids who needed it most, especially my two who hadn't had anyone show up for them.

Fortunately, a couple of the great dads had noticed my loners and had taken it upon themselves to help. I mouthed a *thank you* to Mr. Oster, who was currently holding the sticky hand of a kid who wasn't his and asking about the rhyme wall.

I felt in my element as I drifted from table to table, answering questions for the dads who asked them, and making sure I had something positive to say about each kid, something to brag about. It was easy to do, since they all felt a little like my own. I knew so much about them now. I knew who was quiet and who was outgoing. I knew whose hand would shoot up quickly when I asked a question and who would dip their head shyly and wait for me to ask them what they thought. I knew who was a jokester and who took everything seriously. I knew who had the softest heart and who wore the toughest skin.

They weren't my babies, but in so many ways, they were.

As I walked around that room handing out hugs and smiles, I swore I felt a pair of steely eyes following me every step of the way.

I told myself I wasn't avoiding Will Perry as I stopped at every other table before making my way to his *last*. It was just that he and Ava were in the corner. It was just that they happened to be sitting with three of my best students with fathers whom I knew wouldn't be checking their watch and hauling ass as soon as the event was over. It was just because I had nothing to worry about with that little A-plus table.

It was certainly *not* because I'd had a highly inappropriate dream about him last night, one where he slipped into my bed and raked my nightgown up and dared me to apologize one more time.

It was *absolutely* not because that dream had woken me, or that I had given in to my desires and rubbed myself against the pillow between my legs until I found relief.

And it was one-hundred percent not because any time Ava hugged me, he watched me in a way that made me feel like I was the best thing that had happened to him.

Or that when his daughter wasn't around, I felt those eyes on me in a much more heated manner — in a way that seared my skin and boiled my blood.

Nope.

It was definitely *not* because of any of that.

As the Donuts with Dad event neared the end, however, I could no longer avoid that table in the corner — not that I *was* avoiding — and so, I made my way over with a bright smile, hands folded together in front of my pink skirt with sprinkles on it.

I'd paired it with a white sweater covered in glazed donuts.

The way Will's eyes lingered on me as I approached that table made me feel like I'd dressed to theme a bit *too* well, because I was fairly certain he was tempted to take a bite if I got too close.

God, why did he have to look at me like that?

It was too easy to convince myself that he felt something, too. That he found me attractive. That he found me irresistible.

Which was ridiculous, and likely *far* from reality.

But *was it?*

The room spun and time slowed as I walked the short distance to that table, Will's eyes latched onto me every step of the way. He only let that gaze brush over my outfit for a split second before he held my stare, and he didn't blink, didn't waver, didn't smile or wave.

He just watched me like it was torture to have me coming closer.

He was a sight with his long, chestnut hair down instead of pulled back, the strands of it shaping the hard edges of his jaw. As promised, he wore his jersey to match Ava, but he'd paired it with black joggers and sneakers that made him look both professional and cozy enough to curl up with on the couch.

His golden eyes held both heat and sadness, like there was a war inside him between holding on to the pain of the past five years, and moving forward into a future that was beckoning him to be reborn. The way he watched me made me want to hold him and let him cry just as much as it made me want to straddle his lap and do my very best to remember *anything* from those *Cosmo* magazines I'd read years ago.

"Chloe!" Ava said when I reached the table, and she broke the spell I was under when she hopped out of her seat and threw her arms around my legs before breaking away excitedly. "Look what we made!"

She pointed to the middle of the table where a triangular dome of donuts had been built, a precariously leaning structure of deliciousness that looked as yummy as it did dangerous.

"Wow!" I said, bending at the waist and planting my hands on my knees to inspect the sticky architecture. "You all did this?"

Ava nodded emphatically. "Yep!"

"It was Gunner's idea," Gunner's dad said proudly.

"And look what I drew!" Charlotte said from beside him, nearly knocking down their donut tower in her effort to show me how she'd illustrated the table of people she sat with — as donuts.

I had to cover my mouth not to laugh at the sight of Will as a donut — complete with long flowing hair, a hockey stick, and a scowl drawn with two deep black crayon lines between his googly eyes.

"That," I said, taking the paper from her hands. "Is one for the wall."

She clapped with glee as I left long enough to hang the drawing with a thumbtack on the cork board, and then I rejoined them, having a seat at one of the small chairs between Will and Charlotte's dad.

I got caught up in a conversation with Mr. West about how his daughter had been doing since the death of their dog, that had been around since before she was born. I listened intently and assured him that she was doing great, all while I felt a pair of eyes burning into the back of my head.

Why was it so hard to even look at him?

Eventually, Mr. West released me, and I smiled at the others at the table — finding them all engaged in activities or conversations. Even Ava was bent over a new drawing with Charlotte, the two of them delegating who would color what.

Which left me no choice but to look to my left.

At Will.

There was no avoiding the heat that crept from my neck all the way down to my toes as I turned to face him, and I hoped my smile was the kind that could cover my stupid crush. I hoped it screamed professionalism. I hoped it did *not* scream *hey, I had a wet dream about you last night!*

"So, which donut was your favorite?" I asked.

And then I promptly cringed, and tucked my hair behind my ear only to untuck it, and then cracked my knuckles before grimacing in horror when I realized Will was cataloguing each nervous tic.

I folded my hands together and stuck them in my lap to prevent further embarrassment.

"Don't do that."

Chills swept over my shoulders and down to my fingertips at those gruff words leaving his mouth.

"Do what?"

"Try to make small talk with me when we live together."

I thought I saw a dad at the table ahead of us angle his head at that, like he was suddenly more interested in what was happening at our table.

I lowered my voice and cleared my throat. "Sorry."

Will arched a brow at me in warning.

"What?! I apologize a lot, okay? Get over it."

I waited for him to growl something back at me, but instead, he just... *stared*. His golden eyes held mine captive, like he was searching for something.

And then, he smirked.

It was ridiculous how that tiny, pathetic excuse for a smile made my heart triple its pace, but it did. I felt like I was thirteen again, reading a blowjob scene from a Wattpad story under my covers well after Mom and Grandma were asleep, instead of sitting at a table full of dads and their kids.

Everything this man did now had my skin tingling, my blood pumping faster, my toes curling in my shoes. He dripped with sex appeal even when he didn't try to, and it was becoming a real issue for his new nanny who was trying very hard not to drool over him.

"You're amazing."

I blinked. "Um... what?"

Will gestured one large hand to the classroom, like it was obvious. I took that precise moment to take in how hilariously bizarre this beast of a man looked folded into a little kid's chair.

"I've never seen you in your element," he said. "I mean, not since those first days of school when I was walking Ava in." He paused, his brows inching together. "You really do love this job, don't you. You love these kids."

Neither one of those statements were questions, though he posed them as so.

"I do," I breathed on a smile, looking around the room. I tucked my hair behind my ear again on habit before internally cursing and shoving my hands back in my lap. "These kids, they're so young, so innocent. They're discovering the world for the first time. They're honest — sometimes brutally so," I added on a laugh. "But they're also heartbreakingly kind and gentle. They're raw, like putty waiting for a strong hand to shape them. I like thinking that maybe I can plant some seeds that will grow as they do. I like the thought that some of their best qualities could be molded right here in this classroom."

I laughed a little at myself, hiding my blush as I looked down at my hands in my lap.

"And at the very least, I like knowing that for the hours they're here with me, they can feel safe. And loved. And free to be themselves."

Will was quiet for so long I wasn't sure I wanted to look at him, for fear I'd see him looking at me like I was insane.

Instead, it was awe I found in his gaze when I met it. Genuine, unfiltered wonder.

"Oh, stop looking at me like that," I said on a laugh, shoving playfully at his shoulder — which didn't so much as budge an inch. "You act like it's not *you* who is the amazing one to watch at work. I'm just a teacher — one in a billion. But *you* are a professional hockey player. A goalie. Literally one in, what, thirty?" I shook my head. "I'm nothing in comparison."

That made his scowl deepen, his jaw hard as stone. "You are far from nothing, Chloe. You..."

I hung on that word, on what would come after it, but as if he thought better of what he was about to say, he never finished.

Instead, he shook his head and took a large drink of his water before looking at me again — this time, with somewhat of a cocky smirk and a playfulness in my eyes.

"I didn't realize you watched me so closely at the arena," he said. "Had I known, I would have shown off a bit more."

I snorted. "Please — like you don't know what you look like when you're doing all those... those..." I waved my hand. "Hip thrust things."

He cocked a brow.

"You know, the warm-up humps." My face flushed, and I looked around to make sure no one was listening to us. "You look like you're deflowering the ice, and there's no way you don't know that. There's no way you don't see all those phones recording you during *that* particular part of the warm up."

The corner of his mouth climbed. "Did you just say *deflowering*? What, are we in the seventeenth century?"

I narrowed my gaze at him, fighting back my smile. "There are little ears around."

"For the record, I didn't realize," he said. "But now that I know, I'll make sure to go nice and slow through those stretches. Since they're your favorite."

He winked at me, and I was surprised I didn't fall backward right off that tiny chair my ass was far too large for.

Was Will Perry *flirting* with me?

There was a pause between us before his eyes widened like he'd just had the same thought, and he quickly scowled and stood, abruptly announcing that he was going to use the restroom.

When he came back, the event was ending, and he left with a kiss to Ava's cheek and not a single word to me.

I spent the rest of the day in a haze, not sure if I was teaching my sugar-powered kids anything of use or if I was just mumbling incoherent thoughts at the front of the class.

But eventually, the day was over, the kids were picked up, and Ava and I were tidying the classroom. She loved when I gave her something to do, and currently, she was meticulously wiping down each table with Lysol wipes while humming along to a Mia Love album she'd begged me to put on the speaker.

I, on the other hand, was staring blankly at my laptop screen with my heart thundering in my chest.

I was officially out of my element, and I needed help.

But as a woman whose closest friends were her mother and grandmother — who decidedly would *not* be good confidants for this particular subject — I had to get a little creative.

Fortunately for me, there was a wonderful little corner of the interwebs called *Reddit*.

And right there in my classroom under a vague username and with a little courage from a glazed donut, I posted my first thread.

Help: I'm falling for my boss.

• • •

Ava and I arrived home to a surprise in the form of Maven and Livia in the kitchen with Chef Patel.

Ava ran full-speed at them, hugging each and spouting on animatedly about our day — especially the Donuts with Dad event. I watched with a tired smile as the three adult women tried to keep up.

Eventually, Ava was out of breath, and I ruffled her hair before Arushi was setting her up with a snack at the dining table. I told her she could have twenty minutes of screen time — this strange girl could never get enough of hockey highlights on YouTube — and once she was set up with the iPad, I sank into one of the empty barstools at the kitchen island.

"And how's our favorite teacher?" Maven asked with a smile that told me she already knew.

I laid my head on my arms with a groan. "Let's just say any day that involves that much sugar is a tough one."

Livia chuckled. "I don't know how you do it. The only kid I can stand to be around is that one right there," she said, pointing toward Ava in the next room over. "And even that has its limits."

"What about when I have kids?" Maven asked, crossing her arms.

"Oh, I suppose I can put up with them. So long as you let me spoil them rotten."

"And so long as you keep them away from your toys," Maven shot back.

Arushi raised a brow at that from where she was doing the dishes, and then she nodded at me, her dark brown eyes as warm as ever. "Want me to make you anything? Will said he was going to go to the driving range for a while, and when he's there, it's usually hours."

"Ooohhh, bad man," Maven said. "I know it's bye week, but he could get in real trouble for that."

"Something tells me that man doesn't worry about trouble," Livia said. "And something tells me *you* could use a margarita," she added with a nod toward me.

I sat back up with a sigh. "I'm fine. Just..."

My words faded. I'd created my post on *Reddit*, but so far, had no comments. Looking around at the three women who had become new friends to me, I wondered if I could somehow get their advice without admitting who I was needing advice about.

"Okay," Maven said, her manicured nail pointing right at me. "I know that look. It's not those kids who've got you all flustered."

Livia gasped. "It's a man!"

Chef leaned in. "A man? Um... would we *know* this man?"

Maven and Livia both blanched at each other before grabbing ahold of my arms like I was about to spill the biggest secret in the world.

"Okay, first of all, you three are nuts," I said on a laugh. "Secondly... you *know* Will. Do you honestly think he's the one I'm in my head about?"

Maven flattened her lips at that. "Hmm... okay. Probably not. That man is about as warm as an ice cube."

"But you didn't deny that it's not a man," Livia pointed out. "Spill."

Arushi narrowed her eyes at me like she didn't believe Will was out of the question.

So, I thought fast, and told the best white lie I'd ever created in my life.

In my story, there was a teacher at school. Noah. And Noah was kind of stand-offish, kind of grumpy, but had recently opened up to me. I'd also caught him looking at me in ways that felt... well, like he wanted to lick me from head to toe.

Livia loved that little tidbit.

I proceeded to add that Noah was recently divorced, that there were complications since we worked together, and that I wasn't sure if I was reading too much into things.

There.

That should do it.

When I finished, Maven let out a whistle. "Well, that is kind of complicated. I mean, a coworker is one thing, especially if there are no official rules against it at your school. But a divorced man?" She shook her head. "He might still be hung up on his ex."

I wasn't thinking of Noah anymore, I was thinking of the *real* man at hand. Of Will. Of how he might still be feeling a very complex bag of emotions concerning Jenny.

"Yeah," I said softly.

"Oh, please," Livia interrupted, waving her hands. "No man gets a pass for that shit. Listen, this sounds to me like a classic case of a scared little boy. He likes you. He probably wants to..." she quirked a brow over my shoulder at where Ava was before lowering her voice. "He probably wants to bend you over one of those little desks and twist you up like a pretzel."

"You're so bad," Maven whispered to her on a laugh.

"But he's *scared*, okay? He doesn't want to make the first move and get rejected. So, make the first move yourself," she said, standing up straight and confident. "Be bold, my babe. Real men love that shit."

"I don't disagree," Maven said.

"Neither do I." Our heads swung to Chef Patel, who was finishing up dishes and wiping her hands on a towel. "Maybe *Noah* is out of practice. After all, I'm sure he went through a lot. With the divorce."

Something about her gaze, about the way those words clipped out of her told me she didn't buy my Noah story one bit.

I swallowed but didn't show my cards. Instead, I forced a smile and nodded. "You're right. I... maybe I'll just ask him."

"No, don't ask," Livia said. "*Move.* Grab his hand, or run yours along his back. Hell, go in for a kiss next time you two are alone, if that's what it takes. Just show him you're interested, and if he doesn't take the cue from there..."

She shrugged, and Maven finished for her. "Then he isn't worth your time."

"Thanks," I said, and this time, my smile was genuine. "I'm not used to having someone to talk to about stuff like this."

"We're here anytime," Maven assured me.

"I'm here almost all the time," Arushi said under her breath, which made us all laugh.

And Livia rounded it all off with another low whisper, leaning in close so only I could hear. "And when you and Noah are ready to take things to the next level, you let me know. He sounds a little submissive." She grinned salaciously. "And I know *just* how to handle a man like that."

Chapter 15

You Know Why

Will

Iwished the pool was colder.

I wished I didn't heat it, that I would have thought to cut the heater earlier in the day so that when I plunged into the deep end, it would be frigid.

I wished that the water stung my skin and stole my breath instead of welcoming me like a warm bath because what I needed right now was an awakening.

I needed a cold, hard reality slap.

I needed to stop fantasizing about my nanny.

When I'd returned home from Ava's school event earlier, I'd promptly gone into the garage, torturing myself with a strenuous jump-roping session that left me gasping for air and wincing against my sore ribs.

But the pain didn't last.

Soon, I was in my hot shower, with all my thoughts drifting to Chloe.

Chloe and her sweet mouth that was always sporting the softest smile.

Chloe and her copper hair that she couldn't resist touching, that made *me* want to get my own hands tangled up in it.

Chloe and her hand-sewn skirts that hugged her lush hips. It never mattered what top she wore with those skirts, because baggy t-shirt, oversized sweater or spaghetti strap crop top — it was impossible to hide her soft, supple breasts.

No amount of masturbation could help.

So, I'd quickly dried off, dressed, and spent the rest of the evening at the range.

It was highly frowned upon during the season. Coach didn't want us doing anything where we could potentially injure ourselves. But I kept it mild, just getting in reps and hitting balls as far as I could in my own personal form of therapy.

When I finally dragged my ass home, I dutifully ignored Chloe and her impossibly irresistible smile while focusing all my energy on my daughter. After Ava was down for the night, I disappeared into my bedroom, not willing to chance even a moment alone with Chloe.

I didn't realize how bad I had it, not with the season in full swing and a playoff run on the horizon. When I had practice and games, it was easy to forget about her until I came home. She only existed for brief snapshots of time before I could snuff out every thought of her and focus on my job.

But it was bye week. I didn't have any games. I didn't have practice. I wasn't even allowed at the fucking arena.

And every waking thought, every dream, every second was filled with thoughts of Chloe Knott.

I swam hard and fast laps in the stupid heated pool, pushing and pushing until my lungs were burning and my shoulders ached. Even then, I went for one more, and then one more after that.

By the time I stopped at the edge of the pool, the muscles in my stomach threatened to seize and take me under. Good. I wanted that pain. I wanted to punish myself like Pavlov's dog.

Think of Chloe? Shock of pain.

Imagine her naked? Kick in the groin.

Get hard at the thought of her on her knees? Baseball bat to the knees.

I hung my arms over the tile lining the pool, struggling to catch my breath and staring at the pattern on that tile until my eyes lost focus. I was ready to go for one more round when a movement from the pool house caught my eye.

And I shouldn't have looked.

I should have just continued swimming, minding my own business, and keeping my focus on the task at hand.

But I couldn't help it. I was powerless against the urge to look where I knew she was.

And when I did, I choked on my tongue.

Fuck.

It couldn't have just been her making a pot of tea or reading on the couch. It couldn't have just been one of her stupid cats jumping onto a window ledge.

No, it had to be her climbing out of the bathtub.

Dripping. Fucking. Wet.

The curtains covering the sliding glass door of her bedroom were sheer. There were blackout curtains there, too, but they were shoved aside. She hadn't shut down for the night yet. She probably didn't think she had to. Ava was asleep. I was *supposed* to be the same.

Instead, I was sitting here in the pool like a fucking pervert, unable to tear my eyes away from her perfect, round, soft body.

Distantly, I could hear the sound of music, and I wondered what she was listening to as she carefully climbed out of the deep stone tub. The bathroom was at the back of the pool house, but I had a clear shot of her through the sliding glass door, and even over the bed and through the curtain that was between us, I could see water droplets falling from her hair down over her shoulders, her collarbone, her breasts, and navel and hips.

The lower half of her was out of view, but when she turned to grab her towel, she pressed up onto her toes, giving me the quickest view of her plump, wet ass before it was gone again.

She ran the towel over her hair face first, and I watched every second her drying herself before she wrapped up in the towel completely.

Only then did I blink, reality coming back to me.

Only then did I realize that my hand had drifted beneath the water, that I had my cock pulled free of my board shorts and was stroking myself in long, slow pumps.

"Fuck," I cursed, the word filled with both disappointment in myself and longing not to stop. I rolled my fist over my shaft and watched Chloe looking at herself in the mirror. She hung her towel, assessing herself for a long moment like she was cataloguing all the places of her body that she wished were different. She ran her hands over her stomach, her hips, frowning a bit and making my next swallow harder to take.

I imagined what she'd do if I stormed inside that bathroom right now, if I showed her how hard she made me, how fucking *mad* I was for her. I wondered what sounds she'd make if I ran my hands over all those curves, if I tested the weight of her breasts and thrust my erection into the crease of her ass and showed her how desirable she was.

I was lost in that thought when, suddenly, a dark shadow hopped up and interrupted my view.

And two green eyes were staring at me from the bed.

The gray and black striped cat flicked its tail at me, amused when I jumped a little like I'd been caught cheating on a test. That judgy cat was a wakeup call, though.

What the actual fuck was I doing?

Watching my nanny through the window with my cock in my hand like a goddamn deviant — *that's* what.

With a heavy sigh, I tucked my hard-on back into my shorts and blew out a long, frustrated breath. I continued letting that air out until I drifted down, until my head was under water and that breath turned to bubbles, until all the air left my lungs, and I sank like a stone to the bottom of the pool.

And I stayed there.

I listened to my heart beating in my ears, focused on how my heartbeat slowed the longer I was under that water, felt how I was both weightless and heavier than I had been in all my life in that warm water.

Eventually, my cock softened. My head cleared. All I could focus on was the mental energy it took to fight the urge to push up and out of the water. I harvested my willpower. I challenged myself to stay longer, to make that sip of air last another second, and then another after that.

It wasn't until I felt like I might actually pass out that I gave in, slowly swimming up until my head crested over the surface of the water. I shook out my hair, brushing it back from my face and wiping my eyes before blinking them open.

When I did, Chloe was sitting at the edge of the pool staring back at me.

"Impressive," she mused, a sleepy, sexy smile on her pink lips.

No, it wasn't purposefully sexy. Just sleepy. Curious, Friendly.

But it was still sexy as fuck *to me.*

"I will admit, I was only going to wait about ten more seconds before I dove in to save you. There's a fine line between impressive and stupid."

"I tend to walk that line quite often," I grumbled, and she smiled wider.

I swam a few feet until I could touch the bottom of the pool, but made sure I was still a full five feet from where Chloe sat. The more distance between us, the better — especially with her looking the way she did right now.

Her hair was still wet and clinging to her neck, tiny droplets leaking down and disappearing beneath the hem of her tank top. I never thought I'd wish for that ridiculous fluffy robe of hers, but I did now. It was too much to see her in tiny sleep shorts and that thin top. It was too tempting, all that damp, warm skin.

She hung her feet in the water, kicking them lazily, her hands tucked under her thick thighs. I tried not to notice how her shorts rode up between them, how the fabric seemed to just barely cover her pussy and hips before it was all leg.

Scrubbing a wet hand over my face, I looked up at the clear sky above us for a moment of reprieve.

"Thank you for coming today," Chloe said, drawing my attention back to her. "I can't tell you how much it meant to Ava. She kept running through every moment when we were cleaning up the classroom. She especially loved telling the story of how Charlotte's dad tried to sneakily ask you for your autograph, but she saw it."

I didn't smile, but the sentiment tugged at my dead heart.

"It's Jenny who actually loved donuts," I said, and instantly, I wondered why the fuck that had come to me. But it was better than staring at Chloe in tortured silence while I tried not to check her out. "I hate them, actually."

"No one *hates* donuts."

"They're too sweet."

"Right. And sunsets are too pretty, and kittens are too cute."

"Speak for yourself on that last one."

She rolled her eyes. "Did you tell her that? Ava?"

"No." I frowned. "I didn't think to, honestly."

"You don't talk about Jenny much, do you?"

It was an honest question. A curiosity. But it hit me like a truck, the weight of it crashing into my ribcage and making my next breath catch.

I didn't know why, but I'd never faced the truth behind that assessment. I'd never stopped and realized that I really *didn't* talk about Jenny — not to anyone, least of all Ava.

Her own daughter.

That hit my heart harder than anything ever had, and I found myself stumbling back a bit, blinking, frowning.

"I... I really don't."

"I can understand why," Chloe said, having more grace and forgiveness for me than I deserved. "I'm sure it hurts."

"It did," I confessed. "But it's... easier now. Not easy, but easier. And I should be talking about her more. I should be telling Ava all about her. I should—"

I clamped my mouth shut, jaw working as I fought against the emotion just thinking of her conjured inside me.

"Maybe it's something we can do together," Chloe offered. "We can start introducing Ava to her mom one thing at a time. A food she loved, a place she enjoyed, a song, a movie, a photograph, or memory."

My eyes roamed hers, searching for an ulterior motive to her suggestion. I waited for my senses to go off, for that familiar feeling of detecting when a woman tried to use the death of my wife to get close to me.

But I found nothing.

Nothing but pure, honest intent to do good.

Fuck, I hated that. I loved it. I detested it. I craved it.

I wanted to warn her to shut her mouth just as much as I wanted to shut it myself, to kiss her hard and leave her breathless.

"Sorry," Chloe said, reading my stare as me being upset. Which was fair, since I wasn't sure exactly what I was feeling. "We don't have to. I didn't mean to overstep."

"Stop fucking apologizing."

"Then stop looking at me like I need to apologize."

My eyebrows shot up at that. "Is that how you think I look at you?"

"Is it not true?"

I could see how she was breathing harder now, her chest rising and falling rapidly as she doubled down on sitting on her hands — no doubt to avoid fidgeting. There was something bold in the way she stared at me, like she was facing a fear I didn't realize she had just by talking to me.

"Most of the time, you're glaring at me or storming away from me. Even today, it was like it killed you to say even a few nice things to me. You left the classroom without so much as a goodbye. You've been ignoring me all night. One moment, you're looking at me like I'm... I don't know, a blessing or something. And the next, it's like you wish I'd never been born."

I ground my teeth together, Adam's apple bobbing hard in my throat.

But I couldn't speak.

A flash of earlier that day hit me hard in the chest, when she'd laughed off her job and acted like she was nothing special. I'd wanted to tell her how wrong she was, and I'd started to — before remembering why I never tried to articulate thoughts like that.

I was terrible with words.

It was easier for me to show what I thought and felt through actions, through touch.

But I sure as fuck couldn't touch her.

So what was I supposed to do?

Couldn't she see it? Couldn't she *feel* it, too? When I looked at her, she squirmed beneath my gaze like it was a heat lamp. When I so much as brushed a part of her skin, I swore I heard her suck in a breath and hold it just as I did.

She had to know I was holding back. She had to understand that I wanted her so fucking badly I was making myself sick trying to refrain from giving in. And if she didn't know, if she was waiting for me to say it...

How could I tell her the truth, when I wasn't even ready to admit it to myself?

"You know why I left without saying anything," I finally ground out, the words raspy and harsh.

Chloe's breaths picked up speed, her nostrils flaring. I watched that determination slide over her again, despite how she swallowed and paled a bit.

And then, she pressed her weight onto her hands, lifted herself, and slid into the water.

Fuck.

My heart tripped over itself before starting to race, and it beat faster and faster as I watched her body disappear beneath the water. The line of it rested just under her breasts when she was all the way in, lifting the weight of them, her nipples hardening into peaks.

"I'm afraid I don't know," she breathed, but that breath betrayed her. Everything about her body screamed that she knew *exactly* what I wouldn't say.

Goosebumps spread over her arms and chest.

Her eyelids fluttered.

Her hands shook until she submerged them beneath the water.

She took one small, slow step toward me, and then another, her brown eyes locked on mine.

"Chloe," I warned.

"Mr. Perry."

My next breath flared my nostrils, and I curled my hands into fists by my sides to keep from reaching for her, to keep from pinning those soft hips against the wall of this pool and sliding my thigh right between hers. I wanted to tell her to call me Will, but fuck if I didn't like the way she said Mr. Perry. Fuck if it didn't make me think about bending her over and making her call me all *kinds* of names.

She slid another inch toward me.

And panic sliced me like a knife.

"Stop."

The word shot out of me.

Chloe did as I said.

Her eyes widened a bit like she hadn't expected that, but she didn't dare test any more of what little space was left between us.

I could feel the heat of her body through the water.

One step, and I could close that gap.

One touch, and I could witness those pretty eyes of hers fluttering shut, her lips parting for me.

One moan from her would be all it took for me to surrender, to fuck her right here, right now, and not relent until I'd taken everything she had to give.

But I couldn't.

I couldn't risk Ava losing her just so I could have one selfish night.

And I couldn't risk hurting her — because I knew I would. I didn't know how to do anything else, not anymore.

Still, I couldn't deny myself just one small pleasure.

Tentatively, I took that step, sucking in a breath just as Chloe did when we were close enough for our skin to brush.

Water dripped from my hands as I raised them from the water. I swallowed hard, sliding my hands along her jawbone until my fingers curled at the base of her neck.

She closed her eyes on a stuttering breath, tilting her chin up, waiting.

My heart slugged to a stop at the way her silky hair felt in my hands, at how my jaw clenched hard when I dropped my forehead to hers, our noses brushing gently. She kept her eyes closed for the longest time, and when she opened them, I wanted to die.

I saw every emotion, every want and desire in her luminous gaze.

And I saw every reminder of why I couldn't get involved.

On a sigh, I dropped my lips to her forehead, wincing against the way just that touch alone burned like the hottest flame.

"We can't," I rasped, the words as painful as the truth behind them.

I held my lips against her forehead, feeling how her weight sagged, how her next exhale let out any hope she was holding onto.

And with my declaration final, I released her.

"Goodnight, Chloe," I whispered, and I didn't look back — not when I climbed out of the pool, nor when I swiped my towel off the back of a lounge chair, or when I slid inside the sliding glass door to the kitchen.

I hauled ass to my bedroom, and once I was inside, I let my head fall back against the wooden door with a *thunk*.

And I wondered how the fuck I was going to resist her now that I knew she wanted me, too.

Chapter 16

Easy Fix

Will

"**G**ODDAMN IT!"

I slammed my stick hard on the ice a week later — too hard, in fact, because it broke in half.

The rink went quiet, save for the skates gliding and the heavy breaths of my teammates. I glared at the puck in the back of the net, the fourth one I'd let past me in today's practice, before picking it up in my gloved hand and heaving it across the rink.

Coach told everyone to grab some water and take five, and as soon as he did, Vince and Jaxson skated over to me.

"Don't," I growled.

"Fuck you," Vince shot back. "If this were us, you'd pin our ass against the boards and demand to know what's going on. So guess what, grumpy guy? It's your turn."

Jaxson plopped down onto the ice criss-cross style like a child, leaning his chin on his hands and smiling up at me. "This ought to be good."

I narrowed my eyes at him. "I'm fine. Just a rough day."

"Bullshit," came a voice with the slightest hint of a German accent, and Aleks slid to a stop next to Vince. "You're too tight, *Jeansbügler.*"

The other guys and I blinked at each other, trying to decipher what that word meant. I could easily ascertain that it wasn't meant as a compliment.

"What he said," Jax chimed in, pointing up at Aleks. "Are you injured and not telling us?"

"No. I'm fine."

"Did something happen to Ava?" Vince guessed.

"No. Ava's also fine."

"Uncle okay? Dad?" They kept on, and on, and on, with me answering more and more angrily each time I had to say no again.

But when Jaxson joked, "Need a trip to Boomer's?", the other guys laughed, and for some reason, my amusement died in my throat.

I sniffed, tearing off my gloves and leaning against the goal.

"That's it, isn't it?" Vince said, and his eyes lit up, jaw dropping like he was surprised and thrilled at my unfortunate circumstances. "Holy shit."

"I'm fine," I ground out.

"Bro, this is an easy fix. I know at least five women I could call who would jump at the chance to jump on you." Jaxson acted like he was about to skate off and grab his phone to make good on that promise, but I reached my half-broken stick out to trip him before he could.

"If you flies don't buzz the fuck off," I warned, spitting on the ice. "I'm just having a day. Let's go again."

"It's the nanny."

Jaxson and Vince whipped their heads toward Aleks, who was smirking at me with a devilish gleam in his eye.

My jaw clicked with how much pressure I put on it as I stared back at him with what I hoped he picked up as a warning glare.

"I see the way you look at her when you think no one is watching you," he said. "Like at the game last night."

My throat squeezed, skin prickling like I'd been caught in a murder instead of checking out my nanny. Ava had been begging to come for a game, and since they didn't have school today — some sort of planning day or something — I'd agreed to let Chloe bring her.

Ava had worn her custom-made jersey, and Chloe had sewn a cobalt blue glittery dress to match. That dress had a deep V neck that accentuated her breasts, and it hugged her waist before flaring at her hips — as if I needed the reminder of how lush they were, how much they begged to be held.

I'd never felt so distracted in a game, not in my entire career.

I'd also never felt so determined.

I'd blocked every shot like my life depended on it.

I also might have taken my sweet fucking time doing warmups, since I knew she was watching. Since I knew she enjoyed the view.

And clearly, I hadn't been as suave as I thought when I'd met her and Ava in the friends and family lounge. I thought no one noticed when I watched her laughing from across the room. I thought no one saw how my eyes drank her in, inch by inch, no matter how I reminded myself she was off limits.

"No fucking way," Vince breathed, but he smiled, clapping me on the shoulder. "Oh, the sweet irony of it.

You work all that time to find a nanny who's great at what she does and doesn't have some sort of ulterior motive to get to you through your daughter. And when you find her, it's *you* who's the scoundrel."

I wanted to flick him in the nose, tell them all they were wrong, and skate off in an angry huff. But that would have been admission just the same as my silence. And as it was, I didn't have the energy to fight them or lie.

I was using every bit of energy I *did* have to keep my hands to myself when I was in my own fucking house.

"Still an easy fix," Jaxson said. "Tell her. My bet is she's just as hot for her boss as he is for teacher."

"Not possible," I ground out.

"Why?" Aleks probed. "If you need to get your balls rubbed to be the goalie we need you to be, then don't be fucking proud about it."

"It's not pride, you shit for brains," I barked at him. "It's common sense. She works for me. She's my daughter's caretaker. She's the first *good* nanny I've found in the years I've searched. I'm not fucking all that up just to get my dick wet." I yanked my gloves back on, clamping my mouth shut before I kept listing reasons.

Like the fact that I was still supremely fucked up from Jenny.

"And it's not impacting my game. I performed last night, did I not? We won. I'm having one fucking off day at practice."

"Why do you think you'd fuck it up? Chloe seems nice. You like her." Jaxson quieted a bit, like he was afraid to say his next words. "It... it's been five years since..."

"Don't," I warned again, and this time, I meant it. If he said another word past that, if he *dared* to say her name right now, I'd have his ass laid out on the ice.

Jaxson threw his hands up, and Vince looked down at the ice like he didn't dare tack on his own thoughts.

It didn't matter how long it had been.

Jenny taught me a lot of lessons, but the one that stuck with me the most was that I couldn't survive losing another person I loved. I couldn't even bare to lose another *friend*.

And the easiest way to prevent that from happening was not to make any new friends to begin with — *especially* of the female variety.

"You're right," I said after a moment. "I need to get laid. I'll take care of it."

"He says, as if it's the worst chore in the world," Vince deadpanned.

"Suit yourself," Aleks cut in. "But I think you're making a bigger deal of it than you need to. It's not like you have to marry the girl. Sex doesn't have to be complicated, especially if she's on board with the rules."

"Rules?" Jaxson made a face like that word was a jinx. "Those don't work out well in my experience."

"They do if you set the boundaries and expectations up front," Aleks countered. "She hasn't tried anything with you, right?" He asked me pointedly. "Who's to say she wants anything at all from you? She's young. She's busy. She probably thinks you're hot but has no interest past that. My bet is she wants to keep getting paid just as much as you don't want to have to find a new nanny." He shrugged. "But maybe she wouldn't be opposed to also getting off from time to time."

"Since when are you invested in anyone's well-being on this team?" Vince questioned Aleks, suddenly suspicious.

"I'm not," he said easily. "I just don't want to lose because Pickles here can't perform. I've seen better hands on a digital clock."

Jaxson bit back a laugh at the chirp, and I tongued my cheek, nodding and forcing a breath so I wouldn't take out my winger right there on the ice.

"You've made your point," I said to all of them. "Now fuck off."

I skated away to get a new stick, and Coach McCabe lifted one brow at me in question. I nodded. He nodded. I grabbed a new stick, and we got back to it.

Thank fuck at least *he* understood when I didn't want to talk.

I was somehow able to focus enough not to let another puck past me, but I still wasn't playing at my best. I knew it. My team knew it. Coach sure as hell knew it, and with one squeeze on my shoulder as I passed him on the way back to the locker room, he warned me that I needed to figure it out.

We had a home game tomorrow against Miami, who hammered us the last two times we played them. It was becoming a joke now, that they were our kryptonite, the one team we couldn't win against.

Add in the fact that one of their veteran wingers loved to chirp me and had a knack for getting under my skin, and we *all* knew I needed to be in the best head space to win tomorrow.

I went up to the team gym for a long bike session, telling myself I'd be fine.

By the time I hit the shower, I was convinced I needed to get laid by whatever means necessary. Clearly, my hand wasn't doing the trick. And if I went another week wound this tight, I'd spiral.

I was even desperate enough to actually go out to Boomer's if I had to.

But when I dressed and made it to my car, all I wanted to do was go home.

I was halfway there when I remembered that Ava was having her first sleepover tonight.

The realization made my foot slip off the pedal, my car slowing until I cursed, shook my head, and started driving again before anyone could honk at me. My heart started racing. My mind spun with thoughts that were as dangerous as they were impossible to stop.

Ava was gone for the night. She was sleeping at Charlotte West's house for her birthday. She'd actually been *excited* about it, which I had no doubt was thanks to Chloe and the strides she'd made with my little girl.

I was picking her up tomorrow after morning skate.

Chef Patel had made cupcakes for Ava to take with her, and she'd also pre-made dinner and put it in the fridge for tonight at my request.

Chef Patel had the night off.

My Chef and my daughter would both be gone.

Which meant...

I swallowed as the implications set in, and I wondered how I didn't realize this little tidbit when I'd first agreed to the sleepover. Chloe and I would be alone.

Then again, I *had* told her to take the night off, too.

Maybe she'd take the chance to go sleep at her own place — to get away from me for the night after a week of awkward silences and very clear avoidance.

Maybe she'd go spend time with her family.

Maybe she'd go out with coworkers, or with friends.

Maybe she'd be out on a date.

Even as I thought the options, my heart pounded faster with what I knew was the truth.

She'd be home.

At *my* home.

It would just be me, and her, alone.

When I hit the gas with a little more gusto, I knew I was literally driving myself crazy.

Because when I flew through the front door of my home, I marched straight through it and out to that pool house with only one thing on my mind.

Chapter 17

No Kissing

Chloe

So, here's the thing about my little *Reddit* post.

It had gone viral.

What I assumed would get me a few sarcastic comments and maybe one or two real pieces of advice turned into thousands of people deeply invested in my little predicament.

They were *especially* intrigued after I detailed what happened in the pool last week.

I, of course, had been vague about everything and had changed certain specifics to protect myself.

In my story online, I lived in Wyoming. My boss was a rancher, and I was his ranch hand slash nanny. But I told the truth about what happened in the pool, about how I'd taken my friends' advice to *be bold* and confronted my boss.

About he'd looked like he wanted to eat me right there.

In the good way.

The way one might want to eat a sleeve of Oreos after being on a sugar-free diet for years.

But he'd stopped it. He'd told me I *knew* what he wasn't saying.

"We can't," he'd whispered against my hair after he'd kissed my forehead.

My fingers floated up to that spot like it still burned as I read through comments that had come in overnight.

It wasn't just strangers online whom I confided in. No, the girls had asked for an update on Noah just a couple days after the pool incident, to which I'd replied that I'd made a move and he'd turned me down. They'd been content to let it go.

And since my list of friends *outside* of the new ones I'd made recently consisted of my mother and grandmother, who I knew would have *very* strong opinions on this matter, it had become my favorite part of each day, to pull up *Reddit* and talk to these wise strangers.

And at least the story I'd fabricated for *them* was a bit more similar to the truth.

The advice varied widely, from those telling me to let go of the fantasy and focus on my job, to those who were begging me to test the line with him again. Some swore I'd regret it if we hooked up, that I'd lose my job (which, I confessed in the post, was allowing me to save more money than I ever could have imagined in my life). Others swore that he wanted me just as much as I wanted him, and that if we gave in, we'd end up falling in love, getting married, and having a house full of babies.

I laughed at those — mostly because I knew that option was off the table for me.

I couldn't fall in love. I couldn't be in a relationship. I couldn't have anything with Will Perry because my matriarchy would disown me.

And it might not have made sense to anyone else, but it meant everything to me to have their approval. It meant everything to me to work hard, save money, and provide for myself the way they wished they'd done. With the money I was earning right now, I was opening endless doors of opportunity.

I was close to being able to pay off what was left of my student loans.

And after that, I'd be setting myself up for an easy future — the one they'd always wanted for me.

I wanted to show them that I listened, that I learned from their mistakes, that I was an independent woman with her own career, income, house, and hobbies.

Falling in love with a hot NHL goalie who made more money than God was not the way to do that.

Which left me sighing a bit as I scrolled through the message board because I was racking my brain with one repeating question.

What *did* I want?

What did I actually expect and desire out of this situation?

I liked Will. He was grumpy, sure, and I was failing miserably at my attempt to make him smile. But I respected him. I admired how he was with his team, with Chef Patel, with his daughter, with *me.*

I also had never been so sexually frustrated in my entire life than I was after almost three weeks of living with him.

When I was at my little house, I rarely ever felt like this. Once in a blue moon I'd reach for my vibrator, and usually, I'd feel guilty afterward, like I'd committed the ultimate sin against my family and myself.

But here, it was all I could do not to hump my pillow every fucking night to the thought of my boss.

And I didn't feel dirty about it. I felt... *empowered.* Especially after last week.

He wanted me, he just didn't want to mess with what we had.

It made sense. He'd searched high and low for a nanny he could trust. He'd fought off a dozen women trying to get to him through Ava. I didn't want to be added to that list. I didn't want him to think even for a *second* that I was the same.

Because I *wasn't.*

I didn't want a ring or any kind of promise.

I didn't want the fame or attention that came with being his girlfriend.

I just wanted him to *touch me.*

I wanted to know what it felt like to have those goalie hands on me. I wanted him to prove to me that not every man on this planet was as terrible as the one I let inside me in college.

I sighed, shaking off the thought and the pure impossibility of it as I scrolled through more comments at the kitchen island. I was standing, sipping on a glass of white wine and absentmindedly stroking Nacho's soft fur where he was lounging on the counter. I was also debating deleting the thread and my username altogether. Clearly, no amount of advice was going to help me, because this was just one of those situations that there wasn't a way out of.

I had the hots for my boss, and he evidently didn't think I was too terrible to look at, either.

But we couldn't go any further than that.

I lifted my wine glass to my lips, and then nearly dropped it when the sliding glass door of the pool house slid open so hard it hit the barrier and shook the whole place.

Nacho jumped and scrambled off the counter, paws skittering as he bolted for the bedroom. I saw another blur of gray fur follow him.

Panic gripped me by the throat, and I was already running through all the self-defense I'd learned over the years. I was one second away from breaking that wine glass over the counter so I'd have something sharp to work with when I realized it wasn't a predator who'd burst in.

It was Will.

He stood in that opening like the god of war arriving at a battle, his eyes wild, hair blowing in the breeze, chest heaving. He stared at me for one long, hesitant moment, like he was about to turn around and storm right back out just the way he'd come in.

Instead, his fingers curled around the edge of the sliding glass door, his jaw flexed beneath the beautiful bronze skin stretched over it, and then he took a full step inside.

"Sit down," he ordered, pointing at the dining table.

My pussy fluttered at that command as if he'd told me to drop to my knees and open wide.

I hastily shut my laptop, abandoning my wine and scurrying over to the table. I dropped down into a seat just in time to watch Will calmly, slowly, shut the sliding glass door behind him.

We were alone.

Like... *truly* alone.

Chef Patel had the night off. Ava was at a sleepover.

It was just me and him, and when he turned and slowly prowled closer, the air came alive with electricity and a delicious promise.

Will's hair was still a bit damp from what I assumed was his post-practice shower. I was used to that look. I was used to his routine.

Except tonight, it looked a little more unruly, like he'd been dragging his hands through it in frustration.

My mind whirred the closer he came, and I tried to read his menacing gaze but found myself even more confused. I didn't know if I was about to get fired or kissed senseless.

The first one made the most sense.

The latter one was what I prayed for.

He wrapped his fingers over the top of the chair across from me when he reached the table, taking a long, steely breath before he cracked his neck and sat down. Where I was ramrod straight in my chair, he kicked back in his, long legs stretching out and one finger drumming on the table as he assessed me like I owned something he was prepared to pay a hefty price for.

"Do you want to have sex with me?"

I balked.

Did he... did he really just ask what I think he did?

"Uh..." I stammered, truly concerned I'd misheard him.

"It's a pretty simple yes or no question."

"Then why does it feel like a trap?"

"It's not."

"You answer first."

He flattened his lips. "Clearly, you already know my answer if I'm here asking you."

"Maybe I want to be wooed. That wasn't exactly a romantic declaration."

"I don't do woo and I don't do romance, either. You want honesty? *That* I can do."

He leaned over the table then, folding his massive hands together and leveling his gaze with mine. He spoke slowly, intently, with a rasp like every word burned on the way out.

"Yes, I want to fuck you, Chloe. *Badly*. So much so that I've fucked my hand every night since you've moved in and thought about you waiting on your knees when I came."

Holy hell.

Those words were degrading. They were horrendous. They were the kind of filth that would have had my grandmother clutching her pearls and my mother slapping Will right across his handsome face.

But they did something else entirely for me.

My body erupted with chills that I didn't even try to hide, and I swallowed, somehow holding his gaze even when I felt my entire body flush with heat. I was tempted to play with my hair, so I sat on my hands to keep from doing so.

"Your turn," he said, and even though he'd just confessed to masturbating to the thought of me, he looked like he'd rather strangle me than get me naked. "Do you want to have sex with me?"

I blinked, my throat dry.

"I... this is just... I've never been asked quite so directly," I stammered.

"I think we both know I'm not one to beat around the bush."

I swallowed, nodding, and then held my chin as high as I could. "Yes," I breathed. "I... do."

"You do what?"

"I want to have sex with you."

The words were a breathy, secret confession that felt as dirty rolling off my lips as any curse word I'd ever muttered in the presence of my grandmother.

For a moment, I wasn't sure Will had heard me.

But then I saw it, all the small ways he reacted — the way his Adam's apple bobbed, his hands gripping each other tighter, his nostrils flaring, eyes heating.

"Here's the deal," he said, and he stood, pacing like a businessman about to close on a billion-dollar merger. "Clearly, there is a mutual infatuation between us. I think it's fair to say we've both felt this way for a while now."

I smirked, folding my arms across my chest and leaning back in my chair.

I'd never seen this man so flustered.

I was *very* content to sit back and watch the show.

"But as you are well aware, I went through hell and high water to find a nanny who didn't make me want to pitch myself off the nearest cliff. Ava adores you. I am beyond grateful for what you do for her, for me, for *us* as a family. And the last thing I want is for this arrangement to be put at risk due to us being stupid."

I didn't dare interrupt — mostly because I was highly entertained by watching him fumble his way through this.

"So, here's what I propose," he said, and he sat back down, back straight and eyes hard on me. "Sex. *Only* sex. Whenever we both consent to it and as long as it doesn't interfere with Ava or our business arrangement in any way, shape, or form. No one can know. Not your friends, not my teammates, not Chef Patel, and most of all, not Ava. I need to know that will be enough for you, that you're not secretly hoping for more than that. Because I can tell you, right now, that I can't give it to you."

Every time this man said the word *sex*, my body wound itself tighter and tighter. I felt like I might shatter into a thousand pieces if he said it one more time.

"I can do that."

He blinked, as if he hadn't heard me correctly. "You can... do that."

I nodded, heart thundering with excitement that I tried to tamp down.

"You're okay with just having a physical relationship, with no other ties, no other promises for more," he said slowly.

"Yep."

"This is not a relationship, and never will be," he said again, like he was sure I hadn't heard correctly.

"Good. I can't date anyone, anyway."

He frowned at that, opening his mouth like he wanted details on the *can't*, but then he changed his mind.

His throat constricted, and he leaned forward just marginally over the table.

"No kissing."

"No kissing," I agreed, even though I *very much* wanted to kiss. I understood the boundary. Kissing was intimate — maybe even more so than having sex.

At least, I could imagine. Not that I'd know.

"And you can't fall in love with me."

"*You* can't fall in love with *me*," I repeated, heart hammering even at the thought. I could just hear my mom's disappointment if I told her this job I'd taken to set up my future and stability turned into me being in a relationship I promised her there was no chance of.

Will almost smiled, his eyes lighting with curiosity. "You think I'd be the one to fall in love?"

"Obviously. Have you seen me?"

I gestured to my old, ratty pajamas that I'd sewn back when I first started learning, the pattern a god-awful, multi-colored tie-dye that deserved to die in the late 90s.

I needed a joke right now, because the heaviness in the room was enough to suffocate me.

Will's eyes raked down the length of me, amusement in his eyes. But as per usual, he didn't laugh. He didn't smile.

He *did* grow quiet, though — hesitation furrowing his brows.

"I don't want to be your friend, either," he said.

His eyes met mine, serious and intent.

"I... I've been there before, and I can't do it again. When I say this is just sex, I mean *just* sex." He shook his head. "We have to stop talking about shit. I don't want to tell you about my life, and I don't want to know about yours."

Those last words stung a little, but I shrugged them off.

"Great. I hate friends, anyway."

Will tilted his head to the side. "You hate friends."

"Yep. Isn't that evident by my Friday night plans?" Again, I gestured to my surroundings. "I hear you, okay? No relationship. No friendship. Just sex."

Anticipation surged through me as he grew quiet, as the questions died out, as that three-letter-word hung between us and dripped with temptation.

"You're sure you can do this?" he asked, voice raw and restrained.

I prayed my giddiness wasn't showing, that he couldn't see how every inch of my being was on fire at the possibility of what could happen when I said yes.

"One-hundred-percent positive."

Will's eyes flicked between mine, searching for cracks, for any sign that I was lying.

I held my expression stone cold and unaffected, cocking a brow in a daring tease.

I could do this. I could be sexy. I could be a teasing, alluring goddess.

Because I finally had my answer.

This.

This was exactly what I wanted, what I *needed*, what I could handle.

There was no risk of falling in love. There was no risk of letting a man into my heart only to have him shatter it and leave me broken. There was no risk of disappointing my matriarchy, of following in their footsteps when they'd spent my whole life warning me against it.

I could keep my job, keep the money, keep the security.

Keep the *power*.

And yet, in the same breath, I could have what I'd always wanted.

I could feel what it was to be desired, to be touched and tasted by a real man. Those scenes I'd read in books and magazines, the passion I'd watched play out on television screens...

I could know what it was, even if just for the briefest moment of time.

It was the best of both worlds, and I saw that same realization dawning on Will's face as he slowly stood, making his way around the table to tower over me.

My neck ached as I looked up at him, and his eyes roved over my throat, my collarbone, down to the gaping neckline of my camisole before he dragged his gaze back up to mine. One thick, long finger reached out, tracing the edge of my jaw as his breathing intensified.

"Tell me again that you can do this," he husked, and it was both a plea and a last-ditch effort to get me to change my mind. I felt the doubt warring through him, saw how he was tortured both by the thought of walking away from me right now and by walking into a situation that would ruin us.

I pushed into his hand, into *him* as I stood, chin lifted, chest pressing against the bottom of his, eyes locked and sure.

His hand slid to my neck and his fingers curled around it, like he was ready to stop me and throw me off him if he had to.

Or like he was ready to grip and squeeze and control and *own*.

"I. Can. Do. This," I breathed, punctuating each word by pressing more into his touch.

He let out a shaky exhale, jaw clicking with reserve.

That hand around my throat tightened with just enough pressure to make me moan.

The sound unleashed us both.

And with my blood pumping and heart galloping out of control, Will nudged his thigh between mine and rocked me into the table with enough pressure to bruise where the glass hit my lower back.

I inhaled a gasp at the feel of that thick, hot thigh right where I needed pressure, and Will ran his hand down the front of me, roughly palming my left breast before both his hands gripped my ass and rolled me against him.

My legs shook, another pathetic moan ripping from my throat.

So much better than my pillow.

"*Goddamn,* Chloe," he husked, gripping my ass in two handfuls before he spanked me and groaned at my resulting gasp. "I've wanted to touch you like this for so long, to feel you pressed against me just like this."

He made me roll against him again, and this time, I took over, loving the way it felt, needing more. I rocked and arched until my clit had the maximum pressure, and my eyes fluttered open on a moan just in time to see Will's unrestrained appreciation.

He loosened his grip, letting me ride, wetting his lips and watching where I straddled his leg.

"*Fuck,*" he said, hands roaming up again until one palmed my breast through the thin fabric of my pajamas and the other tightened around my throat.

He forced me to look at him, and it felt both mortifying and hot as hell when I humped his leg again with my eyes locked on his.

"You can come just like this, can't you?" he asked, meeting me thrust for thrust with the pressure I needed to drive closer. "Filthy fucking girl. Fucking my leg. I bet you've fucked your hand just like this and thought of me, haven't you?"

I moaned and closed my eyes, unable to look at him as shame and desire made heat flood my cheeks. *Why* did I love this? My first time with a man, he'd been silent save for some very unattractive grunts and asking me *do you like that* two seconds before he came.

But this...

It was like Will saw what I didn't, like he knew what to say without a word from me to confirm or deny. He was reading my body language, my moans and gasps.

"Don't shy away now," he said, squeezing my neck until I fluttered my eyes open once more. "Take it. Take your first one."

First one?

I was still processing what that meant when Will licked a hot line along the slope of my neck, sucking my earlobe between his teeth and nibbling it as chills rocked through me.

"Your second one will be on my tongue," he promised, his voice low and husky in my ear.

The words were so dirty, so *hot*. I gripped onto his shoulders and bucked against him, wild and hard, releasing whatever bit of shame was still holding on.

I didn't know if this was a dream, a fantasy, or real life.

All I knew was that I didn't want to stop.

Will groaned in my ear as I picked up the pace, and I held onto him like he was my lifeline, rocking and rolling against his thigh with my orgasm mounting more with every bit of friction I found.

"That's it," he praised, and when his teeth clamped down on my lobe again, I whimpered. "Ride my thigh like you want to ride my cock. Show me how good you'll take me when I finally let you."

Jesus Christ.

Those words in my ear. His voice hot and raspy and all-consuming.

I was riding wildly now, and Will must have enjoyed the view of my tits bouncing because he leaned back and pinned his lip with his eyes on my chest as I rolled my hips and tangled my hands in his hair.

I didn't want to wake up.

I didn't want to go back to not knowing what it would feel like to have his hands on me.

I didn't want to abide by this stupid fucking *no kissing* rule, because as my climax crested, I wanted to moan into his mouth, I wanted him to muffle the embarrassing screams that were climbing out of my throat.

Instead, I dug my nails into his shoulders, violently shaking as blood rushed from every corner of my body right between my legs.

I came hard and fast and unbridled, closing my eyes and arching my neck and offering every scream up to the sky. It was an orgasm so familiar, just like the ones I found with my pillow, except hotter, deeper, *more*.

Will took control when I couldn't move anymore, his hands locked on my ass and helping me ride him until I was completely fucking spent. When I was, I collapsed into him, breathing heavy, sweat slicking the back of my neck and chills sweeping over me when Will carefully rocked me once more against him.

"I love the way you look when you come," he said.

The praise made me shiver again, and I felt drunk as I lifted my heavy gaze to meet his.

"I want to see that again."

And then, showing he was even stronger than his muscles let on, he lifted me until I had no choice but to hold tight to his neck and wrap my legs around his waist.

His erection met my center, my pants wet and sticking to me, and he groaned at the proof of what he'd done as he carried me over to the kitchen island.

My backside landed on the cool stone top, and then he slapped the side of my ass.

"Lift."

I pressed into my palms, and he tucked his fingers under the band of my pajamas and ripped them down in one fell swoop.

He peeled them off one leg and then the other, groaning when he saw that I didn't have another layer underneath.

I should have been embarrassed. I should have clamped my knees together and winced at the fact that this man had me spread wide on a countertop with evidence that I'd just come by humping his leg right in his face.

Instead, I reached down into the deepest depths of my soul and tried to find confidence, to hold onto whatever it was I had that made Will Perry look at me the way he was right now.

Like I was beautiful.

Like I was sexy.

Like I was everything he wanted.

Be bold, I heard Livia say, and I embraced that with everything I had.

With his eyes devouring my body, Will wrapped those gargantuan hands around my thighs and tugged me hard until my ass hung off the edge of the counter and my hands shot out to grip whatever I could to keep me steady.

"So fucking wet after that," he mused, and my soul left my body when he swiped one finger through where I glistened for him.

He didn't penetrate me, just teased and played and watched where he touched me like he was committing every inch to memory.

My heart pounded like a drum.

I can't believe this is happening.

I can't believe this is happening.

Will looked up at me, his golden eyes dark and promising, his tongue jutting out to wet his lip.

And when he dropped his mouth to my pussy, I nearly passed out on the spot.

Chapter 18

Sit On Me

Will

Those sweet little sounds would be the death of me.

Every time I touched her, Chloe's breath would quicken or release in a heated gasp.

When I whispered dirty words against her ear, she'd reward me with a whimper.

And when I finally licked my way between her thighs, gliding my tongue flat and hot along her seam, she moaned my name in a way I knew I'd hear echoed in my dreams for life.

I didn't allow myself time to think about what we were doing. I didn't want to give my common sense the chance to tell me all the reasons it was stupid and irresponsible and likely to lead to a crash. Instead, I put my thoughts on mute and let myself be consumed by everything that Chloe Knott was as I unraveled her.

My cock was swollen and aching for her as I took my time between her legs, savoring what I'd imagined tasting for weeks now. She was soaked from her first release, the

195

one she'd worked out with both of us fully clothed and her just rubbing herself against my thigh.

The memory made my dick jump against my pants, begging to be set free, but I wanted to lick another orgasm from her before I got my own.

"You don't even realize how much of a tease you are, do you?" I asked, breath hot against her pussy as I held tight to one of her thighs and snaked my other hand beneath her. I toyed with her entrance with my middle finger, testing just an inch of her and feeling her tighten around me as I withdrew. "Walking around every day and night with that smile of yours, with those eyes..." I bit my lip on a groan at the way she responded to me, the tightening and writhing. "Tempting me with this ass, these thighs, these beautiful fucking tits."

I licked or bit or squeezed each reference I made, loving how Chloe squirmed beneath me. Her eyes were hooded as she watched me over the swells of her breasts still covered by her top. I plucked at the material, at her nipple through it, savoring the shocked cry of surprise she let loose when I did.

"Pull them out for me," I said, and I kept my eyes on hers as I pressed into her cunt a bit more with one finger, flicking my tongue over her clit before covering it completely and sucking hard.

She bowed off the counter, head arching back, breasts an offering to the gods.

"Let me see you play with yourself while I make you come again."

I knew it wouldn't take much. She was trembling already, the same way she did when she rocked herself against my leg. But I wanted to take my time. I wanted to test every theory I had about what she liked until I found the perfect combination.

Hastily, Chloe shoved the thin straps of her tie-dye tank top off her shoulders, pushing still until the fabric bunched at her waist.

And revealed two gorgeous, heaving, perfect breasts.

I groaned, rewarding her with a long suck of her clit as my free hand roamed up and over her thigh, hips, and waist until I could take her in one lush handful. I squeezed and kneaded and rolled her nipple between my fingers in time with my tongue working between her legs. Testing the weight of her was better than I'd ever imagined, and I played with her tit with one hand still teasing between her thighs until I couldn't stand it any longer.

I had to give them my full attention, those breasts that had driven me to insanity.

I climbed up over her, not giving a damn when my back screamed in protest at the awkward way I was bent over the island. I bit my lip and grabbed each of her breasts in a handful, shaking them a bit to watch the way the full roundness of them rippled.

"Fuck," I cursed, and I sucked one nipple into my mouth, smiling against her skin at how her hands flew to my hair and held me there.

"Holy shit," she breathed. "That feels *incredible*."

I didn't know what the other men in her life were doing to make me seem so great at sucking on a fucking tit, but I wasn't complaining. I gave her more, kneading and touching and sucking and licking until she was grinding her wet pussy against my abdomen and begging for relief.

I ripped my shirt overhead, disposing it somewhere on the floor behind me before making quick work of my pants. I left my boxer briefs on, smirking a bit at the sight of Chloe leaning up on her elbows with wide eyes as she took in the view before I had her pinned against the counter again.

I licked my way down between her thighs, settling in and testing what she liked, what she loved, and what would make her come.

She *liked* when I licked her with a flat tongue, when I covered her with heat and let her feel all of me.

She *loved* when I tightened the tip of my tongue to a point and worked her clit with it, when I pressed one finger inside her just up to my middle knuckle.

But when I sucked her clit between my teeth, when I held that pressure and moaned against her while fucking her with my finger, when I used my free hand to roll my fingers around her plump, peaked nipple...

That was the ticket to making her come.

"Oh, God," she breathed. "Oh, *fuck*. Will, I... I..."

Her words were drowned out by the loudest, sweetest fucking screams I'd ever conjured from a woman in my life. They weren't the fake ones I'd heard from girls who performed in the bedroom like it was a porn studio. They weren't shy or subdued, either.

They were raw and real. They were proof of what I was making her feel as she combusted and found her second release.

Her hands fisted my hair so tightly it stung, but I didn't dare break pace. I worked my fingers and tongue against her until her knees fell open, her head hit the countertop, and her breaths shot out in long puffs of exhaustion.

I didn't rush her as she came down. I slowly removed my finger from inside her, massaging the outside of her opening as I kissed her swollen clit. My other hand released the pressure from her breast, and I took the time of her recovering to fully appreciate the view before me.

God, she was fucking beautiful.

Her red-orange hair was splayed out on the counter, her cheeks the most sensual shade of *just fucked fuchsia* — and I hadn't even fucked her yet. I savored the plumpness of that bottom lip she'd been biting, the pink marks my hands had left on her breasts and thighs and hips.

She was an offering, her shirt shoved down to her waist, her pants on the floor beneath me, breasts heaving, pussy glistening.

My cock refused to be ignored any longer, and I reached one hand into my briefs to palm myself as I let my eyes continue their slow perusal of her body.

"You are a wet fucking dream, Chloe," I said, stroking myself and thumbing the bit of precum on my tip until I coated myself with it. "Magnificent. Absolutely fucking *perfect.*"

Chloe leaned up onto her elbows, her eyes wide again as she looked where my hand was in my briefs. When I pulled myself all the way free and rid myself of the fabric, her mouth fell open into a soft *o*, her lashes fanning her pink cheeks as she tried to catch her breath.

Then, her mouth closed, her eyes narrowed into determination, and she was on the move.

Her hands pressed into my chest until I had no choice but to back away from the counter, and she made enough room for herself to slide down off it. Her tits bounced on the landing, and I groaned at the sight, fisting myself a little tighter.

"Let me," she said, and her hands replaced mine as I hissed a curse and let my head fall back.

I had to admit, it wasn't the sexiest thing in the world. She didn't lick along my chin, spit in her hand and fuck me slowly with her slick fingers curled around my shaft. She didn't whisper dirty commands in my ear or slide my cock between her wet lips to let me feel what I'd done to her.

In fact, she seemed... hesitant. *Scared*, even.

Her hands trembled as she took my place, and once she had me in her grip, she seemed unsure of what to do next.

Her breathing intensified as she mimicked what I'd been doing, working my cock in long, slow pumps with her hands covering every inch. She used both, at least, which took many women time to get to. She seemed eager to do what made me feel good, responding to every sound I made and working me faster when I started thrusting my hips into her grip.

I was wound so fucking tight from going down on her, from watching her make herself come against my thigh, that I was pretty sure I could bust right there in her hand.

But I willed myself to hold back, to keep my fucking cool.

Especially when she dropped to her knees and brought all my fantasies of the past three weeks into living color.

"Fuck yes," I praised, sweeping her hair out of the way when she was in front of me. I gathered it in one fist and held it tightly. "Let me feel that sweet mouth."

Again, I swore I saw worry etched in her gaze. So much so that I frowned and nearly asked her what was wrong. But before I could, she quickly opened her mouth — and *dove* onto my cock.

I shuddered from the suddenness of it. One moment, she tentatively held me in soft, unsure hands. The next, she was gagging from attempting to take me all the way down her fucking throat.

"Jesus, Chloe," I groaned, tightening my grip in her hair. My eyes crossed with the effort to stand after feeling her wet mouth and hearing the sound of her choking.

She pulled back, fisting me with one hand and staring at my cock like it was both a puzzle to be solved and a snake to run away from. She went back, slower this time, her hot mouth suctioned around my head and shaft until she gagged again and pulled back, sitting on her knees and looking up at me with a strand of saliva connecting her to my cock.

Fuck me, that was a gorgeous sight.

"I... I want you inside me," she said, breathy, pleading, her eyes wide and rimmed with tears from gagging on my cock, her cheeks flaming pink.

And I didn't even care that it was the weakest attempt at a blowjob I'd ever had. Two lashes of her tongue and one squeeze from her hand had me ready to come without her touching me again — let alone hearing her say those words.

"What was that?" I asked, arching a brow and running my thumb over her wet, swollen lip.

She swallowed, chasing my thumb with her tongue.

"I want you inside me."

I ripped her up in an instant, half pulling her and half carrying her to the couch. There were a million ways I wanted to take her. I wanted her legs on my shoulders and her tits in my face as I pushed inside her. I wanted to bend her over the arm and fuck her from behind. I wanted to prop her ass on the edge of the couch and lay her head on the floor, to spread her legs wide and fuck her like a porn star while she screamed out my name.

But right now, I wanted her to be the one in control.

I stopped only long enough to fish a condom out of my wallet, leaving Chloe sitting on the edge of the leather with her chest heaving as she watched me sheath myself.

"Take that off," I said, nodding to where her shirt was still bunched at her waist.

She made quick work of it, and then sat waiting, hands nervously twisting her hair and pulling it to one side before she sat on her palms.

So many visions paraded in my mind at that sight. I imagined her naked on her knees, sitting on her hands for me, letting me do whatever I wanted to her mouth, her tits, her pussy, and her ass. I imagined tying those hands up to my bed frame so she didn't have a choice but to hold them still while I had my way with her.

She'd said yes.

She'd agreed to the deal.

This was only the first time I'd take her, and the possibilities had me aching for the next time before round one was even finished.

"Up."

I barely got the word out before she was standing, and I took her place on the middle cushion, sinking my back against the leather and reaching out for one of her hands.

"Come here," I beckoned, and I helped her climb into my lap.

She looked unsure as she did, her brows furrowing, lips rolling together as she watched where her thighs straddled mine. She used her hands on the back of the couch to hold her weight off me, and I frowned.

"Sit on me."

Her worried eyes flashed to mine, and she sank just an inch.

My nostrils flared.

"Eventually, you're going to be sitting on my face, Chloe. So you better get used to it. *Sit.*"

This time, she let go, and I moaned when the full weight of her rested in my lap, when my cock slicked between her swollen lips.

"That's it," I said, and I reached between us for my shaft, lifting her just enough for me to press against her entrance. "Now, do it again. Slowly. As slowly as you need to."

Her breathing intensified when I edged inside her. I cursed, she shivered, my cock begged for me to wind my hands around her shoulders and pull her down until I was balls fucking deep.

Somehow, I resisted, busying myself with her beautiful tits and hips, instead. I let her take her time, focusing on the little sounds she let loose as she sank down another inch, lifted, and then found one more.

"Such a good fucking girl," I praised, rolling her nipples between my thumbs and forefinger to help her work me inside her. "Taking my cock just like I knew you could."

Chloe whimpered, letting her head fall back as she lifted and sank another half inch. Each time she coated me with her release, and after what felt like the most excruciating, tantalizing minutes of my life, she finally sat *all* the way down.

For a long moment, we just sat there, Chloe moaning and breathing hard as I pinned her hips in place and felt my cock jump inside her. She hugged me so perfectly, and when I helped her lift up and slide back down, I knew I wasn't going to last long.

I told her as much, cursing out the admission as she picked up the pace and started riding me in slow, rhythmic pumps. Every time she landed in my lap, her breasts rippled. Every time I flexed deeper inside her, she cried out and bowed into me. Every time I groaned, she rocked her clit against my pelvis like that sound was the key to her third orgasm of the night.

For a while, I let her move just like that, driving me wild with each maddeningly slow roll of her body. Her legs quaked around me, her eyes casting up toward the sky before they locked on my gaze.

"Do you like it? Am I... am I doing it right?"

I almost laughed.

I was two seconds away from coming before she could get hers and she wanted to know if she was doing it right?

"I fucking *love* it," I told her, because I was all too happy to praise her if that's what she needed to hear. "Watching you ride me, feeling how you hug my cock."

She moaned, and I used the opportunity to hold fast to her hips and help her pick up the pace. She rocked against me each time she landed, and I flexed in deeper, desperate to find that spot inside her.

When she grew wild and unsteady, I knew she was close. She bucked and whined and let me take the full weight of her, let me control how fast she was bouncing in my lap. And when she came again, her walls tightening around me and her screams echoing off the glass of the pool house, I let myself follow.

I fucked her harder, faster, holding onto her so she wouldn't fly out of my lap as I chased my release. She cried out both my name and God's in tandem, and when the first numbing, all-consuming shock of release found me, I bit down on her shoulder, groaning out weeks of pent-up frustration and tension.

"God*damn*, Chloe," I cursed against her skin, and I held her to me, rocking inside her over and over, deeper and deeper, like I wanted to become a permanent part of that perfect body of hers.

Her nails clawed at my back in a way I knew would leave marks, but I didn't give a fuck. I was consumed by her. I was everything and I was nothing. All the energy in the universe existed inside me right now, inside *her*, and yet we were nothing at all, nonexistent and omnipresent all at once.

Somehow, at some point, my climax receded.

I felt myself slowing where I pumped inside her, sighed a bit as she felt lax in my arms. My cock twitched until it began to soften, but I kept it inside her, flexing in and out like I could catch round two if I tried.

My arms wrapped around her, pulling her against my chest, and I inhaled the sweet scent of her and nuzzled into her neck.

For a split second.

Then, I realized what I was doing and promptly released her.

Chloe flushed when I did, hiding her face behind her chaotic hair as she not-so-eloquently rolled off my lap and splayed out on the couch next to me.

We stayed like that a long moment, both of us breathing and sweating and silent.

Then, Chloe laughed.

She covered her face with her hands, giggling at first before she gave into the loudest, cutest, most addicting laugh. She peeked at me through her fingers, giggling harder when she saw my arched brow.

"I'm sorry," she said, waving me off, and then she collapsed even more into the cushions with a sigh, her arms flopping out to the side. "It's just... *God*. Is that... is *that* what it's supposed to feel like?"

I frowned, blinking, racking my brain to catch up with her words.

"Uh..."

She waved me off again before I could answer, sitting up and pinning her lip between her teeth. "Okay. I... I have a little confession."

She was still fucking giggling while I sat there like I was missing a very big piece of the puzzle.

"Um, so... don't freak out but... that was only my second time."

My jaw hinged open.

Surely I didn't hear that right.

"Your... second time?" I repeated.

"Well, *technically* my first for whatever that magical thing you did with your mouth was," she corrected. "Oh, and the whole dry humping thing."

Her cheeks flamed with the words, and she hid behind her hands.

At least, until I peeled them off and pinned her with a stern look.

Did this woman just tell me that was her first time having someone go down on her?

That it was only her *second* time having sex?

My heart started to gallop, panic threatening to seize me by the throat.

I framed her arms in my hands and pulled her to face me straight on.

"Explain."

Chapter 19

If I'd Have Known

Chloe

Shit.

I'm in trouble.

Will hadn't spoken in a full five minutes since I'd finished telling him the truth about my sexual experience.

We had moved back to the table — me in a new set of pajamas that *wasn't* soaking wet, and him in his boxer briefs and dress shirt, the buttons left open for me to enjoy the view of his hair-dusted chest and muscle-lined abdomen. Nacho and Pepper were still hiding somewhere in my bedroom, but Coconut had sauntered out to join us, flicking her tail and eyeing Will suspiciously from where she curled up by my feet.

I didn't mind letting him quietly soak in the information, not when I had the opportunity to rake my eyes over every inch of him without hurry. Everything had happened so fast, I'd barely been able to register. But now, I could ruminate on the memory of his thick, long, hard cock, how he'd pumped himself with his eyes drinking me in, how he'd fisted my hair when I'd attempted to go down on him without a fucking clue what I was doing.

I internally laughed at myself, cringing a little and hiding my face in my hands.

"What?" Will asked, finally breaking the silence.

"Nothing. Um, do you want some tea?" I asked, hopping up and moving into the kitchen before he could answer. Coconut skittered away, but didn't leave the room. She perched on the back of the couch like she still wanted to keep an eye on us.

I put on the electric kettle and pulled two mugs from the cabinet, plucking out one of my favorite hibiscus teas.

Another long stretch of silence existed between us until I sat down with the tea, and I wrapped my hands around my mug as Will blinked at his, brows furrowed, still digesting.

"Okay," he said, gaze hard when it found mine. "New rule. You need to be fucking honest with me — especially about shit like this."

"I didn't exactly have time to tell you," I pointed out.

"You make time."

"You said you didn't want to know anything about my life."

That made Will's scowl deepen. "Well, I want to know about things like this."

"How am I supposed to tell the difference?"

"Use your common fucking sense, maybe?" Will stood, dragging his hands through his hair as he paced to the sliding glass door and back again. "Chloe, I wouldn't have fucked you like that if I'd have known…"

His frown had shifted from frustration to concern, the line between his brows making me all gooey inside.

"Oh, what?" I teased, arching a brow. "You would have made *sweet, sweet love* to me instead?"

Will flattened his lips, slow-blinking at me.

"Exactly," I said, waving a hand over him before I lifted the hot mug of tea to my mouth and tentatively took the first sip.

Will sat back down, reaching for his own mug but just resting his thumb on the handle rather than drinking from it.

"The shit I was saying to you..." He winced, pinching the bridge of his nose and shaking his head.

I reached across the table and squeezed his wrist until he lifted that gaze to me, and I made sure he saw the sincerity in my eyes when I said, "I *loved* it."

He swallowed. "You did?"

"Will, I came not once, not twice, but *three* times." I widened my eyes and blinked rapidly at him like that should have been all the evidence he needed. "Wanna know how many times I came the first time I had sex?" I held up my hand and made a zero with my fingers curling toward my thumb. "This many."

That made Will's brows bend together in a menacing glare. "Fucking punk. He didn't deserve to touch you."

I ignored the way that fired me up again, releasing my grip on his wrist and sitting back in my chair to sip my tea.

I thought the conversation was over, but after a moment, Will said, "Honesty." He pinned me with his gaze. "One-hundred-percent honesty from here on out."

"But don't tell you about my life," I added. "And don't ask about yours."

"Don't be a smart ass."

"Or what?"

I smirked with the dare, and Will's nostrils flared like he was more than happy to deliver on punishment if I tested him.

"Okay, fine. Here's my first bit of honesty," I said, cupping my mug in my hands and leaning over the table. "I've never sucked a cock before."

"Jesus *Christ*, woman," he muttered, wetting his lips as one hand reached down to adjust himself in his briefs.

One glance under that table showed me why, and my mouth watered a bit at the sight of that thick bulge.

"Can you let me recover before you say things like that?"

"Okay, your rules are getting *very* confusing now."

Will tongued his cheek, and I *swore* something just short of a laugh came from his chest like an exhale.

"I almost made you smile there."

"I smile all the time," he defended, his scowl back in place.

"Oh, sure. The most smiley man I know, hands down."

The mood felt lighter now that the truth was out in the open. Will finally took a sip of his tea — and then promptly grimaced and looked at me like I was insane for liking it. Hibiscus wasn't for everyone.

"Well, I better..."

Will hooked a thumb over his shoulder toward the house, and I smiled down at my tea on a nod.

"Yeah," I said.

I tried to ignore the rush of confusing emotion surging through me as I walked him over to the sliding glass door after he'd dressed.

I wanted him to stay.

But for what?

He didn't want to be friends. I agreed that I was fine with just sex, and yet, there was a hollow ache inside me now that he was leaving. I wondered if it would be so bad if he just sat on the couch here instead of inside. I could turn on an old episode of *Jeopardy*. We didn't have to talk. I could be quiet. We could just be in the same room.

I tampered down those desires, cracking my knuckles before I clasped one hand around my elbow behind my back and stared at my bare feet.

"You okay?" Will asked.

I forced a smile up at him. "I just came three times, Mr. Perry. I'm fantastic."

The corner of his mouth tilted, and he reached forward, thumbing my chin. "I kind of like when you call me that."

"I'll remember that for next time."

His eyes flared like he couldn't wait.

That made two of us.

With one last stroke of my jaw line, Will opened the door.

Before he could step through it, my hand jutted out to catch his arm. "Wait."

He paused, his eyes finding mine.

"I... does this mean..." I swallowed, tucking my hair behind my ear and staring at his chest so I didn't have to meet his gaze when I finished that thought. "Will you teach me?"

"Teach you?"

I glanced up at him through my lashes before my gaze dropped again. "You know... how to... do things."

He was quiet for so long I thought maybe I wasn't making sense, but when I found the gall to look at him again, his eyes were dark and heady, his chest rising and falling in a restrained manner.

"You want me to teach you how to suck my cock, Chloe?"

Fuck.

My body burned, skin flushing the same bright pink it had when he'd made me come.

I nodded. "I want you to teach me everything."

A hot breath shuddered out of him, and he looked away from me and toward the house before giving a curt nod.

"Yes?" I asked.

"Yes," he said.

And then he bolted like if he stayed one moment longer, our first lesson would begin right here and now.

Damn that man and his restraint.

* * *

The next morning, I made the strongest cup of tea of my life and pulled up *Reddit*.

I posted an update.

I shared the latest news, but left out the details.

And I proceeded to ask for every piece of sexual advice the Internet could give me — starting with how to let my boss teach me how to fuck without catching feelings.

Chapter 20

Doing Our Best

Will

I realized, in the week that passed after that fateful night, that I both loved and hated the deal I'd made with Chloe Knott.

I hadn't seen a single flaw with it when I'd taken the approximately ten seconds to think it through as I stormed into the pool house. We both wanted each other. We were alone for the night. If we made a deal for *just* sex, then everything would be great.

And *fuck*, was it great.

I'd thought about that night every moment since.

I couldn't watch Chloe eat her breakfast without thinking about eating *her*. She knew it, too, because when she'd catch me staring at her, those pretty cheeks would flush pink the way I loved them to, and I'd smirk and look away knowing she was thinking exactly what I was.

But as much as I wished I could say everything was peachy, there were complications.

The first being that I had zero fucking clue before I spread her out on the pool house kitchen island that she was practically a virgin.

My body still hummed anytime my brain played back how she'd asked me to teach her, and everything inside me wound tight just begging for the chance. We hadn't found one yet. Between hockey, school, and Ava — there wasn't a whole lot of opportunity to fuck without the high risk of being caught.

Oddly enough, waiting for round two with Chloe wasn't even the most difficult part of this mess. In fact, that part was kind of... *fun*. Exhilarating. I knew the wait would only make the next time I got to touch her that much better.

No, the hardest part was that I fucking *missed* her.

Apparently, when Chloe gave her word, she gave it with her whole chest. I'd told her I couldn't be her friend. I'd looked her right in the eye and made her agree to stop asking about my life and to stop telling me about hers.

And so, she had.

Other than pleasantries, the last week had been devastatingly void of Chloe-isms.

She didn't join me when I sat down to watch *Jeopardy* after Ava was asleep. She didn't bring her current craft projects inside, but rather kept them all in the pool house — away from me. At dinner, she talked to Ava or Chef Patel.

She very carefully avoided chatting with me, unless it was a group conversation.

I knew she still woke up in the middle of the night, but she no longer graced me with her presence in the kitchen or by the pool. She stayed in the pool house, reading a book on the couch or making her own late-night snack before ambling back to bed.

This was the boundary I told her I needed.

It was the boundary I *knew* I needed.

And yet...

Frustration curdled deep in my belly as I put Ava to bed the following Friday night, her head on my shoulder as I read *Broken Crayons Still Color*. She clutched her favorite plush fish to her chest, absentmindedly playing with the fins with her eyes glued to the pages as I turned them.

"Daddy?" she asked when I closed the book.

"Mm?"

"Did Mommy like to read?"

The question knocked the breath out of me.

After the event at school, I'd taken Chloe's advice and told Ava how her mother was the one who loved donuts — not me. My daughter had lit up at the tiny tidbit of information, asking what flavors were Jenny's favorite and whether she had a favorite donut store. That conversation had led to us going to Krispy Kreme bright and early on a Sunday morning and getting all Jenny's favorites for Ava to try — starting with the lemon-filled one.

Before then, Ava had never really asked about her mom.

Then again, she hadn't spoken much at *all* for a long time. That hadn't worried me, not until it was time to start kindergarten and Uncle Mitch asked if I was worried about her falling behind. She wasn't speaking up in class, wasn't comfortable talking to her peers during activities.

But when Chloe had tutored her a bit in the first semester, it helped her tremendously with communication. Since becoming our nanny, she'd somehow managed to make a chatterbox out of my daughter. Ava was gabbing away most nights, and the more she talked, the more questions she had.

Apparently, those questions were shifting toward Jenny.

I wanted to punch myself right in the fucking nose, because this was completely natural for a little girl who'd lost her mom. What *wasn't* natural was how I had done such a shit job telling Ava about Jenny. She should have known so much about her, but I'd been too caught up in my own grief to give her anything.

"It wasn't her favorite thing," I admitted, setting the book in my lap.

Ava kept her head on my shoulder, fingers plucking at the shiny fins of the orange stuffed fish in her arms. "How come?"

"Your mom was always on the go. She loved to be outside, or traveling, or doing something new with friends. That didn't really leave much time for reading."

"Oh," Ava said, nodding.

We were quiet for a long while, and I searched every corner of my dumb fucking brain for something more to say. But I came up empty.

"I'm sorry I don't talk about your mom more," I finally landed on. "I... would you like me to do that?"

Ava shrugged, but then nodded again — like she was afraid she'd hurt my feelings if she admitted that she would very much like to know about her own mother.

"Well, then — I'll do that," I promised, kissing her head. "Maybe we could even plan a trip for you to go up and visit MorMor this summer. Would you like that?"

Another nod, though it was a bit more unsure. Jenny's mother was born in Denmark, and when we'd had Ava, she'd asked to be called MorMor just like Jenny called her grandmother, and so on.

Jenny's mom was around a lot in the beginning, when Ava was born, and then again when Jenny passed. But since then, we've only seen her twice — and both times, she came to Florida. I had never taken Ava up to Wisconsin where Jenny was born and raised. I'd never made an effort for Ava to have any sort of relationship with her aunt or her cousins, either.

I guessed since my family was so small and didn't really make an effort to see one another, I just thought that was normal.

"Okay, then. I'll work on that. And again, I'm sorry if I haven't..." I clamped my jaw shut, chewing on the words I didn't know how to say.

"It's okay, Daddy," Ava whispered, and she looked up at me with those beautiful green eyes, the same shade as her mom's. "We are doing our best."

My throat constricted, jaw tight as I did everything I could not to break into a million fucking pieces right there. I nodded, kissing her forehead once more before I climbed off the bed. I tucked my daughter in as she yawned, and with an *I love you* and *goodnight*, I clicked on her night light and slipped out the door.

I stood in the hallway for a long moment afterward, eyes shut and head resting against the wall.

Some days, I really sucked at being a father.

My heart ached wondering what it would be like if things had happened differently — if Jenny were still here. A flash of what could have been hit me like a life in fast forward. I imagined bath times full of adventure and giggles and water splashing everywhere. I saw Ava traveling and exploring with her mom — beach days, theme parks, markets, and bike rides. I saw a life where I had a friend by my side to help in this wild thing called parenting. She would have been so much better at it.

Emotion stung my eyes when I finally opened them, and I sniffed, standing straight and composing myself.

The conversation with Chloe in the pool resurfaced in my mind again.

"Maybe it's something we can do together. We can start introducing Ava to her mom one thing at a time. A food she loved, a place she enjoyed, a song, a movie, a photograph, or memory."

I swallowed past the knot in my throat, pushing off the wall behind me and making my way downstairs like a zombie. Soft laughter wafted up the stairs as I descended, and when I rounded into the foyer, I found Chloe and Chef Patel at the small dining table — each with a glass of wine in hand.

"I can't believe you made a *scarecrow father* and hid him in your closet for years," Chef said on another laugh, shaking her head and looking at Chloe as if seeing her for the first time. "What did your mom do when she finally found it?"

"Oh, what she thought was even worse," Chloe said. "Arushi. Are you ready for this?" She paused, waiting, and then shook her head like she still couldn't believe it herself. "My mother, bless her, *swore* that I'd made that damn scarecrow as a boyfriend — and that I was doing *sinful things* with a pair of overalls stuffed with straw."

"No!" Chef covered her mouth as a peel of laughter slipped through. "Stop it, you're kidding!"

"I wish I was. It was already mortifying as it was to admit that I wanted a father figure badly enough to stitch something so hideous together. But to then have my mother assume I was hiding some sort of pleasure doll?"

Chloe rolled her eyes on a groan as Arushi burst into another fit of laughter. "I never recovered. Even now, I have hives under my hoodie just thinking about it."

She shoved the sleeve of said hoodie up as if to illustrate, and Chef squeezed her wrist before wiping tears from her eyes.

Chloe looked beautiful.

She always did.

Tonight, she wore a lavender hoodie that read *Half Teacher, Half Tea* on it. It was paired with flimsy gray sweat shorts that rode up between her thighs in the most delicious way. Her hair was pulled into a tiny bun on top of her head, though it was short enough that the bottom half of it fell out of the hair tie and hugged her neck, instead.

I stood in the hallway and watched her smile for longer than I should have.

She had the best fucking smile.

Why couldn't I say shit like this to her?

Why couldn't I tell her how much I missed her asking me questions and telling me her weird stories, how badly I wanted to make her smile just the way she was right now.

Words were broken for me. They always had been.

Then again, maybe it wasn't just words. Maybe it was my heart, my soul, my ability to care for another human being without the fear of losing them.

It wasn't just Jenny, although that was the freshest wound. But I'd lost my mom. I'd lost my father, even though he was still alive. And there was only so much loving and losing a person could do before a piece of them just... broke.

I'd meant what I said to Chloe that night in the pool house. I couldn't give her a relationship. I couldn't be her friend.

What I'd left out was that I *wished* I could.

Like right now, I wanted to ask her about her father. I wanted to know why she never knew him. Did he pass away? Did he leave her and her mom? Did her mom leave *him*?

But I didn't have the right. I was the one who put the boundaries in place, and they needed to exist.

Especially because I was a starved man when it came to her, and I'd do anything, play by *any* rules just to have the chance to hear her moan my name again.

"I think I missed quite the story," I said, finally joining them in the dining area.

The words announced my presence, and Chef beamed a smile my way, gesturing for me to sit while she immediately jumped up to grab me a glass of milk.

Chloe, on the other hand, flushed a deep red and looked down at the table, untying her hair only to tie it back up again. It was still just as messy as before, and she seemed to not know what to do with her hands once she was done. She glanced up at me with a worried expression once Chef was gone.

"I'm sorry, we were just chatting. I can—"

"Stop," I told her, hating how she was already moving to stand and hide away in that fucking pool house. I wanted to burn it down so she had no choice but to stay here. "This is your home, too."

She swallowed. "I don't want you to think I'm trying to... I was just..."

"Chloe, it's fine. I—" I stopped myself before I could finish that sentence, which was *I miss you being here.*

Or maybe it was *I don't want you to feel like you have to hide.*

I didn't mean I never want to talk to you ever.

I didn't mean any of it at all.

I... don't know what I mean.

Instead, I cleared my throat just in time for Chef to join us again, handing me the glass of milk before she took a seat with her wine.

She patted the chair next to her, arching a brow at me and casting a curious look between me and Chloe.

I was thankful she didn't ask whatever questions I knew she wanted to in that moment.

"Actually, I'm glad you're both still here," I said, nerves firing to life as I decided to go through with the harebrained idea I'd had on the way down the stairs. "I need your help."

Arushi paused where she was lifting her glass to her lips, her wide eyes such a dark brown they nearly blended in with her pupils as she blinked at me.

"Did you just ask for *help*?" She sat her glass down and dug her phone out of her pocket. "Sorry, I need to record the date and time."

I leveled her with a look.

"Ava just asked about Jenny."

That made both her and Chloe pause, the two of them exchanging a glance before Chloe asked, "What did she say?"

"She wanted to know if Jenny liked to read."

Chef's eyes got a little misty when she smiled, covering her heart with one hand. "Oh, that sweet, sweet child."

"After you and I talked, I told Ava about how much Jenny loved donuts," I said to Chloe. I didn't miss how Arushi narrowed her eyes when I referenced Chloe and me talking. "And I think now she's curious. She's thinking about all the things I've been too much of a coward to say."

"You're not a coward," Chef staid instantly. "You were a grieving husband and a new father trying to figure it out."

Those words hung heavy on my shoulders for a long moment. All I could do was nod.

"Well, I've been thinking more about what you said," I finally croaked, clearing my throat before I found Chloe's gaze. "About introducing Ava to Jenny one thing at a time."

"Oh?" Chef tapped the table between us. "What's this plan? I want in."

"I mentioned that maybe we could slowly tell her more about Jenny," Chloe said. "You know, share her favorite song or watch her favorite movie. Do the things she loved to do."

"This is a *wonderful* plan," Chef said gleefully, her eyes bright and wide when she flashed them back to me. "What do you have in mind?"

"Well, that's why I wanted to talk to you both. Chloe, is there any chance in hell you could get off work next Monday?"

Chloe made a face like she wasn't sure. "I mean, I haven't taken vacation since I started working at this school. So, *technically*, yes. I have the time. My only concern is that it's only a little over a week away. But I can certainly make the necessary calls. As long as there is a sub available, I don't see why not."

"You haven't taken a vacation?" Chef repeated, brows inching together. "Like... ever?"

"I love my job," Chloe said with a shrug. "And I get the summer off. Besides, where am I going to go? What am I going to do?" She waved a hand toward the pool house. "Play games with my cats? Answer the many male suitors who come to call?"

Arushi smirked. "I bet there *would* be many male suitors, if you ever went out to meet them. *That's* what we need," she added with a snap of her fingers. "A girls' night out. I'll bet Maven and Livia would jump at the chance. Maybe next time Grace is in town—"

"What about you, Chef Patel?" I interrupted, cracking my neck and hoping it came off just as me being sore and stiff from last night's game, and not that I was two seconds away from hauling Chloe up over my shoulder caveman style and taking her to my room so I could lock her up and ensure *no man* ever looked at her again.

Chef's smirk tilted my way now, an amused glint in her eyes.

Damn her.

"I work for you," she pointed out sarcastically. Then, she pretended to be concerned, her bottom lip protruding. "Sore neck?"

"I'm fine," I grumbled, and I looked away from her before she could chuckle into her wine glass.

"Why?" Chloe asked. "What's going on next Monday?"

"I'll have Sunday off, and we'll have a later, lighter practice that Monday. The schedule has been crazy lately, and we're closing in on the end of the season over the next couple of months. Coach has been pretty insistent that we take time away from the rink when we can."

The women in front of me nodded.

"So, I was thinking..." I grimaced, grabbing the back of my neck and wondering if I even wanted to say these words. Because once they were out, there'd be no turning back.

"What?" Chef asked impatiently, snapping her fingers. "Come on, spit it out, I don't have all night. My brothers are having a Carrom tournament, and I have ten minutes before I need to leave or I'll lose my chance to take all their money again."

"Oh, what's Carrom?" Chloe asked excitedly.

"It's a tabletop game, kind of like finger billiards — but with small disks. I'll explain another time when Mr. Turkey isn't edging us with the possibility of pulling his daughter out of school for a day of hooky for some mysterious reason."

Two pairs of eyes swung back to me, and I scratched my neck before letting out a long, heavy sigh.

"There were many places Jenny loved to go on a day off," I said. "But, from the second she moved to Florida, one place trumped everything else."

I looked up at the ceiling, another flash of Jenny assaulting me like a bright blinding light. I saw her wide smile, my hand in hers as she tugged me through the most godforsaken place on the planet — with the most idiotic mouse ears on her head.

With another exhale, I brought my gaze to Chloe. "Disney World."

The table was so silent I could hear the dishwasher running in the next room.

"Disney World," Chef repeated, deadpan, like there was no way she'd heard me correctly.

"*Disney* World?!" Chloe echoed, her mouth falling open on a smile as she clapped and bounced gleefully in her chair.

"Disney World," I said again.

And then I was tackled in a hug so fierce I nearly flew off my chair.

Chapter 21

Tell Me What You Want

Chloe

"Well, I have to say, it's an honor to finally meet you," I said a few nights later, greeting Mitch Perry in a hug that he seemed much better equipped to handle than his nephew. "Ava has talked nonstop about you since the beginning of the school year."

"She gives this old man too much credit," he said, flashing a warm smile when he released me. Mitch was at least twenty years Will's senior. He possessed so many of his nephew's features — the sharp jaw, wide shoulders, crinkles at the edge of his eyes. But his expression was warmer, his smile easy and natural where Will stood behind him with his usual scowl.

"Thanks again, Unc," he said, handing over the large purple backpack with all of Ava's belongings for the night. "She's really excited."

"Are you kidding? I'd never pass up the opportunity to spend a night with my girl. I hate how busy work has been lately. It should ease up for a while now. Then again,

I guess if I had been more available, we might not have you around," he added with a wink my way. "Also, is it you we have to thank for how smiley my great niece is? Because the sight about knocked me on my ass."

"Yes," Will said at the same time I said, "Oh, no."

Will's eyes caught mine, a warning glare like he'd fight me if I tried to hide from the compliment.

"Ava is like a new person, thanks to Chloe. She's really come out of her shell," Will said. "Still loves hockey, though. So I hope you're prepared to watch a game tonight."

Uncle Mitch sighed and looked up at the ceiling. "I would rather take her to the arcade and suffer the stickiness and noise that comes with that than sit through another fucking hockey game."

Will smirked. "I'll pray for your eardrums, then."

Mitch eased his hands into his pockets, rocking up on his toes and peeking into the house a bit more. "So, uh, is Arushi here? I swore I could smell her amazing cooking from outside."

"She just left about an hour ago," I said, and I didn't miss the disappointment on his face. Will and I shared a curious glance, but before either of us could remark on anything, Ava bounded down the stairs.

"Okay, I'm ready!"

She had the hockey uniform I made her clutched in her arms, and she beamed up at the three of us in a way that made it hard to remember the kid she'd been at the beginning of this semester.

"Pumpkin, I'm not sure you need that," Will tried, ruffling her hair and nodding to the jersey. "Sure you don't want to leave it here so I can wash it and have it clean for you when you get home?"

"It's not smelly," she defended, sniffing it for good measure. "And I gotta show Uncle Mitch!"

"I can't wait to see it," Mitch said, bending to her level and offering to carry it for her. She reluctantly handed it over, and then he told her to go get herself situated in the car and he'd be right out.

Ava shot out like a bullet, belting a Mia Love song at the top of her lungs as she swung the back door of Mitch's truck open and climbed up. She was big enough to know how to get herself into the booster seat and buckle up, but I watched her from the doorway just in case — and I knew Mitch would double check when he got out there, too.

"Hey, have you, uh... have you called your old man lately?"

I stiffened at the mention of Will's father, but kept my eyes on Ava so as not to pry into a conversation not meant for me.

"Not lately," Will admitted. "He okay?"

"Sure, yeah. Just misses you."

"Phone works both ways."

Mitch sighed. "I'm not arguing that, just... you know him. He does his best. Like the rest of us."

There was a long, understanding silence between uncle and nephew, and I glanced over my shoulder just in time to see them embrace in a hug that spoke of years and years of history.

Interesting, how Will never really spoke about his dad, but I knew he watched *Jeopardy* every night he was home because it was something he and his father used to do together. There was clearly some fondness there — but, maybe some pain, too.

I longed to know more, but knew I couldn't ask.

Mitch squeezed his shoulder. "Alright. I'll drop her off at school in the morning."

With a smile and nod of his head as he passed me, Mitch let himself out. Just as I expected, he double checked that Ava was safely buckled before climbing into the driver seat. Ava waved excitedly as they pulled out of the drive.

And then it was just the two of us.

It wasn't necessarily an uncomfortable quiet that fell over the house once that truck was gone, but it was... heavy. Charged. Like if I touched a blanket I'd get an electric shock.

Will shoved his hands into the pockets of his joggers, but he didn't move his large frame out of my way. I shut the front door behind me, my back against it, but still, he stayed put.

He was still the same man who dropped his daughter off on the first day of school, and yet, so much about him had changed. His hair was a little longer now, the stubble on his jaw a little more coarse. He didn't look as tired as he had when I'd taken this job. His eyes were brighter now, his skin glowing a rich bronze, his cheeks full instead of hollow.

But his golden eyes were still as sad as ever.

I wondered if that would ever change.

"Tuesday night," he said — as if I wasn't aware.

I smiled. "Yep."

"Plans?"

I snorted at that. "Oh, of course. A five-course meal with a guy I met on Tinder, and then hitting the club with my girls."

Will frowned a bit, like he wasn't sure if I was joking or not. I rolled my eyes.

"I have a half-finished puzzle and a true crime podcast cued up," I said. "You?"

"Nothing."

I nodded, heart spiking a bit at the implication behind that one word. Chef had already gone for the day.

We really would be alone — just the two of us.

The last time that was the case, I'd dry humped his thigh.

"Um... did you want to talk anymore about the plans for Disney?" I asked when he didn't budge from where he stood. "Before I go over to the pool house?"

"I think the plans for Disney are pretty set."

I nodded again.

He still didn't move.

Scratch that — he *did* move, but not out of the way. He stepped toward me, his eyes flicking between mine as the space between us slowly evaporated.

"Think your puzzle can wait another night?"

"Uh..."

"Because I find myself in quite the teaching mood."

He punctuated that last word with a final step in front of me, his body towering over mine, eyes alight with a tease and a dare and a promise.

The scent of him was intoxicating, the warm spice of his body wash mixed with faint hints of leather and rope. I wondered if that was from his hobbies in the home gym or if there were more exciting lessons than I anticipated waiting for me.

My heart had gone from a steady beat in my chest to an erratic, wild animal thrashing against the cage made by my ribs. I wondered if he could see my quickened pulse when his eyes dipped to my throat, if he could sense my excitement the way a lion might sense its prey.

It had been over a week since we'd had sex. Honestly, it had been over a week since we'd looked at each other for longer than two seconds without one of us breaking the gaze. I'd felt a bit like walking on eggshells, unsure of if I was welcome inside any more for fear of crossing one of his boundaries.

I'd agreed not to divulge our little secret to anyone, and so I'd made sure not to speak of it to the girls — even though I desperately wanted to. I debated using the whole "Noah from school" storyline to work around the rule, but I was a bit worried one of them would see right through me.

Maven was wicked smart. Livia was observant as hell. Grace, though she was on the go, seemed to be the kind of girl who could sniff out the truth without trying.

And I was pretty sure Arushi was already onto us, so I *really* needed to keep it together around her.

Fortunately, my *Reddit* fans were all too eager to share their advice. They were now immensely invested in my story, and while there was still a good portion of them rooting for us to fall in love — a laughable impossibility — the vast majority of them were rooting more for me to get my back blown out.

And they had *fantastic* advice for how not to catch feelings, starting with the number one rule Will had already put into place. No kissing.

Still, I'd had a hard time acting normal around him ever since I'd had his tongue between my legs. Any time we were in the same room without anyone else present, I'd find an excuse to leave. I didn't want to impose on his boundaries, and I also didn't know how to just go back to casual conversation. Besides, he'd made it clear he couldn't be my friend... so what was there to even talk about?

But now, we were alone again — and every nerve-ending sparked at the thought of what that might mean.

"Is that so?" I asked, trying to tease him but failing when the words came out all breathy and desperate.

The corner of his lips tilted up just a fraction of an inch as he stepped even closer. My chest brushed the top of his abdomen, and when he removed his hands from his pockets, one reached for my hip and tugged me into him as the other confidently traced the slope of my neck.

God.

How did he do that? How did he turn it on so fast, so effortlessly?

One moment he's Mr. Dad, all professional and hands to himself.

And then the second we're alone, he's touching me like I'm his, like I always have been, like those massive, calloused hands don't belong anywhere else.

"What do you want to learn?" he mused, skating the back of his knuckles along my neck before tracing them across my collarbone.

Goosebumps raised in his wake, and the rest of my body reacted to that touch and his words like he was a music conductor, and I was the waiting orchestra. My eyelids fluttered, breath catching in my throat, nipples hardening to a point beneath my sweater.

"Everything," I breathed.

His eyes lit up with humor and hunger in equal measure, and I didn't know which sensation pulled more of my attention — the strong, warm hand covering my backside with a gentle squeeze, pulling me flush against him, or the thumb of the opposite hand running a slow, gentle line along my bottom lip.

"Starting where?"

My brain tried to fire, to send the signal for syllables, consonants, and verbs that would form words and allow me to speak. But when Will slid both hands up to frame my neck, his fingertips sliding back into my hair and curling there until he tilted my head up toward his, it was all I could do to remain standing.

It felt so fucking good to be touched by this man. To have him grip me and move me and *look* at me the way he was now.

"I... well, I guess..."

"Come on, Chloe," he encouraged, thumbs gliding along my jaw. "Open those pretty eyes and tell me what you want."

I felt drugged as I did what he said, my lids heavy, pulse beating against his palms.

"I want your mouth on me again," I whispered, my eyes falling to that magical mouth as my neck burned with the admission. When I dragged my eyes back to his, I swallowed. "And I want you to teach me how to do the same to you."

His nostrils flared, grip tightening where his hands curled in my hair.

"You said you liked it," he commented. "Last time, when I told you what to do." He kept one hand in my hair and slid the other to the front of my throat, forming a collar but resting it gently, without any pressure. "When I called you filthy and praised you for every dirty thing you did."

I shuddered out my next breath, light-headed and leaning into his touch. "Yes."

"You have to tell me if you change your mind," he said. "If I go too far, if I do anything you don't like. Understand?"

I nodded, anticipation buzzing through me like a live wire.

"Verbally, please."

"Yes," I said instantly, swallowing and feeling his hand tighten as I did.

"That's a good girl."

The words washed over me in an exotic, pleasure-soaked wave.

I pressed up onto my toes, mouth on track for his. I wanted him. I wanted him so fucking badly I couldn't think straight.

I forgot about the no kissing rule until our lips were centimeters apart and he squeezed my throat hard, pushing me back until I was pinned against the door.

His breath was hot on my lips, his eyes flicking between mine beneath furrowed brows before that gaze dipped to my mouth. If I didn't know better, I'd think he was tempted to kiss me, too.

But he pushed himself away, putting distance between us, his hand still clamped around my neck.

"Sorry," I murmured, skin heating with how horrified I was at my slip.

"You can show me just how sorry you are when I let you suck my cock."

Fuck.

"Get undressed," he demanded, stepping back and taking all his heat with him. "Then go to the kitchen. I'll be there in five minutes, and I want you on your knees waiting for me. Tie your hair up and sit on your hands."

He left with me gaping and blinking and trying to log everything he'd said.

I stood frozen for a breath before I launched into action, hastily shedding my sweater and slacks. I'd sewn those slacks, and right now I was cursing myself for the marks they left on my stomach and thighs when I took them off. No one ever had to see that but *me*, so I'd never thought anything of it. But now, I was all too aware of every inch of my body as I left my bra and panties behind, too, and tiptoed to the kitchen.

It was warm outside, but the air conditioner blew relentlessly, and a chill swept over me as I looked around the kitchen. I didn't know where he wanted me, so I walked to the middle and carefully sank down onto the cold, hard floor.

My knees stung a bit as I tried to get comfortable. I nearly forgot about my hair, and I cursed before tying it up in the best ponytail I could manage for how short it was.

Sit on your hands.

I frowned, trying to figure out what that meant. I was on my knees. But when I heard footsteps coming from the hallway, I shoved my hands between my thighs and my calves, sandwiching them there and trying not to have a fucking heart attack at what was about to happen.

I looked up just in time to see Will prowl into the kitchen, slowly and confidently without any sort of rush. He paused at the island and let his eyes roam over me.

My mouth instantly watered.

I'd seen Will in many outfits that conjured a tingle in my belly. I'd watched him warm up in his full hockey gear, seen him freshly showered in a tailored suit after a game, ogled him while he jump-roped in nothing but basketball shorts, admired the muscles of his back as he swam laps in the pool.

But I'd never seen him look more delectable than he did right now.

He still had on the light wash jeans he'd been wearing all afternoon, but the Henley t-shirt he'd paired with it was gone now. It was just those damn jeans, not even the band of his briefs peeking out from beneath them.

Is he even wearing briefs?

It didn't look like it — not with how a hard, long outline of a bulge was pushing against his zipper.

I took my time appreciating every valley and mountain of muscles that lined his abdomen, chest, and arms as my eyes drank him in. He was breathing just as heavy as I was, his eyes dark and focused on where I was knelt in the middle of the kitchen and waiting for him to tell me what to do next.

I realized he'd pulled his hair back, too.

It was in a low bun at the nape of his neck, a few strands loose and framing his jaw.

He looked like he meant business, like he was showing up for game five of a playoff series and his team was one win away from clutching the Cup.

There was a low, appreciative groan in his throat before he started walking toward me. He didn't stop until his bare feet were at my knees, and my neck burned with the effort to arch and meet his gaze.

Why was seeing this man in nothing but jeans so fucking hot?

Since *when* did a man's bare feet make me clench my thighs together?

I was convinced Will Perry could have made anything sexy. Playing chess, hopping on a pogo stick while naked, taking out the garbage. It didn't matter.

He just oozed sex appeal. He didn't even have to try.

"Now this is a pretty sight," he mused, running his thumb along my jaw before tilting my head up even more. "This is how I want you when I teach you how to make me come."

A shiver rocked through me, and Will smirked at the evidence when my nipples pebbled into hard peaks.

"But I want you dripping first."

I would have grimaced at the foul word if it wasn't so fucking hot coming off his lips, and he offered me a hand, helping me stand as the blood slowly rushed back to my legs.

Will held my arm above my head then, having me twirl slowly with his eyes raking over every inch of my naked body. He inhaled slow, exhaled even slower, and shook his head.

"Gorgeous," he breathed.

And I felt it. I *felt* beautiful beneath his gaze.

"Put your hands on the island," he said when he released me. "And bend over."

Nerves sparked in my belly as I did what he said. My hands splayed the cool countertop, and I bent just an inch, looking over my shoulder to where Will was...

Reaching into the freezer?

I frowned, even more confused when he pulled a white-plastic wrapped Popsicle from a box. He shut the freezer door and turned toward me, taking in the view of me waiting for him.

"Slide those hands out," he said, ripping the package open to reveal a bright orange Popsicle. "And *bend* so I can see more of that sweet ass of yours."

I followed the command, and though I felt exposed and vulnerable, I also felt the distinct rush of power coursing through my veins.

Will Perry could have any woman he wanted, but he was weak for *me*.

He walked around to the opposite side of the island first, leaning on his elbows with a wicked gleam in his eye and a perfect view of my cleavage. He waved the Popsicle side to side before sucking it between his lips.

And I knew I was insane then, because my pussy fluttered at the sight of this man eating a fucking frozen treat.

"Mm," he mused, and then he withdrew the Popsicle and offered it to my lips. "Taste."

I opened my mouth, keeping my hands in place and letting Will control the depth. He let me taste just as much as he had, just the tip. The popsicle was sweet and citrusy, and when he pulled it away, I licked my lips to taste the remnants of it.

Will smirked, circling the island until he was standing behind me. He pressed the top of his foot against the inside of my right ankle until I opened my stance, and then he did the same with the left. I had no choice but to spread, and when his erection pressed through his denim against the swells of my ass, my eyes fluttered shut on a moan.

And then, shot wide open — because an icy burning sensation ran along the back of my neck.

I gasped, pulling away, but Will pinned me against the counter with his hips until the Popsicle was pressed against my skin once more. It was wet and sticky and cold, and violent chills raced from where he touched me all the way down to my toes.

I bit my lip and squirmed, both hating the way it felt and yet curious about what it was doing to my body, too. I was ready to cry out and beg for relief when suddenly the cold was gone.

And was replaced by a hot, wet mouth.

Will licked and sucked along the same trail he'd made with the Popsicle, moaning as he lapped up the sticky sweetness and sent yet another wave of chills washing over me. The sensation of his warmth covering the bite of the cold was too much. I arched into him, moaning when he tongued his way up to my earlobe and sucked it between his teeth.

"More?" he mused.

"More."

My answer was a breathy plea, and Will removed all his warmth before I felt that Popsicle along the back of my neck again. This time, he dragged it up to the top of my jaw and brought it all the way down to my chin.

Which meant when he chased that line with his mouth, he was kissing all along my neck and jaw until his lips hovered just below mine.

I whimpered at the tease, at how close and yet how far he was from taking my mouth for his own. But the noise died in my throat and was replaced by a yelp when suddenly, a shock of cold circled my nipple.

I yanked away from the touch, but again, Will chased me, pressing that wet, icy Popsicle against my pebbled flesh. He'd wet it with his mouth again, which made it glide like butter as he circled my nipple and smiled against my neck as my peak grew harder beneath his torturous touch.

"Will, please," I whined, the pleasure bordering a little too close to pain.

Instantly, the Popsicle was gone, and he lifted one hand up and out of the way so he could turn me just enough to suck my breast into his mouth.

I gasped and groaned and let my knees go weak, let him hold the weight of me as I surrendered to how it felt to have him massaging my breast with his tongue and that lingering coldness still present.

Just as soon as relief came, it was gone again.

He repeated the sensuous torture on the other breast, like he was afraid one might be jealous of the other. I was ready to scream and kick and thrash when he finally relented and rewarded me with the warmth of his mouth, and then my legs were trembling, and I was melting into him.

Over and over, again and again, he dragged that melting Popsicle across my skin and brought me the most curious mix of pain and pleasure. Only when it was a mess did he haphazardly toss the Popsicle into the sink, and then he whipped me around to face him and held out his sticky fingers.

"Suck me clean."

A hot shot of electricity zipped down between my legs, and I squeezed my thighs together as I opened my mouth and let him stick his fingers in one by one. I sucked the orange sweetness from each one while his eyes flared and drank in the sight.

"Let's see if I've got you where I want you," he mused, and he ran his clean hand down the front of my body roughly until he could slip it between my thighs.

I had no choice but to open for him again, and we both moaned in unison when his fingers skated easily through where I was wet and turned on.

"That's a good fucking girl," he praised.

He held my eyes and lifted those fingers to his lips, licking each one while I watched.

Fuck.

"And I thought the Popsicle was sweet," he said. "Are you ready to ride my tongue, Chloe?"

"God, yes."

The closest thing I'd ever seen to a smile washed across that man's face, and he carefully sank down onto the kitchen floor before pulling me with him.

I waited for my cheeks to burn, for embarrassment to make me murmur and hesitate and ask him if he was sure. But after that whole scene with the Popsicle, after the way he looked at me and licked me and tasted me on his fingers — I couldn't find anything but pure fucking want inside me.

Will helped me straddle his face, his hands on my ass and adjusting me until he had me right where he wanted me. He kissed the inside of each of my thighs, moaning when I stretched my hands out to brace myself on the drawers above his head.

"You just keep giving me the best views," he groaned, biting the tender flesh of my inner thigh with his eyes cast up at my breasts hanging above him. "You ready to talk me through what you like?"

"No," I answered honestly, because talking at this point seemed like the most difficult thing in the world.

He smirked and ran his tongue along the crease of my thigh, just inches from where I really wanted him.

"You've got to tell me what you like, what you need," he said. "Part of having great sex is being confident. It's knowing what works and asking for it. It's knowing what *doesn't* work and steering me away. Everyone is different. Help me discover *you*."

I nodded, panting, unsure if I could do what he was asking but *absolutely* sure I wanted to try.

Will nosed my clit, his scruff rubbing against my vagina as he settled in. He started with slow, lingering strokes of his tongue from my opening up to my clit. There was little pressure there, but *fuck* was it hot to feel his wetness covering me, to feel him breathing against my skin. My legs shook as I dropped down, spreading my legs wider and silently asking for more.

Will arched one brow, continuing the same slow assault.

He wanted me to say it.

"That feels good," I admitted, biting my lip when he squeezed my ass and rocked me against his flat tongue. "But I want more."

"More," he breathed, the vibration teasing my core. "Where?"

"My clit."

Will answered with a satisfied grin against my pussy before he was sucking my clit between his teeth. I gasped, gripping onto the drawers harder and trying not to give in to my urge to rock against his face.

But he pulled me down onto him, eagerly devouring me, his hands kneading my ass as he began sucking my clit in tiny little pulses.

"Oh, *fuck*," I breathed, and I couldn't help it now. I met his tongue with a thrust of my hips. "Yes. *Fuck*, yes, like that."

Will moaned, and again the vibration of it made me see stars. My climax was already tickling the edges of my vision after the teasing, the cold and the hot, the words, and this fucking *man* beneath me.

"You're not going to hurt me," he said, breaking his touch to a sad whimper from me. He kissed my clit and smiled at how I shivered when he did. "Fuck my face, Chloe. Because I promise — I plan to thoroughly fuck yours."

"Oh, *God*."

He sucked my clit into his mouth again, and I let go. My hands flew into my hair as I sat upright and gave into my need to rock against his touch. I bucked like a wild bull, savoring the little groans Will rewarded me with.

But I needed more.

I played with my breasts, rolling my nipples between my fingers and thumbs and moaning when I remembered Will's mouth there.

More.

I still needed more.

"Finger me," I breathed, and this time, embarrassment *did* shade my cheeks. I couldn't even open my eyes to look down at Will when I said the words. I just kept writhing against him, seeking the last little bit of whatever it was I needed for the flame to catch.

Will maneuvered me until he could snake one hand between us, and without a tease, he plunged one thick finger deep inside me and curled it against that magical spot.

"*Fuck!*"

I was unhinged now, rolling against him and savoring every sensation. He sucked my clit in a steady, unrelenting rhythm, his finger pumping in and out of me once, twice, before he'd leave it submerged and wiggle it in just the right way to coax my orgasm to the surface.

I sat down more, wanting him deeper, needing more, more, *more*. And Will answered in every way. He filled me with another finger. He sucked my clit and held it there, rewarding me with pulse after pulse of pleasure. And when I creaked one eye open and then the next, my gaze traveling down, that was all I needed.

He was ravenous.

I watched his fingers working, his mouth latched onto me, his golden eyes dark and searing and fixed on me.

And I combusted.

"God, Will, *yes!*"

I cried out those words over and over, in various order and at every decibel that existed. When I could no longer rock myself against him, Will took over, working me with his tongue and his fingers as I shook and screamed and moaned out every last second of my release.

Panting filled the air as the last of the climax left me, my chest heaving, hair wild where I'd run my hands through it and destroyed the ponytail I'd fixed it into. I trembled violently when Will withdrew his fingers, and then I was laughing, rolling off him until the cold tile was against my hot, slick back.

"Wow," I breathed, body tingling, mind numb and lagging. "*Wow.*"

Will rolled over, wiping his mouth before the edges of it curled up just a bit. His eyes roamed over me, and then that same dangerous heat slid into his gaze.

"Fix your hair," he said, standing. "And get back into position."

I swallowed, both exhausted from coming and enlivened by the thought of bringing him the same pleasure.

I scrambled up as quickly as I could, ignoring my body's protest. I pulled my hair back into a tight ponytail again, sat on my knees, and wedged my hands between my thighs.

Will was at the freezer again, and he plucked another Popsicle from its wrapping.

This one was red.

The outline of his erection was even thicker against his jeans now, and I felt the nerves slide into my stomach when I remembered just how big he was.

This wasn't going to be easy.

But I wanted it. I wanted to unravel him. I wanted to watch him come, to know I was the one who made him feel good.

I felt like I was back in college as I straightened my back, angled my chin up at him, and let determination slide into any cracks fear had produced.

Will bent into a deep squat right in front of me, his eyes on mine as he held the Popsicle with one hand and slid the other between my legs. He had to dig between my thighs to find what he wanted, and when he felt how slick I was, he bit his lip on a groan.

"Dripping," he confirmed. "Just what I wanted."

He stood, his denim-restrained cock right in my face as he stared down at me over the ridges of muscles lining his abdomen.

"Open your mouth. Wide. Tongue out."

And the real lesson began.

Chapter 22

Filthy, Naughty, Perfect Little Thing

Will

I turned to ash at the sight of her.

My body burned, a yearning, searing, unbearable heat consuming me as I towered over her and watched her part her plump, rosy lips.

Her cheeks and neck and chest were flushed from her climax — the climax *I* had given her. Her hands were trapped between her thick, beautiful thighs. Those wide brown eyes were fixed on me, excited and eager to learn, but tinged with a hint of something uncertain. It was impossible not to let my gaze wander, slow and greedy.

"What a sight you are," I mused, lowering the red Popsicle until the tip of it brushed her nipple.

She jolted at the sensation, the Popsicle still frozen with flecks of frost on it. But it melted at the contact with her skin, leaving a pink mark as I trailed it from one breast to the other, loving the way Chloe wiggled and writhed — both seeking the touch and running from it.

She didn't speak. She *couldn't* — not with her mouth open and waiting, pink tongue spread flat and ready.

Slowly, the Popsicle skated up and across her collarbone, along the slope of her neck, until I ran it along her bottom lip, the top of it grazing her tongue.

"I'm not going to teach you how to suck any man's cock," I told her. "I'm going to teach you specifically how to suck *mine*."

Her breathing intensified, puffs of warm air defrosting the Popsicle where I held it before her.

"Because — and let me make this crystal clear — while I am fucking you, you are only mine to fuck. And I am only yours. Understand?"

She nodded, eager and impatient.

"First, I want you to tease me," I said. "Wrap those perfect lips around the tip and taste."

Chloe bent forward enough to capture the tip of the Popsicle, and my nostrils flared when she closed her mouth around it. I could tell she was swirling her tongue, and my cock jumped at the need to switch places.

"Good," I told her. "Now slide a little deeper, and suck."

I could see the tentativeness in her expression as she withdrew, lips to tip, and then dove a little deeper. Her cheeks hollowed out and a sucking, popping noise filled the kitchen.

I groaned.

"*Fuck,* yes, Chloe. Just like that."

She preened when I said her name, rolling her tongue around the maybe inch and a half she'd made wet before she closed her mouth and sucked again.

"Now, you're going to make it real wet and sloppy," I told her. "Spit on it, and take it deeper."

Chloe swallowed, her eyebrows folding together before she withdrew from the Popsicle and stared at it like a challenge. She closed her mouth and swirled saliva, and then she spit, coating the Popsicle before she wrapped it up in her mouth again.

This time, she slid it in about halfway and gagged.

"Sorry," she said, pulling off and hanging her head.

"Eyes up here."

Her gaze snapped to mine.

"Do not apologize," I warned. "I will only tell you once."

I teased her lips with the Popsicle as she stared up at me, shame and the remnants of her orgasm still staining her cheeks.

"I'll show you how to use your hands for what your mouth can't fit," I explained. And then I lowered just half a foot, staring down at her as I forced the Popsicle into her mouth. She let me in, licking and sucking and keeping her eyes on me. "Besides, I fucking *love* when you gag."

She whimpered, the sound vibrating through the Popsicle all the way to my hand.

And that was it.

I'd had enough of using a fucking prop.

I pulled the Popsicle away, savoring the sucking noise she made when it released from her lips. I didn't even look as I tossed it into the sink. I would deal with that later.

Right now, my only mission was to hear her make that gagging noise with my cock halfway down her throat.

"Lick your lips clean," I told her, and I watched her do so slowly as I plucked the button free on my jeans and slid the zipper down. I stood right in front of her as I maneuvered the denim down my thighs and let it fall at my ankles.

These jeans were custom made for me — had to be, because hockey had carved my ass and thighs into fucking massive heaps of stone.

When they pooled at my feet, I left them there.

And Chloe gaped when she realized there wasn't another layer separating us.

I fisted my erection, stifling a groan at the first bit of contact. I was so worked up after her riding my face and that little Popsicle lesson that I felt like I could pump five times and blow. Part of me wanted to. I wondered what she'd look like with a shiny pearl necklace, her doe eyes all wide and innocent as I painted her.

But she wanted to learn.

And I'd be a lying sonofabitch if I said I didn't get off at the thought of being her first, of being the one to teach her.

"Show me you know what to do," I said, releasing myself.

Chloe's hand shook a bit as she reached out, her palm warm when it wrapped around my base. I sucked in a breath when she touched me, my cock jumping against her touch, and then her eyes were fixed on me.

She leaned forward, pressing my crown against her tongue.

My eyes rolled all the way back.

"Yes," I breathed, fisting one hand in her hair. I wrapped it around the hair tie struggling to hold back her locks and cradled her skull so I could guide her if needed. "I love when you taste my cock."

She moaned, wrapping her lips around me and sliding down an inch. That vibration, the coolness of her tongue from the Popsicle, the eagerness with which she took me…

it was enough to have me all the way fucked up in just the first sixty seconds of this blowjob.

Just like I'd taught her, Chloe swirled her tongue, tasting and teasing with her eyes on me. When she pulled back and dove a little deeper, she sucked, her cheeks going hollow, and the pressure made me groan and fist her hair tighter.

"Such a quick learner," I breathed. "Such a good fucking girl."

That egged her on, and she pulled back, looking at my cock only long enough to spit on it before she was tasting and sucking and diving deeper.

Her brown eyes held mine until she gagged, her eyelids fluttering shut without her control, and she pulled back with those eyes watering and her cheeks flushing a deeper shade of red.

"*God*, yes," I praised, thumbing her jaw. "Do that again."

She teased and played and made me wet, and then she gagged.

"Hold it," I begged, using my fist in her hair to show her what I meant.

I only held her there for two seconds before I released and let her pull back.

"That is so fucking hot, Chloe," I told her, and I nearly forgot my own fucking rule as I bent and gripped her chin, pulling her mouth close to mine.

I wanted to reward her with a kiss.

For a long moment, I debated it, my eyes on her swollen mouth as she panted and waited.

But I released her, standing again and wrapping a hand around my cock to guide it back to her mouth.

"Now, you're going to make it wet again," I said. "Spit on it, gag on it, and then use your hands to coat my cock with your saliva."

She nodded, though she seemed unsure, but she did exactly what I asked. I moaned when she sucked and swirled, cursing at the gag, and when her warm hands wrapped around me and covered me in her spit, I let my head fall back, eyes on the ceiling.

"Jesus Christ," I muttered, dragging my heavy gaze back down to her. I ran my hands into her hair, holding on with both of them to show her what to do. "One hand at the base, the other on top of it," I said. "Cover the rest with your mouth."

She covered me completely when she followed those directions, and for a moment, I just savored the sight of her bent over and taking me, her ass a perfect heart shape from this angle, her hair a mess in my hands.

"Now," I said, covering her hands with my own. "Twist your hands and pump them up and down, working them with your mouth. Like this."

I illustrated for her, twisting her hands in opposite directions and pushing them up toward her mouth until she nearly released my tip. Then, I'd drag them back down, and her mouth followed, sucking me in as deep as she could.

"*Fuuuuck*," I groaned. "You suck that cock so well, don't you? I knew you'd be good at it. I knew you'd love it."

I released my grip, hands finding her hair again, but I held on lightly, letting her be in full control.

"Now, look at me."

Her eyes were glossy when they met mine.

"Make me come, and swallow it when you do."

She bit her lip, her gaze sliding to my cock long enough to watch her hands work me and fit her mouth to just the right spot. Then, with her gaze locked on me once more — she went to work.

Her hands twisted and slid against my shaft. Her tongue swirled, tasted, and flicked. Her lips closed around me, and she sucked like she wanted to drain me.

She was about to.

"Firmer grip," I managed to croak out as my orgasm burned at the edges of my vision. I felt the beginning of it, the numbness, the all-consuming need to take over. I wanted to grab onto her hair and slam my cock right into her throat, but I wouldn't. I never would. I wanted her to have control. I wanted to let *her* get me there in the slow, torturous way she was.

With a moan and more gusto than I expected from her first time, Chloe sucked and licked and worked me with her hands like an A-plus student. She gagged and held me there before working me faster, and I groaned and shuddered and chased that heat teasing all my senses.

And then, the woman released me, working me with her hands like a goddamn pro as her lips dripped and her eyes pleaded.

"Come in my mouth, Will," she breathed. "Show me I did a good job."

"*Fuck*," I ground out, and she covered my cock with her mouth just in time for me to give her what she'd asked for.

I hadn't expected those words. It was *me* doing the dirty talking. It was *me* teaching the fucking lesson. But hearing her beg for it, knowing she wanted my release just as badly as I'd needed to give her hers... it unleashed something carnal inside me.

It surprised her when I came. I knew, because her eyes shot wide and for a moment, I thought she was going to pull off me. But she kept pace, kept her hands and mouth working as I cursed and panted and groaned out every wave of my release.

My hands gripped in her hair — not controlling, but holding on to keep from spiraling off the fucking planet.

She was so goddamn beautiful it hurt.

And I knew nothing would ever compare to this. Nothing ever had before, nothing ever would after.

I was shaking and sweating by the time my orgasm subsided, and I reached back for the island to hold onto with one hand and keep myself steady as Chloe's eyes looked up to me, unsure of what to do next.

Without me saying so, she gently let me go, licking me clean on the way.

Her hands hit her thighs, leaving wet, slippery handprints.

And she swallowed.

"You filthy, naughty, *perfect* little thing," I mused, wiping her bottom lip with my thumb as I shook my head.

She smiled against my touch, her gaze now alight with excitement and glee. "I did it!"

A laugh burst from my lips — well, as much of a laugh as I ever let free, anyway — and I reached down, gently helping her stand.

I tucked her hair that had fallen from her hair tie behind one ear, swallowing as I took in the sight of her freshly fucked mouth, the pink marks still lining her breasts where I'd dragged the Popsicle across her skin.

"You did, indeed," I murmured. "Now let me get you cleaned up."

It wasn't a request. I could tell by her reaction to every word and demand that she'd enjoyed our play time, but I was also aware that her experience was practically nothing. I wanted to make sure she felt okay, that she knew I respected her and adored her.

Shit.

I swallowed as that last thought found me, ignoring it somewhat as I tugged Chloe back to my bedroom.

I didn't miss how she looked around while I ran the shower. She'd never been in there before.

No woman ever had.

Without a word, I helped her step under the warm stream of water, and then I stepped in behind her. The rain shower covered us from above, and Chloe sighed, letting her head fall back as she savored every drop.

"Are you okay?" I asked, reaching for my shower gel. I hoped she wouldn't mind that it wasn't a feminine scent. I lathered some in my hands and waited for her response.

"I'm fucking *incredible*," she said, smiling at me and wiping the water from her eyes.

I smirked. "I'll say."

I waggled my brows as she laughed, and then I began to gently massage her, working the lathered foam over her shoulders, across her breasts, over her stomach and hips and thighs. I didn't sexualize her while I did. I cleaned her, caressed her, soaking up the sated moans she let free and the soft smile on her lips.

"Thank you," she whispered, and when I caught her gaze, there was true appreciation there.

"I think I should be thanking *you*."

"No, I mean it," she said, frowning a bit as she looked at my chest. "I never knew it could be like this. I always thought..." She shook her head. "You make me feel powerful. Sexy," she added, her gaze finding mine. "Wanted."

My throat was tight as I rinsed my hands and then her.

How the fuck had she not *always* felt that way?

"What happened," I asked. "The first time you…"

She snorted. "Oh, God. Do you remember the little comment I made that time we were watching *Jeopardy*, about my head hanging off the bed?"

My jaw clenched.

I'd thought that was a joke.

Chloe shook her head. "It was awful, Will."

Why did I love it so much when she said my name like that, like we were old friends, like we were lovers?

That very thought struck a violent chord inside me that made me regret asking.

I wanted to know more about her, and yet I knew it was dangerous to know anything at all.

I'd had a friend with benefits before.

She turned into my wife, the mother of my child, and then she died.

The thought was sobering just as much as Chloe's story. She washed her hair and chattered away, telling me about the first, and only, man she'd been with. It was some stupid college boy who'd lasted all of six seconds. He obviously hadn't even thought about her pleasure, let alone acted on it.

I listened, but I'd be lying if I said my mind hadn't gone elsewhere.

Mostly to the place it always went when I needed protection.

"I'm sorry," I said when she finished. I reached around her to turn off the water.

"Don't be," she assured me. "It made my life less complicated, to have that as my first experience."

She stepped out and grabbed one of the towels I'd hung for us, wrapping herself in it.

"It set realistic expectations. It proved to me what my mother and grandmother had always wanted me to know."

"And what's that?"

She shrugged, a sad smile on her lips as she glanced at me over her shoulder.

"That love isn't real, and men can only give so much. In the end, I have to take care of myself."

My heart cracked.

I wanted to tell her she was wrong.

I wanted to tell her that *I* would take care of her. That *I* would make her feel good, make her feel wanted, make her feel... *loved*.

But I couldn't.

Because here I was, serving as yet another layer of proof to back up her theory.

I held Chloe's gaze, and I swore she was waiting for me to say something, too. I willed my mouth to open.

But I couldn't lie to her.

Apparently, it was much easier to lie to myself.

"I'm going to make some food," she said, tearing her gaze from me. "Want any?"

"No, thank you. I'll heat up the leftovers Arushi left later."

Chloe nodded, and I tried to ignore the disappointment I saw in her, the disappointment I felt in my chest.

"Well, then," she said, spinning and throwing me a seemingly unbothered smile. "See you around, coach."

She saluted with a wink.

And then she was gone.

Chapter 23

Cruel, Isn't It?

Chloe

"**A**bsolutely not."

I chuckled, trying and failing to pull Chef Patel from where she was rooted in place on Sunday. Just like Will had promised, we were at Disney World, soaking up his full day off and staying the night in Orlando. We'd make the drive back home tomorrow morning before his late practice.

Our VIP tour guide, Juan, was busying Will and Ava with some fun facts about the Mad Tea Party — the ride Chef was refusing to partake in.

"You're being such a Will right now," I said. "A real turkey!"

"I will hold your things," she offered, grabbing the backpack I had full of snacks, water, sunscreen, and other items I thought we might need. "And will be waiting right here when you get done."

"Come *on*, Arushi," I begged. "You already sat out on Space Mountain *and* the Barnstormer."

"And you did just fine on your own, didn't you?" She pursed her lips. "I will be right here."

"Fine," I said with a heavy sigh. "But I'm going to make you ride *It's a Small World* as punishment."

"That damn song will be stuck in my head all day."

"Sure you don't want to do the teacups instead?"

She considered for a moment, then shook her head and lifted her chin. "I'll survive *Small World*. But I'm *not* letting you twirl me around and make me vomit on this thing — especially after that hideous pretzel and cheese we just had and called *lunch*."

"Mmm, I want another pretzel!" Ava said, popping up beside me with her eyes wide with glee. She'd been like that all morning, from the moment we'd stepped foot inside the park. It was almost impossible for me to remember her as she was before now, when I first started as her nanny. Gone was the child who barely smiled, barely laughed. It was as if once she realized how nice it felt to do both, she decided she never wanted to stop.

Today, her brown, wild hair was tamed into two long pigtails on either side of her head. The only way we'd been able to convince her to leave the hockey uniform at home was to promise to buy her a brand-new shirt once we got here. She proudly wore a pin on that pink Tinkerbell shirt that said *First Visit!*

"Maybe later," I offered. "Or should we save room for some Mickey Mouse ice cream?"

"Oh! Ice cream!" Ava clapped and bounced, and then Will was joining us, his brows set low over his eyes.

How this man could scowl at the happiest place on Earth was beyond me — but he'd managed to all day.

We'd wrangled him into a t-shirt that Chef Patel and I had made that said "Disney Dad" on it — though he'd refused us once we'd tried to complete the look with a pair of Mickey ears. The shirt was almost too small for him, but only in the way that made the muscles of his arms impossible to ignore. I knew he had to be tired after a late game night, but perhaps the win had given him energy. Or perhaps he was just so excited to bring Ava here that he'd *make* the energy, if he had to.

Even through his grumpiness all morning, it had been the sweetest thing to watch him hold Ava's hand as our Juan led us safely around the park. He did his best to ignore the other guests as we passed them, especially when they pulled out their phones to take photos of him. A few had asked him for autographs and selfies, much to the dismay of Juan, who was doing all he could with security in tow to give us an unbothered experience.

But Will had handled it all in stride, smiling for the pictures and scribbling autographs before turning his attention right back to his daughter.

I'd listened intently all morning as he'd told her about Jenny's favorite park — Magic Kingdom. We'd started in Tomorrowland, because it was how Jenny always started, and Ava had jumped for joy when she was just barely cleared as tall enough to ride Space Mountain. Will had dug up an old, printed photo of him and Jenny on the very same ride — Jenny smiling and yelling with her hands in the air while Will looked scared to death beside her.

It had gotten a good laugh out of all of us.

The morning zipped by in a rush of rides and food and games, along with Ava shopping her little heart out at every gift shop we passed. Our tour guide and Will were both loaded down with bags — bags Chef Patel happily held while we did most of the rides without her.

It turned out she had a major fear of rollercoasters, and also a fear of throwing up.

But I could tell that regardless of whether she rode the rides or not, Ava was happy Chef Patel was with us. She skipped and held her hand and chatted her ear off between rides, pointing at everything we passed and forcing Chef to take a picture with her and Goofy when we found him signing autograph books.

It had truly been a magical day so far — and now, we were ready to tackle the teacups ride.

At least, Ava and I were.

Arushi was sitting out, and the way Will was frowning at the ride, I wasn't sure we wouldn't have to beg him to join us, too.

"We could skip this one," he offered grumpily. "We still have lots of park to cover before the fireworks."

"But you said Mommy loved this one," Ava reminded him, and I covered my smile with a hand as she tilted her wide eyes up at him.

No *way* could he say no to that look.

Will heaved a heavy sigh, looking up at the sky before he rubbed his daughter's head. "You're right. Let's do it."

"Yay!" Ava jumped into the air, clicking the heels of her light-up sneakers together before she hurriedly dumped her stuffed Dumbo into Chef's waiting arms and took off in a sprint toward the line.

Juan took off after her as Will and I jogged to catch up. We were escorted to a shorter line, and were ushered onto the ride the very next round.

It would have been impossible for us to do Disney World the way I had in the past. Even with a tour guide and security, we'd had guests taking photos and hollering out to Will every chance they got. The more people made a scene, the more the guests around them asked who we were and got out their own phones.

Anyone who was a hockey fan knew him.

Anyone who *wasn't* wanted to — because he was famous. He was a professional athlete. He was someone to take a picture of and post online and brag about being in the same vicinity of.

It was madness.

Our tour guide had offered several times for us to walk the park underground through the tunnels the staff used, but Will wanted Ava to get the full experience.

Even if that meant fending off the fans who spotted him.

"This one, this one!" Ava said, sliding into a teacup.

She scooted all the way to the back of the little bench surrounding the small round table center, and I took her left side while Will took the right.

"So the cups just spin on their own?" Ava asked when the ride attendant came by to shut the door to our teacup.

I was still chuckling at Will trying to get comfortable with how long his legs were. His knees were practically up to his chin as he grunted and forced them into the tiny space between the seats and the table in the middle.

"Yep," he grated, and he gave me a warning look not to say otherwise.

I smiled mischievously. "Actually—"

"Chloe," Will threatened.

It sent a shiver through me, and I found myself wondering if he'd find a fun way to punish me the next time we were alone.

I couldn't even find it in me to be ashamed for those dirty thoughts — not since our first *lesson* in the kitchen last week. I felt that tantalizing burn of the Popsicle on my skin long after it had melted and we had cleaned up.

The entire thing was cemented in my mind, a delicious memory that replayed time and time again.

I still couldn't get over it, how it felt to have his hands on me, to have his *mouth* on me. And how he'd managed to make me enjoy going down on him when I'd always thought that sounded like the worst thing in the world was beyond me.

I hadn't just enjoyed it — I'd *loved* it. The way he looked at me, the sounds he made because of what I did to him, his hands gripping my hair and my name on his lips when he came undone... it was the most beautiful haunting.

The only disappointment I felt was when I thought about the shower after, when I wished for Will to tell me something he already told me he never would.

Sex was different with him — but that was all it was. Just sex.

As much as I was happy to agree to that, I'd be lying if I said I didn't long to know him better, to curl up next to him after what we'd done and fall asleep in his arms, to wake up in his bed and see his crooked smile that wasn't ever really a smile.

I tried to head the warnings and advice of the experts on *Reddit*, the ones who reminded me time and time again to lock up my feelings after we fooled around. *Don't ask questions and don't stick around*, they said. *Don't open up, and don't mistake the way he touches you for anything more than lust.*

But they weren't there.

They didn't see his heavy eyes drinking me in, or feel how his touch turned tender the moment we both found our release. They didn't witness how those filthy words turned to gentle hands washing me in the shower, didn't hear the way his voice trembled a bit as he asked if I was okay afterward.

It was all so confusing, I couldn't even pretend I wasn't in way over my head.

So, I chose to ignore it all and just live in whatever moment was right in front of me.

Presently, that was the opportunity to teach Will's daughter how to get the most out of the teacup ride — and watch her father squirm in the process.

"See this table?" I said, ignoring Will's groan of frustration as I showed Ava what to do. "Once we get going, this table will control how much and how fast we spin. We can go and go and go in one direction and then switch it to the other — like this."

I demonstrated with my hands, showing how to spin one direction and then the other.

Ava bounced in her seat, the pigtails I'd wrangled her hair into that morning honestly too cute to handle in that moment. I knew now from the many photos of Jenny that Will had scrounged up that Ava had her mother's eyes. They were bright green and full of curiosity.

"You ready?" I asked her as the ride began.

"Ready!"

"We really don't have to— *ergh!*"

Will's rebuttal was cut short by the first spin, and his hands flew to the table Ava and I were turning as fast as our little hands would let us.

The ride started slow at first, and then it picked up speed, our teacup rotating us so quickly, the world blurred. Ava fought against the force of gravity to hold onto the table, spinning and giggling as her little face turned red.

"Change, change!" I chanted, and Ava and I grabbed the wheel as hard as we could, the teacup lurching to a stop before we began swiveling the other way.

Will looked green, his hands jutting out to stop us from turning the table more. "Alright, that's enough."

"Come on, Daddy! Spin! Spin!"

Just as I suspected, Will couldn't resist his daughter — not when she was having what I was pretty sure was the best day of her life.

Reluctantly, and with a dramatic growl, Will used his massive grip to help us pivot the table. The teacup swirled with more speed and intensity than it had with just me and Ava spinning it, and eventually, Ava threw her hands up in the air and let out the sweetest peal of laughter.

It was the kind of moment that stuck in your mind like glue, a core memory of an innocent child without an ounce of stress or worry on her shoulders. She was free. She was living.

She was happy.

The corner of Will's mouth tilted up, and we shared a look across the teacup.

As if the world wasn't already blurred beyond us, the look he gave me made it feel as if there was no world at all outside of this three-foot circumference. His honey eyes held fast to mine, questions and declarations unsaid.

Time slowed, Ava's laugh ringing out loud and lovely in the background as Will swallowed, his brows furrowing together.

Just as soon as the moment had come, it was zapped away, the ride slowing to a halt while Ava panted and clapped and demanded to go again.

We toppled off the ride in a dizzy daze, Ava and me laughing as we walked side to side in our attempt to make it back to where Chef Patel and Juan were waiting for us without falling over.

"How was it?" Chef asked, handing Ava her Dumbo toy.

"Amazing!" Ava and I answered at the same time Will said, "I think I'm going to be sick."

That earned a laugh from Juan and a wrinkled nose from Arushi, and then we all regrouped and headed on our merry way.

We zipped through Fantasyland and Liberty Square, pausing for a bit on Tom Sawyer Island while Ava took a nap in her dad's arms. Chef Patel seemed grateful for the break, stretching out her legs and soaking up the sunshine while she dozed off in a little nap of her own.

Will and I sat silently next to each other, watching the boat travel back and forth, the people spilling onto the island and walking around a bit before piling back on to head back toward the rides and attractions.

It was the kind of day that made me happy I lived in Florida. The rest of the country was battling blizzards and freezing rain while we had a sunshiney day, the temperature in the seventies and a cool breeze flowing through the trees. It wasn't a very busy day, either, especially considering it was a Sunday. And having the VIP tour made it easy to get through the park without much hassle of waiting in lines.

When we traipsed over to Adventureland, Chef accompanied Ava to the little girls' room and Juan took his own leave. Will and I stood guard of all our belongings.

"It's a very nostalgic place, isn't it?" I commented, smiling at the sight of a family passing by — the mom pushing the stroller while a little boy rode on top of his dad's shoulders.

"You come here a lot as a kid?" Will asked.

"Once."

"Only once?"

"My mom wasn't exactly a huge fan of Disney," I explained.

"And I thought *I* was the scrooge," Will mused. "Who doesn't like *Disney*?"

I sighed, smiling even though my heart hurt a bit at the memory. "I begged my mom for the longest time to come here. She would never let me go when my friends invited me with their families. But one summer, between fifth and sixth grade, she finally brought me. It was just me and her." I shook my head. "It was one of the best days of my life and one of the worst, too."

I paused, unsure of whether to continue or not. I knew this was crossing a boundary Will had so clearly spelled out for us.

But then again... he'd asked, hadn't he?

"Everything was fine until we passed by the Bibbidi Bobbidi Boutique. You know, where you can get your hair and makeup done and they dress you like a princess?" I laughed a bit to myself, staring down at my dirty white sneakers. "I wanted to do it *so* bad. I remember watching the other girls come out of the castle after getting their makeovers and just *whining* for my mom to please, please, *please* let me do one, too.

"But, to my mom, it was the equivalent of me asking to do cocaine," I said. "She loathed the Disney princesses. She never wanted me to watch their movies. In fact, the ones I *had* seen were because I snuck them at my friends' houses and just didn't tell Mom."

"Why did she hate them?"

"Because the women were dependent on men," I answered, lifting my gaze to meet his. "Especially the older movies. It was all about getting married, giving up everything for love. Cinderella was just a poor stepchild until she found a prince. Ariel gave up her voice and mermaid tail to chase Eric on land." I shrugged. "In my mom's eyes, the men *saved* them — and the women wanted to be saved. That was the ultimate sin to my mother and went against everything she wanted to teach me."

"What about Tiana, though?" Will argued. "She was a bad ass."

I chuckled. "Okay, first of all — *love* that you know this. That movie had just come out, actually, right before our visit here. But my mom wouldn't know how much of a bad ass Tiana was, or see the badassery in *any* of the princesses because she made her mind up about them years ago. I mean, come on — look at Jasmine! She was the ultimate baddie. She stood up to her father, refused to just be married away as a prize... and the way she played Jafar in the end?" I shook my head. "And Mulan? Hello? She literally fought in war. She was a hero!"

I shrugged, watching my toes again as I kicked a rock around.

"Anyway, it didn't matter. Part of the reason my mom didn't bring me here was because she was a single mom fighting to make ends meet as it was. Disney is expensive. And me continually begging to be turned into a princess set my mom into a rage. I can't blame her, not entirely, anyway. She had done so much to bring me here and I was just too young to understand." I paused. "She dragged me out of the park kicking and screaming. I wanted to stay for the fireworks. We hadn't even made it to all the rides. But she was done."

Will let out a soft sigh. "Disney *is* expensive," he

agreed. "I'm sure it was hard on her, being a single mom. But... gotta say. She sounds like a real man hater."

"Grandma, too," I said. "But they have their reasons. My grandfather and dad gave them plenty. I think they raised me the way they did out of the goodness of their hearts and a fierce need to protect me. They wanted me to be stronger. And, in a lot of ways, I'm thankful for that. Because I *do* feel independent. I feel like I can sit comfortably in my own company. I can be alone without being lonely. I can provide for myself and experience happiness without it being dependent on a partner."

"You don't ever think it would be nice to share it all with someone?"

The question knocked me off guard — so much so that any response I might have had got lodged in my throat.

I forced a smile up at him. "What about you? Did you ever come here as a kid?"

I saw in his frown how much he wanted to press me about his previous question, but he respected the nonverbal cue I gave enough to let it go.

"I grew up in Maine," he offered as way of explanation. "Not as easy to just drive across I-4 and get here."

"Fair," I said.

"I came a few times with Jenny once she moved to St. Pete, though." He seemed contemplative at that, but instead of going into more detail about his late wife, he turned the conversation back to his family. "I do remember Mom wanting to do a family vacation here, but even with both of them working hard, like you said... it was a lot of money to try to save up. And then I got into hockey, which is an expensive sport for even a well-off family." He paused, swallowing. "And then mom got sick."

The words hung between us, weighted and painful.

"When she passed, Dad didn't really know what to do with me, I don't think. He put all his spare money into making sure I had hockey, though. Looking back, especially as a father myself now, I don't hold anything against him. He was doing the best he could. He couldn't give me much in the way of words or affection, but he sacrificed a lot to make sure I had a team, a coach, a sport, a way to spend my time. He was just trying to survive and make sure I was okay."

"That had to be so hard," I whispered.

Will shrugged. "Kind of cruel, isn't it?" His eyes found mine. "I lost my mom, and now Ava has to live without hers. Your mom never had a father, and neither did you."

"I guess all we can do is make the most of the hand we're dealt," I said. "Kind of like what Ava says to you, right? *We are doing our best.*"

Will's eyes flicked between mine, a ghost of a smile on his lips. It was like he wanted to laugh it off and nod and agree with me just as much as he wanted to cry and pull me into his arms and feel broken together.

In the end, Ava came barreling toward us, and the conversation ended with words unspoken.

Chapter 24

Fairy Godmothers

Will

"Should we grab dinner somewhere before it gets dark?" Chef Patel asked, checking the time on her watch. "Then we could circle back to the rides we haven't done before the fireworks."

"Fireworks!" Ava echoed, spinning with her hands up in the air.

"We have a reservation for you at Be Our Guest," Juan said, eyes on his clipboard. "But it's not for a couple hours yet." His eyes flashed to me, and I knew it was because he was unsure of whether he should be the one to reveal our surprise or if it should be me.

I liked Juan. He was a young kid, wide-eyed and bushy-tailed with a view of the world that I envied. He and his family had moved here from Venezuela when he was just a baby, and he had this infectious energy that revolved around making the most of every day. He smiled and told us facts about the park and led us around like this was the best job in the world and he was the happiest man alive.

It made me wonder, for the first time in five years, why the hell I was so grumpy all the goddamn time.

I nodded to him, letting him know I'd take it from here. Clearing my throat, I dropped down to one knee so I was on Ava's level. "How about we grab a snack, and then... how would you feel about becoming a princess?"

Ava's eyes grew wide, and I tried and failed to calm the knocking of my heart against my chest as I felt Chloe's gaze on me from above.

"A princess?" she repeated softly.

I nodded. "You get your hair done, your makeup, and you get to pick whatever princess dress you want. You even get a tiara," I added.

"What's that?"

"It's a beautiful, sparkling crown that sits on your head," Chloe filled in for me, her voice full of wonder as she dropped to her knee beside Ava.

She was so fucking pretty. Of course, she couldn't have just worn jean shorts and a t-shirt like the rest of us. No, she'd spent the last week sewing a romper for the occasion. It was a mix of a rich purple and a sea green, the pattern somehow childlike and adorable, yet fitting for an adult. Maybe it was the way it cinched her waist and framed her breasts, modest but in no way hiding her curves. Across the chest, she'd stitched the words *Most Magical* and there was an embroidered image of the castle beneath the font.

I tried not to focus too hard on the way her thighs stretched against the fabric as she twirled one of my daughter's pigtails. "You'll love it, little angel bug."

Chloe's eyes found mine then, and I swallowed, nodding in lieu of a smile.

"I can really be a princess?" Ava asked.

"You sure can. But we better hurry. The kind Fairy Godmothers who will turn you into a princess are agreeing to stay later than usual just for us," I said.

"Really?!" Ava's mouth dropped open, and then she grabbed me by the hand and tugged me off the ground. "Let's go!"

"Are they ready for us?" I asked Juan.

He was texting away on his cell phone, but nodded and smiled. "They should be once we get there. Let's stop and get a snack like you said and we can head that way."

"I'm going to be a princess! I'm going to be a princess!" Ava chanted the words, skipping around us before she stopped dead in her tracks and looked up at Chef Patel. "Do you want to become a princess, too, Chef?"

"Oh honey, I'm already a queen," Arushi said, patting her head. "Have been for years."

Ava giggled.

My heart lurched into my throat, Juan arching a brow at me before nodding encouragingly.

"Actually," I said. "How would you feel about Miss Chloe becoming a princess with you?"

Ava gasped at the same time Chloe's head snapped toward me, confusion in her wide eyes as she frowned and tried to make sense of what I'd said.

"It's... I'm too old," she whispered, keeping a smile on so as not to upset Ava. "They have an age limit."

"Sometimes, exceptions can be made," Juan said for me, since apparently my voice was too unstable to make a peep.

Chloe's lips parted, her eyes softening as she swiveled toward me. She blinked once, twice, and then her eyes were watering.

"You did this for me?"

Fuck.

"For Ava," I said instantly. Sniffing, I tucked my hands into my pockets on a shrug. "But I thought she might not want to do it alone."

Chloe read right through the lie.

Her lips wobbled as she pressed them together, her eyes glossed, disbelief painted in her every feature.

And then she launched herself into my arms, wrapping hers around my neck and squeezing tight as she let out a deliriously happy squeal.

"Thank you," she whispered, her grip unrelenting. "This is the nicest thing anyone has ever..." She shook her head, pulling back but not away. "Well... just, thank you, Will."

It was impossible not to catalog every point where her body met mine, from her hips in my hands to her breasts pressed against the bottom of my chest. My nostrils flared as I stared down into her impossibly deep brown eyes, eyes that were surveying me as if I was a puzzle she couldn't quite figure out.

What the fuck am I doing?

The words echoed in my mind as time stretched between us.

I was breaking my own damn rules.

Those rules had been set for a reason. They were to protect Ava, to ensure Chloe and I kept things professional, that we didn't get ourselves into a murky situation.

They were to protect *me*.

And yet here I was, asking her about her life, desperate to know her better, relentless in my pursuit to find a way to make her smile and feel cared for for once in her life.

"This is going to be *the best!*" Ava said, jumping up and down and breaking the spell between me and Chloe.

Chloe broke away with pink cheeks, tucking her hair behind her ear before she grabbed Ava's hand and let her lead the way toward one of the snack carts. Juan escorted them, reading off some options for food before our appointment, and I hung back for a moment trying to catch my breath.

Chef Patel stepped right in front of me with her arms full of bags, one thick, black eyebrow hiking into her hairline.

"Shut up," I said, circling her to catch up to the group.

"I didn't say a word."

"Didn't have to."

"No, I certainly did not," she agreed on a laugh.

I subtly flipped her off behind my back.

That only made her laugh harder.

• • •

An hour and a half later, Ava and Chloe looked like the remnants of a glitter bomb.

Ava was a golden yellow from head to toe, the dress she chose that of Belle. She was admiring the smattering of stars and glitter on her cheeks as the Fairy Godmother assigned to her placed a tiara on her head. My daughter gasped as the final piece slid into place, the crown sitting perfectly on top of the little bun they'd fastened at the top of her head with a yellow ribbon.

She looked up at me as if I'd hung the moon.

"Daddy, *look*!"

"I see," I said, smirking a bit as I came up behind her. She turned back to the mirror and I placed my hands on her shoulders. "You look absolutely beautiful, Pumpkin."

"Oh, no pumpkin unless she's out past midnight," the Fairy Godmother said, ever in character.

"Let's get a picture of you," Chef Patel said, helping Ava out of her chair.

"What about Chloe?!"

"She'll be right out," one of the other Fairy Godmothers assured her. "She's almost dressed."

Juan had pulled some *big* strings for this. The boutique was normally booked out weeks, if not months, in advance. But he'd somehow convinced a few of the employees to stay late and make room for us. I tried to tip them — not just once, but several times — but they declined every single one of them.

They seemed genuinely happy to help us, though; the Fairy Godmothers smiling as they watched Chef Patel snap photo after photo of Ava, who was striking poses and giggling at Chef's commentary as she did.

Not only had they made an exception for us timing wise, but they'd also let me book a service for Chloe. The boutique was meant for little girls — not adults — which meant there were no adult-sized chairs or costumes. But like their reputation suggested, the employees made magic happen. They dolled Chloe up just the same as Ava, and then came in last minute with a surprise princess gown covered in a white garment bag.

At least they let me pay for the dress.

As we waited for her reveal, I watched Ava, heart heavy and slow as I wondered what had happened to her over the last few months.

She had completely transformed.

Just a year ago, she was barely speaking. Months ago, she was barely smiling, *never* laughing.

Now... she was a kid.

She was happy and smiley and carefree. She didn't wear the weight I unintentionally put on her. She didn't emulate me the way she had for so long.

No, it seemed she favored Chloe's energy now.

That struck me like a bat to the head. Chloe had swung into our lives so unexpectedly, and she'd done so with a mission. She hadn't just taken on the job as Ava's nanny with pity or with the mindset that she could make a buck. She didn't want anything from me — not fame or a quick ticket to money or a relationship past the professional one we had.

She didn't want anything *at all* other than to make Ava happy, and me by proxy.

That was a kindness so pure and selfless that I couldn't quite understand it.

But I was thankful. I was grateful for her time and her energy, for the way she knew how to get my daughter out of her shell better than I ever could. I would never be able to truly pay her enough for how she'd knocked sense into me, too — how she'd brought to light the ways I could introduce Ava to her mom without wanting to hurl myself off a cliff in the process.

Chloe was healing us, just by existing.

That thought was dancing in my mind when Ava and Chef Patel stopped their dance party on a gasp, Ava's hands flying to cover her mouth as they stared at something behind me.

When I turned, I understood why.

Chloe appeared to glide out of the dressing room, the mirrors all around the boutique reflecting her in a kaleidoscope of beauty. Her russet hair hung in loose, wavy curls around her chin, one side of it pinned up with a light pink seashell. Her makeup was a little less glitzy than my daughter's — a more refined look, as if she really were a princess joining us for dinner.

I had no idea where they'd conjured the dress they found for her, but it fit as if it had been tailored with her in mind. The skirt that hung to the floor was a shiny, pearl pink. A darker shade, similar to the color her cheeks turned when she blushed, hung over her shoulders and cinched her waist before slowing out in two puffs from her hips.

On anyone else, the thing would have been ridiculous. But on her...

It was breathtaking.

"*Sundar*," I heard Chef whisper somewhere behind me, and while I was still stuck in a haze, Ava whizzed past me and slid to a halt right in front of Chloe.

"Wow," she breathed, blinking up at her.

"Wow is right," Chloe said, tapping the tip of Ava's tiara. "You look amazing, princess."

"No, *you* look amazing."

"No, *you*," Chloe argued back, and then they were plucking at each other's clothes, dishing out compliments and giggling like best friends.

Chef approached them with her phone in hand, gesturing for them to get together for pictures. She snapped away while I watched from behind her.

I couldn't take my eyes off Chloe.

And when her gaze slid to mine, I felt that familiar faltering of time, the way the world stuttered to a quiet whisper around us.

Juan tapped me on the shoulder, shaking me from the moment as he informed me we needed to get to our dinner reservation. It was madness as Chloe and Ava thanked the employees profusely for their work, and after a dozen more pictures with the Fairy Godmothers and a hundred blown kisses, we were all but running across the park to Be Our Guest.

We were immediately escorted to our dining table once we made it, and after dinner, we rushed to the Seven Dwarfs rollercoaster ride before finding our spot for fireworks.

I never got the chance to tell Chloe how gorgeous she looked.

But as we rode the water taxi to our hotel, I caught her shy gaze from across the boat. The lights reflected off the water, and in her warm eyes, my daughter sleeping with her head resting against Chloe's shoulder. Chloe smiled at me, just the corner of her mouth lifting, and need coursed through me like a wild, rushing river.

I wondered if Fairy Godmothers really did exist.

I wondered if mine had sent Chloe to me.

And I hoped she could feel my intention as I returned her gaze, as I let my eyes travel the length of her, knowing her skin was turning that lovely shade of red I loved so much even though it was too dark to see it.

I wanted her to melt from the heat in my stare.

I longed for her to let me show her what I could never say with words.

There was only one way I knew how to do exactly that.

I was ready for another lesson.

Tonight.

Chapter 25

Not for Long

Chloe

Once I flopped down on the bed in my hotel room, I found it nearly impossible to move again.

Exhaustion washed over me like it never had before, humming in every bone and muscle of my body. My legs and feet ached, my eyelids were too heavy to peel open. I barely had the energy to text the cat sitter and watch the adorable videos she had sent of my three rascals getting into trouble like always.

And yet, I wore the biggest smile.

There were no words for what an amazing day it had been.

And while Will had almost made me burst into tears with what he did for me at the boutique, what replayed in my mind most were images of Ava. I smiled wider and wider as I remembered her squeals of laughter, how she ran to each character we found to fill her autograph book, the way her eyes grew round and mesmerized in each show and on every single ride, how she threw her arms up and screamed — fearlessly — on every rollercoaster she was tall enough to ride.

It was the most perfect day, one I knew she'd never forget.

I'd sent a few pictures throughout the day to the group text with my mom and grandmother. They hadn't met Ava yet, but I hoped one day they would. I also hoped they'd see from the pictures that I was doing my job, that I was safe, that Will wasn't a threat the way they thought he was.

Grandma commented on how adorable Ava was, and Mom said she liked my princess look — though I didn't miss her pursed lips when she said it. Maybe the fact that they hadn't dressed me specifically like any of the Disney princesses made a slight difference, but she still didn't look thrilled.

They both begged me to come visit soon before the call ended, which I promised I would.

I groaned when my phone pinged, thinking it was them and hoping like hell they wouldn't ask if I had time for a phone call. But when I looked at my phone, a tired smile crept over my face at the text from Maven.

Maven: I just saw a photo of Will Perry on Instagram.

Livia: ... okay?

Maven: AT DISNEY WORLD

Maven: WITH HIS DAUGHTER

Maven: AND HIS CHEF

Maven: AND HIS NANNY *wide eyes emoji*

Livia: Daddy P at Disney World?! This can only be the work of a certain teacher we know.

Grace: I love y'all, but it's not even six AM where I am. Muting you until I'm a human later today and I'll catch up. *kiss emoji*

I chuckled, typing out my response.

Me: Believe it or not — this was his idea.

Maven: My jaw is on the floor. Did he have fun?

Me: Would I know if he did?

Livia: LOL grumpy ass goalie. I bet Ava had a blast, though.

I sent through some pictures, which got a flurry of responses that made me glad Grace had turned her notifications off. Otherwise, no way would she be able to get back to sleep.

Maven: It's been too long since we've seen you. I think we should plan a date.

Livia: Yeah, I need an update about this hottie at your school.

Maven: Noah!

Me: Not really much to tell...

Maven: I call bullshit. The way you looked in the photos I saw on Instagram today? You were glowing.

Livia: Ah, it's that freshly fucked look.

I swallowed, typing and deleting about a dozen things. What the hell did I say to *that*?

Maven: I'm telling Vince we're doing a barbecue. We'll do it at Will's, since we all know he'll find an excuse not to come if it's anywhere else.

Me: Arushi and I can help with this ambush. I'll text you when we're back home.

Livia: Love it. Night, babes!

I let my phone fall to the side, smiling up at the ceiling as exhaustion made it feel like I was sinking farther into the bed.

I had friends.

I had friends who thought to text me, who wanted to make plans to see me.

And not just the girls, but Arushi, too. I'd barely had time to work on any of my puzzles or crafts lately, between hanging out with Chef, spending time with Ava, texting the girls, and getting... *lessons* from Will.

Who even *was* I?

Eventually, I managed to peel myself off my bed, rolling over until my feet hit the floor. I groaned when I stretched my toes on the carpet, and then carried myself step by painful step to the bathroom. My fingers worked the seashell clip in my hair until it came loose, my hair spilling free, and I rubbed the spot with a content sigh.

My reflection was one I didn't recognize, not just because I was still in the princess gown with glitter and a full face of makeup, but because something had shifted in me on this magical day, too.

I couldn't name it, but I could feel it.

I was unfastening the pearl earrings the boutique had provided me when a knock sounded on my door.

Will stood on the other side of it, his face as worn and tired as mine and a bottle of champagne in his fist.

Instantly, my heart jumped into my throat.

"Hi," I said more breathlessly than I meant to, my body already coming alive just at his presence.

"Hi," he echoed. "May I?"

He gestured toward the open door between us, and I slid to the side so he could let himself in.

Unlike me, he'd already changed, his hair drying in messy waves and the fresh scent of his shower gel meeting my nose as he passed by. He had on light gray joggers and a black Ospreys t-shirt that was made for Gasparilla weekend.

He wasn't wearing shoes.

And I internally rolled my eyes at myself, because once again, I was drooling over this man's feet.

"Ava asleep?" I guessed. She and Will were staying in the room right next to mine, and Chef in the room on the other side of that.

"She begged for a sleepover in Arushi's room. Pretty sure they both knocked out before I even finished my shower," Will confirmed. "I found us some champagne," he said once I let the door shut behind us.

I walked toward the bathroom again while he flopped down in the swivel chair at the desk that was piled high with the random things I'd strewn out of my suitcase. My heart was beating in my ears as I tried to figure out this confusing man.

He'd set all these boundaries, all these *rules*... and yet today, we'd talked and talked. He'd found a way to make one of my childhood dreams come true, for fuck's sake.

How was I supposed to figure him out?

"Us?" I asked as I unfastened my necklace and set it next to the earrings. "You don't drink."

"I don't drink *often*," he corrected. "But I'm in the presence of a princess. Feels like the perfect time to make an exception."

I snorted on a smile, reaching behind me for the zipper of the dress. Except it was harder than I thought to grasp. The Fairy Godmothers had helped me dress, and therefore, I hadn't realized I'd have to twist my arms and elbows in the most unnatural ways to try to reach the zipper at the top of my neck.

I strained a bit too hard in my attempt and winced, but managed to grab the zipper and pull it down a couple inches. When it reached the middle of my shoulder blades, I lost it again, and had to switch positions to reach for it from the bottom, instead.

"Jesus Christ," Will muttered, standing and crossing the room in long strides. "Let me do that before you break yourself."

"I've got it."

"I'm not doubting you do, but it might be easier if you just let me." He paused when his fingers found the zipper, his eyes on mine in the mirror as he arched one beautiful brow. "Unless you're too independent to accept help from a measly man?"

I elbowed him, which earned me a grunt that almost sounded like a laugh.

The moment he slid the zipper down my spine, though, all humor left me in a little gasp. I sucked in air and held it like my last breath as his warm knuckles skated from my shoulders all the way down to my hips. That zipper didn't need to move as slowly as he dragged it, but he seemed to be in no rush, seemed to be savoring every centimeter of that trail.

When I looked at him in the mirror, it was in time to watch his throat constrict.

And then he released me.

"There," he said. "Wasn't so hard, was it?"

"I think my feminist card has been revoked, actually."

Will shook his head, and then surprised me with a playful slap of my ass that made me yelp and drop my jaw in his direction. He just smirked and leaned around me, plucking the plastic-wrapped bathroom cups from where they sat by the mirror before he turned and made his way back toward the desk.

He popped the bottle of champagne while I dug through my suitcase for the t-shirt and panties I'd brought to sleep in. For a split second, I felt a little embarrassed at the thought of changing with him in the room, of parading about in just my underwear with him here.

But then I remembered he'd had me naked, on my knees, and making me prove to him how wet I was less than a week ago — and any embarrassment left me like the air from a quickly deflating balloon.

"You were great with her today," Will said as he carefully poured the two cups of champagne. It fizzed like crazy, so he alternated between the two in slow tilts of the bottle. "Ava."

I shimmied out of the dress, carefully hanging it in my closet like the priceless gem it was before I stripped out of the panties and bra I'd worn all day. Deciding it would be disgusting to sleep like this, I turned on the water for the shower and stepped in.

I noted the way Will's back tensed a bit when he heard the sound, but he didn't turn around.

"Do you want me to leave and let you get changed?" he asked.

"Like you haven't seen me naked," I shot back, and then I stepped into the shower. "Just taking a quick one. Anyway, what do you mean *I* was good with her?" I asked, speaking loud over the water. "Did you not see the way she looked at you all day? I think you just secured father of the year."

Will didn't answer — or if he did, I didn't hear him. I quickly washed my body and my hair before climbing out of the shower and toweling off. I'd left my t-shirt and panties on the bathroom counter, and I slipped them on with a sigh before making my way to where Will sat at the desk.

He was watching me with his jaw tight, the little muscle in his cheek flexing as I strode over to him and snatched the cup of champagne his hand wasn't nearly folding in two with its vise grip.

"Thank you for this," I said, tilting it to my lips. The bubbles were light and refreshing, and combined with how I felt after a hot shower, I couldn't help but hum my delight.

Will was just staring at me, subtly shaking his head. "Fucking hell, woman."

"What?"

"Don't *what* me," he growled. "You just paraded your beautiful, wet, naked ass in front of me, and then the only thing you cover it with is this?" he asked, tugging at the hem of my thin, oversized t-shirt.

"I have panties on, too," I argued.

"Not for long, you don't."

Heat rushed along my neck as Will set his champagne to the side — which I was fairly certain he'd barely touched — and then his hands were on my hips, a needy intake of air rumbling through his throat as his fingers fisted in the fabric of my shirt and he pinned me against the desk.

"That so?" I asked, and I wished I sounded like a confident little tease, but the words came out breathy and light. "Because I was kind of thinking I'd have this glass of champagne and go to bed."

"Mm," Will mused, running the tip of his nose along my neck as I struggled to hold onto the cup of champagne in my hand, my eyes fluttering closed, neck arching to give him better access. "Tired?"

"Exhausted."

"Too exhausted for another lesson?"

His words rumbled right below my ear, and when he nipped at my earlobe, a wave of goosebumps shot from that point of contact all the way down to my toes. I couldn't hide how my body reacted to him, how my nipples hardened into peaks and my legs widened enough to let him slip his thigh between them.

I tilted my chin toward him, our lips hovering less than an inch apart. It was as if he were a magnet and I was a flimsy piece of metal, because I lurched toward him, lips on track for his, a desperate need to kiss him filling me in a way I couldn't ignore. I wanted to taste the sweet bubbles on his tongue, wanted to know what it would feel like dancing with mine.

I somehow managed to stop myself just before we made contact, and I rolled my lips together, swallowing. "What did you have in mind?"

He was so close, I couldn't read his expression, couldn't see his eyes clearly. But I could see his mouth, the way his lips parted, how his breath was as shaky as mine.

"Other than you, nothing much."

He dropped his mouth, narrowly missing mine as he kissed and licked along my chin, down the column of my neck and across my collarbone. I arched and moaned and gave up on trying to hold my champagne, setting it on the desk and sliding it out of reach so I wouldn't knock it over.

"Tell me what you want to learn," he urged, fisting my t-shirt in his hands.

My brain was shooting blanks.

I blinked over and over, trying to focus on a single thought past the fact that his tongue was gliding along my skin and his erection was pressing into my stomach.

"Well," I breathed. "My first time, I... it was missionary," I said, swallowing. "And then with you, I was on top."

"And what a vision it was," he growled against my skin, rocking his hips into me. I gasped at the sensation, at how hard I made him, at how he'd abandoned the champagne and any attempt at conversation the moment he saw my body because I'd undone him.

To have that kind of power...

"Maybe... perhaps we could try..." I reached for the words past the spell he was weaving on me with every touch, but my eyes rolled back, and a moan ripped through me when he palmed my breast through the fine fabric of my t-shirt at the same time his thigh rubbed between mine.

"You want to test out some new positions," he guessed.

"That," I confirmed on a breathless nod.

I thought I felt his lips curl against my skin, and then his hands slid roughly up under my t-shirt, piling the fabric on his wrists until I had no choice but to lift my arms and let him strip it overhead.

He groaned when I was bared to him, flinging the shirt somewhere behind him as his eyes raked over me. He plucked at the band of my boy shorts next, but I pressed my hands into his chest and shoved him backward.

"You first. I'm more naked than you."

He arched a brow. "Then fix it."

I swallowed, holding my chin high to feign the confidence I wasn't sure I felt as I stepped forward to meet him. Mirroring his movement, I slid my hands under his shirt, and the moment my hands pressed against his hard, muscled abdomen, he shivered and groaned.

I smiled, biting my lip as I pushed the fabric up to reveal him inch by blissful inch. "I love the sounds you make when I touch you."

"Well, I love when you touch me, so we're even."

I wasn't as fluid as he was at undressing someone, but when I got the t-shirt up to his chest, he took over for me, reaching behind him with one hand to grab the neck of his shirt and rip it the rest of the way off. He reached for me as soon as it was gone, large, strong hands sliding into my hair as he tilted my head the way he wanted it so he could kiss and bite along the slope of my neck again.

"You better not leave any hickies," I warned.

"Or what?"

To prove he wasn't scared of my threat, he bit down hard and sucked my skin between his teeth until I hissed and arched into the touch.

Okay, maybe I was completely *fine* with a hickie, actually.

Maybe I liked the thought of him wanting to mark me like that, to claim me in a way that was so public and feral.

No.

I mentally slapped myself as all the advice from my internet friends on *Reddit* surfaced in my brain.

This was how I'd get hurt.

Thoughts like that was how I'd muddy the already shallow water we were swimming in.

To punctuate that slap, I tore away from his touch, sliding my fingers into the band of his joggers and briefs and pulling them down together in one fell swoop.

His cock sprang forward when I did, and because I'd taken his pants all the way down to his ankles, I was face to face with the monstrous thing.

I swallowed, taking in every inch of it before I glanced up at Will.

The corner of his lips lifted, but his eyes were heated and heavy, his chest rising and falling rapidly as he took in the sight of me below him.

I didn't give him the chance to kick out of the pants. Instead, I dropped to my knees, wrapped him in my fist, and swirled my tongue around his crown before he could make a single move.

"Jesus Christ," he gasped, one hand flying to the bed behind him to steady himself as the other reached into my hair and gripped tight. He held me still for a moment, not allowing me to move, like he was afraid he'd come in my mouth right then and there if I did. "Woman."

I pulled back and looked up at him innocently. "What?"

With a growl, he pulled me up by the arms and tossed me onto the bed as if I weighed nothing. He looked almost pissed as he stepped out of his pants, and then he was descending on me, climbing up the bed between my legs with a wicked gleam in his eye.

"*I* get first taste," he said, and then he used his shoulders to spread my thighs wide, kissing and biting along my inner thighs. "Understand?"

"Yes, sir," I breathed, writhing beneath him.

"You said those same words to me the first time you came to the rink, you know," he mused, nosing my clit before he teased me with one feather-light lick. "Made me want to fuck you against the glass and give you a thousand reasons to say them."

His confession unleashed a gasp, and then his tongue wrenched a moan from deep inside me as he dragged it from my opening up to my clit. He hummed with the motion, the vibration adding to the pleasure, and my legs shook as he repeated the movement again and again.

"So fucking sweet," he said, fingers digging into my thighs to hold me still as he worked between them. He sucked my clit the way I'd told him I liked during our last lesson, the little pulses driving my orgasm to the surface faster than I thought was possible.

"No," I whined, wiggling away from him.

He stilled, arching a brow at me. "No?"

"I don't want to come like this."

Will slowed his perusal, but still licked and kissed me in lazy sweeps. "How do you want to come, Chloe?"

When he said my name, a shiver rocked through me, and I rolled my fingers over my hard nipples as if *my* touch could do anything to relieve the ache there.

"I want you to fuck me, Will," I panted, squirming, confidence soaring through me when those words elicited a groan from him. "I want you to fill me up."

His groan was deep and guttural, one I felt echoing through my bones as he kissed his way slowly up my body.

He let his lips graze my thighs, my hips, my stomach, and breasts before he settled on top of me.

For a long moment, he stared down at me, his eyes flicking between mine as the playfulness slowly disappeared from his gaze. One hand swept the hair from my face, and he thumbed my jaw.

"I didn't get the chance to tell you how beautiful you looked today," he said.

My heart thumped twice hard in my chest, a dangerous percussion that I wanted to lean into as much as I wanted to run from screaming.

"It's just makeup," I whispered.

"No," he said instantly, shaking his head, his eyes following the trail his thumb lined on my lip. "It's just *you*."

The words had no sooner left his lips before he was kissing along my neck, and I had no choice but to bow off the bed and into his touch. Soft moans and breaths leaked out of me unbidden, and I savored every little touch of his skin against mine until he rolled off me long enough to retrieve a condom from his joggers.

My pulse picked up as I watched him sheath himself, the imagery hotter than I ever knew it could be. I always pictured a nervous, fumbling college boy hurrying to put a condom on before he rushed to what was next. But Will was slow and purposeful with every move he made, and this was no exception. He kept his eyes fixed on mine, his lips parting as he rolled the latex in place and groaned at the feeling of his fist around his shaft.

It lit me up from my very core, and I squirmed under his gaze, desperate to be connected again.

"You're going to need to use your words again," he told me as he crawled back onto the bed. He braced his knees between my thighs, opening me wide for him. "Tell me what you like, what you don't. We can try as many positions as you want."

"What about you?" I asked breathlessly. "What position feels good for you?"

"I promise, I'll be able to come no matter how I fuck you, Chloe," he husked. "Right now, I'm more focused on *not* coming until you do."

I bit my lip on a smirk. *Why* was that so hot, to know I could conjure that worry in his mind, that there was even a chance of it.

Will's eyes were hooded and dark as he lifted one of my ankles to his shoulder. He kissed along the inside of the soft skin there before hiking my other leg up, too. Then, he pressed forward, his hands framing my shoulders as his erection pressed against the back of my thighs.

It was a delicious stretch, and my heart galloped as he kissed the inside arch of my foot with a mischievous gleam in his eyes. "This okay?"

I nodded.

"Words."

"Yes," I breathed.

Balancing on one hand, he reached between us with the other, and I felt him align his crown at my entrance. He toyed with me first, sliding himself up and down through my wet slit before he notched himself in just a centimeter — enough to hold him there as he placed his hand on the bed again.

His eyes held mine as he flexed his hips, and I gasped at the first inch, the searing pain of stretching to fit him blurring with the mind-numbing pleasure of feeling him penetrate me. I didn't miss how his eyes flared at my reaction, at how he seemed to grow even harder inside me.

"Okay?" he asked.

"Yes," I breathed, and I palmed his ass in my hands, pulling him in deeper.

We groaned in unison as he slid another inch, and then he pulled out, my body instantly craving the fullness of him before he edged himself back in. He was deeper this time, and I moaned and released my grip on him to twist my hands in the comforter, instead.

Again and again, he withdrew and flexed, filling me more and more each time. When he was fully seated, he stayed there for a long moment, both of us breathing hard and soaking in the way it felt to be rooted together.

"Perfect fucking fit," he growled against my calf, biting the flesh as he withdrew his hips and flexed all the way in again. "Like you were meant for me. Like this cunt was made in my honor."

"Jesus," I whispered, eyes rolling up to the ceiling as he rocked in hard enough to make me see stars. "It feels so good."

"You feel tight as fuck like this," he said, and he picked up his pace, pumping in and out of me with my legs rested on his shoulders, my body bending in half. "You always feel so fucking tight."

I loved the position, the way he hit deep with every thrust. I loved watching his dark eyes as he flexed into me, the way his mouth opened, and groans of ecstasy slipped through him.

But I needed... *something*.

"Talk to me," he coached.

I bit my lip and frowned, trying to figure it out. "I want to touch myself."

"Mm," he mused. "You want to rub your clit while I fuck you?"

"Yes," I whimpered, my cheeks flaming, and Will pressed up onto his knees. He grabbed my ankles, keeping my legs hiked but spreading them wide and continuing his rhythmic thrusts.

Fuck.

This view completely demolished the one before it.

Now, I could watch the roll of his body when he fucked me, how his abdominal muscles flexed and released with every pump. I felt his grip on my ankles, his eyes raking over my newly exposed flesh. We both watched together as my breasts bounced each time he slid into me, and I moaned when I finally allowed myself to touch them, to roll my nipples in my fingertips and stir my climax closer to the edge.

"*God*, yes, baby," Will groaned, feral and unhinged. "Play with those beautiful fucking tits for me."

Baby.

The nickname made a shock of electricity shoot right to my pussy. It was so intimate and sweet, and yet somehow, he said it in such a filthy way that it unraveled me. It was like he wanted me to be his, or like I already was.

I gave in to the position, letting my eyes close and my neck arch before one hand reached down between my legs and stroked my clit. I fired up to life easily, and I knew without much testing that I could come like this. I could come *right now* if I wanted to.

But I didn't.

I wanted to play, to experiment, to learn.

Instantly, I pulled my hands back, my chest heaving, orgasm cresting only to recede again with a frustrated howl.

"I like this," I breathed. "But I want to try something else."

Will smirked. "You edging yourself, baby?"

I didn't even know what the fuck that meant, but I could guess, and when I nodded, Will hummed his approval in a kiss against my ankle. Slowly, he released me, lying down on the bed next to me before helping me climb into his lap.

Except I didn't straddle him normally.

Instead, he maneuvered me until I was facing away from him, my knees spread over his hips, hands bracing just above his knees on his thick, muscular thighs.

"I want to watch this ass bounce as you ride me," he said, palming said ass in two lush handfuls. He gripped hard and groaned as he made me jiggle, and then his hand came down in a quick slap that made me gasp and arch and writhe.

I tried not to remember much about my first sexual experience, but one thing I could never forget was how that boy had eviscerated me and my reputation afterward. I could still hear him telling his friends that he'd fucked a fat girl and it wasn't that bad. I could still vividly remember his face when I took my clothes off, how he hadn't wanted to look too long.

It had taken me a long time to come back to loving my body after that, but I did. I loved myself fiercely. I found so much beauty in my thickness, in my curves and rolls. I was like Aphrodite, damn it.

And I knew without a second thought that Will felt the same way.

He appreciated me with every look, every touch, every taste.

"Sit on me," he begged, guiding my hips until I felt the crown of him pressing inside me. I was so wet from him fucking me before that I slid down easily, and we both groaned at the reconnection, his hands roaming over my hips and ass before he slowly started to help me move.

I liked this position, too. It felt completely different than the one before it — I wasn't quite as full, but the friction of my clit against his balls every time I rocked my hips was so fucking good I didn't miss the deeper connection.

At first, I used my thighs to really lift and sit, but eventually, the rub of my clit against him was too exquisite to deny myself. I sat more fully, rocking on him and feeling his cock deep and seated inside me.

"I could definitely come like this," I breathed.

Will moaned and bucked into me, and *that* sent him deep enough to make me gasp.

"*Yes*," I breathed. "Like that."

He thrust again, taking the work off me as I focused on finding that sweet contact that coaxed my orgasm to the surface. I felt it burning up my veins, my blood pumping faster, heart racing as the edges of my vision blurred.

But before it could catch, I lifted, hovering above him with my legs shaking and a whimpering cry wrenching from my throat. My orgasm was already coming, the beginning of it tingling through me, and now that I'd stopped all contact, my body was convulsing in protest.

"Fucking hell, Chloe," Will said, sitting up to wrap his arms around me. He palmed my breasts and kissed along my spine. "You're torturing yourself."

"I want more."

"More?"

"Another position."

He smiled against my shoulder blade. "Masochistic little thing."

But he answered my plea, flipping me back into the mattress with another appreciative smack of my ass. This time, he had me on my stomach, and he kissed down my back, over my hips, and along each swell of my ass before he hiked my hips up.

I arched my back, knees planted against the mattress but my face still in the pillows as he fit himself to me. He played with me again, sliding his crown between my lips and running it up and down before wedging himself inside me.

He slid in hard and fast and deep — so fucking deep I cried out and fisted the sheets like I'd spiral into space if I didn't hold onto them for dear life.

"Fuck," I screamed, but a moan rode out of me on the next breath. "So deep."

Will groaned his agreement, withdrawing and flexing inside me all the way to the hilt again. It stole my breath when he did. He was so impossibly deep like this, enough so that I felt him hitting edges inside me never before touched.

"Too much?" he asked, slowing his pace.

"No," I said. "Yes. Maybe?"

Will kept his pace slow and even for a while to let me adjust, and then he pressed his weight into me from behind until I had no choice but to drop to the bed. I was flat on my stomach, but then he hiked my left knee up toward my chest, using his knees to spread me wide.

As soon as he slid inside me again, I knew this was the jackpot.

My hips were lifted just enough from my knee being perched for me to slide my hand down and rub my clit in slow, torturous circles. Will balanced on the hand behind me while using the other to snake under me and fondle my breast. We both moaned when he palmed me, testing the weight, and then he was toying with my nipple and flexing into me in slow, smooth, steady pumps.

"Oh, *fuck*," I breathed. "This. *God*, this."

Will was speechless now, his face twisted up as he pressed his forehead against the back of my head. I was arching and reaching for him, and he seemed to be doing everything he could not to come.

That spurred me on.

I rubbed my clit with more pressure, rocking into my hand each time Will rocked into me. He was so deep, and he was *everywhere* — his lips kissing my hair, his hand massaging my breast, his cock filling me with enough depth to bring stars to the edge of my vision.

This time, my orgasm crept up slowly, like it wasn't sure if I was teasing it again, like it didn't trust me to let it loose. But the more it came on, the more it took over, the less control I had.

It prickled my skin at first, and then numbed my toes and fingers, working slowly toward my core. Heat battled with ice in my veins. Pleasure sparked so electric that I cried out, chasing the sensation, my hand wild between my legs as my entire body trembled with the effort to catch the fire.

And then the earth shook, a star exploded in the universe of my soul, and I came like I'd never come before.

It almost hurt at first, and I whimpered Will's name as he grunted and kept his pace to drive me home. On the heels of that pain was the most consuming pleasure I'd ever experienced, the kind that swallows you whole and takes you to another realm. I moaned and screamed his name, begging for more as much as I willed it to stop — but the waves kept coming, crashing over me again and again until I was drowning and shaking and pleading for air.

"*Fuck*, Chloe," Will groaned in my ear, and then he plunged deep, spawning on the last of my climax just as he caught his own. I wanted to live inside a cave with the sounds he let loose, to hear those moans and pants of ecstasy echoing off the walls of my heart forevermore.

I loved to undo him. I lived for that rush of power and pleasure as he spilled inside the condom, inside *me*, his shoulders taut, arms trembling, breath sawing in and out of him in uneven bursts.

Eventually, he stilled, and I collapsed into the bed, heaving and sweating and smiling like a fucking loon. I moaned when Will flexed inside me one last time, and then he withdrew, both of us hissing at the loss.

He rolled onto the bed beside me, and I creaked one eye open, smile widening as I took in the sight of him breathing so hard it was like he'd just played two back-to-back games.

"Jesus fucking Christ, woman," he cursed, one hand on his chest and the other sweeping through his hair. He let his head fall to the side, eyes wide like I was insane. "I think you might be the death of me."

I just giggled, kicking my feet with the soreness of him still lingering between my thighs.

"Thanks for the lesson, coach," I said, lifting up onto my elbows to wink at him.

He groaned, thumbing my chin as his eyes raked over me. It had to be a sight — my cleavage against the bed, my face pink from being freshly fucked.

"Pretzel."

"Excuse me?"

"That's the name of the position," he mused. "Pretzel."

"Pretzel," I echoed, and my tongue skated out to taste his thumb when he ran it over my bottom lip. "I definitely like that one."

"I can see that," he mused. "And the others?"

"I liked them, too."

"I'm beginning to wonder if there's anything you don't like."

When you leave.

The words danced on the tip of my tongue, twirling against the back of my teeth and begging to be set free.

I swallowed them down, instead.

We were quiet for a long while before Will made the first move, groaning his way out of the sheets before he was helping me stand, too. We showered together, and just like the last time, he washed my body and my hair as I moaned and leaned into his strong, gentle touch.

But as soon as we were dry, he was dressing.

As soon as he was dressed, he was gone.

And as soon as he was gone, my mind was racing, heart aching, every cell in my body warning me that I was lying to myself.

I told him I could do this.

I told him I didn't want anything more.

But the voices of my matriarchy were being drowned out more and more by the voice inside me screaming that he could be different, that this didn't have to have rules, that *we* could be more.

And I didn't need *Reddit* to tell me how stupid and delirious those thoughts were.

Chapter 26

House of Matches

Will

I was sick.

And not just in the way that I knew already — which was that I couldn't get Chloe out of my head, not for a single fucking second.

I was playing with fire when it came to this little arrangement of ours. I kept my heart guarded about as securely as a raggedy old wooden fence would, because no matter how I tried to put distance between us, I couldn't help but give in to the desperation I felt to get closer.

No, I wasn't just that kind of sick.

I was *sick* sick — as in down with the goddamn flu.

This was what I got for going to a theme park in the middle of cold season, I supposed.

I'd been relatively fortunate over the years as a dad, all things considered. Somehow, even when Ava brought home germs from school, I managed to tough it out. I could play with a stuffy nose or a headache. I could even suffer with a fever and a stomach bug.

But the flu was something Coach didn't fuck with.

The last thing he wanted was for anyone else on the team to catch it, for a group of us to be down with body aches, fatigue, and a fever. I'd seen guys play even *days after* having the flu, and it was hardly ever to their full capacity.

And so, when I'd shown up to practice sick as a fucking dog three days after Disney, Coach had ordered me to see the team doctor. I thought they'd tell me the same as usual — it's a virus, hydrate and rest and don't push too hard.

Instead, I'd tested positive for influenza, and I'd been sent home without the option to stay even if I wanted to.

And I did. I *needed* to stay, to be at practice, to be on the flight to our next away game.

We had twenty games left of the regular season.

Twenty.

In hockey, that might as well have been one.

The race for the playoffs was too fucking tight for me to be out. It was almost impossible for us *not* to make the playoffs at this point, but these next twenty games could mean the difference in having home ice advantage and top seeds versus being a wildcard.

That's how close the teams in our division were. That's how much every game mattered at this point.

I'd thrown a fit when Coach told me to leave. I'd been even more pissed when I missed our away game against Pittsburgh and we lost. It didn't matter that my backup played great, that it really wasn't his fault for the L. I still felt the responsibility of it weighing on me.

As it was, I was laid up on the couch on my final rest day, grumpier than I ever had been and scowling at the television as I played the latest episode of *Jeopardy*.

I had clearance to return tomorrow, as long as I was feeling better. And to be honest, Coach and I both knew that even if I *wasn't* feeling better, I'd still be there.

Fortunately, I actually was on the mend, my body aches less severe, fever lowering, cough receding, throat no longer making it feel like I was swallowing razor blades.

I knew I had Chloe to thank.

When I'd been sent home, she'd launched into action like a nurse, forcing me into bed and bringing me everything I could possibly want or need to recover. She'd insisted Chef Patel not come to the house, to prevent her from getting sick, too. That meant Chloe was cooking for us. She'd also taken over completely with Ava, on top of teaching five days a week, and had cleaned the house with disinfectant more in the last few days than I'd ever done in the years I'd lived here.

"The last thing you need is for Ava to get sick next," she'd warned my first sick day home, wiping down the TV remote with a Lysol wipe.

And I'd tried not to give in to my urge to pull her into me, to thank her with an embrace since my words were fucking broken.

It was such as simple act of care, but the fact that she wanted to keep my daughter well, that she was considerate of Chef, that she so easily stepped up to the plate to handle everything I would have worried about... it was something I'd never take for granted.

But unfortunately for me, Chloe *also* didn't want the flu, and she kept her distance — physically, anyway — and made sure to wash her hands thoroughly after any time she came into my vicinity.

Perhaps that was what pissed me off most about this entire scenario.

Here I was, home, no practice, no games, no responsibilities... and I couldn't even spend my time fucking Chloe into oblivion.

It was hard to think about anything else after our night in Orlando. I had been plagued by the image of her riding me reverse cowgirl ever since, haunted by the way her legs shook violently when they were hitched on my shoulders, and she denied herself a climax in the name of testing other positions. I could close my eyes and still feel how she tightened around me when she finally relented, could replay the most intense orgasm of my life as I let myself follow behind her, both of us gripping onto each other tight and riding out the waves.

The flu wasn't the most dangerous part of this situation.

No, it was that Chloe was taking care of me, and that I couldn't help myself but to talk to her when she brought me food or ran a hot bath on my behalf.

I'd spent the last three days laid up, but I'd also spent them learning her.

She told me about her days at college, about how she had wanted to be a teacher for longer than she could remember. I listened intently as she told both hilarious and horrifying stories of her early teaching days, and I memorized the way her eyes grew distant when she talked about some of her troubled students who stayed in her heart still.

I asked about sewing and her strange fascination with true crime podcasts. She pulled up photos on her phone of what she called her early "Pinterest fails" before she started figuring things out. I passed the time with eager questions, never feeling like I knew enough.

What was even more terrifying was that I opened up to her, too.

I told myself it was the fog of having the flu that loosened my lips, but I'd be a lying sonofabitch if I said I didn't want to share with her every time she shared with me. I didn't shy away when she asked about my early hockey days, or my mom, or the strained relationship with my father. I smiled when I told her about Uncle Mitch, how he'd stepped in when Dad had gone hollow. I chomped at the bit to tell her about playing in college, about my first years bouncing back and forth between the AHL and the NHL.

I didn't even shy away when she asked about how I was after Jenny died.

I told her everything — from the way I broke down and nearly lost my spot on the team to how I rose above the grief and became the best version of myself on the ice.

But how I felt like I'd lost myself as a father in the process.

Every new story she shared with me, I felt my heart crack. Every story I shared with her, I felt the crack widen. Over and over again, the cycle repeated, and I found myself making room for her to slither in, to make a nest, to make a home.

I found myself wanting to make a home in her, too.

And then, like the colossal asshole I was — I'd shut down.

I didn't know why Chloe stayed. One moment, we'd be talking and she'd be laughing and I'd be leaning in for more. The next, fear would spike through me, the memory of Jenny so fresh in my soul that I couldn't escape it.

It was a trauma response too significant to play off, one no amount of therapy or self-awareness could fix.

I was just... fucked. There was no way around it.

And I knew I was hurting her.

When we had sex, I left immediately after. When the talks got too deep, I'd close myself off to her and be a grumpy sonofabitch until she left me alone. I wasn't too blind to see the hope in her eyes turn to disheartened pain every time this happened, but I was too emotionally stunted to do a damn thing about it.

My brain would beat me senseless as soon as I was by myself, reminding me with every menacing thought that I could wind up back where I was four years ago if I wasn't careful.

That was always enough to sober me.

I couldn't go back to that man. I couldn't risk losing my team, my daughter, all because I couldn't keep myself in check.

More than that, I couldn't bear the thought of fucking everything up so royally that Chloe wanted to quit.

Because even if *I* could survive her leaving, I wasn't sure I could say the same for Ava.

My daughter loved her. I knew that without needing to hear it. It was in every mannerism of my little girl... from the way she held Chloe's hand to the way she said goodnight.

As it stood, Chloe and I had an understanding. We both agreed what we were and what we were not, what we never would be.

If I could stick to that, we would all be okay.

So, I vowed to remind myself of that fact every chance I got.

I could have her in this small way, but I had to keep my head on straight. I had to protect my daughter, protect Chloe, protect myself.

This was a house of matches that was one wrong move from going up in flames.

I was only half-focused on the television as Ken Jennings read the four-hundred-dollar answer in the category the contestant had chosen. He said something about a right-wing group from the 40s named after the first Cold War victim, and I mumbled, "What is the John Birch Society?" at the same time as the contestant.

There was no joy when Ken confirmed the contestant and I were both right. I just blew my nose and let the tissue fall to the ground beside me, my nose so raw now I wanted to die every time I touched it.

I was ready to climb into bed, but wanted to make sure Ava got down okay before I did. Chloe had gone upstairs more than an hour ago to get her settled.

Another ten minutes of the show went by. I was fast-forwarding through a commercial break when suddenly, music thumped from a speaker upstairs.

It was a Mia Love song, loud and obnoxious as ever. I frowned, ready to grump for them to turn it down, that it was too late for this shit. But the music grew louder and louder, like the speaker was moving toward me.

And indeed, it was.

I looked up at the top of the stairs just in time to find Chloe and Ava strutting down in matching costumes — which consisted of dresses made with more pink sequins than should have ever existed in the whole *world,* let alone this house. They even had matching shoes, which were god-awful turquoise house slippers in the shape of a... narwhal?

Ava barely contained her giggles as they danced down the steps in sync, hopping down two steps before they'd wiggle their hips and back up one step, then repeat. Chloe held onto the speaker while Ava held onto the railing.

They both about lost it when they saw my face.

But the show continued, and as much as I wanted to keep my scowl in place, it was impossible to do when I saw my daughter like that. How long had I wished for a lightness in her, for her to be a fucking *kid*?

Chloe had released that side of her in mere weeks.

When they made it to the living room, Chloe set the speaker on the coffee table before hurriedly running back to her place next to Ava. It was just in time for the bridge, and they looked at each other, nodding their head as if counting down the beat.

As soon as the chorus began, they broke out in a synchronized dance.

It started with them hopping up into the air and crossing their feet. When they landed, they used their new position to do a swivel turn and wink at me over their shoulders. The chorus was something about being a woman in a man's world, about being unapologetic and loud and weird. Chloe and Ava hit some new move with every word, including a twisted-up version of the hand jive along to the lyrics *kick some ass*. When that final word sounded, they both covered their mouths with wide eyes instead of lip-synching it.

At this point, the TV remote lay abandoned by my side, the episode fast-forwarded all the way to the end on the television. I watched with amusement bubbling through me as the two weirdos continued dancing, each move more bizarre than the last.

Chloe stood behind Ava, both of them straight as a board, and then they broke out into opposite waves, thumbs over their shoulders and goofy grins on their faces.

When they hopped up only to somersault in opposite directions, the music grew to a crescendo, and the finale came with Chloe encouraging Ava to run at her. My daughter leapt with a mix of fear and unfaltering trust in her little eyes, and Chloe grabbed her wrists, swinging her up and onto her shoulders in a feat that made my jaw drop. It was like an acrobatic circus move or a swing dance — maybe a combo of the two.

They threw their hands up in victory as the song ended, and then there they were, both of them panting in the middle of the living room with their final poses held strong.

It lasted only a second before Chloe was helping Ava off her shoulders, and they were high-fiving each other and squealing over how they'd done it, they'd pulled it off, they'd even nailed the landing. Chloe held onto Ava's hands as she bounced excitedly around her, eyes wide as she replayed the whole routine like it hadn't just happened.

And my chest locked.

I thought it was a heart attack at first, and I bolted up from where I was reclined on the couch, clutching my abdomen as the unfamiliar sensation seared through me.

But before true concern could set in, a strange noise barked out of me.

A laugh.

A... *laugh*.

It rattled the rust off my rib cage, the first roll of it shocking me.

And then the girls pivoted toward me, their necks nearly snapping in the process. Their eyes were wide, their conversation and excitement muted.

And I laughed again.

I bent at the waist, coughing a bit like my body didn't fucking remember how to do this properly. That made me laugh even harder, my hands braced on my knees, eyes watering.

God.

I was laughing.

Really laughing.

I peeked at Chloe and Ava, who stood completely still and gaping at me in the middle of the room. It sent another rip through me, and I fell over sideways on the couch, clutching my stomach as I laughed and laughed and laughed.

It hurt as much as it healed. It was as painful as it was a relief.

I didn't know I even *could* laugh anymore.

But here I was, unable to keep it together after a ridiculous dance routine put on by my daughter and her nanny.

I was still trying and failing to school myself when the girls blinked and looked at each other.

"Daddy's laughing," Ava whispered, shaking her head. Then, her eyes doubled in size, the biggest grin I'd ever seen spreading on her face as she started jumping with Chloe's hands in hers. "Daddy's *laughing!*"

They squealed together before they were barreling toward me, and I held up a hand, unable to tell them through the fit of laughter to stay away from me. I was still sick, even though I probably wasn't contagious anymore.

But they didn't care.

They tackled me, Ava flinging her arms around my neck as Chloe squeezed me in a tight hug around my waist.

I shook with a laugh that was nearly silent now, like an old wheezing man who couldn't catch his breath. And there we were, a pile of giggles on the fucking couch as Ava and Chloe tickled me and squealed and celebrated like we'd just won the Stanley Cup.

In many ways, I knew this was even better.

"You're laughing, Daddy! You're laughing!" Ava squeezed me tight.

"I can't believe it," Chloe mused, releasing me to sit back on her heels and wipe the tears from her eyes. She stared at me for a moment longer of disbelief, and then she jumped up, thrusting her finger into the air like a superhero. "I'm baking a cake!"

"I'll help!" Ava yelled instantly, jumping off my lap to chase after Chloe as she ran toward the kitchen.

"I think this calls for Funfetti," Chloe said, pulling a box from the pantry. "Wouldn't you say?"

"And *tons* of sprinkles!" Ava confirmed.

Then, she whipped around, her little eyes on me before she sprinted toward where I was still trying to gain my composure. She grabbed my hands in hers and tugged until I stood, and then she was dragging me to the kitchen.

"Come on, Daddy! We're baking a cake!"

"It's a school night," I said pathetically, blinking away the tears that laughing had formed in my eyes.

Chloe and Ava both protested against my weak argument, and I threw up my hands in surrender, sliding into a barstool at the island to watch them bake.

As Ava measured out ingredients, Chloe's gaze caught mine over her head, a sense of wonder in her brown eyes. She smirked, shaking her head, her cheeks shading the prettiest pink.

And my heart sank to my feet.

Because in that moment, on a seemingly insignificant Sunday night, I felt the power of something I thought I'd never experience in my life.

Family.

Chapter 27

Noah Balboa

Chloe

It was a warm, sunny day about a week after Will was feeling better that we ambushed him with a barbecue at the house.

He was grumpy about it for all of ten minutes, glaring at me and Arushi for our role in it all while his teammates carried in coolers full of beer and meat. But a few kisses on the cheek from Maven, Livia, and Grace, combined with Ava being *supremely* thrilled that she had swim buddies for the day, made the frown between his brows slowly disappear.

The guys had practice earlier in the day, but had the rest of the afternoon and evening off before tomorrow's practice. Then, they'd be on a flight to Atlanta.

I didn't know how they did it, how I could look around the backyard and find so many seemingly calm and collected men when I knew they felt the stress of the season weighing on them. Then again, they loved hockey. This team was like their family.

And the Cup was within reach.

I knew that was driving Will, and I imagined it was the same with all the guys. Tampa hadn't won the whole thing since early in the 2000s, even though our team had had many winning seasons.

Maybe this was the year.

Carter Fabri had flown in from New York for a few days, making the most of a break he had in his AHL season. It was my first time meeting the kid I'd heard Will refer to as the closest thing he had to an annoying little brother, and I adored him within the first ten minutes.

He was like a giant golden retriever.

He smiled wide and unapologetically. He goofed around like he didn't have a care in the world. Where Vince and Jaxson were cocksure and Will was grumpy, Carter was kind and funny and sweet.

Presently, he and I were in the pool with Ava, playing a very intense game of Marco Polo that had her bursting into a fit of giggles every time Carter managed to evade her. She'd call out *Marco*, he'd call back *Polo*, and when she'd launch herself across the water, he'd skate away just in time for her to hear his splash.

It was absolutely adorable.

Around us, the party was in full swing. Music wafted over the pool from speakers above the outside kitchen. Chef Patel was on the grill, clamping her tongs at any man who tried to take her place, while the rest of the crew either worked on setting up sides, snacked on the appetizers we had out, or chatted away in the shade of one of the many umbrellas.

Grace was in Jaxson's lap in a lounge chair, both of them soaking up the sun and struggling to keep their hands — and mouths — off each other.

It wasn't until Vince went by and flicked Jaxson hard on the ear that they broke apart.

When Arushi called Ava up to eat, I helped her dry off, high-fiving Carter before he ambled toward the guys, and I made my way to where the girls were congregating around a bottle of champagne on ice. Livia poured a tall flute for me and handed it to me as soon as I arrived under the shady pavilion, wrapping a beach towel around me.

"For you, beautiful," she said, bowing a little as the glass left her hand and slid into mine. "You are too cute with her, by the way."

"Seriously. I think that little girl's eyes turn to stars when she looks at you," Grace offered with a smile and lift of her sun-kissed cheeks.

I took a sip of the champagne, all of us watching where Chef was helping Ava pile her plate up.

"She's the best kid," I said softly.

"Truly," Maven agreed. "And I'm not sure I've *ever* seen that man so happy."

She nodded to where Will was standing in a circle with Carter, Vince, and Jaxson. Vince was showing them some kind of golf stance before Jaxson jabbed him hard in the ribs and nearly sent him toppling into the pool.

When Will laughed, the girls gasped, and I didn't miss how the guys balked at their goalie.

"Did he... did he just *laugh*?" Livia asked, blinking. She looked like a million dollars, white bikini blazing against her rich brown skin, nails painted a glossy red, gold hoops hanging from her ears and a body chain that matched draping from her neck down to her hips.

"He's been doing that all day," Grace said, shaking her head. "Jaxson and I were talking about it. Specifically, about how that never happened before *this one* came along."

She nudged me in the hip, drawing my attention back to them. When I saw the way they were all smirking at me, I flushed.

"Oh, stop," I said, waving them off, but I couldn't hide my victorious grin at the sight. I'd accomplished my mission of making that grumpy oaf laugh, and now that I had, it seemed he couldn't *quit* laughing.

It was the best.

"No, *you* stop," Maven said, her smoky voice teasing and light. "Girl, we are not blind."

"Or stupid," Livia added with a tilt of her glass to her lips.

"That man can't keep his eyes off you. And you light up like a sky of fireworks every time you catch him looking." Maven folded one arm over her lean stomach, balancing the elbow of her other arm on her wrist with the champagne flute hanging daintily from her fingers. "Care to share with the class what *that's* all about?"

Shit.

I hoped the panic I felt racing through me didn't show on my face, that the roll of my eyes and easy smile on my lips was convincing. One of Will's number one rules was that no one find out about us.

And no matter how badly I yearned for advice from these girls, I wouldn't betray his wish.

Even though I desperately wanted to. I wanted to pull them to the side and divulge every detail. I wanted to see if *they* could figure him out, if they could tell me why one minute he was worshipping my body and laughing in my sheets and asking about my life, only to shut down and run from me in the next breath.

I wondered if they would know the layout of this game better than I did, if they'd be able to see something I didn't.

Because everything in my body, heart, mind, and soul said that Will Perry wanted more from me than just sex, that *we* were more than just sex.

But any time I'd lean too far into that belief, he'd remind me with his words, with his actions that we had a deal.

And that deal was sex and sex only.

"Listen," I said, lowering my voice and leaning in like I had a big secret.

The girls all widened their eyes and leaned in, too, ready for me to spill.

"I don't think there is a woman on the *planet* who does not think that man is hot," I said on a laugh. "Including me. So, yes, sometimes I blush a little when he looks at me. Can you blame a girl?"

"Hell no," Livia said. "That man has Daddy Energy in more ways than one, if you know what I'm saying."

Maven rolled her eyes and elbowed her best friend. "Okay, so... are you two... you know?" She waggled her brows.

And I *prayed* I was putting on the best show of my life when I shook my head on a smile, glancing at Will before pulling my attention back to them.

"He's my boss, nothing more. I'm here for Ava. And honestly, I'm just glad I could prove to him that he could find a nanny who doesn't want anything from him, because I'm pretty sure he was convinced that wasn't possible."

The girls all deflated in sync, which made me laugh. Grace was even pouting a little as she took a sip of her champagne.

"Well, as much as I wished for a different answer to

that," Maven said with a sigh. "I'm actually really happy to hear that response. Will... he's quiet, you know? He doesn't really let anyone in. But we all knew he needed help for a long time. We all knew he was struggling."

"And now that he has you?" Grace smiled, squeezing my arm. "He's a completely different person."

I returned her smile, cheeks heating as I glanced over my shoulder at Will.

I froze when I realized he'd been watching me, too.

The guys were talking, but he stared right through the gap of Carter and Jaxson's heads, his eyes pinning me in place.

"I feel the same way," I said honestly.

My heart rate spiked when Will smiled at me like he knew what I was saying even from across the pool.

And then I blew out a breath and turned back to the girls. "This has been life changing for me. I have Ava, Will, Arushi — and you three," I said, poking each of them with a smile. "I've never had girlfriends before."

"Aw," Grace said, wrapping me up in a tight hug for what a slight little thing she was. "I feel this so hard. I was the same way before finding this crew."

"Well, you're one of us now. Even if Will messes things up, you'll always have the girls," Maven promised.

"Yeah. Like if he *messes up* your bed sheets," Livia murmured. "Or your hair, or your—"

Maven pinched her, and I smiled, shaking my head.

"Chloe is a professional," Grace said, waving her shoulders side to side. "Besides," she added with a wicked grin my way. "She's got *Noah*."

Livia and Maven shared mischievous looks, and now the three of them were bouncing on their heels waiting for me to update them on the hot teacher at school.

317

The hot, non-existent teacher and a story I had yet to come up with.

But I pretended to melt away from them in a shy smile, hiding my face until they were begging for details.

Anything to steer them away from the truth.

• • •

Will

Chloe was impossible to ignore on an average day, but on a hot, sunny one in nothing but a black bikini custom-fitted to her incredible body?

I was fucking ruined.

I couldn't keep my eyes off her and I knew it. From when she was playing with Ava in the pool to when she was laughing with the girls as they drank champagne and snacked on fruit, my gaze was glued to her.

I thought I'd gotten away with it, that I was somehow slicker than I felt because no one had called me out yet. But just when I was confident in that, Carter had to go and ruin it all.

The large group of us ate at the long outdoor dining table under the shade by the grill. I forced Arushi to join us, especially after she worked so hard all day on not just hamburgers, but steak and ribs that were out of this world.

The conversation floated from Vince and Maven's wedding to our playoff race, the afternoon fading into evening with everyone smiling and laughing and having a great time. Even I couldn't hold my displeasure at the surprise barbecue for long — not when Ava was this happy, when the guys were relaxing when they very much needed to, and most of all, when Chloe was smiling so contently.

After dinner, the girls worked on helping Arushi tidy up — despite how the guys and I had tried to do it ourselves. They insisted it was so they could gossip and to leave them alone.

I smiled when I watched Chloe give Ava a list of jobs to do, knowing that would make my daughter feel better than if she'd told her to go play.

God, she just *knew* her. Like she always had.

Like she was her own.

I was lost in that thought as Jaxson ribbed Carter about how he'd been ogling our dentist all day. Carter tried and failed to deny it, his voice pitching up a few octaves.

And then, the punk escaped further interrogation by throwing me under the bus.

"Besides, if anyone is ogling anyone here, it's our goalie."

I whipped my head toward him, narrowing my gaze.

"I mean, he's practically fucking his nanny with those sad eyes of his every time she walks by."

I punched him hard in the chest, which earned me laughs from Vince and Jaxson as Carter rubbed the spot. He shrugged his shoulders and mouthed *sorry*, like I should have been understanding that he was just doing what he had to do to get the conversation to steer away from him.

"He's got a fair point there, Daddy P," Jaxson said, taking a pull of the IPA in his hand. "I've seen you smile more today than in the entire time I've known you."

"Fuck the smiles. You've been *laughing*," Vince pointed out, like it was the equivalent of seeing a trick shot. "Does our new friend Chloe have anything to do with that?"

I slow blinked at them with my lips in a flat line, refusing to entertain the question.

"Oh, he's got it *bad*," Carter said, shaking his head on a drink of his beer.

"I do not have *anything*," I argued. "Other than, finally, a competent nanny who my daughter adores."

"I don't think Ava is the only one doing the adoring," Jaxson said with a wag of his brows.

Fortunately, I was saved from the hellish conversation and having to blatantly lie to my friends when the girls joined us. Grace jumped on Jaxson's back while Maven slipped under Vince's arm, planting a kiss on his cheek before he was beaming down at her.

Carter tried to put his arm around Livia, who simply arched a perfect brow at him and blinked. I found it hard not to laugh as he cleared his throat and pretended it was just a stretch before folding his arms over his chest.

Chef Patel was entertaining Ava, watching her hold her breath in the pool for all of three seconds before she'd pop back up. Arushi, bless her, acted like it was the most fascinating thing in the world. My girl was lucky to have her.

And then, there was Chloe.

She stood across from me, right between where Maven and Livia were, her skin a bit pink from the sun. My heart ached a bit as I watched a smile bloom on her face at something Carter said, and I willed myself to look away before anyone else caught on to how gone I was for her.

Because I was.

I was so fucking gone it wasn't funny.

My focus rested entirely on not letting that little fact show — to my teammates or to myself, if I was being honest. It took so much effort that the conversation felt muted to me.

Until the second Livia slammed me back down to Earth with one stupid name.

"Are you really going to make me leave tonight without even a single detail about Noah Balboa?"

The question was aimed at Chloe.

Which made no fucking sense.

"Noah Balboa?" Maven asked on a laugh.

"What?" Livia shrugged. "Hot teacher with an awareness of his trauma? That screams big dick energy to me."

"Who's Noah?"

I tried to ask the question casually, but the way everyone's heads snapped in my direction, I had a feeling the words came out more gruffly than I was aiming for.

Chloe shrank under my gaze, tucking her hair behind one ear. "He's just a friend."

"A teacher friend at her school," Grace corrected.

"Who is apparently very hot, divorced, and tripping over himself trying to tell our girl Chloe here that he's into her," Livia added.

"And I mean honestly, who could blame him?" Maven asked. "I'd trip over myself, too."

There were some laughs at that, and then I thought I heard Jaxson asking Chloe for details. I thought I heard Vince telling them all to bug off and leave the girl alone, to let her keep her dating life private. I thought I heard Carter say something about how *nothing* was private in this little group of friends.

But I couldn't be sure of any of it.

Because I was barely breathing, staring at Chloe with a war of emotions raging inside me.

She was into a guy at school.

He was into her.

My blood boiled at the thought, throat tightening, ribs refusing to expand and give my lungs the room they so desperately needed. Jealousy and anger surged through me like rival tidal waves, each of them battling for the top spot.

But on the heels of them was a deep, horrible sadness.

Because I knew this was a good thing.

Chloe was the most incredible woman I'd ever known. Every man *should* be tripping over themselves to get her attention. *She* should be crushing on a man who can give her what she deserves.

I wanted her to be happy.

But fuck if I didn't want her to be happy with me.

The reality that I couldn't make that a reality was more sobering than any ice bath I'd ever taken. I stared at her from across the circle, all my friends' laughter subdued like I was drowning under water and watching from the bottom of the pool.

Chloe was blushing and giggling at something someone had said, her eyes on her feet.

But then, they lifted to mine.

Her smile fell, the color draining from her face. She swallowed beneath what I knew was a hard stare from me, one powered by the jealousy and rage I couldn't quell.

Somehow, I forced a breath.

And then, I forced a smile.

"Well, before you two get serious, I think you better bring him by the house," I said, hoping the joke would play off, that I could somehow make it sound like a tease, that I could somehow convince her I was unaffected. "I promise to only polish one gun while I grill him."

There was a pause from the group, and then Carter burst into a laugh that made everyone else release, too. He clapped me on the shoulder, shaking his head.

"Will Perry, forever playing the role of Daddy," he said with a grin. "Stop playing, though. You don't own any guns."

I cocked a brow at him. "That you know of."

And with that, the conversation turned away from Noah the Hot Teacher.

I waited long enough until I could make the excuse that I needed to get Ava down to sleep, and then I snuck away, holding my shit together as I got my daughter cleaned up and into her bed. The sun and water had her falling asleep before I could even read a full page of a book, and when I slipped out of her room, I walked slowly down to the guest one down the hall.

Then, I grabbed the first pillow I saw, and screamed into it as loud as I could.

Chapter 28

Before You Hated Him

Chloe

I had a new definition of March Madness.

No longer did I associate the words with the college basketball tournament. Now, they would forever be tied to how quickly that month flew by in the house of Will Perry.

Once he was over the flu, he was a man focused on one thing and one thing only: the playoffs. As the Ospreys raced toward their chance to fight for the Cup, he grew more and more intense. I knew how much he wanted this, how much the entire *team* wanted this. It was evident in every move they made.

I did my best to support him in every way I could.

Just like when he was down with the flu, I ensured things at home were covered. And if I was being honest with myself... I *loved* that I was helpful, that I could alleviate some of his stress and provide comfort, even if in a small way.

I ran the house like a manager, coordinating Chef Patel and the housekeepers while also playing my role as nanny. When spring break rolled around, I filled it with activities and adventures for Ava. Will joined us whenever he could, but it was a busy time for him, and I ensured Ava didn't have a moment to feel sad at his absence because we had so much fun on the schedule.

But just because his focus was on the team didn't mean Will wasn't present with us. Every week we brainstormed until we thought of another way to introduce Ava to Jenny through something she loved to do. We had a movie marathon day during spring break with all her favorites. We took Ava to a taco truck Jenny loved one Saturday afternoon before a game. Will dug out photographs from Jenny's life, and Ava and I crafted beautiful frames and fun ways to display them around the house.

I'd never found Will more attractive than when I witnessed him being a great dad even when he had a full plate.

And when Ava was sound asleep, all that attentiveness turned to *me*.

It never mattered how tired he was, how late a game ran, or how ragged he felt after two back-to-back away matches. It also never mattered how tired *I* was, how busy I was with teaching and handling things at the house.

Somehow, Will always found the energy to slide into the pool house, pin me against the nearest wall, and drive me mad with his touch.

And I apparently never ran out of energy when it came to him.

Some nights, he was slow in his perusal of me, teasing me and offering *lessons* in everything from foreplay to going multiple rounds. Other nights, he was quick and needy, stripping me and taking me hard like I was the key to draining all the stress coiled in his body.

My favorite nights were the ones where he stayed.

They came more often than they should, more often than I knew he wanted them to. I thought he'd pulled away from me a bit after the barbecue, but it had lasted only a couple of days before it felt like he couldn't resist me.

God, how I loved that feeling.

He was always watching me, always waiting for the first moment he could get me alone. After hours of exploring each other, we'd lay in my bed or stand in my shower until the water ran cold, talking and laughing like we had nowhere to be in the morning.

Laughing.

I still couldn't get over that breakthrough.

The first time the sound had come from his chest, it was as if it had been wrenched free against its will. He was still sick then, and the laugh had rattled his chest in-between coughs.

But now, that laugh came more freely, like once the first one was released, the others couldn't wait to follow suit.

He laughed when I attempted to be sexy and alluring in a strip tease, only to trip on my pants and fall against my bedpost, yelping at my stubbed toe and bruised knee. He laughed as he kissed those injuries and I mewled beneath him, like it was the most adorable thing. He laughed when I lathered shampoo in my hair and styled it in a mohawk, rocking out on an air guitar and singing a terrible rendition of an old Fall Out Boy song.

When I made a joke, when Ava snorted milk out of her nose, when Chef poked at him for being grumpy... all the times he never laughed before, he laughed now.

I cherished each one like it was the first.

And with every laugh, with every night that passed between us, I found it harder and harder to see the line we'd drawn in the sand.

I willed my heart not to hold onto every smile he shared with me, not to latch onto every word he said on the nights he stayed late and opened himself to me. I tried not to read into it when he asked about *my* life, when he broke his own rules and seemed to hate the moment he had to leave when it finally did come.

Still, we hadn't kissed on the mouth — that was one rule we had followed strictly.

And at this point, I was pretty sure it was the only thing saving me.

I couldn't believe a whole month had passed by like this, in a routine I never thought I'd find with a man I never imagined a place with.

March Madness — that's what it was.

I felt like a completely new woman as I walked the sidewalk that led to my mom and grandma's house on the evening of my mother's birthday. Things had been so busy with school and Ava and Will that I hadn't seen them since before I moved into the pool house.

I wondered if they'd see what I felt, if they'd take one look at me and catalog all the ways I was different.

But before I could even open the front door, it flew open, and grandma tackled me in a hug that almost sent the cake I'd baked for mom flying out of my hands.

"There's our girl!" She hugged me tight, inhaling my scent like I'd been pronounced dead at sea and then just showed up alive. "Oh, let me get a good look at you."

She framed my arms in her hands, pulling back and shaking her head on a smile. I waited for her to narrow her gaze and sniff out the fact that I was getting my back blown out weekly by my boss, but before she could, my mom shooed her out of the way and took me in her own embrace.

"Sweetheart, my little Chloe Bear," she said, and as much as we had our moments, just the sound of my mom's voice like that turned me into a little girl again. I melted into her hug, heart full as I squeezed her back. "It's so good to see you."

"Good to see you, too, Mom," I said. "Made your favorite," I added, holding up the cake saver once she released me.

"Red velvet?!"

"With the buttercream icing."

"You're too good to me."

She kissed my cheek, and then Grandma took the cake from my hands and Mom looped her arm through mine, guiding me inside.

The house my matriarchy shared was just right for them. Nestled into a vibrant senior community complete with a golf course, swimming pool, and club house that hosted Bingo weekly, their home was a three-bedroom, one-story ranch house with the classic Floridian flare. The outside was painted a bright turquoise blue, the barrel-tiled roof a rustic brick color, and palm trees framed the driveway and sidewalk up to the house.

Inside, both personalities shone through. My mother was a tidy woman, minimalistic without the urge to hold onto much. The house was always spotless, even if she wasn't expecting me, and each piece of furniture was carefully selected and decorated with sparsity in mind. The entire house had the feel of a model home, like anyone could walk into it and live there for a month without feeling out of place.

My grandmother's personality showed with the kitchen being the only messy space allowed in the house. She was always in there baking or cooking or rolling out bread dough, and she had so many gadgets from the TV buy-on-demand programs that there was hardly any counter space left.

There were only a dozen pictures on the walls, and all of them were of us. My school photos. Our girls' trips. Holidays throughout the years.

None of them showed my father or grandfather.

"Let's play Rummy now and eat cake later," Grandma declared, putting the cake in the kitchen. She stopped long enough to pour us three glasses of lemonade before she led the way to the dining room table already set up with cards. "We have so much to catch up on."

"Yes, like how your grandmother here has a new enemy at water aerobics."

"Worse than Genevieve, if you can believe it," Grandma mumbled.

"No one is worse than Genevieve," Mom argued.

Grandma snapped her fingers as she took her seat. "Oh, you need to tell her about the Bingo drama, too."

"Lord, that'll take all afternoon. And besides, I want to hear about my daughter," Mom said, beaming at me as Grandma started shuffling and dealing the cards. "It's been so long. *Too* long. Tell us everything. How's school?"

"How's that sweet little girl you're nannying for?" Grandma asked.

I waited a beat, arching a brow, because I knew *one* of them would ask what they really wanted to.

Grandma didn't take her eyes off the cards, but her expression was prim. "And is that *father* of hers behaving himself?"

There it is.

"I was wondering how long it'd take you to spit it out," I teased.

Grandma rolled a shoulder noncommittally, almost like she didn't really care. But the way she peered over her glasses at me told me otherwise.

"Well? Is he?" Mom probed.

I sighed. "Just like I told you two when I first moved in, Mr. Perry is a professional. He is respectful of me in every way."

Except when he has me on my knees gagging for him, but they didn't need to know that.

"And this opportunity has been life changing."

In more ways than you two will ever know or need to know.

"Life changing." Grandma snorted. "How so?"

Wordlessly, I slipped one hand into the cross-body bag I'd sewed from scrap fabric and retrieved a check. I set it right in the middle of the table.

Mom snatched it before Grandma had the chance, and her eyes nearly bulged out of her head. "Chloe May," she breathed. "What have you done?"

Grandma took the check from her hands and gasped. Her eyes snapped to me in a narrowed accusation. "What is this? Is he making you sell drugs?" Her face went ashen. "Oh, God. Are you... are you his *whore?*"

I choked on my lemonade, wiping my mouth with the back of my wrist as I gaped at her. "Grandma!"

I hoped she couldn't see through the blush furiously shading my neck right now, because while it wasn't what she thought, Will *had* called me his little whore the other night.

And I'd loved it so much I'd come on command.

"Well, how else do you explain this?!" She held up the check and waved it around like a piece of evidence.

A check for thirty-thousand dollars.

"He pays me five-thousand dollars a week," I explained.

It was their turn to choke.

"What in the—"

"*How*?!"

"He's the starting goalie for one of the best hockey teams in the league," I reminded them, picking up my cards like it wasn't a big deal.

Like I didn't still have a panic attack every time that money hit my account on Friday.

"Like I said, he respects me — more than the school system ever will. He recognizes how difficult being a nanny is and he just happens to be in the position to pay me well. Very well."

"Outrageously well," Mom stated, plucking the check from Grandma in disbelief. "Why are you giving this to us?"

"Because I don't need much," I said quietly. "And you two have done so much for me, sacrificed your entire lives. I thought this could set you up for a while. I thought... maybe this could pay off my student loans."

They grew silent, Mom's eyes watering as she and Grandma exchanged a look.

It was a look of surprise, of wonder.

Of pride.

"I know how hard it was for you," I said to Grandma. "To raise Mom on your own. And Mom, for you to raise me. And I know you sacrificed probably more than I even understand to put me through school. So... this is me paying you back."

"Oh, Chloe," Mom tried.

"Or you could do something fun," I said before she could argue. "Take a cruise or go on one of those bus tours you keep talking about. Besides," I added — and damn it if my brain didn't realize my error before I'd even fully made it. "Will takes care of me, so I don't need..."

Shit.

I let my voice fade, unable to even look at them as the uncomfortable silence fell over us.

"He takes care of you," Mom repeated, incredulous.

Grandma snorted. "Here we go."

"Chloe, please tell me you're smarter than that," Mom said, setting the check down and shoving it aside. "Please tell me you've learned better after all we—"

"Oh, relax, Mom. I didn't mean it like that. I just meant that for the time being, he's paying for rent at my old place and I don't pay for the pool house. I may be moving in there permanently if all continues to go well."

"Permanently?!" Grandma gasped.

Shit. This was not going well.

"I just mean that I love the job and he seems to be happy with my performance, so—"

"Oh, I'll bet he is," Mom muttered.

I let out a frustrated sigh. "Listen. You two may not understand it, but this is something I want. It's something I very much enjoy, okay? I get to teach, like I love to do, without worrying about making ends meet. I get to spend time with Ava, who is an incredible little girl I know you two will love and adore once you meet her. I get to spend time on my crafts, share my art with Ava. I have a friend in Arushi. Hell, between her and the team and the girls, I have more friends than I've *ever* had — ever. And I have a wonderful boss in Will Perry."

And a wonderful stash of orgasms, too.

"Now, I know you have your opinions. I know you have your *reasons* for those opinions. But I am..." I vibrated with frustration. "Frankly, I'm sick and tired of you projecting your issues onto me. I'm tired of you not listening when I tell you that I am fine. No, that I'm *fantastic*."

I was trembling now because never had I ever raised my voice to these women.

"I have money set aside for me and will continue doing so, but I wanted to do this for you because I love you," I yelled. Realizing my voice was raised a bit *too* high, I cleared my throat, holding my chin up as I played my first card. "So take it or don't take it, but don't shame me for feeling happy for the first time in my life."

The words shocked me as much as they did them, and Grandma shared a look with Mom before they both let out a long breath.

"It's very kind, honey," Mom said. "Thank you. We are... honestly, blown away by the gesture. We never expected you to pay us back. We took on those loans because we wanted to." She paused. "And yes, we worry about you."

"That will never change," Grandma added.

"And I just... I don't want you to fall into any kind of trap. Men like that, who are rich and talented and powerful, they're even better at playing the game. They're the kind who will make it seem like you're so irresistible they can't help themselves when it comes to you. They'll make you feel *different than the other girls*," Mom said.

Grandma tutted. "Only to then make you feel crazy when you start to fall for them, like they never gave you a reason to believe they felt anything more for you than that you were a good lay."

Sandpaper coated my mouth at that.

It hit a little too close to home, and suddenly, I felt like a foolish little girl.

"But I'm sure he's not like that," Mom hurriedly added, reaching over to squeeze my wrist. "And I will say... this whole situation does seem becoming on you. You're glowing. Really. You seem as happy as you say you are."

"Have you noticed she hasn't been doing her usual nervous tics?" Grandma added. She beamed at me. "You seem confident, my love. It's a wonderful look."

For a while, we just played our cards in silence. I felt my heart rate settling, though there was still a bit of defensiveness hanging on — along with that foolishness as I overanalyzed everything that had happened in the last few months.

I didn't want them to be right about Will.

Then again, how could they be, when Will and I had made an agreement? I knew what I'd signed up for. I'd signed up more than willingly.

He may not have been able to give me a relationship, but he was giving me something I'd always wanted — experience. He was showing me how good it could feel, to be wanted and desired, to find a physical release with someone who made you feel comfortable and safe.

So then why did it hurt to think about a day coming where he called that out, where he confirmed that was all we were?

And how long could this last?

I knew *I* didn't have any interest in dating anyone else, but did he?

The thought made my stomach bottom out. I couldn't imagine the day he brought another woman home, holding her close to him and introducing her to Ava.

Would I just have to smile through it, be their nanny on family vacations?

Would I quit?

Could I quit, leaving Ava after how close we were now?

Tears pricked my eyes, and I sniffed them back, blinking into the present. "I think it's time for cake," I said on a forced smile, and before Mom or Grandma could notice anything, I shoved my chair back and hopped up, ducking into the kitchen for a brief reprieve.

By the time I was serving the cake, I had my shit together — if only temporarily. We lit candles and sang to Mom, finished our game of Rummy, and ended the evening with White Russians in the living room.

As the night winded down, I found myself looking at the pictures on the wall.

"What did you love about Grandpa?"

The question stopped Grandma's rocking in her chair, and Mom's hand hovered where she'd been lifting her glass to her lips. They shared a look.

"Before you hated him," I clarified. "Before he left. You had to have loved something about him."

"Well, I was a foolish woman," Grandma grunted, staring at her half-full cup.

"Please," I whispered. "I'd love to know something about him. Something good."

I knew the request shocked them. For my entire life, I'd been content to only hear that men were useless, terrible things, and that I should steer clear of all of them. I'd accepted that my grandfather and father both abandoned us, that they were good for nothing.

Maybe it was introducing Ava to her mother that had me feeling sentimental. Maybe it was the sick part of me that wanted to believe in love. Or maybe it was just that I didn't know anything about the men I came from, but I felt a suddenly insistent urgency to know now.

Grandma sighed, rocking again and staring at her hands wrapped around her cup. "Your grandfather loved to paint."

"He did?" I asked with wonder.

She nodded. "He was damn good at it, too. Some days he'd sit on our front porch when the weather was nice and paint all day. He'd start with a blank canvas and end with something so beautiful, it would take my breath away."

I smiled at the imagery, wondering if he would paint the sunrise or sunset, the flowers blooming in the yard, or maybe a portrait of Grandma.

I wondered if that part of me that loved to create came from him.

"He never sold his paintings, either," Grandma added, her voice a bit quieter. "Proud man that he was. He never found anything he did to be good enough. But any time someone in the community asked him to paint for them, he'd do it. For free. Happily. Even when we didn't have two red pennies to rub together, he'd find a way to get supplies and make it happen." A smile touched the corner of her lips. "He was good in that way."

"I didn't know that," Mom said softly.

Grandma shrugged, sipping her White Russian, her job complete and her content to never talk about Grandpa again.

"What about Dad?" I asked Mom.

She blew out a loud snort. "That man wasn't good for anything."

Grandma agreed with a hum in her throat.

I leveled Mom with a look. "Come on. There had to be something, otherwise you wouldn't have made a baby with him." I gestured to myself. "And you *did* make a pretty awesome baby, if I do say so myself."

That earned me a smirk, and then she let out a heavy, annoyed sigh. "Oh, I don't know... he was charming, I suppose."

"He loved to get you into trouble," Grandma chimed in. "Always testing his luck."

Mom softened at that, almost smiling. "He did. Maybe that was what I liked most about him. Where I was always playing it safe, he was looking for risks. He never liked being comfortable. He always said when you were comfortable, you stopped growing."

My heart pinched. I didn't know how much I really needed to hear about my father until Mom said those words.

"They may not have been all bad," Mom said sharply, like she could see my daydreaming eyes. "But they left. They *left*, Chloe May. At the end of the day, that's what speaks the loudest of their character. It doesn't matter if Grandpa loved to paint or if your daddy loved adventure. They walked away from their partners, from their children."

"Which just goes to show that it doesn't matter how great you think a man is. They're all selfish in the end. Only looking out for themselves." Grandma shook her head, draining the last of her drink. Her eyes held mine when she finished. "Which means you better look out for *you*."

Chapter 29

The Monster

Will

It was late by the time Chloe got home.

Ava was long asleep, and with an early practice tomorrow morning — I should have been, too. Instead, I was watching video of Jacksonville, who we'd play on Saturday, pretending not to have half my focus on the pool house.

I was making mental notes of how one of the team's forwards attacked on goal when a light flickered on. I'd missed her making her way through the gate and across the yard, but looked up just in time to see her dropping her purse and keys by the door before she disappeared inside.

I needed her tonight.

I needed to touch her, to hold her, to smell her and hear her sigh.

That fact alone scared the ever-loving fuck out of me, but it was true. I'd needed her more in the past month than I'd ever needed any woman in my life.

What was most surprising was that she showed up without me even having to voice it.

Just like when I was sick, she'd stepped up in every way as I focused on the team and our playoff race. She was running this house and this family like it was her full-time job.

I used every chance I could to thank her for it.

I told her with words — though they were feeble and insignificant. *Thank you* just didn't seem like enough. So, I told her with a weekly bonus, too.

But my favorite way to thank her was by making her come.

I had memorized it now, the series of events that led to her release. I could close my eyes and picture her flushed skin, her fluttering eyes, the shape of her body as she spread and opened and invited me in. I knew the sound of her sighs, her whimpers, her deep moans as she drew closer and closer. I could feel the way her nails would rip into my flesh, could never forget the precise way she tightened around me in little pulses when she finally gave all the way in.

She was all I thought about other than hockey and my daughter these days.

When I had a great game, I couldn't wait to celebrate with her. When I had a shit practice, she was who I wanted to get lost in.

Every waking moment, every sleepless hour — it was her.

I forced myself to wait twenty minutes before I shut my laptop, turning out the kitchen light and making my way across the pool deck to her door. I knocked softly, letting myself in when I didn't hear a response.

"Chloe?" I called out, making sure I didn't surprise her.

"Back here," was the answer, a soft, almost sad reply that came over the gentle sound of a bathtub filling.

Nacho ran right up to me, circling my feet with his bushy orange tail. I smirked, bending to pet him behind the ears until he was purring, and Pepper was coming over with a croaky *meow* to demand his own pets.

Coconut sat on the back of the couch, eyes narrowed, tail flicking. I wasn't trying to win over those asshole cats, but the other two had warmed up to me quite nicely.

Still, I counted it as a win when Coconut let me pet her once before she meowed and hopped off the couch, sauntering away with her tail high.

I made my way toward the sound of the water next. When I stepped into the bathroom attached to Chloe's bedroom, I found her staring at her feet propped on the edge of the tub, the water pouring between them and bubbles covering her all the way up to her collarbone. Only her neck, head, knees, shins, and feet were above the water line.

She didn't startle when I entered. Her eyes were hollow and empty as she turned to look up at me, and she forced the most pathetic attempt at a smile before her eyes were on her toes again.

My chest tightened.

You should go.

The three-word warning echoed in my mind like a police siren, the warning clear.

But I couldn't leave her.

I just... *couldn't.*

Wordlessly, I stripped out of my pajamas, tossing them on the floor before I slowly turned the water faucets off. Then, I moved to stand behind Chloe, sweeping her damp hair off her neck in a silent request for permission to join.

She sat up just enough to let me slide in behind her, the massive tub fitting us easily as I lowered myself down. The water rose dangerously close to the top, but I didn't care if it poured out and onto the floor. I wanted to be there with her — connected, touching, feeling.

Once I was settled, I pulled her flush against me.

And we both sighed.

It was like coming home, the way we melted into one another. No words were needed. Just being there together was enough.

Again, fear prickled the back of my neck, but I ignored it.

I couldn't help the fact that I was already hard just at the sight of her, let alone the feeling of her slick body nestled up against mine. But I didn't act on my impulse. Instead, I helped her relax into me, finding her shoulders with my hands and rubbing the tense muscles as she sighed and sank deeper into the water.

"That feels nice," she whispered, a little moan escaping her when my thumbs worked into her rhomboids.

I kissed her hair, had a moment of panic for how easily that gesture came to me, and cleared my throat. "Rough night?"

"No, actually," she said. "It was lovely. We played cards and had cake for Mom's birthday."

"But?"

She sighed. "But... yeah, I guess it was a rough night, in some ways."

I swallowed, a moment of silence passing between us while I worked her shoulders and watched what I could see of her expression from this angle.

341

"Want to talk about it?"

It was something I shouldn't have asked. While we clearly had crossed many of the original boundaries I'd made that first night in this very pool house, we had still been careful. Any time conversations ran a little too deep, one of us would change the subject or mount the other to turn our attention elsewhere.

Just like the no kissing rule, there was a reason I set the guideline that we couldn't be friends.

Because friendship and fucking often felt a lot like a relationship. Sometimes, it felt a lot like love.

I knew from experience.

My heart thumped hard in my chest as I realized I asked because I *wanted* to, because whether I liked to admit it or not, Chloe was already my friend.

She was more than that.

God, she was so much more than that.

She was...

"No," she answered, saving me from my spiral, from the panic gripping me hard by the throat.

She covered her hands with mine, moving them lower, beneath the water, until one was cupping her breast, and the other was slipping between her thighs.

"I want *this*."

I groaned as she moved my hands the way she wanted, rubbing herself with me as her pawn.

I knew exactly what she needed — it was what I needed, too. Not words. Not therapy.

An escape.

Whatever stress coiled in my body from work, whatever pain was passing through Chloe after seeing her family tonight... we held the key to releasing it all, to finding relief, in just a single touch.

My cock twitched against her back as I cupped her hard between the legs, rubbing my palm against her under the water. The soapy suds added the perfect amount of lubrication for me to glide and slip, and Chloe let her head fall back on my shoulder, her eyes closing, mouth parting.

"Yes," she breathed, bucking against my touch. Her hands reached behind her for me, twisting in my hair. "I love when you touch me, Will. I love the way your hands feel."

I groaned at the sound of my name, at the breathless way she said it.

"Grab my throat," she begged, squirming beneath my touch under the water.

"*Fuuuuck.*" The word dragged long and low out of me, and I kept one hand working between her thighs as the other slid up her chest until I could wrap my fingers around the column of her neck. "You like when I choke you, baby?"

"Yes," she panted, wetting her lips. "Harder."

I squeezed, just enough to make her whimper, to make the blood rush to her face. It was hot as fuck, and the way her pussy clenched around my middle finger told me it turned her on as much as it did me.

"You know who I really want to throttle?" I asked, squeezing a bit tighter. "Noah."

She stilled under my touch, and then a soft laugh slipped through her lips. "Who?"

"The guy at your school," I clarified. "The one the girls were talking about."

Just saying this guy's name made my entire body vibrate with jealousy. I'd done my best to put it out of my mind since the barbecue — especially because Chloe had never brought him up to me, and clearly, I was getting any spare time she *did* have.

But I'd be a lying sonofabitch if I said I didn't think about it.

"I want you to date, Chloe," I said, rubbing her neck with my thumb as I slid my finger deep inside her, out, and in again. She moaned at the touch, body slick and sliding against mine. "I want you to be happy. But, *fuck*, I don't want to share you."

The admission had my next breath harder to take, but I tried not to focus on it. I tried to keep all my attention on where she was writhing against me, instead.

"He isn't real," Chloe breathed, arching her ass against me. "I made him up."

"You... what?"

"I made him up," she repeated, covering my hands where I held her. She gripped me tight, both of us groaning when I pushed my finger inside her again. "The girls were convinced I was smitten over someone, so I created Noah."

Chloe twisted in my arms a bit, enough that our eyes met.

"You're the only one touching me, Will. You're the only one I *want* to touch me." She swallowed. "The only one I want to touch."

My nose flared with possession, my eyes searching hers before she turned again, body pressing against mine in a silent plea for more. And *fuck*, it shouldn't have made me happy. It shouldn't have felt so good to hear her say that.

I didn't deserve it.

But I desired it all the same.

She couldn't speak anymore, not when I gave her what she asked for, her every breath being cut short by my grip. I kept it just loose enough for her to be okay, but tight enough to give her what she needed, and I slid my palm under the water up to her tits. I played with her nipples, taking my time with each swollen, beautiful breast before my hand dove back down again, applying pressure against her clit.

She bowed off me, hips thrusting up and nearly out of the water as she chased that friction.

I licked a slow, sensual line behind her ear before sucking on her lobe, nipping it with a growl. It sent chills over her skin, and her entire body trembled when I pressed my palm against her clit again and smoothed her up and down.

"Look at you," I mused, smiling against her neck. "So desperate to come. So fucking needy."

She mewled, and one low, whispered word escaped through her rosy lips.

"Please."

My cock hardened even more at the plea, and I rocked it into her as I squeezed her throat a bit tighter. Her nipples were taut, face red with effort as she bucked against my hand.

Water sloshed out of the sides of the tub as I began to work her harder, faster, my palm sliding up and down before I'd bundle my fingers at that sensitive nerve ending and torture her with quick circles.

Our bodies were slick, sliding against one another as she whimpered and chased her orgasm. I could tell she was close — so fucking close — but she couldn't quite get what she wanted.

All at once, I released her, pulling my hands from her throat and between her legs. I gripped onto her hips and started lifting.

"Stand up."

Chloe was in a daze, her eyes fluttering, body trembling at the loss. But she did as I said, using the sides of the tub to help her stand as I gave her a boost. When she was up, I turned her to face me, guiding one foot to the edge of the tub behind my shoulder.

I fully planned to immediately go to town on her, but now, I couldn't help but take a moment to appreciate the glorious fucking view.

Her body was soaked, bubbles clinging to her curves and sliding down to the water in slow rivulets. Her plump breasts heaved with every breath, her face flushed, eyes heavy as they stared down at me and waited for what I'd do next.

"Goddamn, Chloe," I praised, running my hands up her calves, her thighs, until I could palm her perfect ass. "I could stare at you forever. I could live and die right here, just like this."

"Please make me come first."

I blinked, and then a laugh barreled out of me. Gone was the Chloe who shied away from asking me for what she wanted, who didn't even *know* what to ask for in the first place.

I wet my lips and pulled her down to my mouth. "Yes, ma'am."

I thought I saw her smirk, but then her face went blank — eyes widening before snapping shut, mouth opening, neck arching and legs violently shaking. I ran my tongue over her swollen clit, teasing her only a moment before I rewarded her with the sucking pulses I knew she loved.

"Will," she whined, dropping lower until I took more of her weight. I hummed against her cunt and sucked harder. She was already close. She just needed to be filled.

Carefully, I toyed with her pussy with one thick finger before driving it inside. She was so wet, not from the bath but from *me*. It made it easy to plunge another finger in, and I curled them in time with the rhythm of my mouth on her clit, ignoring the way my arms burned and my neck ached at the angles and effort.

I was a fucking hockey player.

If there was one thing I had, it was stamina in spades.

It didn't take long for Chloe to become a wild animal. She fucked my face in her desperation to find release, and I gave her the same energy back. My fingers slid in and out, curling, fucking her deep while my tongue worked her clit. I swirled it and latched my mouth onto her, sucking and licking and moaning so she could feel how much I loved to be here, how badly I wanted to make her fly apart.

And fly apart she did.

Her hands shook where they braced her on my shoulders, nails biting into the muscle as she cried out. She bucked her hips and trembled so hard she nearly collapsed, but I held her tight, not letting her back away from my mouth or my fingers as I gave her every last wave of that climax.

She screamed my name and a dozen curse words, shaking and rocking against me. And when she finally found the end, her orgasm receding, her head snapped forward, eyes hooded as they latched onto me.

I pressed a light kiss against her clit, helping her bring her leg off the edge of the tub and right herself as I removed my fingers from inside her.

She shook her head on a sated smile.

Then, she turned, offering me a sensational view of her glistening backside before she lowered into the water. She stayed on her knees, leaning forward, one hand on the edge of the tub and the other holding her steady under water. She looked over her shoulder, her wet hair sticking to her neck and cheeks and lips in rustic strands as she batted her lashes.

And she didn't even have to ask for what she wanted.

She wiggled that perfect ass side to side, the bottom of it gliding over the water, a beckoning grin on her pink lips.

I inhaled a long groan of a breath as my hands moved to palm her, sliding up and over the slick swells of her ass in admiration. I smacked one cheek and then the other, biting my lip at the resulting wave of each.

With a growl, I moved her forward enough for me to stand. I needed to grab a condom, which was a real fucking inconvenience in this moment.

As I searched for the nearest towel, Chloe's hand shot out to touch my leg. "Where are you going?"

"Condom," I managed.

She bit her lip. "What if we..."

Her voice faded, but her eyes finished the question for her.

My heart kicked hard in my chest at the thought of fucking her raw, of taking her without a barrier between us.

I knew this woman's body inside out. I knew she had a thin little bar on the inside of her left arm where her birth control was implanted. I knew she wasn't fucking anyone else but me.

That made another rush of adrenaline spike through me, possessiveness a heady drug fogging any other thought.

"You know I'm not with anyone else," I told her.

"I know."

"You know I'd never be unsafe with you."

"I know."

She pulled at my leg, urging me down, her spine glistening, heart-shaped ass begging me to relent. It was the conversation we needed to have before taking a step like this, to ensure we were being smart, being safe with one another.

But it was also a conversation I never thought we'd have.

She was rooted so deep in me, I knew whether I admitted it or not that I'd never be free of her.

I ignored that reality as I sank back into the warm water. Enough of it had been slopped over the sides of the tub now that her pussy rested just above the waterline.

With a thick swallow, I fisted my cock and pressed my crown against her, sliding between her slick lips as we both moaned and shivered together. When I wedged inside her enough to move my hands, I found purchase on her hips, and slowly drove inside.

I ceased to exist.

Like a black hole had swallowed me up and delivered me inside a new universe altogether, I felt my body bending and warping from the inside out, all my awareness zeroing in on where her pussy hugged my cock for the first time without anything between us.

I hissed and groaned and savored the panting breaths Chloe let free. Her back arched, eyes rolling shut, and when I slid out and back in, deeper, we both cursed.

"Oh my God," she moaned, and while I was content to stay just like that, fitted together, Chloe slid off my shaft and back down in a slow claim. "Oh my *God*."

"You feel fucking remarkable, Chloe," I managed, my voice so low and gruff I almost didn't recognize it. It was like every breath was being strangled by the new sensation of having her fully, like every cell of my being was locked onto where we were connected.

"I knew it would be different, but holy shit," she breathed. I had my hands loosely holding her hips, letting her control every fluid movement. Watching the way I disappeared inside her beneath the full shape of her beautiful ass was enough to make me come after just a few pumps.

I stared up at the ceiling, willing myself to hold on and not give in yet.

For a long while, Chloe paced us, moaning and panting as she slid off me and back on in a slow, torturous rhythm. Every time she'd back up, her ass would pop against my abdomen, the flesh rippling.

"It's so hot watching you like this," I praised, hands gliding over her ass as she continued working toward her second release. My words made her moan and pick up speed. "That's it, baby. Faster."

Her ass slapped against me, sloshing the water in the tub as she fucked me harder. The more she moaned, the longer I watched that gorgeous sight, the closer I was to coming. It was climbing up my spine like an inevitable storm now, lightning cracking in my veins, thunder rolling through my bones.

But then Chloe slowed, making me groan in a mixture of pleasure and pain.

Was she edging *me* this time?

"I... I've been thinking about another lesson," she said quietly.

I didn't miss how she'd gone shy on me again, how her cheeks were pink as she looked over her shoulder at me. I also couldn't think of another single lesson we could have at this point, but I was curious.

"Yeah?"

She nodded, and I grabbed ahold of her hips, grinding deep inside her before withdrawing in a slow, measured tease.

"Tell me."

"Sometimes, when I... when I play with myself... I..."

She bit her lip, wincing a bit like she was mortified to even admit what she wanted.

That got me really fucking curious.

"Show me," I said. "Show me what you do."

Chloe swallowed, balancing her weight on the hand pressed against the bottom of the tub. Her other hand slid over her breast, down her side and hip before slicking over her round bottom. She gripped my cock where I'd pulled out of her, both of us moaning as I slid back inside, and she had no choice but to move that hand.

And then, she was toying with her ass.

My breath hitched in my throat, my next swallow impossible to take as I watched her. Her fingers circled the hole as I withdrew and slid inside her again, and as I did, she pressed just the tip of her middle finger inside.

I nearly blacked out.

"You want me to fuck you here," I asked, using my thumb to move her finger out of the way. I circled her ass without penetrating, just toying with her, asking, seeking.

I thought I saw her nod.

"I need your words, baby."

"Yes," she whimpered, and I rewarded her by pressing my thumb against that entrance, applying just a tease of pressure. "Yes, *please*."

I muffled the curse that ripped out of me, wetting my lips as my heart raced in my chest. It was one thing to fuck her without a condom, but to have her beg me to fuck her ass in the same night?

I didn't know how long I'd last.

"Do you think you can come like that," I asked, pressing my thumb inside her. I only went to the first knuckle, but she rewarded me with a deep moan.

"Absofuckinglutely," she breathed.

I smirked, but couldn't find it in me to laugh — not with my cock deep inside her cunt and my thumb edging more inside her ass. It took every ounce of focus I had not to come, not to give into my own urges and slam into her, hard, over and over until I found mine.

"It might hurt," I warned.

"Go slow."

I nodded, withdrawing from her pussy as we both moaned at the loss. I replaced my thumb with the crown of my cock, teasing the hole, using the slippery suds and water to lubricate that sensitive area.

I pressed in, just enough to stretch her around my head, and Chloe moaned louder than I'd ever heard.

"Holy fuck," she breathed.

I stilled. "Should I stop?"

"No," she said incredulously, and then her hand reached back for my ass, pulling me toward her until I slid in a half inch. "Oh, *fuck*."

My eyes crossed at how tight she was, at taking her in this forbidden way. I didn't know what turned me on more — the sight of her bent over in the tub, the way she'd been bold enough to ask for this, or the fact that she trusted me to be the one to take her like this for the first time.

The combination had my veins burning, and I pressed in more, sliding in a full inch before I withdrew and slid in another.

Chloe hissed at the fullness, her hand slowing me, and I took her cue. I was in no fucking hurry to get her there. I was enjoying every blissful second of this.

Slowly, centimeter by centimeter, heated breath by heated breath, I worked my cock inside her. Chloe moaned and panted the deeper I got, and once I was all the way in, she squeezed her ass around me.

"Oh, my God," she breathed, looking over her shoulder like she wished she could see the view I had. "You're fucking my ass."

"And you're taking it so damn well," I said, sliding out and back in as we both groaned. "Stretching for me, hugging my cock so fucking tight."

"Fuck, I want to come."

She didn't wait for me to tell her to do so. Her hand shot down between her thighs, and she spread them as much as she could in the tub, rubbing her clit in slow circles as she moaned and gave me control.

I fucked her in time with her own movements, slowly at first, and then a little faster as she rubbed her clit with more speed. I didn't know what I expected, but it wasn't for her to come so fast and so hard.

"Shit, Chloe," I praised as she took my cock and touched herself, her moans growing louder and louder. "Look at you, coming while I fuck your ass. You filthy fucking thing."

"Yes," she whined, and then she was a mess of moans and curse words and my name.

That was all I needed.

The sight of her rocking her ass to meet me, her tits bouncing and flinging water, her neck arched and mouth open as she cried out her release... it was lethal.

I fucked her harder, deeper, plunging into her once, twice, three times before I caught my own release. She gasped at the fullness but was still riding her own orgasm, so I didn't dare stop — not even when my own climax took me under, drowning me and filling me with life at the same time.

My body burned. The universe expanded and snapped back to this room alone. All the blood in my body rushed to my cock, and I buried myself inside that woman until she'd drained every last drop of me.

"God*damn*," I groaned, slowing, thrusting inside her and withdrawing almost to the edge before I pushed out again.

When I did, a bit of my cum leaked out of her, and I moaned again.

Carefully, I withdrew completely, but before she could move, I grabbed Chloe by the hips and held her there.

"Squeeze your ass, baby," I said through my panting, my racing heart, my bleary vision.

When she did, cum dripped out and down, sliding over her thigh, between her legs, covering her in me.

I was a feral fucking animal at that sight.

"You are un-fucking-real," I said.

I wrapped my arms around her, kissing her back and taking her weight until we were both collapsing into the water, clinging to one another, hands in each other's hair, lips against skin, hearts racing out of control.

Somehow, I ended up reclined against the back of the tub, and she was in my arms, her head on my chest, body melting into mine.

She peeked up at me, blinking, her eyes wide and face flushed.

We stared a long moment, and then I smiled, and she

smiled, and we both laughed as she buried her face in my chest, and I wrapped her in a tight embrace. Whatever sour emotion had been clinging to her when I stepped into this room was gone now, and all the stress from my day had disappeared, too.

"Well, that was fucking incredible," I said with a grumble against her hair.

She giggled and shook her head, her face still covered by my chest. "I... I *really* liked that."

The confession was mumbled, but I lifted her chin to look at me, holding her gaze with my own. "Don't ever be ashamed of what you like in the bedroom, what you want. Especially not with me."

Something flashed through her, and she nodded.

Then, her eyes fell to my lips.

My heart stuttered to a stop, chest tightening until it was painful.

And I wished I would just kiss her.

I wished I didn't feel my rib cage crushing my lungs, that I had more control over how the anxiety and fear spiked in my body at just the thought.

But I was powerless against it.

It was engrained in me.

It was years of pain, of suffering, of rebuilding to who I had finally managed to become — all of it resurfacing and shutting down every door I had managed to creak open since I'd walked into this bathroom.

I cleared my throat, putting distance between us. "Let's get cleaned up."

I couldn't look at her as I helped her stand, couldn't find a comforting word to say as we took a shower and washed each other before she wrapped up in her robe and I dried off with a towel and we climbed into her bed.

She rested her head on my chest, and I played with her wet hair, my eyes on the ceiling and hers somewhere across the room.

And I hated myself more in that moment than I ever had in my entire fucking life.

Because I was just counting down the minutes before I could leave.

What the fuck is wrong with you?

I knew the answer, I just didn't want to admit it. I didn't want it to be true. I didn't want to be controlled and ruled by tragedy, by trauma, by a physical response to intimacy that I had no goddamn power over.

This was why I'd drawn boundaries. *This* was what I'd been afraid of.

And yet, I'd broken my own rules. I'd been just as guilty in this as Chloe was.

Maybe more so.

And here we were, silence stretching between us, lines blurred, hearts too involved.

"I'm going to head in," I said, my voice a low croak as I maneuvered her off my arm.

I sat up, but before I could stand, Chloe's hand wrapped around my forearm.

I stilled, taking a calming breath before I glanced over my shoulder at her.

"Will," she breathed. "Don't you... can't you stay?"

Fuck.

I closed my eyes, nostrils flaring, trying to reach for that part of me that had opened to her. I tried to *stay* open, willed myself to be calm and kind and understanding. I willed myself to do what she asked, tried to convince myself how I would love it, too.

But it was like a monster breaking free from the flimsy cage that held it at bay, like I was being taken over against my will. I felt it happening, and yet I was powerless to stop it.

The doors slammed shut.

The walls grew tall, lined with barbed wire.

The monster roared.

It didn't even feel like me as the scowl slid into place, as my jaw hardened, the muscle beneath it popping against my skin.

I met her gaze. "Are you sure you're still okay with this?"

It was as if I'd slapped her.

Her head snapped back, lips parting before she zipped them shut again. She swallowed, her eyes dropping from mine in shame at the same time she released my arm.

I thrashed against the monster, wanting to reach for her, to apologize instantly.

But I was a prisoner inside my own soul.

"Of course," she said. "I'm fine, I just... I don't know, I'm being silly." She gave a pathetic excuse for a smile, waving me off as her eyes glossed. "Go. I'll see you tomorrow."

She hurried off the bed without letting me see her face again, ducking inside the bathroom.

And the monster dragged me out of her sheets in a numb daze, hauling across the back yard until he could lock me in my castle once more.

This time, it felt like he threw away the key.

Chapter 30

You Good?

Will

April came like Christmas, like a holiday that always seems so far away only to surprise you with its arrival as if it happened quickly and unexpectedly.

Eight games.

We had *eight games* left until the playoffs.

The pressure was so high, the tension thicker than I'd ever felt.

Coach was strung out, his usual cool façade interrupted by bursts of outrage when we fucked up in practice.

Aleks was focused on the ice, but was up to his usual shenanigans *off* the ice — which meant our PR team was busy cleaning up after him nearly every week when we were trying to focus on the games ahead.

Vince and Jaxson were wound just as tight as I was, the three of us trying to wrangle the team into one that could win the whole thing.

There was no question on whether or not we'd make it to the playoffs now. We were in.

We'd have a chance to fight for the Cup.

Now, it was about staying healthy, finishing strong, and securing our spot as top seed. That meant home ice advantage for four games instead of three in the seven-game series that made up the playoffs. Playing on our own ice, having our home crowd cheering for us — it meant everything. It could be the difference between winning it all and going home in the first round.

For so long, I'd worked with this team for this exact moment. Years and years of building, working hard, making adjustments. Finally, we just... clicked. We had the right players. We had the momentum. We had the energy, the drive, the luck.

And my focus was fucking shot.

When I was at the rink, I was there. I was in it. I was with my team, all my awareness on the goal I protected, on the players I was trying to lead to our first championship in decades.

But instead of that focus coming with me when I went home, it evaporated instantly the moment I crossed the threshold.

Because when I was home, everything revolved around Chloe.

Chloe, who had twisted me up so fiercely I could barely breathe in her presence. Chloe, who had infiltrated my home, my family, my *heart*. Chloe, who had become close friends with my chef, who had become *best* friend to my daughter... maybe even more than that.

Chloe — who had barely talked to me in more than a week.

Since that night in the bathtub, she'd pulled away from me.

It was the smart thing to do. It was what we both needed — namely *me*. Clearly, I was barely holding onto the reins of our arrangement. But somehow, I'd managed to keep myself on the other side of that line we'd drawn. I hadn't stayed that night. I hadn't given in.

Because of that, I'd completely lost her.

I felt it in the way she could barely look at me the next morning, at how every smile she gave me now was weak and lined with a sheen of pain.

In the process of saving myself, I'd hurt her.

It was so clear, so evident, and yet I couldn't figure out what the hell to do about it.

She wanted this, too. She'd told me as much. *I don't date. I don't want friends*. We were on the same page. Where my reason stemmed from Jenny, hers came from her family, from her desire to be independent and to make them proud of her and her decisions.

But suddenly, it didn't feel like our reasons were so clear. It didn't feel like they made fucking *sense* — not anymore.

I was frozen, unclear in my own feelings and unsure of my next move. I felt her pulling away more and more each day. We didn't flirt anymore. We didn't touch. We barely spoke — just enough to communicate about Ava.

I missed her so badly, even when we were in the same room.

And yet I didn't have the fucking right to.

It didn't matter that she'd agreed to just sex. I couldn't call her on that, couldn't hold her to it — not after all that had transpired in the months since we'd made that agreement.

We both knew it was more than that now.

The difference was that it seemed like she could face that fact — and all I knew how to do was run from it.

Florida was already warming, the promise of a brutal summer evident in the humidity making my hair stick to my neck as I sat on the park bench and watched Ava playing on the slide with Chloe. It was a rare Sunday off — one very much needed — and it was too beautiful of a day to be stuck inside.

It was Chloe's suggestion to use the day to get back to our mission of introducing Ava to Jenny through things she loved to do. Immediately, this park had come to mind.

Jenny used to come here at least once a week. It was her favorite place to escape from the rush of the world, to take a moment to breathe. The park was shady and quiet, lined with giant oak trees garnished with Spanish moss and a creek that bubbled as background noise just past the picnic benches. It had been more run down when we used to come here together — a forgotten oasis that the local residents didn't have time or money to improve.

It had changed in the last five years of my absence, though. The old playground had been updated, the picnic tables and gazebos restored, and a new walking and biking trail had been made to run along the creek that eventually led to a river three miles north. The improvements meant the park was busier now, but it was still as gorgeous as ever.

I hid under the brim of my hat and behind the dark frames of my glasses. So far, no one had bothered us. Then again, the dozen other people we shared the park with seemed to be in their own little world, too. There was a family of four eating lunch by the creek, a couple running the path with their dog, a mom watching her kids just a few years older than Ava as they threw a Frisbee.

"Daddy, look!" Ava called, and I snapped my attention from where my eyes were losing focus in the trees to her just in time to watch her fly down the slide on her stomach. She giggled the whole way down, somersaulting at the bottom and popping up with wood chips stuck in her hair and all over her clothes.

"Perfect ten!" I called, grinning, but my heart was racing a bit after watching that tumble. "Be careful, okay?"

"I am!" she promised, and then she was running over to Chloe, who smiled down at her and said something as she ruffled her hair. They were best buds now, two peas in a pod.

When Ava ran off again, Chloe walked toward me, her hands in the pockets of her powder blue sundress and her eyes on her white sneakers. She'd pulled her short hair half up today, and the breeze blew the strands this way and that as she crossed the park.

Wordlessly, she took a seat at the opposite end of the bench from me. She couldn't have put any more distance between us if she tried. In fact, I was pretty sure half her ass was hanging off the edge of that bench, that if I lightly pushed against her shoulder, she'd topple off.

"Thank you for today," I said, stretching my arm over the back of the bench as I reclined back. The tips of my fingers brushed her neck when I did.

She leaned forward to avoid the touch.

"It's a beautiful park," she said. "I can see why Jenny loved it so much."

I nodded, heart squeezing under an iron fist at the mention of her name.

Everything in me wanted to shut down in that moment.

The hair on the back of my neck stood on end. My heart kicked in my chest. My lungs struggled for air.

But for the first time in five years, I didn't grant my body's wish to run, to avoid, to cease operating.

Instead, I forced a breath that seared my lungs on the way down.

And I talked.

"I came here once after she died."

Chloe stiffened, tucking her hands under her thighs. She didn't say anything, but her chin tilted toward me, and though I had my eyes on Ava playing with another little girl her age, I knew Chloe was looking at me.

"I sat right here on this bench and cried like a fucking baby," I admitted, patting the wood. "It was maybe a week after she'd passed, when my uncle and some of my teammates' wives were helping me with Ava while I tried to navigate my new life. Jenny's mom was here, too. I think. Or was that a couple weeks later?" I paused, trying to recall. "To be honest, I don't remember a lot about that time. Isn't that so shitty?" I shook my head. "Ava was this beautiful baby, growing more and more every day, and I couldn't even be fully present for it. I was a zombie."

I swallowed, my throat constricting as I watched Ava laugh and try her hand at the monkey bars. She fell after the third one, but immediately sprang back up and started again.

"I wouldn't have made it through without all the help I got, and yet I could barely thank the people who were helping me. I was practically mute. I don't remember how or when it happened, but slowly, over the years, I started living again. I showed up for Ava as much as I could. I came back to my team and played harder than I ever had. My mentor helped me on that front, reminding me that when I didn't have anything else, I had hockey. I had the Ospreys."

I chewed the inside of my cheek for a moment, the emotion of those early years washing over me. Again, everything inside me begged to shut down, but I refused.

I *wanted* to share this with Chloe.

I needed to.

"When I came here, when I was crying so hard I could barely breathe... all I could think about was how Jenny meant more to me than I ever told her."

The confession slammed into my chest hard enough to make me pause.

"We always said we were just friends. But we were *best* friends. And we shared the same bed. And we had fun... *God*, did we have fun. Without Jenny, I was too serious for my own good. But she reminded me to play, to *live*. I loved her, Chloe," I said, finally turning to face her. Her eyes were glossy when I met them. "I loved her with my whole heart, and it kills me every day that I lost her. That Ava lost her. That maybe, if we would have been more careful, if she wouldn't have gotten pregnant... she'd still be here."

My nostrils flared, throat tightening.

"And then I feel like a monster because I know even if I could go back in time and choose that option — I wouldn't. And neither would Jenny. Because then Ava wouldn't be here."

"Oh, Will..."

"Jenny would have been so much better at this than I am," I continued on a laugh, shaking my head. "Motherhood would have just come easily to her. She never would have worried. She never would have stressed. With her, it would have just been another adventure."

A moment of quiet passed between us, both of us watching where Ava was playing before I began to speak again.

This time, my voice shook.

"I miss her every day," I whispered. "But I have another confession to make, one that might affirm what a terrible person I am."

"You're not a—"

"Because I miss her, I do," I said, turning to face Chloe. "But I miss you more."

Chloe's face paled, her eyes wide, lips parting. "Me? But I'm right here."

"No, you're not. You haven't been since..."

I swallowed, sucking in a breath. My voice no longer shook. It no longer *worked*. How did I tell her what I was still trying to figure out myself?

"Chloe, I—"

But before I could say another word, a blood-curdling scream ripped through the park.

Chloe and I both jumped up off the bench, heads snapping toward the playground.

Ava was on the ground, clutching her ankle and wailing in pain.

It all happened so fast. My heart leapt into my throat, feet turning to stone and rooting me to the spot where I stood as the worst-case scenarios played out in my head like a movie reel.

Chloe sprang into action, taking off in a sprint. She was already bending down by Ava's side by the time I managed to take one slow-motion step.

I couldn't breathe.

I couldn't form a single word.

I could barely walk, could barely drag myself through the slog of invisible liquid that seemed to be holding me back from my daughter.

The closer I got, the more I saw her anguish. Her face was bright red, her hair covered in wood chips, cheeks stained with tears, and fresh ones leaking out of her eyes. She cried and cried.

She cried for *me*.

"Daddy! Daddy!"

Ava writhed in pain as Chloe soothed her with a hand on her head, and when I finally made it to them, they both looked up at me.

Like I had the answer.

Like I would know what to do.

I should have. I *should* have known what to do. I should already be moving.

Why can't I move?

I stood there frozen, blinking at where Ava's ankle was already swelling before I dragged my gaze to her face, her wailing like a muted cry now against the beating of my heart in my ears.

Finally, I looked at Chloe, who had her brows pinched together, her eyes flicking between mine.

Silently, she reached out for me, her hand wrapping around my wrist.

She squeezed it, something in her eyes soft and reassuring.

"It's okay," she mouthed.

And then she turned back to my daughter and saved the day.

"Okay, my little angel bug. Look at me. That's it. Hi," she said with a smile. "Did you fall off the bars?"

Ava nodded, crying harder.

"Okay, it's okay," Chloe said, smoothing a hand over Ava's hair. "It's alright. Show me where it hurts."

Ava pointed to her swelling ankle, her voice garbled when she said, "It popped."

My heart raced double time, but Chloe just nodded, her hands slowly, softly, coming to the injured area. "That happens sometimes. Can you tell me how bad the pain is. On a scale of one to ten, how bad does it hurt?"

Ava sniffed, and as if the question calmed her, like it gave her something else to focus on, she leaned back on her palms, taking one long, slow breath.

"I don't know. Maybe seven?"

"Seven," Chloe repeated. "You're so strong. Okay. Here's what we're going to do. I'm going to pick you up, okay? We're going to go get your leg elevated and put some ice on it. We're going to wrap it up with some fabric I have in the car, to give it some compression. And we're going to go see the doctor. Okay?"

Ava's lip wobbled. "Am I going to die?"

I felt like I was living an out-of-body experience as Chloe bit back a laugh, and she swept my daughter's hair out of her face, framing her cheeks.

"Not today, angel bug. You're okay. I think you might have sprained your ankle, but we will let the doctor take a look at it. Right now, I want you to know you're being so brave and so strong. And your dad is here, and so am I, and we're going to get through this together. Okay?"

Ava sniffed and nodded, and then she was letting Chloe take her in her arms.

Chloe looked back at me after a few feet to make sure I was following.

Just like she said, Chloe did all the steps she should have, repeating them out loud as she performed each task so Ava knew what was happening. She checked in on the pain. She told Ava how good she was being. And before I knew it, we were in the SUV, Ava strapped into her booster seat with her ankle wrapped in fabric holding ice from our cooler in place. She sniffed, her tears dry now, but she was still groaning in pain, wincing and clearly uncomfortable.

Chloe was in the driver seat.

She fired up the engine, turned to me and laid her hand on my forearm. "You good?"

Her words brought me back to life.

I felt everything snap into place, like the fall had knocked me out of orbit and Chloe's hand on my arm, her words, her eyes were the gravity that brought me back home.

It was the same two words I often asked my teammates when I knew something was off. It was the familiarity of them that had me nodding, that had me squeezing her hand in return before I angled myself over the seat and looked back at Ava.

"How you doing, Pumpkin?"

My throat was raw when I spoke, but it seemed as though hearing my voice gave my daughter even more strength.

"I'm okay, Daddy," she assured me. "I'm strong."

"Yes, you are," I agreed on a weak smile. "Daddy's here, okay?"

I reached behind me, grabbing her little hand in mine and holding tight. I didn't let go the entire way to the hospital.

And my eyes never left Chloe.

Chapter 31

Need You

Chloe

I felt like a rag doll that had been dragged behind a truck and flung into a raging ravine by the time I was sneaking out of Ava's room that night.

The adrenaline that had kept me alert for hours had long crashed, and I felt the remnants of it tingling beneath my skin as I carefully shut her bedroom door and tiptoed down the hall.

A heavy sigh filled with relief left my chest as I descended the stairs, running a hand back through my messy hair.

As I expected, it was a bad sprain. My guess was that she'd rolled that ankle when she came down on it. The doctor gave us a prescription for a low dose of ibuprofen and sent us home with the usual orders: rest, ice, elevate.

Ava had been an absolute trooper. In fact, by the time we left the ER, she was making the nurses laugh, happily accepting treats as her father handled the outtake paperwork and pulled the SUV around to pick us up at the door.

The media had caught wind of the situation — which was supremely shitty, because that meant someone at the hospital had leaked it. When it was time to leave, there were reporters lined up and wanting to interview Will, to know what happened and have it aired on the evening news.

He had handled it like a pro, shielding both Ava and me from view as the camera shutters flashed. It was a stark contrast to how he'd been at the park. There, I knew he'd been in shock. But once we were on our way to the hospital, he came back to himself, back to the man with a plan.

Though he'd been silent most of the evening.

The media, blessedly, didn't follow us home. Once we were here, Ava had wanted a bath and a book. Now she was passed out, holding tight to her favorite stuffed fish and gently snoring.

What a week it had been.

Between the chaos today and the absolute mess of emotions I'd lived in since the night with Will, I was so strung out I wasn't sure I even qualified as human anymore.

There was no way around the truth.

He'd hurt me.

When I'd asked him to stay, when he'd thrown our arrangement in my face, asking if I could still *handle it* like I was losing control...

It was like having the warnings of my matriarchy thrown right in my stupid face.

I couldn't look at him after that, not without my stomach bottoming out and my heart threatening to seize in my chest. He had to have known I was already hurting that night, that I'd needed him. We'd found escape in each other. We'd found a release.

But I'd needed him to stay.

And he didn't.

I didn't know how to handle it, didn't know what to do. *Reddit* had been no help. All they'd done was berate me for being stupid, saying how I'd failed at fucking without feelings.

They were right.

I'd deleted all my posts, deleted my username, and pulled up the group text with the girls. I'd typed everything out — the truth — but in the end, I deleted it all.

I'd never felt so alone.

Until today, when Will had opened up to me about Jenny at the park. I didn't even have time to analyze what that meant, what he was trying to say before Ava got hurt.

I miss her, but I miss you more...

When I made it downstairs, there was a soft light glowing in the kitchen. My body ached as I made my way over, and I found Will with his palms on the kitchen island counter, his eyes on a glass of amber liquid that looked completely untouched.

"She's down," I said, wincing a bit as I slid onto one of the barstools. You would have thought *I* was the injured one for how my body was protesting the movement. "Took two times reading that new book she loves so much, but she's sleeping now."

I looked at Will when he didn't respond. He was just staring at the glass, his jaw tight, chest slowly inflating and deflating.

"Hey," I said, reaching across the counter to grab his wrist.

His eyes flicked to mine when I did.

"She's okay," I assured him with a soft smile. "You raised a tough kid. If anything, I bet she'll be bragging about this tomorrow."

I chuckled a bit, and Will looked at where my hand was on his wrist before he pulled away completely. I frowned as he stood there, just... *staring* at me.

Then, slowly, like a predator creeping in on its prey, he rounded the kitchen island until he was standing just inches from where I sat.

He gazed down at me, the heat of him radiating off his skin in waves that made chills sweep across my arms.

"Will?"

His jaw flexed at the sound of his name, and he took another step, slipping into the space between my legs as his hands reached for me. They slid along my jaw, over my cheeks, until his fingers were in my hair and cupping my neck and tilting my chin.

My eyelids fluttered at the feel of him, at the overwhelming waves of electricity that coursed through those hands and into my soul.

His throat constricted, eyes searching mine, thumbs gliding along the line of my jaw.

He tilted my chin more, until my neck was arched, my eyelids heavy as I watched him bend. His dark eyes were locked on mine, never faltering, his hands strong and steady where they held me in place.

Will pressed his forehead to mine, inhaling a long, slow breath and letting his eyes shut at the contact. It was as if he were breathing me in, memorizing me with his hands as his fingers curled in my hair.

He swallowed, jaw muscles popping, nose flaring like he was battling a war I couldn't see.

And then he lowered his mouth to mine.

And he kissed me.

Shock zipped up my spine, replaced quickly by a longing so deep and intense that it hummed in every inch of my veins. I sucked in a breath at the same time Will did, like we were resurfacing after being under water for years.

Oh my God.

He's kissing me.

He's kissing *me.*

His lips were warm and firm against mine, his hands holding me to him. My heart seemed to float away on a cloud the longer we were connected, and when he peppered that kiss only to start a new one, it soared to another universe.

I'd had this man in so many ways. I'd had him on his knees for me, been on my knees for him. I'd had him inside me. He'd had me twisted up in dozens of positions. I'd had him in beds and in baths and against kitchen counters.

But none of it compared to how it felt to have his mouth take mine.

Slow and intentional, sweet and needy. His soft lips met mine time and time again, exploring, discovering. The first time I parted my mouth and his tongue swept inside to taste mine, I moaned, a shock of pleasure ripping through me.

I pressed up out of the barstool and into his touch, into the kiss, my body igniting at the low groan in his throat when I did. One hand stayed firmly in my hair, his thumb still caressing my jaw, as the other snaked around my waist and pulled me into him. He couldn't get me close enough. He wanted more when there was nothing more to take.

And yet I wanted the same, like if I could strip my entire self and bestow it at his feet — I would.

"Will," I breathed against his lips, his name a question and an invocation.

"Fuck the rules," was all he answered, and then we were moving.

Blindly, we bounced down the hallway, me stepping on his feet as he dragged me along without wanting to break the kiss. When we'd hit a wall, he'd press me into it, dragging that kiss along my jaw and down my neck before he'd claim my mouth again.

Each time he did, we both moaned together, the next kiss always sweeter than the last.

He was everywhere, his hands on my body, thigh pressing between mine, hips caging, chest breathing hard in time with my own. I ceased to exist outside of his touch.

It was all consuming, a fiery surrender and a shock of light against a dark sky.

I knew we were in his room only by the way his scent invaded me. It was his body wash and leather and rope and that particular smell that was just *him*. The scent completely enveloped me when I was laid down in his sheets, and my heart ricocheted in my chest.

He'd never fucked me here before.

The only time I'd been inside this room was for a shower after our first lesson, and even that had been brief.

There was nothing rushed about this.

Will took his time, like time was all we had, slowly peeling our clothes off one article at a time. My dress, slipped over my head and left in a puddle on the floor. His shirt, pulled over his head with one hand behind his neck. My bra, unclasped and shoved aside. His shorts, button unfastened, zipper tugged down, fabric ripped to his ankles before he was descending on me again.

He punctuated each new loss of clothing with a parade of kisses along the newly exposed skin until we were both bare and trembling, holding onto each other in the darkness of that room as if it were our first time.

"Need you," he managed on a low, rough breath as he slid between my legs. He kissed me hard with the admission, his brow furrowed, heartbeat labored where I felt it thrumming through his chest. "Need you so fucking much."

I dug my nails into his back to signal that I felt the same — that I'd maybe felt it longer than I'd ever admit.

I didn't know what it meant, that he was breaking his own rules, that he'd opened up to me today and he was kissing me tonight, and that when he slid inside me, we both cried out and clung to each other.

But I knew it meant *something*.

There was a monumental shift. I felt it in every thrust of his hips, with every slide of him inside me, with every kiss he pressed along my jaw, my collarbone, and most of all, against my lips.

He moved slowly and with purpose, like he was trying to write poetry with every measured flex. There was no dirty talk, no commands, no filth whispered into my ear.

It was sensual and deep, our connection that night. It was a joining of souls. It was a white flag of surrender, a victory cry from a hard-fought battle won.

Will pressed up onto his elbows so he could lock his eyes on mine, and those honey wells held my gaze as he continued to fuck me slow and deep. The sensation of having him looking at me like that felt more powerful than anything happening below our waists, and it sent me spiraling.

I came without trying. I came with a whimpered cry and my eyes squeezing shut and my heart pounding out of my rib cage as the slow waves washed over me.

Will came right behind me, his groan low and reverberating through my throat as he kissed me there and flexed harder, deeper, burying himself in me like he never wanted to leave.

Then, he was kissing me again, his mouth on mine, tongue seeking access until I let him in. He stole what little breath I was holding onto with that kiss, and then he was moving inside me again, his release slicking me and making round two so easy to begin.

He pulled me on top, and I rode him just as slowly as he'd taken me, until he was leaning up, pulling me against him, kissing me deep as we both found a second release.

I didn't know what time it was when we finally cleaned up.

I didn't know what was racing through his mind as he washed me and kissed me and dried me with a soft towel before leading me back to bed.

I didn't know what tomorrow would bring.

But I knew that this time, he asked me to stay.

This time, he curled his hot, massive body around mine and pulled me into him, fitting us together like puzzle pieces.

This time, he held tight, like he would never let me go.

This time, we fell asleep in each other's arms.

This time was different.

Everything was different.

And I was unafraid.

Chapter 32

A Good Man

Chloe

Scratch that.

I was afraid.

I was very, *very* afraid.

The morning came too quickly, too harshly, the sunlight streaming in through the windows of Will's room. We hadn't thought to shut the blinds last night, and I winced a little as I sat up in the bed, my head aching.

Shit.

What time was it?!

I ripped the covers off me, quickly dressing and not thinking about the fact that I'd be parading about in yesterday's clothes as I ran down the hallway and up the stairs to Ava's room.

When I creaked the door open, I saw she was still sound asleep.

I let out a long breath, watching her for a moment before I silently shut the door again. Will had decided she wouldn't be going to school today, and after what happened, I called in and used my second vacation day of my career so that I could stay home with her.

I decided to let her sleep a little while longer. Judging by the sun alone, it was likely around seven-thirty or eight. After all the adrenaline yesterday, she could use the extra rest.

We all could.

And with that thought, the night came rushing back to me.

I pressed my back against the wall, heart racing as I closed my eyes and a flash of Will struck me behind the lids.

My own hands traced where his had been, washing over my neck, my collarbone, my lips. I still tasted him there, still felt the bruising pressure of his mouth seeking mine.

He kissed me.

I blinked open at the realization, chest tight and mind whirring.

The last week and a half had been so strange between us. After our last night together, I couldn't help but pull away from him... because just like my *Reddit* friends had warned, I knew I'd started falling for him.

Hell — I had already fallen. Hard. A face-planting, knee-skinning type of fall that left you bruised and bloody for life.

I thought putting distance between us was the right thing to do. The *Reddit* advice flew in faster than I could read it before I deleted everything, but it all echoed the same sentiment — pull away. Go ghost. Don't talk to him, don't confess feelings, and *definitely* don't get naked again, not until you pull your shit together.

His words from yesterday floated through me.

I miss her, I do, but I miss you more.

And then he'd kissed me.

And last night, that wasn't a lesson. That wasn't fucking.

That was making love.

That was sensual, slow, every move intentional.

I frowned, blinking rapidly and trying to keep up with my mind as it spiraled.

Because he was already gone this morning.

I tiptoed down the stairs, and when I heard rustling in the kitchen and the sound of voices, I breathed with relief again. He probably just got up to check on Ava. He was probably in the kitchen with Chef now, waiting for me.

What would he do when he saw me, I wondered?

Would we smile and wink and keep our secrets like always?

Would he pull me into him, kiss me in front of Chef, claim me for more than just the nanny he fucks occasionally?

Did I... want that, too?

That last question was both the easiest and the most difficult to answer. My heart, my *soul* responded with a resounding *yes*. I wanted him. *God*, I wanted him more than anything.

And yet there was a loud voice in my head, maybe two of them, reminding me of all the reasons it was stupid to even admit that to myself, let alone out loud.

I tried to school my features as I rounded into the kitchen, but when I stumbled upon Chef and Uncle Mitch, my steps faltered.

Uncle Mitch was in the kitchen with Arushi, laughing as they cracked eggs together over a mixing bowl. He pretended like he was going to lick his fingers and she swatted his hand away, shaking her head and calling him stupid, but with eyes that said she thought he was anything but.

It felt like a private moment, but when Chef saw me enter, she didn't act surprised. She simply smiled wider as she rinsed her hand and dried them on her apron.

"Good morning, sunshine," she said. "How's our girl doing?"

I blinked, looking around like Will would manifest out of thin air. "Still sleeping," I managed. "I'll wake her here in a bit."

"It's okay, might as well let her sleep. She didn't wake up when Will checked on her earlier, either. Poor thing is probably beat," Uncle Mitch said, crossing the kitchen to where I stood after he'd washed his own hands. He pulled me into a hug that I felt rather stiff inside before he framed my arms in his large hands.

He looked so much like Will, it made my chest hurt.

"How are *you* doing? Must have been quite a scare."

"I'm okay," I said, the lie coming a bit too easily.

He gave me a look like he knew better. "Well, Will called me this morning, asked if I'd come spend the day with Ava. He thought it might help her feel better to have this old clown around while he was at work." He winked. "Besides, he was pretty adamant that *you* take the day off."

I blinked. "Oh."

"He said you really stepped up to save the day yesterday," Chef chimed in.

And that was the crack that broke the dam inside of me.

He just... left.

He left without a word.

He left without talking about what happened last night, about what this meant, about what the hell we *were* now.

Which left *me* feeling like I'd overanalyzed it all, like it didn't matter.

Fuck the rules, he'd said. But maybe he meant just for the night.

Need you, he'd whispered. But maybe he just needed the release.

I'd read too far into it already, making a fool of myself in the span of twelve hours.

Mom would be so disappointed. Grandma would suck her teeth and shake her head.

I was a simpering idiot.

My eyes flooded so quickly I couldn't do a damn thing to stop the tears before they were streaming down my cheeks. I swiped them away as quickly as they came, but it was too late.

Mitch and Arushi shared a concerned look, and then Chef was wiping her hands again, hooking me by the arm and tugging me out into the back yard. She barked some orders for Mitch to take over in the kitchen, and then we were outside and she was hugging me in the shade near the pool.

"Okay. This is not about Ava," she said, squeezing me tight as more tears fell. "What's going on?"

I sniffed as I pulled back, shaking my head, emotion clogging my throat and making it impossible to speak. But Chef Patel wasn't taking no for an answer. She stood there with me, letting me cry, letting me feel it all while she rubbed my arms and waited.

"Oh, sweetie," she said after a while, her thick brows folding inward. "You love him."

I covered my face and cried harder, ashamed by the possibility that she might be correct.

"I'm a foolish girl," I whispered.

"Stop that." Arushi pulled me to sit in one of the lounge chairs, taking the one next to me and folding my hands in hers. "He loves you, too, silly."

I barked out a laugh at that.

"Don't laugh me off," Chef said. "I know that man, okay? I've had four years in this house with him, with his grumpiness and general disdain for the world. But you?" She smiled, shaking her head. "You made him smile again, made him *laugh* again. You brought the light back in. Not just for him, but for all of us — for me, for Ava. You may not be able to see that clearly, but I can."

"He left," I said, sniffing and bringing my eyes to her. "We... last night, we..."

Chef made a *tsk* noise, but her disappointment wasn't toward me. "He is such a *bewakoof.*"

The corner of my mouth lifted, because I didn't need to know the literal translation to know she was calling him an idiot of some kind.

"It's fine," I tried, wiping my nose with the back of my hand. "We had an... agreement of sorts. And this is what we agreed to. It's just that last night, something... well, he..."

I groaned, slapping my forehead at the stupidity of it all. Was I really going to say *he kissed me, so I thought it was different?*

Chef leaned down to catch my eyes. "Start from the beginning, and tell me everything."

Every part of me wanted to scream *no, thanks*, but at the same time... I *needed* to talk to someone about it. And Arushi and I had become friends, *good* friends.

How long had I wished for friends like her, like Maven and Livia and Grace?

So, after a deep breath, I let it all spill.

I told her about the tension between Will and me in the beginning, about the night we'd made a deal. I told her about the rules, how they'd been bent even from the beginning, how we violated the *let's not be friends* part almost immediately. I told her about why he'd booked the boutique for me, about how he'd opened up to me about Jenny, about all the nights we stayed up talking and laughing, about how he'd kissed me, and what he'd said...

Fuck the rules.

When I finished, I felt like hiding, but Chef wouldn't let me.

"Listen to me," she said, taking my hand in hers. She seemed to be struggling to find the right words. "I am not making an excuse for him, okay? I want to make that clear. I am so upset with him and how he handled this morning that I have a right mind to storm down to the arena and pull him back here by his ear." She shook her head. "But, if I know him the way I think I do, my bet is that his mind is just as stirred up as yours." She squeezed my hand. "My bet is that he just needs a moment to get his thoughts together."

I let out a sigh.

It felt dangerous to hitch a wagon to that little bicycle of hope.

"You have the right to make whatever decision you need to for yourself," she continued. "And I want you to do that without any influence from me. But, for whatever it's worth... I think he loves you, my dear. I think he loves you so much it has scared the ever-living shit out of him. And I think he's probably blocking shots at the rink this morning, jumping rope, and killing himself on an exercise bike trying to work through the mountain of thoughts in his head. He's scared — just like you are. He doesn't want to ruin anything, least of all what you have with Ava. He's treading carefully. But," she said. "That doesn't give him a right to not ease your mind, to not *tell* you that's what's going on and let you in. It's unfair for him to just leave after a night like you had with him. So, if you see this as a red flag and you don't want to hear him out, I won't blame you." She shrugged. "But I hope you'll give him a chance to surprise you."

We were both quiet for a long moment, and I laughed a little, running her words over in my head.

"This advice is so different from what I would receive from my mom and grandma," I said, giving her a wry smile. "They'd be calling him all kinds of names, telling me they were right, making me regret ever questioning their way of life in avoiding men altogether."

"Well, sometimes bitterness can eat us alive," Arushi said. "And everyone makes the choices that feel right to them. For some of us, that means blocking the source of what hurt us and never taking a risk again. For others, it means picking ourselves up, dusting ourselves off, and getting back on the horse."

I nodded, considering.

"Listen, I also don't have the best track record with men," Chef confessed. "But I think I know a good one when I meet them. I think I can tell pretty quickly what lies at the heart of someone. And I can tell you in all honesty, without hesitation, that Will is a good man." She arched a brow at me. "I think you know that already, too."

"I do," I said, rolling my lips together. "But just because he's a good man doesn't mean he's ready to be a good partner."

384

"Oof," Chef said, tapping my hand as she stood. "I can't argue that. I think you need some space to think. And maybe a trip to see your family."

"They'll just yell at me."

"Then let them yell," she said. "But find your own voice, too, Chloe. You have a strong one. And you have something to say, something *worth* saying. It's okay to disagree with them. And it's okay if they disapprove when you do. Because let me tell you something — having their approval will mean nothing if you lose your own happiness in the process."

Those words hung over me as Arushi left to head back inside.

In fact, they stayed with me all through breakfast. Ava joined us in bright spirits, and I helped her with her ankle before she and Uncle Mitch were laid out in bean bags in the living room with her favorite show on the television. He and Chef both urged me to take the day off like Will had suggested, and after a shower, changing into fresh clothes, and feeding my fur babies — I decided they might be right.

I was still hurt by Will leaving without a word that morning, but after talking to Arushi, I realized that I might be jumping to conclusions. I was built to do that. It was in my blood, drilled into me by two women I looked up to and respected all my life.

But was there no room for understanding, for compassion, for realizing that just like I have baggage and won't always be perfect... the same is true for him?

Still, I didn't even know what he was thinking. Maybe he really *was* just an asshole, and he'd come home later and act like nothing happened, like last night was just another night of *our deal*.

Even as I thought it, that possibility felt weak.

Regardless, I wouldn't know until later, and right now, I needed to take my own time to figure out what *I* wanted.

And to do so, the first thing I needed to do was face my past.

So, I snatched my keys off the counter, hugged everyone goodbye for the day, and headed to Mom and Grandma's.

Chapter 33

Heartless Fucking Pricks

Will

I needed to go home.

It was after two in the afternoon now — far past the end of practice and any excuse I had to stay at the arena. My body was weak, rebelling against my whirring mind as I pushed myself to exhaustion on one of the bikes in the team gym.

I'd shown up earlier than necessary, rolling in at seven when practice didn't even start until nine. After practice, we had a meeting pre-scouting our opponents for tomorrow's game, and then most of the team had stayed for an hour or two of training before leaving.

But I was still here.

Vince and Jaxson invited me to Vince's beach house to get away for a while, but I declined.

Coach checked in on me, making me promise not to work myself into the ground before the game tomorrow. Still, I stayed.

kandi steiner

Now, I had sweat dripping into my eyes, hands weak on the handlebars, legs aching as I pedaled slower and slower, my energy leaving me in monstrous waves now. But I wanted the pain. I wanted the fatigue. I wanted to feel *anything* other than the gaping hole in my chest.

I was a fucking coward.

I'd woken in the middle of the night with my chest so tight I thought I was having a heart attack. The reality of what I'd done with Chloe was like a thousand knives to the gut, and I'd curled into a ball on the floor of my bathroom until my breathing had somewhat steadied.

As soon as it had, I'd dressed, slipping out into the living room without saying a word to Chloe. She'd looked so peaceful sleeping in my sheets, and the longer I watched her, the more I longed to just climb back in with her.

But she deserved more than that.

She deserved me knowing what to say when we finally spoke. She deserved me having a decision made, a plan, an apology... an explanation.

I didn't have any of that in the early morning light, so I left her with a kiss on her forehead and a silent promise that I'd have something worth her time when I returned.

I'd checked on Ava, called in Uncle Mitch, let Chef Patel know that I wanted Chloe to take the day off, and then... I'd left.

It made perfect sense when I did it.

I justified my actions with excuses that felt sound. I just needed a little time to think, to work through what this meant, to know what to say when I saw her. I'd just get through practice and then I'd suddenly know what to do.

But the longer I was at the rink, the more I worked my body into the ground, the more I realized it wouldn't stop my mind from racing. It wouldn't change the fact that I didn't *know* what all this meant or what came next.

I only knew that somewhere along the way, I'd fallen in love with Chloe Knott.

And that wasn't a part of our agreement.

I should have stayed this morning. I should have worked through it with her. I should have confessed that I'm an idiot and that she makes me want to break every rule I've ever made.

But I was afraid.

I was afraid of not having control, of not being the one with everything handled.

I was afraid of repeating a past that still haunted me to this day, of hurting her, of putting her in danger somehow just by becoming involved with her.

There was so much riding on what happened next. If I confessed my feelings for her, would she even reciprocate them? Would she want what I do?

To be together?

The best-case scenario was that she would, and even that would leave a host of questions — her employment with me, her living situation, her job at the school once she was in the media limelight...

Ava.

My chest tightened at the thought of my daughter, of how this would impact her.

Because the worst-case scenario of me telling Chloe how I felt would be that she *didn't* want what I want, that I crossed a line and now she's uncomfortable.

That now she wanted to leave.

And even if the best-case scenario happened, there was the very real possibility that Chloe and I may not work out in the long run. And then where would that leave us?

Where would that leave my daughter?

The other option was to lie to her, to say last night meant nothing, that the last few *months* had meant nothing.

The best-case scenario *there* would be that she agreed, that we'd laugh it off and go back to whatever kind of normal we could find after. The worst case would be that I hurt her, that she admits there's more to it for her and she can't continue the way we have been.

And in both situations — it was still a lie.

A lie I couldn't live with.

A lie I wasn't even sure I could mutter at this point.

My mind was a hot, seeping mess of thoughts like these, one whipping in before the previous thought could even pack its bags. This was what I had been so afraid of from the beginning. It was why I told myself to stay far away from her, to not entertain my desire for her.

But I had.

And that desire wasn't born from wanting her body alone.

It was from wanting *all* of her.

I loved her.

I knew it before I even admitted it silently to myself, and yet the thought hit me like a train. I stopped pedaling, hanging my arms on the bars and resting my head between them in defeat.

I fucking *loved* her.

I loved her positivity, her light, her humor. I loved how strong and independent she was, how she'd created a life on her own without needing attention or validation from anyone else. I loved that she knew herself so fully, that she was so unapologetic in her hobbies, her philosophies, her way of life.

I loved the way she loved my daughter.

I loved how she'd brought the sunshine into our lives, how she'd made that giant house a home.

I loved the way she laughed, the way she found a way to make *me* laugh again. I loved her crazy midnight existential crises and her asshole cats.

I loved how she knew what I needed before I ever had to say it, and how she let me in when everything inside her said she shouldn't.

I'd taken that trust for granted this morning.

I should have said *something*, but I'd clammed all the way up.

And now, as the hours ticked by, it felt like it was too late to fix it.

Once again, I was frozen, a prisoner of my own stupidity.

The gym door opened without a sound, the only cue a brush of cold air drafting across my heated skin. I dragged myself to sit upright, mopping my face with a towel before I looked over my shoulder.

Aleks Suter looked grumpier than me when he sauntered in, his brows furrowed, teeth practically bared as he slung his bag into a corner. As the final push before playoffs did to all of us, he was thinner than when the season started, his muscles more pronounced from days and days of skating nonstop.

He walked over to me without a greeting, standing directly in front of my bike and folding his arms over his chest.

"Listen to me, and listen to me well," he said, not giving me a chance to tell him to fuck off before he kept on, his voice growing louder. "I understand you're usually the one who whips guys into shape around here. I saw it when

I first joined the team and for many months after. I know when someone is distracted, you call them back to the task at hand. I know when someone is having issues off the ice, you're the one who talks them through it until there's a solution that doesn't impact the team in a negative way. I know you're a leader. But right now, you're falling apart. You're held together by a single thread. I don't know who else sees it, but I sure as shit do, and we're going to squash whatever is going on right the fuck now. You're not leaving this room until you talk it out. Because we have eight games left before the playoffs, Perry, and I'll be damned if I let you ruin my shot at the Cup after all I've been through to get to this point."

I blinked, both unamused and impressed by his outburst. "You finished?"

"Yep. Your turn." He hopped up in the bike seat next to me, leaning his back against the handlebars and waiting.

For a long moment, I just glared at him. Who the fuck did he think he was, coming in here and demanding *shit* from me? He was a punk, one who had been a real pain in my ass since he first arrived. Even now, he was stirring up media bullshit in a time when our team needed to focus.

And what did he mean after everything *he'd* been through?

Smoke came out of my ears as I tried to figure it out. I knew he'd had a rough go on the team he was with before, but it was *his* fault. And likely, the reason they'd choked in the playoffs three years in a row was because he was too busy being a sideshow to be there for his team.

Or maybe I was seeing it wrong.

Maybe there was more to it.

"What do you mean, *after all you've been through?*"

"Nope," he said instantly. "Not about me. This is about you."

I flattened my lips. "I'm fine. Working through some personal things."

"Great. I'm all ears."

He kicked back even more, crossing his arms again.

The bastard.

Sweat came faster than I could wipe it away, and I knew I'd pushed too hard. I'd pay for this in the game tomorrow. I needed an ice bath and some soft tissue work at the very least.

"I don't have all day," Aleks prompted when I took a while to speak.

I sighed. "We're not friends, Suter. And this is personal. So, just trust me when I say I'm fine and I'll work it out."

"No can do," he said. "Vince is tied up with wedding shit. Grace is in town, so Jaxson isn't an option either. That means you get me."

I flattened my lips, ready to walk out if I could get my legs to work. But then he asked a question that made it impossible to move.

"It's the nanny, isn't it?"

Shit.

My face must have answered him where my words couldn't, because he grinned, shaking his head and arching a brow. "I knew it. Let me guess — you took my advice to get your dick wet but *didn't* take my advice to set up rules. So now you've got your feelings all involved."

"Fuck you," I spat, gripping him by the shirt. I pulled his face to mine. Just him talking about her like she was the kind of girl you could fuck and forget made me seethe.

"Not all of us are heartless fucking pricks like you are, okay?"

His face went neutral at that, the corner of his lips curling before they fell. I thought I might have struck a nerve. I was about to apologize when he shrugged and laughed.

"Yeah, well, look where having a heart got you."

I glared at him a moment longer before releasing him and sinking back into my bike seat.

"You knew before you even started hooking up, didn't you?" Aleks asked. "You knew she was different. You knew you wanted more from her."

I swallowed.

"Wanna know how I know?" Aleks continued. "Because I think we're more alike than you want to admit. And I think you know how to scratch your itches when necessary without ever crossing any lines into this territory. You could have easily gone to Boomer's. You could have fucked a puck bunny and left it at that. But you found a way to fuck *her*, instead."

He held up his hands when I snarled at him.

"I'm not saying that disrespectfully," he said quickly. "I'm just saying, you knew. You liked her then. You wanted her and you didn't just want sex, even if you did set rules."

"I did," I ground out.

"Sure, and how fast did you break them?"

Goddamn it, he was good at this.

He chuckled when I didn't answer. "How bad is it?"

"Bad," I croaked.

"Come on, tell me," he said, waving his hand. "The sooner you get this out, the sooner we can both move on. God knows I don't want to be here any longer than I have to smelling your stinky ass."

Maybe I was possessed in that moment, or maybe I was just too exhausted to fight — because for reasons unbeknownst to me... I told Aleks fucking Suter everything that had happened between me and Chloe.

I don't know what I expected as I laid it all out. I watched his face for signs of judgment, but found none. When I finished and he was all caught up, he was quiet for a long time, nodding and scrubbing the five o'clock shadow on his jaw.

"You want to know what I would do?" he asked. "Or do you want me to tell you what I would *want* to do, but wouldn't be strong enough for?"

I frowned. "Both."

"Well, if it were me, I'd fire her," he said. "Because you're in love with her, Perry. Plain and simple. And you're right. There's a very real possibility one of you, if not both of you, gets hurt in this. She changes her mind. You change yours. And with Ava in the picture..."

My throat closed in on itself at the thought of letting Chloe go — both as our nanny and as the lifeline I didn't realize she'd become to me. "And the other option?"

The muscle in his jaw worked for a moment as he looked at me like he wasn't sure he could voice it. Finally, his voice lower than before, he said, "I'd own my mistake of leaving without a word this morning, I'd chase her down wherever she is, and I'd throw myself at her feet. I'd admit I have no fucking idea what I'm doing but that I want her, consequences be damned. I wouldn't count all the ways it could go wrong. I wouldn't let fear hold me back. I'd believe in love."

I swore, I saw a thousand ghosts dancing in his eyes as he spoke, like he wasn't just talking about me and Chloe.

"You don't believe in love?" I asked.

"I believe love is very rarely reciprocated, and it's reserved for men much better than me."

His expression hardened before I could question him more on that, and he hopped off the bike, clamping a hand hard on my shoulder.

"Look — all I can say is that I've known you the least amount of time out of everyone on this team, and even *I* can see how good this girl has been for you. For your family. I can also see that *not* giving in to your feelings for her has twisted you up into a fucking knot. So, let me ask you this — when I proposed the option of losing her altogether, did it make you sick to think about?"

"Positively ill."

"Then you already know the answer. What happened with Jenny..."

I stiffened at her name, and I wouldn't have thought it was possible had I not seen it with my own eyes, but Aleks softened, frowning, taking a moment to consider his words.

"It was fucking brutal, man. I... I'm sorry you had to go through it. Life handed you a real shit card with that, and I don't blame you for never wanting to go through anything like it again. I'm not going to sit here and tell you everything with Chloe will be a fairy tale, and I have no idea what her lifespan will be. Sure, you might lose her. But hell, we could all lose someone. It's a possibility every single day. That's why they stitch shit on pillows about hugging everyone you love and making the most of every moment."

I almost laughed.

"So yeah, I don't know what will happen or how long you'll have with her. Maybe forever. Maybe just a few months. But I do know that my goalie ain't no fucking bitch," he said with a smirk. "And you're a better man than I am, than most are. So, don't let fear fuck this up. Don't lose her because of *what ifs*."

"But what if she doesn't want this?" I shot back immediately. "I told you about her family, about her past... and here I am already proving her theory correct."

"So grovel, you dumbass," Aleks said simply. "And then do your best every day to prove her wrong, to prove her mom and grandma wrong, too. And if she doesn't accept that, if she doesn't want more, then you respect it and you move the fuck on. Jesus," he added, shaking his head and releasing his hold on me. "Alright, are we done with this? I'm breaking out in hives. And you smell like dog shit."

I chuckled, nodding. "Yeah, yeah, we're done." I stood, wincing as every muscle in my body protested when I did. I clapped him on the back. "Thanks, man. I think I was wrong about you. You're not the little shit I thought you were."

"Don't get excited," he said, shrugging me off. "I'm exactly who you think I am."

"Seems like you're being who you *want* me to think you are — who you want everyone to think you are."

"Like you said before, we aren't friends, Perry," he said, and he was already walking for the door when he shot over his shoulder. "And we'll all be happier if we keep it that way."

He left without another word, and the silence of the team gym covered me, my ears ringing in the quiet.

I looked up at the mirror, at the sweat dripping off me, at my hunched shoulders and ragged, red eyes.

I was a wreck. I was so much less than what Chloe deserved.

And yet, I felt the burning in my chest to be better.

For her.

For Ava.

For our family.

I showered quickly, ignoring the pain racking my body, and then I was on the phone as I packed my bag and headed for the team parking lot.

"How's Ava?" I asked Mitch when he answered.

"Oh, bounced back like the trooper she is. She's sore, I can tell, but she's strong. We're making popcorn and settling in for another movie."

I nodded, chest on fire as I all but sprinted for my car. "Is Chloe there?"

"No, she took the day off like you told her to." He paused. "Why?"

"I need to talk to her."

"You finally going to tell her you're in love?"

That stopped me in my tracks only for a moment before I opened my trunk and slung my bag inside. "Sure am."

Uncle Mitch let out a rich growl of a laugh, and I swore I heard Chef Patel laughing in the background, too. It was a bit early for her to be there prepping for dinner, but maybe she'd wanted to stay with Ava. She loved her like her own.

"About damn time!" she called.

"I hope my daughter is in the other room?"

"She is," Mitch confirmed. "But my bet is that she knows it, too, you dummy."

"Okay, we can all take turns calling me names later. Any clue where Chloe went?"

"Her mom's," Chef answered.

Double shit.

I knew from all Chloe had told me just how her mom and grandmother felt about men.

I guess I was about to experience their wrath in real time.

Chapter 34

What's Left of Me

Chloe

The screaming had stopped.

To their credit, Mom and Grandma had refrained from all the *I told you so's* I'd expected from them. Mostly, it was them yelling the more I told of the story, saying how selfish and awful Will was, and how he'd set a trap for a naïve young woman and how they'd hang him up to dry by his toes.

I'd stuck up for him at first, but the more they went on and on, the less I knew what to say. They had a comeback for everything, reasons built by decades of experience that I didn't have.

So, once again, like I had that morning... I just felt like a foolish little girl.

It seemed to soften them, the more they realized I didn't want to argue. It was like I was a poor fox that had stumbled upon a bear trap they'd warned me about in the woods. They were mad because they were afraid, but really, they just wanted to make sure I was okay.

Grandma had made tea while Mom assured me it would all be okay. She said nothing needed to be figured out right now, and that I should stay with them for the night. I hadn't really agreed, but I hadn't declined, either.

I didn't know what to do.

Now, hours later, it was quiet in the house, Grandma tinkering with a new bread recipe in the kitchen while Mom and I watched an old *Gilmore Girls* episode. My head was in Mom's lap, her hands playing with my hair as I cried silently and swiped the tears away before they could hit her leg.

My heart felt like it was being crushed inside my chest. I couldn't stop reliving last night, couldn't stop replaying the last few months and looking for clues that what my mom and grandma said was right. Did he really just use me?

It didn't sit right, the thought of that possibility. I knew from the moment he stormed through the pool house sliding glass doors that first night that it was more. I could see it in his eyes, could sense it in the way he took me, the way he touched me, the way he drove me over the edge of desire.

Even before that, I could see the admiration in his eyes when he saw me working at the school, could feel the way he'd soften whenever he observed me with Ava. I thought about the nights in the house watching *Jeopardy*, the mornings at the breakfast table, the games, the pool...

And through all of that, I never saw any signs that Will was some horrid man just out to bang his nanny.

It just wasn't who he was.

Chef Patel's words were what I clung to more than anything — perhaps foolishly. I wanted to believe she was right, that he was just scared like I was, that he needed a moment.

But my heart kept banging against my ribs and reminding me that she could be wrong.

It was nearly four o'clock now, and I still hadn't heard from Will.

Mom laughed at something Lorelei Gilmore said, her belly jiggling against my head and drawing me back to the present. I watched the screen with my eyes losing focus, and then, the doorbell rang.

"I got it," Grandma called.

Mom barely acknowledged it, and I was too weak to move from where I laid.

That was — until I heard a familiar, deep voice.

I shot upright, eyes wide and hands flying up to try to tame what I knew was a wild bird's nest of hair.

"What?" Mom asked, alarmed, but I was already on the move.

I wiped my face just in case there were any tears still there, hands smoothing over my wrinkled dress as I rounded the living area into the foyer.

My legs stopped working as soon as I saw him.

Will stood in the doorway, his expression solemn and sincere as he said something to my grandmother. When he saw me, he stopped mid-sentence, his eyes taking in what I knew to be a haggard appearance.

But he looked at me like I was everything.

His eyes were wide, brow creasing a bit like he immediately wanted to hold me and erase the pain I knew was laden in every feature. He looked like just as much of a mess as me, his face long, fatigue written all over him from his tired eyes to his slumped shoulders.

But *God*, he was still gorgeous.

He was still the man who had framed my face last night and kissed me oblivious. He was still the father who cared more for his daughter than anything in the world. He was still the starting goalie for a playoff hockey team, the friend who bought me, a grown woman, a makeover at the Bibbidi Bobbidi Boutique.

King of my heart.

Said heart thumped faster when Will took a step, his eyes locked on mine, jaw tight.

But Grandma pressed her metal spatula into his chest, keeping him from moving one more inch.

"You've got a lot of nerve showing up here," she grumped at him, and I didn't need to see her face to know it was the one I used to get when I'd make the mistake of talking back to her as a child.

"Grandma," I hissed, rushing the rest of the way down the hall. I tried to scoot her aside, but the old woman was built like a brick house.

"You go on back inside, Chloe May, I'll handle this one."

I groaned, pinching the bridge of my nose when she started tapping her spatula against her other hand like it was a baseball bat and she was the leader of a street gang.

"Who is it?" Mom called, on her way to join us.

Great.

"If it's Marv again, I already told him we—"

Mom's words cut off when she joined us in the hall, and she narrowed her gaze before pulling me behind her like she had to save me.

"I know you aren't stupid enough to show your face here after what you've put our little girl through," Mom seethed.

My face was flaming hot as I grimaced and caught Will's gaze through the blockade my matriarch had made around me. *Sorry* I mouthed, embarrassment flooding my nervous system.

But Will just smiled, the corner of his lips lifting before he stood taller, shoulders squared, and looked right at my mom when he said, "I'm afraid I am, ma'am. Stupid, that is."

His eyes met mine again.

"Stupidly in love with your daughter."

$$\cdots$$

Will

I felt like a bunny rabbit trying to infiltrate a coyote's den.

Chloe's mom glared at me harder after the words left my mouth, and her grandma clucked her tongue like I was an idiot. I wasn't here to argue that.

Instead, I kept my focus on Chloe, watching as her lips parted when I confessed what I'd known to be true far longer than I wanted to admit.

She was an absolute wreck — the most beautiful mess I'd ever seen. Her hair was matted and wavy, sticking to her neck and chin, the back of it fluffed up behind her like she was a pissed-off bird of some kind. Her face was ashen, save for the blush that touched her cheeks, and even with the distance between us, I could see evidence that she'd been crying.

I hated myself for that, for making her wonder where my head was all day long. I found myself again longing for a time machine to go back to this morning, to have climbed into bed with her and pulled her against me and woke her with a dozen kisses before telling her the truth.

That I was scared.

That I didn't know what to do.

That I didn't know how to act, now that the rules had been blown to smithereens.

But I couldn't go back. I only had right here, right now — and apparently, we had an audience.

"Chloe, you know I'm no good with words," I said, swallowing at the truth of that statement. "I never have been. It got worse after Jenny passed, and to be honest, I never cared. I never felt like I had a thing to say. Not until you came into my life."

Chloe tried to squeeze through the barricade her mom and grandmother had made, but they snuffed her out, both of them arching a brow at me.

"But I'm going to try," I continued. "For you. I'm going to try to voice what I should have a long time ago. I'm going to try to be better in every measurable way. Because that's what you deserve. It's what you make me want for myself. You..." I swallowed, shaking my head. "You have burrowed into my heart so deeply, it feels like you've always been there. It feels as if my heart would cease to beat if I lost you."

Chloe's eyes welled with tears, her nose flaring as she covered her lips with shaking fingertips.

"One day, I was just a shadow of a man going through the motions, surviving. And the next, I had you. Suddenly, I was awake. Suddenly, I was smiling, and laughing, and longing for someone in a way I didn't know was possible. You... you altered my fucking chemistry, Chloe. You obliterated the dark haze I'd existed in for *years*. You brought in the sun."

"Language, young man," her grandmother warned, but I didn't miss how she was now leaning against the door frame, her spatula lowered, her guard down.

"Apologies, ma'am," I said, offering her a sheepish smile before my gaze was on Chloe once more.

I wanted to hold her. I wanted to sweep her into my arms and be able to touch her as I confessed every last word.

"I knew even when I set those flimsy rules between us that they were useless. That *I* was powerless against the way I already felt for you. I tried, Chloe. I did. I tried to stay away from you. I tried to keep us both from this... this pain, this foreign territory. I knew you weren't looking for a man. I knew you didn't want to date anyone. I knew I wasn't *worth* dating, that I was so fu—" I swallowed, noting the warning glare from Grandma. "Messed up that I couldn't be the man you deserved. But it didn't matter. Not my best intentions, not my futile attempts to keep us both safe by drawing out the do's and the don'ts." I shook my head. "Because you are not the kind of woman any rule applies to. You are the exception. You are the one they're meant to be broken for."

Chloe smiled, crossing her arms over her stomach as her bottom lip wobbled.

"I'm sorry I left without a word this morning. I'm sorry I was too much of a coward to stay and work this out with you. I thought taking a little time and space would somehow make the answers magically appear. But the truth is I have *no idea* what comes next. I don't know how we navigate the new road ahead of us. All I know is that the second I kissed you, everything changed.

"Maybe we'll only make it a few months. Maybe I'll give you my last name and we'll grow old together. Maybe it'll be something in-between. Whatever it is, I know that it's worth any pain that might come, any challenges, any roadblocks. And I know I want this. I want you. I want *us*."

My hands were shaking now, but I held her gaze, held my promise.

"I want your ridiculous fuzzy robes in the morning and your tea-breath kisses. I want your laughs with my daughter and your midnight existential crises. I want your cat hair on my clothes and your imprint on my heart. I want to watch you make a mess of our house with every new creation, want to listen to every wise word you share with my daughter who I know loves you more than even I do already. I want to feel you in my arms at the end of every night and inhale the scent of you on my pillow at the start of every morning.

"I'm going to screw up, that I know without a doubt. But I can also promise you that I will always make it right after. I will always come back to you, better than before, until I am everything you deserve and more. I will care for you, the way you care so fiercely for everyone around you. I will make you a home. I will protect you, and always make sure you have all the room you need to roam."

I took a step toward her, not breaking through the human barricade, but standing tall on the other side of it, holding her gaze with the weight of the world resting on my shoulders.

"I will love you, Chloe, with every broken shard of what's left of me. And I will rebuild with you — *for* you. If this is what you want. If you feel the same. And if you don't, I will let you go." I shook my head, throat tight as I whispered. "But between you and me, I am a very selfish man. And I... I don't want to let you go. I don't want to

407

live another moment without you. All of you. In every way you'll be mine."

When the last word was said, I realized how hard I was breathing, how much my hands trembled before I shoved them into my pockets.

A quiet hum fell over the four of us, though in my mind, it was only me and Chloe in that moment. It was just me, standing there with what little I had to offer, and her, holding the power to crush me or make me whole again.

She rolled her lips together, sniffing before she tried to shove through her mom and grandma. For a moment, they resisted her. I saw them share a look, one I couldn't quite read.

And then they parted like the Red Sea.

Chloe blinked, like she was surprised she didn't have to fight them.

"I don't know about you," her grandmother said to her mom. "But Gerald never said anything like that to me."

Chloe's mom let out a puff of a laugh, waving her hand. "Please. Brian would sooner chew off his own foot than say a damn nice word about me."

They both softened a bit, like they were in their own world, and then Chloe's grandma pulled her into a hug, and her mom turned to look at me.

"If you hurt her..." she threatened, not even needing to lift a finger for me to feel the warning loud and clear.

"You have full permission to take me out," I said. "In whatever way you want. I accept baseball bat to the head or being run over by a car."

The woman's mouth tilted at that, like she wasn't sure how she felt about me yet — but she was warming.

"Come on, Mom," she said, looping her arm through the older woman who shared so many similarities. "Let's leave them to it."

She stopped only long enough to touch her daughter's cheek, thumbing it and whispering, "Be careful with that heart of yours."

Then, the women left us, and Chloe rushed into my arms.

I pulled the door shut before crushing her to me, inhaling her sweet scent — chai and sugar and crayons. I clung to her like she wasn't real, burying my face in her neck before I finally set her feet back on the ground.

"Okay, *what* was all that?" she said, sniffing and smacking my chest playfully. "*I'm not good with words* and then proceeds to wax poetry?"

"Honestly, I think I blacked out."

She chuckled, winding her arms around my neck. Her eyes searched mine, her brows folding in. "You love me?"

I nodded, sweeping her hair back and running my thumb along her jaw. "Think you can love me back?"

"Hmm... maybe. You are pretty talented with a Popsicle..."

She smiled with the tease, pressing up onto her tiptoes until her mouth melted with mine. I slid my hands into her hair to hold her there, breathing in that kiss, that woman, that moment. I never wanted to let her go. I never wanted to remember what it was like before her.

"I love you already," she whispered against my lips. "I fell for you long ago — even though everyone on *Reddit* warned me against it."

I blinked. "Um... did you just say Reddit?"

Her cheeks flamed, and she slid her hand down to mine. "I'll tell you about that another time."

"I think I'd like to know now," I insisted as I followed her to the car. She bypassed hers, a silent agreement passing between us that we'd worry about getting it later.

"Well, you'll have to wait. Because right now, I want to go home."

"Home," I echoed, holding the car door open for her.

She paused long enough to press her lips to mine with a smile. "Home."

Chloe slid inside the passenger seat, and I drove her to the house just as she asked, but I knew the truth.

Home was wherever she was.

Chapter 35

You Little Brat

Chloe

The dinner table was alive with laughter that night.

Uncle Mitch and Chef Patel sat on one side, Ava and I sat on the other, and Will was at the head. Despite her ankle still being swollen and tender, Ava charmed us with her stories of the day, making a recovery day of watching movies sound like a safari adventure.

I didn't miss the way Mitch watched Arushi when she spoke, didn't miss the way she flushed when she realized he was watching her, either. When our eyes met across the table, I lifted a brow in question, but she just sucked her teeth and waved me off.

I'd cleaned up a bit when we'd arrived, making sure my face and hair didn't show evidence of the hellish day. In all honesty, it felt like a lifetime ago already, like it was something I hadn't lived at all.

All the pain had been erased, word by word, thanks to the man to my right.

He barely took his eyes off me throughout the dinner, and when I told the story of how Coconut came to join my little family, he hung on every word like it was gospel.

Then, as we all laughed together, he covered my hand on the table with his own.

My heart leapt into my throat when he did, soaring into the sky and sinking into my gut at once. It was the most incredible, powerful feeling, to be claimed by him like that, to feel the action behind every word he'd spoken earlier. And yet, it was new, unfamiliar, terrifying.

Chef and Mitch grew quiet when it happened, sharing a look over their wine glasses before they went back to eating with little smiles of victory on their lips. And when I chanced a glance at Ava, she was completely unbothered. She smiled at the gesture, and then proceeded to kick her feet under the table while she did her little happy dance she often did when mac and cheese was on the menu.

Will squeezed my hand in his, and I bit my lip, disbelief dancing with the most unbridled joy in my belly.

After dinner, Mitch helped Chef clean up, and then they were headed out the door. Will and I spent time with Ava, who was very sad her father wouldn't play a game of paper towel hockey with her until she'd rested her ankle for at least a week. But she settled for a book and an imaginary cookie baking with her teddy bears, and then she let us tuck her in, already falling asleep before we could turn on her nightlight.

It was just the two of us, then.

Wordlessly, Will wrapped my hand in his, tugging me down the stairs and into the dark hallway that led to his bedroom. We'd no sooner made it through the door before he was shutting it behind me, pressing me into it, and kissing me senseless.

His lips warmed mine, and I sighed, melting into his touch like it was the first time. The tension in his shoulders relaxed, too, like he'd been waiting for this moment, for the second he could get me alone and touch me how he wanted to.

Like always, he was all-encompassing, his hands traveling the length of me before they were in my hair and cradling my skull. He had the power to make me feel so small and yet so cherished, protected and revered.

"I love you," he whispered on a sigh, punctuating the declaration with a long, deep kiss.

"You just want to hear me say it back."

He grinned against my kiss, spinning me and backing me up to the bed. "You caught me. Now give me what I want."

"Say please."

I fell back into the mattress, and he was immediately crawling over me, his lips marking every inch on the way up to my mouth.

"I'll beg all night, if that's what you want."

I moaned when he hiked my thigh up and pressed his desire against me, his mouth claiming mine.

"Please, Chloe," he growled, rolling his hips and sparking a wave of chills. "Say it."

"Fuck me, Daddy," I whimpered, writhing against him.

He balked, whole body freezing as I grinned and bit my lip.

Then, he was laughing, shaking his head and digging his fingers into my ribs. "You little brat."

"Mmm, gonna spank me?"

He tickled me mercilessly, until I was thrashing and nearly crying from laughing so hard. I pushed until he let me climb on top of him, and then I straddled his hips and framed his head with my hands in the mattress, lowering my mouth to his.

"I love you, you impossibly frustrating man," I said, kissing him between each word. I ground against his erection with a sigh. "Now give me what *I* want."

"Yes, ma'am."

We were all hands after that — fingers sliding buttons through fabric, zippers unzipping, clothing being shed left and right. We laughed as we maneuvered one another, the dance not graceful or sexy in any capacity, but then we were bare to each other, warm bodies pressing against one another and trembling with need.

I clawed at his back when he flipped me into the comforter and began kissing his way down between my thighs. I wanted him inside me, impatient as ever, but he just grinned against my skin and took his sweet time making me writhe beneath him.

Every press of his lips against my skin was searing hot, a branding iron I didn't want to run from. I longed for his name all over me, for him to leave his mark for me and all the world to see.

"I'm going to taste this sweet cunt every fucking day for the rest of my life," he rasped, licking me with one hot, flat strike of his tongue that had me bowing off the bed.

"I don't think you've clued me in on this plan," I panted, whimpering when he began working that expert tongue against me. "No ring on my finger."

"Yet," he growled, and then my thighs were prisoners to his strong grip, and he was feasting while I moaned and held onto the comforter for dear life.

Yet.

The word sent electricity soaring through me, the thought of being his forever a strong enough notion to make my knees quake and my heart give out.

But all thoughts raced from me the more he worked his tongue and fingers in the perfect way to unravel me. I came on his tongue, trying not to scream too loud as he held me against him and didn't relent until I was falling lax and struggling to catch my breath.

Even then, he blew hot air over my sensitive clit and kissed along my inner thighs until I was grabbing at his shoulders and pulling him up. I rolled onto my stomach, bending one knee toward my chest and looking over my shoulder with my ass offered to him like a prize.

I fucking loved this position now. Ever since that night in the hotel room, it was one of my favorites. I knew by the way Will groaned and bit his lip that it was one of his, too. His hands reached for my ass, palming it in the appreciative way he always did before he was lining himself up where I wanted him most.

He slid inside me easily, my pussy wet from his mouth and my release. When he filled me to the hilt, we both gasped and moaned — me loud enough that he was covering my mouth with one hand and grinning against my ear.

"Shhh," he said, and my eyes rolled back as he withdrew and flexed inside me, slow and measured.

God, it felt so good. *He* felt so good. I couldn't even recall the awful experience I'd had the first time in college — not now. Will had eviscerated every touch before his, had wiped any memory that wasn't his hands on me from my mind forever.

He peppered kisses along the back of my neck as he thrust in and out, both of us moaning and breathing heavily, climaxes mounting. I could have come again, but Will was wound tight, and soon he was picking up his pace and burying himself deep until I was moaning into the pillow and he was up on his knees behind me, hands gripping my hips as he fucked me wildly.

I preened under his praise as he came, fighting back his own groans as his body stilled inside me, his release pumping out in rivulets that leaked out of me when he withdrew and pushed inside one last time.

He owned me.

This man *owned* me, body and soul.

Will withdrew all the way reluctantly, kissing my shoulder before he was rolling off the bed and hustling into the bathroom. I heard the water run, and then he returned with a warm washcloth, running it between my legs as I moaned and stretched like a cat.

When we were both cleaned up, he wrapped me in his arms under the buttery sheets, his legs tangling into a pretzel with mine until I was giggling beneath the prison he'd made with his body.

"Can't breathe," I teased, my voice muffled by his chest.

"You're still running that mouth of yours, so I call bullshit."

"Hey, what happened to all those promises about taking care of me?"

He swatted my ass. "I think I fulfilled that duty tonight."

I chuckled, burrowing into his arms and sighing contently. We were quiet for a long while, his fingers running through my hair, mine drawing shapes on his back. I'd never felt so whole.

"So, what's next?" I finally asked.

Will released me enough to let me lay into the pillows, and he propped his head up on his palm. "What do you want?"

"Well, I think we should tell Ava."

"Agreed." He frowned. "What do you think she'll do?"

I sighed, watching where my finger drew a line along the dusting of hair on his chest. "I won't even pretend to know. But whatever her reaction is, she'll have us there to work through it all with. That's the best thing we can offer."

He nodded. "What do you think about moving into the house?"

I smiled. "You want me to?"

"Isn't it obvious?" he asked, tightening the grip of his legs around me.

"I don't want you to get sick of me."

"Impossible."

"And what about the cats?"

"Move them in, too. I'll give them their own room. I'll make this whole damn house a cat tree if that's what you want."

I snorted. "Coconut would be pleased."

"She likes me."

"She doesn't like anyone."

He shrugged. "Just wait, you'll see. She'll be purring in my lap watching *Jeopardy* in no time."

We talked like that for what felt like hours, going over logistics that felt like we were talking about what we'd do if we won the lottery. Then again, I guessed in a way, I had.

Eventually, we both grew quiet, and Will's eyes darkened as he traced the edges of my face with his thumb.

"I'm going to mess up sometimes," he whispered. "I know I will."

"And I'm going to need constant reassurance from you," I combatted. "There's always going to be a part of me questioning if this is real, if I'm going to wake up one day and you'll be gone."

His frown deepened. "I would never leave you, Chloe."

"And one day, I'll believe that wholeheartedly," I said. "But for now, I'm battling against a lifetime of being told and thinking that all men do is leave."

He nodded, a long sigh leaving him before he leaned down to press his lips to my forehead.

"I can't wait to prove that theory wrong," he said. "I'm going to stay. I'm going to stay so damn hard."

I laughed, wrapping my arms around him and squeezing tight. "And I'm going to be there through all the mess ups to remind you what a good man you are."

"Fuck, I love you."

"Yeah, yeah," I teased, and then he was tickling me and wrapping me back up in a straitjacket of legs and arms and kisses.

Everything I'd ever known was blown out the window that night, a new life beginning — one better than any I'd ever dreamed.

And under the mountain of that man, I whispered words I'd never tire of, no matter how I teased.

"I love you, too."

Chapter 36

Learn My Lesson

Will

A week passed in a tornado of hockey and home.

I showed up at our home game the next day more focused than ever, Aleks smirking at me like he knew before I said a word that I'd taken his advice. He didn't ask, just patted me on the helmet on our way out for our morning skate with a muttered, "Atta boy."

The team was on fire. We smoked our opponents that night, three to zero. Our next two games were away — one in Toronto and one in Buffalo. We lost the first in overtime, but showed out in the next, and returned home with a determination to finish out the season strong and play our asses off for the Stanley Cup.

When I wasn't with the team, I was all in on Ava and Chloe.

Ava was a champ with her injury, doing what we asked her to do in terms of recovery without whining or complaining one bit. She was better every day, and our biggest challenge was convincing her she wasn't ready to go back to playing as hard as she was used to.

"You would be back on the ice if it were you," she'd shot at me one night in argument, and Chloe and I had battled back laughter.

The little shit was right, and unfortunately for me, she was just like her Pops.

Chloe had been sleeping in the pool house, but she was slowly moving things inside — including the cats, who now roamed freely throughout any room they desired. She'd been busy with school, the year picking up after spring break as summer drew closer and closer.

Now, it was another home game day, and in-between my post-morning-skate nap and my report time at the arena — Chloe and I were telling Ava about us.

Where I wore my nerves on my sleeve as we gathered her at the dining room table, Chloe looked calm as ever. She smirked at me, squeezing my wrist with one comforting hand before she started talking.

Ava was dressed and ready for the game, excited to be able to attend since it was a Saturday night. It was also the first time she'd been able to wear her hockey jersey since she got injured. It made my heart squeeze to see her in my number, to feel the excitement radiating off her.

I knew once I got her into hockey this summer, I'd never get her out of it.

I hoped she'd find a home in it just like I had, that I could bear witness to her playing in a women's league down the line.

She and Chloe were chatting away about the game, how Ava couldn't wait to get popcorn and throw her stuffed animal on the ice when we won. Chloe told her she'd have to explain the rules to her like always, and Ava was groaning and pretending it was an inconvenience when I knew she secretly loved it.

Eventually, Chloe turned to me, arching a brow with an encouraging dip of her chin. "Well, I'm going to use the restroom before we leave. I'll be right back."

She squeezed my shoulder as she left the room. We'd both decided that it would be better for me to tell Ava alone first, to give her a moment to process between the two of us.

But with Chloe gone now, I was as scared as ever. That woman really had become a lifeline to me.

I took a deep breath, leaning my elbows onto the table. "Before Daddy goes to the rink, there's something we want to talk to you about."

Ava was kicking her feet under the table, but they stopped swinging at that, her little eyes flicking to mine. It was wild, how kids could pick up energy like that. She knew what I had to say was big, that this wasn't normal for us.

"Okay," she said tentatively.

"You know how Chloe has been living out in the pool house? How we hired her to be your nanny back in January?"

Ava nodded with a wide grin. "It's been the best."

"It has been," I agreed. "And we've all been hanging out a lot, haven't we?"

"Mm-hmm," Ava said. "We're best friends!"

My heart squeezed, and I looked up at the ceiling a moment before bringing my gaze back to hers. "We sure are."

I watched my daughter for a long moment, praying what I said next would bring her comfort and happiness and nothing else. But this was all foreign territory to me.

"What would you think about Daddy and Chloe maybe being more than friends?"

Ava frowned a bit, and I realized that wasn't the best terminology. How the heck would my five-year-old daughter know what I meant when I said that?

Fortunately for me, Chloe slid back into the room then, leaning against the door frame with a soft smile.

"You know how we watched *Tangled* together, and how much you loved it?" she said, crossing the room to sit next to Ava again. Ava nodded excitedly, and Chloe smiled. "Well, your dad and I are like Rapunzel and Flynn."

Ava's eyes widened a bit, her gaze floating to me before she smiled and hid her face. "You mean you two like to *kiss*?!"

"Maybe," Chloe teased, tickling Ava, who squirmed and laughed and finally dropped her hands from her face to look at us again.

"Do you love her, Daddy?"

My heart nearly burst out of my chest, and I blew out a long breath, reaching over to grab Chloe's hand in mine. "I do," I whispered. "Very much."

Ava smiled, looking between us, and then she shrugged, kicking her feet. "Okay."

"Okay?" I asked.

"Do you have any questions for us?" Chloe added. "Anything you want to know?"

"Does this mean you're going to stay forever?"

Chloe smiled, running a hand through my daughter's hair. "I think it means that's a possibility, yes. And for now, I'm at least going to move into the house with you guys. Would that be okay?"

"Into my room?!" Ava clapped.

"No," Chloe said on a laugh. "Into your dad's room, but I'll be up there every night with you to play and read before bed. Deal?"

"Deal."

We talked for a while longer, Chloe knowing what questions to ask better than I did. But in the end, Ava was just excited. I knew one day she might have more questions — especially when it came to her mother. But I also knew that with Chloe by my side, we could handle it.

We could handle anything that came our way.

When it was time for me to head to the arena, I kissed Ava on the forehead, and then I brought Chloe into my arms, a little nervous to kiss her for the first time in front of Ava. But I did it, savoring each kiss like it was the first and the last and promising I'd find them after the game in the family lounge.

"Go get 'em," she said, squeezing my arm when I released her.

But before I could walk out the door, Ava screamed, "Wait!"

She tugged at Chloe's phone peeking out of her jean pocket — I couldn't stare too long, because this woman in fucking *jeans* was apparently my ultimate undoing. She had gone on some shopping trip with Maven, Livia, and Grace last weekend, and if I thought seeing her in the custom-created dresses she made was torture, it was nothing compared to a well-fitted pair of denim.

Ava turned to me. "Before you go, can we take a family picture?"

I scrubbed a hand over my mouth, emotion strangling my next breath. All I could do was nod, and then she was running to get Chef Patel from where she was cleaning up in the kitchen after making me my pre-game meal.

Ava dragged Chef into the room and handed her the phone, and then Chloe was tucking herself under my arm, and I hiked Ava up in the other, and we leaned together for our first photo together.

"Say *hockey!*" Chef said.

"Hockey!" we all chimed together.

Arushi smiled as she clicked a few photos, and I swore I felt another smile, one that wasn't in the room with us, but rather watching from somewhere above. I knew I'd never get the chance to hear her say it, to know for sure... but my heart told me Jenny would be happy to see us all together.

She'd be happy I was introducing our daughter to her, happy with who our daughter was becoming.

Happy that *I* had somehow found my own happiness, too.

As soon as the photo was taken, Ava was calling Chef in to join us, not taking no for an answer. I held Chloe's phone in my hand as far out as I could to capture us all in one selfie, the smile on my face so foreign and yet so *right*.

Ava was clawing at my arm to see the photos as soon as we dispersed, and I lowered my hand so she could see, swiping through each one.

"Wow," she breathed on a little smile. "We really are doing our best."

When I handed Chloe her phone back, I kissed my girls one last time before heading out the door.

And I made a vow to learn my lesson.

I made a vow to print and frame those photos tomorrow, and to paint every wall in this house with the memories of us.

Chapter 37

Happy Beginnings

June
Will

Skates cutting into fresh ice.

The puck gliding before a *clink* sent it flying.

My heart pounding in my ears, fast, but steady.

Chirps from my teammates.

Curses at missed attempts.

The crowd chanting and screaming.

The satisfying *plunk* of a puck hitting the bar and bouncing off.

The even more satisfying buzzer when we scored.

This was the symphony of the fifth game of the final round in the Stanley Cup Playoffs, and it was music to my ears.

Three periods had happened in what felt like a blink of an eye. It was impossible to be fully present in a game like this because every ounce of energy was tied up in doing what you came to do. Our wingers were focused on scoring. Our defensemen protected me. I protected the goal. And as a team, we fought tooth and fucking nail to clinch the win.

We were ahead three games to one in this series, and if we took it tonight... it was over.

The Cup was ours.

Tampa buzzed with an energy I'd never felt from the city I knew and loved, not in all my years on the Ospreys. We battled it out to a sold-out crowd, all of them ready with fish in hand to make it rain on the ice. Banners hung from skyscrapers and city banks. The lights on the riverwalk twinkled blue and white. Every radio station and news outlet were tuned into *this* game, to this period, to these final minutes.

If we lost, we'd still have a chance — but our next game would be in Sacramento. Traveling back and forth between the west and east coast was brutal for even our most seasoned players, and when Coach huddled us up in the locker room before the game, we were all in agreement.

We were winning this thing.

Tonight.

I knew I looked like a wild animal from the outside, my eyes as wide as they could go as I took in every slash of the puck and every change in direction from each player on the ice. My heart skipped before tripling its pace when the puck was suddenly heading my way, perfectly in the control of Sacramento's center.

He drilled toward me like he was going to take the shot himself, but as I crouched low and prepared to block, I spotted the right winger cutting past Jaxson.

The center passed, the winger wound up with all his might before knocking the puck toward me, and I snapped into action like I could read his mind.

My left leg shot out, putting me practically in a middle split, and the puck hit my shin guard before popping back.

I didn't have time to celebrate the block before I was

in position again, another shot coming from the left winger who was waiting for the rebound. This one I covered with my glove, stopping the play to the roar of nearly twenty-thousand Ospreys fans.

It was thunderous, a rumbling I felt in every inch of my body as I sniffed and tossed the puck to the ref. I nodded at the acknowledgements that came from my teammates, but then we were back in action.

There were only three minutes left in the game, and we were tied one to one.

I didn't want overtime. I wanted to win *now*. But it wasn't up to me. All I could do was play my part, block every shot that came my way and pray that one of our guys could get a shot in at the other end of the ice before the final buzzer.

Our only goal tonight belonged to Vince, who had taken the lead of most goals in the league by the end of our regular season. It was only his second year playing, and if the way he was showing out was any indication, he had a long, record-breaking career ahead of him.

But he'd come up short every shot he'd taken since that first one tonight, and frustration rolled off him in plumes as I watched him send the puck toward Sacramento's goalie. It hit him right in the middle of the chest, and Vince let out a scream, banging his stick on the ice before Jaxson was skating over to mutter something into his ear and clap him on the shoulder.

This wasn't the time to lose our cool.

This was the time to fucking *kill*.

Another minute passed with our guys scrapping it out with Sacramento's. When Suter was tripped on his advance down the ice toward the goal, the crowd roared, and so did my teammates both on the bench and on the ice when the ref didn't call the penalty.

I held out my gloved hands, slowly lowering them down again and again in a symbol for my team to calm.

There was still time to play.

Even through his mask, I could see Suter's bloody grin when he looked at me. He spit on the ice, letting the refs know in a not-so-subtle way that they'd fucked up, and then he went right back to the game.

I knew then it was over.

I knew by the way he glided across that ice like a jaguar, his shoulders tight, neck bobbing left and right like he was just out for a stroll. He checked one of the Sacramento players hard against the glass, stealing the puck and driving it down the ice. He passed it to Vince only for Vince to dangle the puck and pass it right back to Suter.

Suter, who was in perfect position to the left corner of the net.

Suter, who made it look easy when he hit that puck, when his stick connected and drove it into the net.

Suter — who made the score two to one with less than thirty seconds left.

The resulting cheers from the fans were deafening. Even I threw my fist up from the goal, watching as Vince and Jaxson all but tackled Suter in celebration.

Holy fuck.

We're about to win the Cup.

The realization had my heart picking up pace, my hands trembling a bit as I crouched in front of the goal the moment the puck was back in play. Sacramento pulled their goalie, subbing in an extra winger to try to score and get us back to a tie, but our guys were ruthless. We blocked the puck, stole it, and sent it firing down the ice for an empty netter.

Less than a minute later, the final buzzer sounded.

And all hell broke loose.

• • •

Chloe

It was a mad house after the final buzzer — which had sent Ava screaming into my arms and immediately made us both start bawling. We were in a suite with Maven, Livia, and Grace — along with some other friends and family members of teammates.

We'd all lost our damn minds at the win, and then security was covering for us as we all rushed to get down to the ice.

Maven hooked her arm through mine, the four of us linking together so we wouldn't get split up. These women had become like family to me — well, that was, after they yelled at me incessantly for keeping my relationship with Will from them for so long.

Thankfully, I'd made up for it by spilling all the details in the end.

These girls *lived* for dirty details.

Since then, we'd gone to dress fittings with Maven, had days at the beach, and even gone shopping together — which was new and surprisingly fun for me.

"We won! Daddy won!" Ava kept repeating as I carried her through the chaos, balancing her in the arm not linked with Maven. The crowd was thick outside of the suites, and all the way until we were in the tunnel under the stadium.

Even then, media snapped photos and shoved cameras in our faces while we fought through.

Ava was a bit heavy in my arms, but I didn't dare put her down. I held her tight, smiling at her through the madness. She was beaming in the new jersey I'd made her for the playoffs — navy blue and white but with glittery gold trim and outlines in honor of her favorite pop star, Mia Love.

Chef Patel and Uncle Mitch had wanted to be closer to the action for the game. I felt my phone buzzing in my pocket and knew it was her wondering where I was. Security led us through the locker room, and when we pushed through the tunnel, Arushi screamed from where she was leaning over the top.

"Can you believe it?!" she screamed, reaching for Ava as Ava did the same. They high-fived with all of us gaping and shaking our heads.

"Crazy!" I screamed back.

Mitch leaned over Chef and gave Ava a ruffle of her hair. I smirked a little at how Chef blushed at his nearness. I was pretty sure we *all* knew they were much more than friends at this point, but I'd let her tell me on her own time.

"Go, go!" Chef Patel called down to us. "Go give that grumpy man of yours a big celebratory kiss!"

Ava drew out a long *ewwww* in a tease, and then she was bouncing in my arms the closer we got to the ice. Once we were against the glass, she pressed her hands against it and screamed for Will.

We had to wait until we had the go ahead from the team staff. Maven was clutching Livia's arm beside us, both of them fighting back tears, and Grace was standing on the cleared Ospreys bench waving her arms around like a wild animal and hollering for Jaxson.

When he saw her, the biggest grin I'd ever seen on that man split his face. He sprinted across the ice on his skates, skidding to a stop at the boards and hauling Grace over his shoulder before he was skating off again.

That was the only green light the families waiting needed.

We poured onto the ice, Maven running for Vince and slipping the whole way. The woman had at least been smart enough to wear sneakers — though she'd argued with all of us that the heels she wanted to wear would look better. She jumped into his arms when she finally made it to him, her legs around his waist and him spinning her to the tune of whistles and cheers from the fans still watching the celebrations.

Ava and I searched for Will. He was no longer where he'd been talking to a news reporter when we'd been making our way toward the glass, and I didn't see him anywhere near the Cup — which was currently being toted over Aleks Suter's head as he did a victory lap around the ice as best he could with how crowded it was.

I frowned, searching, heart racing a bit the longer time passed when suddenly Ava and I were tackled in a hug from behind.

"Daddy!"

Ava squealed the greeting, wiggling out of my hold until she could hop down onto the ice. Will was beaming, a Stanley Cup Champ hat covering his sweaty hair as he bent down to one still-padded knee. Ava was in his arms the moment that pad hit the ice, and he wrapped her up tight, kissing her cheek.

When she pulled back, tears were streaming down her face, the emotion too strong for her little heart to handle.

"Hey, now," he said on a laugh, hugging her again.

"You did it," she garbled. "You did it, Daddy. I'm so proud of you."

My heart melted at the sight, and Will nuzzled into her before he was looking up at me, his eyes soft, a content, confident smile on his lips.

When Ava finally released him, he stood, sweeping me into a sweat-drenched hug that I would have gone into happily. I didn't care that his hair was dripping on my arm when I draped it around his neck, or that he smelled like a locker room when I pressed my lips to his.

That sweaty beast of a man who'd blocked thirty-nine shots tonight was *mine*.

"Hi, baby," he whispered in my ear, and then he was pressing a kiss to my hair that made me shiver as much as the nickname did.

I was distantly aware of the cameras on us, but in the last few months, I'd learned not to pay them any mind. This was part of dating the best goalie in the league, and now, he was a Stanley Cup winner.

Let them all watch. Let the rumors fly. Let the women be pissed.

They could all eat their hearts out.

"You were fucking *incredible*," I screamed over the noise, holding tight to him. "Absolutely unreal."

"I'm so glad you were here."

"I wouldn't miss it. It was insane."

"I can't believe it."

"I can."

He laughed, and we kept babbling back and forth, incoherent mutters of disbelief that got lost in-between the thousands of kisses we shared. When he pulled Ava into his arm, he wrapped the other around me, carefully moving us through the crowd.

Will was stopped a couple times for short interviews, and of course, tackled by his teammates as they celebrated their win. I hugged the girls when I passed them, holding especially tight to Maven — who was extra emotional with her wedding just a couple weeks away now.

Eventually, we made it to the Cup, and a few of the Ospreys shoved it toward Will until he carefully put Ava down and picked the behemoth thing up over his head. The fans cheered, Ava jumped up and down clapping, and I smiled, shaking my head and watching my man beam in a way I'd never seen him before.

Pictures snapped from every direction, and when he sat the Cup back on the ice, he gathered Ava and me around it for a photo. Ava was leaning against the Cup, the thing bigger than she was, and Will bent down next to her while I stood over his shoulders. He covered my hand with his, the other holding onto his daughter, and while the cameras went off, he was looking at Ava or at me — never at the lens.

When he stood, he groaned a bit, the soreness from the game settling in. Then, he gasped, clutching onto the edge of the bowl at the top of the trophy. "Shit!"

"What?" I asked, gripping his shoulder in a panic. I searched for signs of where he was hurt, but he just shook his head.

"I think I dropped something in the Cup."

I frowned, looking at the thing — which was deep enough to fit a baby in, but shallow enough that anything dropped in there wouldn't be lost.

"Okay, well, just get it out," I said on a laugh, and I peeked inside to see what it was.

The moment I did, I froze.

kandi steiner

Because inside that shiny silver bowl was a shiny gold band — sporting an even shinier marquise diamond.

I couldn't move. I couldn't breathe. I couldn't do anything but wrap my white knuckles around the edge of that trophy and stare with my mouth open like one of the stuffed fish still littering the ice.

Distantly, I was aware of a warm hand on my back, and then another sliding in to retrieve the ring. I followed it as Will pulled it free, and then I gasped along with everyone around us when he dropped to one knee.

Ava screamed, jumping up and down like she'd been in on this secret all along. She clasped her hands together in front of her face and watched me anxiously, her smile big enough to split her face.

It was too loud for him to profess his love for me, to say the things I could read so clearly in his hope-filled eyes as he watched me from that ice with a soft, almost nervous smile.

But I didn't need words — not a single one.

I knew.

I knew how much he loved me, it was written in every action he'd shown me since the day I moved into the house. I knew every vow he could make before he even had the chance to make it. I knew this man meant forever when he told me I was his, and I knew the way my heart beat only for him that he was it for me, too.

He just sat there on one knee, holding that ring in one hand and my hand in the other, waiting.

Tears sprang to my eyes, and with a dozen cameras trained on us, I rolled my lips together and nodded.

Will let out a breath like he'd been unsure, like there was any chance in hell I'd say anything but a resounding *yes*. He slid the ring on my finger, and then stood, framing

434

my face with those strong, magical hands of his and kissing me for the whole world to watch.

We only had a moment before Ava was wrapping herself around my legs, and I bent to hug her, too, wiping the tears from my eyes. She pulled at my hand until she could see the ring, and then she was chattering on and on about wedding planning and where we'd do it and who would come and *could she please wear her jersey?!*

And I marveled at how one little offer to help out a student's dad after school had turned into the most life-changing six months of my life. I wasn't scared in that moment. I didn't feel the impending doom of every warning my mother had bestowed on me since my birth.

I knew, without a doubt, that in my story?

The man would stay.

The woman would have her independence while being cared for, too.

The child would have her parents, all of them.

And this family would have a happy ending — but not for a very, very long time.

We had too many happy beginnings to have first.

The End

Epilogue

Wide Awake

June 29th
Chloe

"**W**ait a hot damn second," Livia said, steepling her long, sparkly nails on the cocktail table between us. "You mean to tell me that you asked strangers on fucking *Reddit* for advice when you had us literally chomping at the bit to know what had you all dopey and smiley?!"

I chuckled, sipping my martini. "Listen, it wasn't my brightest idea. But I couldn't exactly tell you the truth of what was happening."

"Yes, you could have, bitch!" Livia stomped her heel. "Don't you understand? We're like a vault, this group."

"That's true," Grace confirmed, stirring her gin drink. "They kept it locked down when no one knew about me and Jax."

"Okay, well, I know that *now*," I said. "But I wasn't sure back then! I've never had girlfriends, okay? But I've learned my lesson, and I promise to never withhold juicy details again."

"Better not," Livia said with a pointed look, but she was grinning despite her stern warning. "I'm just glad to see you two so happy. I'm happy to see *that one* happy at all," she added with a nod toward Will. He was taking photos with the guys, all of them in tuxes and balancing a dazzling Maven in their arms. She laid across them like their arms were a chaise lounge, queen energy radiating off her. "I wasn't sure he had that emotion capability."

"And let's not forget about this *rock*," Grace chimed in, grabbing my wrist so she and Livia could fawn over my diamond. I flushed and pulled my hand away, waving them off.

"It was an interesting road," I said, but my heart swelled when I looked over at Will just in time to see him laugh. The photographer snapped away, and I melted, because those smiles and laughs came so easily to him now, as if they'd never left. "But it was well worth the ride."

"What about you, little miss?" Livia probed Grace. "Think there will be a ring on your finger any time soon?"

"Better not be," she said. "Listen, don't get me wrong. I love that man. I *know* he will be my husband. But I'm in absolutely zero rush to get married, have babies, and settle down. I've got too many adventures to have first."

"Fair enough," Livia said.

"What about *you*?" I asked Liv, waggling my brows. "Will I ever get to see Doctor Young settled down?"

"Listen, the only jewelry you should ever hear me talking about are nipple clamps and dog collars. If I start babbling about anything else, check my temperature."

I flushed a deep red while Grace stifled a laugh, and then a pair of slender arms draped around my shoulder and Livia's, Maven joining us at the table.

"Okay, I know I'm usually the one with a camera around my neck, but I swear to God, if I have to smile for one more picture, my cheeks are going to divorce my face." She rubbed her cheeks but couldn't help still grinning. "Why does smiling hurt so much?!"

She was absolutely stunning.

Her dress was a sparkling A-line boho dream, the base of it cream, the fabric draped over it white, and every inch of it studded with the most beautiful crystals. The neck of it cut deep between her cleavage, and the bodice hugged her slim waist before flowing down to the floor in the most gorgeous flowy skirt I'd ever seen. It made me jealous of the designer who'd dreamt it up, even more so of the seamstress who got to bring it to life.

The sleeves of the dress were long, hugging her all the way to her wrists. Her hair was slicked into a chic bun, the baby hairs framing her face in intricate designs, and though her makeup was stunning, it was soft so as not to hide her freckles or the natural beauty she held so effortlessly.

From the diamonds studding her ear lobes to the candles on each cocktail table, every detail of this wedding had been so meticulously thought out and brought to life.

I'd gasped when Will and I had walked into the boathouse arm in arm earlier after the ceremony. It was like walking into an enchanted forest.

Plants lined every glass wall of the boathouse, the natural light from the setting sun casting a soft glow that was only enhanced by the candles floating everywhere. Pottery of all shapes, colors, and sizes held those plants — a beautiful combination of the two souls wedding one another.

It was a boho dream without being too much, elegant and earthy without being pretentious. It felt as cozy as it did magical, and from Maven's breathtaking entrance to Vince's teary-eyed vows, I'd been enraptured.

"Here, drink this. It'll help." Livia offered her martini to her best friend, and once she took a long drink, Maven sighed, flashing us her dazzling smile.

"I love you bitches. I'm so glad you're all here."

"Love you, too... *sister!*" Grace squeezed Maven tight with a squeal. "God, I've always wanted a sister. Now we can team up on Vince."

"Oh boy," said a deep voice, and Vince joined us with his eyebrow arched high. He looked as handsome as ever, his suit a rich brown like the earth, his golden hair styled, the hair on his jaw trimmed to perfection. He could have walked out of a *GQ* magazine. "Why do I feel like I walked into a trap I didn't realize I set?"

"Don't act like you don't love it, brother," Grace said, pressing up onto her tiptoes to kiss his cheek. "You'd be lost without us."

"I won't argue that," he said, and his arm slid around his wife's waist, a dopey-eyed smile on his face. "How's my wife?"

"Ready to dance with you."

"Shall we let the band know?"

"We shall," she said. "By the way, when are we going to the courthouse to change your last name?"

She smiled with the tease, and all of us grinned because we were in on the joke from when they first met. Vince had thrown all his lines at Maven in his pursuit of her — including that *when* they got married, not if, he would take her last name.

"First thing Monday morning, if that's what you want."

Maven shook her head, a sexy grin aimed at her husband as she leaned into him. "You know I'd never let you. I love wearing your Tanev jersey too much."

"That makes two of us," he growled, nipping at her neck as she playfully shoved him away. And then Maven was blowing kisses at us while Vince toted her toward the band.

Jaxson and Carter joined us then, and as they chatted with the girls, my eyes scanned the room for my fiancé.

Fiancé.

I didn't think I'd ever get used to that.

When I found him, he had Ava on the dance floor, doing some goofy dance that looked more like he needed to pee than anything else. I smiled on my way over to them, and as soon as I joined them, Ava grabbed me by the wrist and pulled me in to join.

"Daddy's doing the running man!"

I arched a brow at *Daddy*, who was still hopping around like a loon. "Is that what that is?"

Ava giggled as Will let his hands fall to his sides with a *slap*. He feigned insult, and then he was tickling me, wrapping me up in his arms with kisses running up and down my neck while Ava laughed and attempted to tickle my stomach.

It was impossible for my heart not to swell in moments like these, when I was all too aware of how perfect things were, of how my life had done a complete one-eighty in six short months.

I loved these two more than I loved anything in the world.

The band announced the first dance, and so we cleared the floor, hugging the edge of it and watching as Vince and Maven swayed to a French song I wasn't familiar with.

Soon, others were joining in, and Carter took Ava out on the floor to dance while Will swept me into his arms.

"So," he said, his eyes drinking me in. "Is this what you want, too? A big, elegant wedding?"

He was dressed in the same suit as Vince, all the groomsmen matching, and I loved the way the rich brown of the suit and the dark green accents played with the honey color of his eyes. His hair was pulled back in a neat bun at the nape of his neck, his jaw peppered with stubble.

He was so hot. Would I *ever* stop drooling over this man?

"Is it what *you* want?" I asked.

He shook his head. "Nope, I asked you first."

I sighed, looking around at the unspeakable beauty. "It's... stunning. But I don't know. I think I would die if I had this many people to entertain. And this many people looking at me when I said my vows."

"So, something smaller?"

"Much smaller," I said. "As in... maybe just us and Ava?"

"What about Arushi and Mitch?"

"Oh, of course. I mean, especially since the way they're moving, they might be asking to do a double wedding."

"No way. They can get their own," Will growled, but he smirked despite it.

"And of course your teammates. And the girls."

"Your mom and grandma."

"Yes, and your father."

He frowned at that, silent for a moment before he nodded. "I'm going to ask if he wants to come spend some time with us in the offseason," he said. "He hasn't seen Ava in so long."

"Will," I said with a smile. "I love this idea. Think he'll go for it?"

"I don't think I'll give him a choice. It's hard for both of us, always has been, but... he's the only dad I have, you know? The only parent I have left. I don't want to live separate lives anymore."

"My bet is he doesn't want that, either."

He shrugged. "I guess we'll find out. You know, it's *you* who gives me the courage to do this. After seeing how much you've opened up to your mom and grandma recently, how much progress you've made with them..." He shook his head, awe in his eyes. "You amaze me."

"Easy, it's mostly the therapist doing the hard work," I said.

"No. It's you," he argued. "And them, too. It makes me excited, thinking maybe my father and I could make the same strides."

"You will," I promised, and I kissed him for good measure to seal how much I believed it.

After Will and I made things official, I realized I had a lot of things to work through when it came to my family. By some miracle, I convinced Mom and Grandma to do therapy with me. I wasn't sure if they agreed because they were bored or because they knew we needed it, too, but I was thankful either way. We'd all made such great progress — together and separate — and every day, we worked toward a healthier family dynamic.

One that didn't involve so much *men are trash* talk.

They'd even started hanging old photos, ones I was surprised they kept. Mom showed me one of my father, with me sleeping on his chest, that nearly brought me to tears.

I hated that he didn't stay, but I was old enough now to understand that maybe he just wasn't ready for me. Maybe he wasn't ready for any of it. I found grace and forgiveness for him even if I also still held pain.

And that healing was for me — not for him.

Will and I swayed for a while without another word, laughing at how Ava was dancing circles around Carter — literally.

"What else do you want?" Will asked after a while.

"What do you mean?"

"I mean, what do you want in your life, Chloe soon-to-be- Perry? Do you like the house we're in now, or do you want something different? Do you want more cats? A dog?" He swallowed. "Kids?"

My heart jolted in my chest, cheeks heating as I smirked and tangled my fingers in the hair at the nape of his neck. "I love our home. Our three asshole cats are plenty for me. No dog."

He nodded with each one, his eyes flicking between mine. "And the last one?"

I rolled my lips together on a smile. "If you're asking if I want your babies one day, the answer is yes. But for right now..." I added, leaning in close so I could whisper in his ear. "I'm having more fun practicing how they're made."

Will groaned and pinned my hips with his gargantuan hands, nipping at my bottom lip as he kissed me. "Consider me available for practice any time."

"Such an overachiever."

"Gotta stay in shape somehow in the offseason."

After the first dance, dinner was served, and then we watched as Maven danced with her dad and Vince danced with his mom. Will held my hand through it as I willed back tears knowing we'd never get that same chance.

But it was okay.

Our family was different, it was born of both tragedy and magic.

But it was *ours*.

In just a couple short weeks, we'd be celebrating Ava's birthday. Then, we'd be taking her to hockey tryouts. We'd have the whole summer to spend together before another season started up, before the school year was in full swing again, and I intended to make the most of every second.

As we danced the night away, surrounded by our family and friends, I didn't fidget nervously even once. I didn't try to hide behind my hair. And I knew without a doubt that there wouldn't be a midnight existential crisis waiting for me once my head hit the pillow.

I was living in a world better than any I could have ever dreamt.

I was wide awake.

And I couldn't wait for what came next.

Epilogue Two

Aleks

She wanted to hit me.

I wanted to kiss her.

That was how it had always been with us.

"This is just... great. Just fucking perfect," Mia said, throwing her hands up in disbelief before she sank down into my giant bean bag with a huff. As soon as she realized where she was sitting, she hopped up with a frustrated growl before stomping over to the couch, instead.

She buried her face in her hands, shaking her head.

"What am I going to do?"

As much as I secretly loved seeing her flustered, that was usually only because I was the one getting under her skin. In this instance, I hated it, because she was upset over something I had no control over.

Usually, I'd toss a smart-ass remark at her and smirk as that perfect mouth of hers gaped open at me, as her cheeks turned red and that little vein in her forehead popped. I knew exactly how to push her buttons, how to make rage pour through that normally put-together woman.

But right now, that side of me I always kept tied up in the basement of my cold, dead heart was thrashing, urging me to go to her, to pull her into me, to hold her and find a way to make it right.

I kicked that motherfucker hard enough to knock him out, snuffing the lights and reminding him why he was locked away in the first place.

Her dark hair fell over her shoulders in a silky curtain as I took the seat next to her. I hovered one hand over her slender back before I carefully, slowly, rubbed it. "I'm sorry."

Mia froze under my touch.

There it was again, that shock of electricity between us, that zap of heat I felt any time my body made contact with hers.

But just when I thought she might melt into that touch, Mia yanked away, uncovering her face so she could properly glare at me. Those sharp blue eyes of hers narrowed into slits. "Well, you should be. This is all your fault."

And just like that, we were back to sparring.

"My fault?" I gaped at her, smirking even with my mouth open because I wanted her to feel as ridiculous as she was being. "Mia, it's a fucking hurricane. What the hell am I supposed to do about it?"

"You're the whole reason I'm here instead of in New York to begin with. I'm doing all this to save your ass! And now, I have to cancel a sold out show at Madison Square Garden."

The truth of that seemed to hit her full force, her face going white.

"Oh, God," she whimpered, burying her face again. "I have to cancel a sold out show at Madison Square Garden."

Any desire I did have to comfort her was receding now, held at bay by her accusation. "Saving my ass," I repeated, tonguing my cheek. "So, this is all about me suddenly? I'm the big bad wolf and you're just doing this to be a little saint, huh? Nothing at all in it for you?"

"Oh, shut up," she spat, shoving me away. I barely budged.

"Because I'm pretty sure this was your publicist's idea," I reminded her.

"Well, your agent is the one who made me come here for your stupid game!"

"Made you?" I stood, jaw tight. "You are a woman with free will, Mia. In case you forgot. No one can make you do anything."

She looked up at me then, her eyes softer, something in the relaxing of her jaw telling me I'd struck a nerve without trying.

It reminded me so much of when we were younger that I had a hard time taking my next breath.

For a split second, we were both eighteen again.

She was begging me to kiss her.

I was begging her not to let me.

I knew even then that we were wrong for each other.

I knew even then that we'd break each other's hearts if we ever tried to be more than friends.

"Whatever," she said after a moment. The word was resigned, not laced with any sort of edge, and that upset me more than if she'd screamed it.

I could handle her yelling at me.

I couldn't handle knowing I'd hurt her — even with all the practice I'd had over the years.

She sniffed, waving her hand in the air like I was a waiter. "Do you at least have some tequila or something?"

"Need to get drunk to face the truth?"

"That I'm stuck in a high-rise condo with my fake fiancé with a hurricane barreling toward us?" She stood, a saccharine smile on her tight lips. "Um, yeah. Drunk is the bare minimum."

She stormed past me and into my kitchen then, and I took a deep breath, letting it out as slowly and calmly as I could as I folded my hands together and rested them on top of my head. I stared up at the ceiling, debating converting to the first religion I could think of just to see if there was a god who could save me.

Mia needed to drink to get through this, and I needed to sit on my fucking hands.

Because she wanted to hit me, and I wanted to kiss her.

And with the two of us forced to stay together for the night, I had no idea how the hell I was going to keep up the charade of anything I felt for this woman being fake.

What happens when the biggest popstar
in the world and NHL's bad boy enter into a fake engagement
for a massive publicity stunt?
Find out in Save Your Breath
(https://geni.us/saveyourbreath),
book 4 in the Kings of the Ice series.

Can't get enough of Will and Chloe? **Catch up with them in
this bonus scene** (https://kandisteiner.com/bonus-content/),
featuring Ava's first hockey game and an update on how Will
and the cats are doing.

Fall in love with the other Kings of the Ice couples!
MEET YOUR MATCH
(https://geni.us/meetyourmatchkoti)
Book 1
TROPES:
Pro Hockey Romance
Forced Proximity
Opposite Sides of the Track
Interracial/Multicultural Couple
Workplace Romance
Enemies-to-Lovers Vibes

WATCH YOUR MOUTH
(https://geni.us/watchyourmouth)
Book 2
TROPES:
Pro Hockey Romance
Teammate's Little Sister/Brother's Best Friend
Road Trip
Forced Proximity
One Bed
Age Gap
Opposites Attract
Forbidden

More from Kandi Steiner

The Kings of the Ice Series
Meet Your Match
One Month with Vince Tanev: Tampa's Hotshot Rookie – twenty-four-seven access on and off the ice. The headline says it all, and my bosses are over the moon when the opportunity of a lifetime lands in my lap. Of course, they aren't aware that they're forcing me into proximity with the one man who grates on my last nerve.

Watch Your Mouth
My brother's teammates know not to touch me — but that doesn't stop me from daring Jaxson Brittain to be the first to break the rule.

The Red Zone Rivals Series
Fair Catch
As if being the only girl on the college football team wasn't hard enough, Coach had to go and assign my brother's best friend — and my number one enemy — as my roommate.

Blind Side
The hottest college football safety in the nation just asked me to be his fake girlfriend.
And I just asked him to take my virginity.

Quarterback Sneak
Quarterback Holden Moore can have any girl he wants.
Except me: the coach's daughter.

Hail Mary (an Amazon #1 Bestseller!)
Leo F*cking Hernandez.
North Boston University's star running back, notorious bachelor, and number one on my people I would murder if I could get away with it list.
And now?
My new roommate.

The Becker Brothers Series
On the Rocks (book 1)
Neat (book 2)
Manhattan (book 3)
Old Fashioned (book 4)
Four brothers finding love in a small Tennessee town that revolves around a whiskey distillery with a dark past — including the mysterious death of their father.

The Best Kept Secrets Series
(AN AMAZON TOP 10 BESTSELLER)
What He Doesn't Know (book 1)
What He Always Knew (book 2)
What He Never Knew (book 3)
Charlie's marriage is dying. She's perfectly content to go down in the flames, until her first love shows back up and reminds her the other way love can burn.

Close Quarters
A summer yachting the Mediterranean sounded like heaven to Jasmine after finishing her undergrad degree. But her boyfriend's billionaire boss always gets what he wants. And this time, he wants her.

Make Me Hate You

Jasmine has been avoiding her best friend's brother for years, but when they're both in the same house for a wedding, she can't resist him — no matter how she tries.

The Wrong Game

(AN AMAZON TOP 5 BESTSELLER)

Gemma's plan is simple: invite a new guy to each home game using her season tickets for the Chicago Bears. It's the perfect way to avoid getting emotionally attached and also get some action. But after Zach gets his chance to be her practice round, he decides one game just isn't enough. A sexy, fun sports romance.

The Right Player

She's avoiding love at all costs. He wants nothing more than to lock her down. Sexy, hilarious and swoon-worthy, The Right Player is the perfect read for sports romance lovers.

On the Way to You

It was only supposed to be a road trip, but when Cooper discovers the journal of the boy driving the getaway car, everything changes. An emotional, angsty road trip romance.

A Love Letter to Whiskey

(AN AMAZON TOP 10 BESTSELLER)

An angsty, emotional romance between two lovers fighting the curse of bad timing.

Read Love, Whiskey – Jamie's side of the story and an extended epilogue – in the new Fifth Anniversary Edition

Weightless

Young Natalie finds self-love and romance with her personal trainer, along with a slew of secrets that tie them together in ways she never thought possible.

Revelry

Recently divorced, Wren searches for clarity in a summer cabin outside of Seattle, where she makes an unforgettable connection with the broody, small town recluse next door.

Say Yes

Harley is studying art abroad in Florence, Italy. Trying to break free of her perfectionism, she steps outside one night determined to Say Yes to anything that comes her way. Of course, she didn't expect to run into Liam Benson...

Washed Up

Gregory Weston, the boy I once knew as my son's best friend, now a man I don't know at all. No, not just a man. A doctor. And he wants me...

The Christmas Blanket

Stuck in a cabin with my ex-husband waiting out a blizzard? Not exactly what I had pictured when I planned a surprise visit home for the holidays...

Black Number Four

A college, Greek-life romance of a hot young poker star and the boy sent to take her down.

The Palm South University Series

Rush (book 1)
Anchor (book 2)

Pledge (book 3)

Legacy (book 4)

Ritual (book 5)

Hazed (book 6)

Greek (book 7)

#1 NYT Bestselling Author Rachel Van Dyken says, "If Gossip Girl and Riverdale had a love child, it would be PSU." This angsty college series will be your next guilty addiction.

Tag Chaser

She made a bet that she could stop chasing military men, which seemed easy — until her knight in shining armor and latest client at work showed up in Army ACUs.

Song Chaser

Tanner and Kellee are perfect for each other. They frequent the same bars, love the same music, and have the same desire to rip each other's clothes off. Only problem? Tanner is still in love with his best friend.

Acknowledgements

This series wouldn't be possible without Rhiannon Gwynne and her husband, Josh Brittain. I feel like I owe y'all an even BIGGER thank you this time around, because you were helping me while also getting ready to welcome your first child into the world! Thank you for the interviews about what it's like to be a professional hockey player as well as the WIFE of a professional hockey player. I would screw this up without your guidance.

To my husband, Jack – I would not have been able to do this one without you. Thank you for being the most incredible husband and partner I could ask for as I struggled to write through my first trimester and then made up for it when second trimester energy hit. I already know from how you love me that our daughter will be the luckiest girl in the world. I love you.

To my momma, Lavon, and my bestie, Sasha – thank you both for always being there to celebrate the great times and suffer through the bad ones together. I love you both.

To Tina Stokes, my Executive Assistant and dear friend – thank you. When I wrote this dedication, I had you in mind, because there's no one in this world who is as giving, kind, and caring as you are. I am so lucky to have you on my team and in my life as a friend. Thank you for all you do. I love you.

A huge thank you to all the amazing women in this industry who have been my writing buddies through various parts of this book. Laura Pavlov, Brittainy Cherry, Catherine Cowles, Willow Aster, Lena Hendrix, Elsie

Silver, Maren Moore, Jessica Prince, Karla Sorensen – I'm honored to be on this journey with you.

Thank you to the crew at OSYS Studios for bringing these books to life in audio. Each book gets better and better with you at the wheel!

To Isabella Bauer – thank you for the endless laughs and your constant belief in me. I'm so happy to have you on our team!

To my team of beta readers: I really put y'all through it with this one. Between deadline changes and this being the biggest book in the series so far, you handled every curveball like the pros you are, and I truly believe we made magic together. A huge and heartfelt thanks to Frances O'Brien, Elizabeth Turner, Sarah Green, Allison Cheshire, Kellee Fabre, Sarah Green, Marie-Pierre D'Auteuil, Janett Corona, Jayce Cruz, Gabriela Vivas, Anna Ana López, Carly Wilson, Nicole Westmoreland, Anna, Lily Turner, Diana Daniel, and Jewel Caruso. I am so happy to have you all on my team.

This book was special in that it featured a representation of a group of people I think are true superheroes – teachers. I want to thank Koko Casey and Kelsey Muller for helping me get it right! Your interviews and beta reading feedback were crucial in making *Learn Your Lesson* what it is, and I truly thank you.

In addition, I want to thank my amazing team of sensitivity readers. Your input is simply put, invaluable, and I am so grateful for your time and energy. Jacqueline Branche, Nagma Bordoi, and Stuti Patel – THANK YOU!

To the team who helps bring my vision to life: Elaine York with Allusion Publishing, Nicole McCurdy with Emerald Edits, Nina Grinstead, Kim Cermak, the whole team at Valentine PR, Shaye Lefkowitz and Lindsey

Romero with Good Girls PR, Ren Saliba and Staci Hart with Quirky Bird Cover Design – THANK YOU. From editing and formatting to photography and promotion, it truly takes a village. I'm so thankful for each and every one of you.

To my unborn daughter: hello, baby girl. This was the first book you and I wrote together, and it was the most special experience that I will never forget. I felt you growing inside me (usually by way of extreme nausea LOL) and it made it so real when I was writing Ava and her relationship with both Will and Chloe. I cannot wait to meet you, sweet little angel, and to watch you flourish. I love you already.

And finally, to YOU, the reader. The fact that you've read all the way to these acknowledgements shows what an incredible human you are. And I just want you to know that none of this would be possible without you. There isn't a day that goes by that I take any of this for granted, that I don't pinch myself and send gratitude bombs into the universe. Thank you for reading my books, for posting about them on social media, for leaving reviews, and for reading indie, period. I am eternally grateful for you. Come find me on the social media platform you love the most and let's be friends.

About the Author

Kandi Steiner is a #1 Amazon Bestselling Author. Best known for writing "emotional rollercoaster" stories, she loves bringing flawed characters to life and writing about real, raw romance — in all its forms. No two Kandi Steiner books are the same, and if you're a lover of angsty, emotional, and inspirational reads, she's your gal.

An alumna of the University of Central Florida, Kandi graduated with a double major in Creative Writing and Advertising/PR with a minor in Women's Studies. Her love for writing started at the ripe age of 10, and in 6th grade, she wrote and edited her own newspaper and distributed to her classmates. Eventually, the principal caught on and the newspaper was quickly halted, though Kandi tried fighting for her "freedom of press."

She took particular interest in writing romance after college, as she has always been a die hard hopeless romantic, and likes to highlight all the challenges of love as well as the triumphs.

When Kandi isn't writing, you can find her reading books of all kinds, planning her next adventure, or pole dancing (yes, you read that right). She enjoys live music, traveling, hiking, yoga, playing with her fur babies and soaking up the sweetness of life.

Connect with Kandi:

NEWSLETTER: kandisteiner.com/newsletter
FACEBOOK: facebook.com/kandisteiner
FACEBOOK READER GROUP (Kandiland): facebook.com/groups/kandilandks
INSTAGRAM: Instagram.com/kandisteiner
TIKTOK: tiktok.com/@authorkandisteiner
TWITTER: twitter.com/kandisteiner
PINTEREST: pinterest.com/authorkandisteiner
WEBSITE: www.kandisteiner.com
Kandi Steiner may be coming to a city near you! Check out her "events" tab to see all the signings she's attending in the near future: www.kandisteiner.com/events

Printed in the USA
CPSIA information can be obtained
at www.ICGtesting.com
LVHW042049190424
777911LV00004B/662

9 781960 649256